Dead of Nyte

By

Jearl Rugh

Published by
CreateSpace Independent Publishing Platform

First Printing August 2013

ISBN-13: 978-1491092637

Printed in the United States of America

Cover Design by Jearl Rugh

The weak can never forgive. Forgiveness is the attribute of the strong.

— Mahatma Gandhi —

Prologue

1968

The blast ripped Dirk from a pleasant dream about a family he'd yet to know in future he hoped to live. As the images dissolved with the sleep webs, his heart responded with an anxious cadence, and an unwelcomed but all too familiar despair usurped his euphoria. Tucked in behind a tree on a small rise, he rolled to his stomach. The plastic grips on his rifle filled his hands, but offered no guarantee of safety no matter how much his mind grappled for it. With the sights pointed in the direction of the thundering peal on retreat into the distance, Sergeant Nyte stared through the barrel-mounted Starlight night-vision scope, and scanned the field not thirty meters out. Six green heat signatures, warm from the life he'd just stolen from them, lay victim to the tripwire of a single M18 Claymore mine.

The fading stars against the black canopy marked the beginning of the second day of a three-day recon mission. It was the first day of Tet Nguyen Dan, the

1

celebration of the Vietnamese New Year. With a two-day cease fire, most of the allied troops took a reprieve from the fighting. Nyte's squad, though, had been assigned to keep eyes and ears on the ground. They had observed not one confirmed slither of enemy movement—until now.

Nyte lifted the scope to scan the near proximity eager to find that the blast would be the end of it, like his men just a few scouts on patrol. But disappointment mingled with dread as he saw scores of men crouched and running for cover across the open field to a tree line fifty meters away. He drew several deep breaths of tepid jungle air, but there just wasn't enough oxygen to subdue the uneasy fear for the lives of his men clawing at his now fully conscious mind.

During the next two unsettled minutes, while he scanned the bush in front of him for each of his men, he hoped his squad would remember the mission briefing he had given before they left base. *"Don't fire unless you're absolutely sure they're shooting at you, and not firing to see if anyone's home. Returning fire throws open a door wide enough to drive a battalion of tanks."* With each one hunkered behind whatever cover they could find, he crossed himself and flung a prayer to the creator of those stars above that they'd be safe if the force on the other side of the clearing decided to ring the doorbell.

When the enemy's first volley erupted, Nyte rolled to a sitting position, rested his back against the tree and waited with his finger on the trigger of his M16. After thirty seconds, when the rain of hot lead stopped tearing through the jungle, he pursed his lips and forced the breath he now realized he'd been holding from his lungs. Raising the scope again, he peered around the trunk and glanced over the enemy. Their green glow indicated they were waiting for a response. *With luck they'll collect their dead and move on.*

But the calm was broken by automatic weapon fire to his right. Jerking the scope around to see who had engaged, he found Hal standing with his rifle at his hip, John Wayne style, spraying short bursts toward the opposite stand of trees.

Over the last day, Nyte had felt a gnawing disquiet for Hal who had landed in Southeast Asia three days ago. On his first mission, he said he was "here to kill gooks," but after a day of playing duck and cover with every sound the jungle uttered, Nyte knew his nerves were as taut as the E string on Jimi Hendrix's Fender Stratocaster.

Proof of life was just what Charlie needed, and after getting three bursts off, without a noticeable flinch, Hal tipped backward like a felled tree spraying the rest of his magazine in a single stream into the air. Once on the ground, he ceased all movement.

Twenty minutes and countless rounds later, the sulfuric trace of spent gunpowder came with Nyte's every breath. Behind the far trees, dawn painted the black horizon with a deep blue brushstroke. He looked again to the position of each man who had trusted him with his life. The carnage he now witnessed brought the bitterness of bile to his tongue. At least five of his men's confidence had been betrayed.

Wolf on the far left flank was still returning fire but favored his left shoulder. Lefty writhed in the dirt with his hands clutching his stomach as if his guts were spilling out. Besides Hal, on the far right Boomer, the explosives expert, lay still as stone. And in the center of

3

the line just ten meters below Nyte, DJ, the radioman, sprawled motionless.

While the firefight raged, Nyte had kept vigil on the body-heat signatures in the tree line. Vietcong reinforcements had been gathering from adjoining sectors like spotted hyenas on the scent of a kill. Because the morning light threatened to expose just how few of Uncle Sam's GIs opposed them, at any moment, Nyte expected to see a wall of pajama-clad AK-47-bearing guerillas swarm from the trees behind a frenzy of fire power.

Since no air cover had arrived once the shooting started, Nyte thought DJ must have been taken out about the same time as Hal. With so many of his men already dead or wounded, holding their position for much longer gave no hope of anyone's survival, which meant they wouldn't fulfill their mission—to report that Charlie was not on holiday. *I need that radio.*

The thick brush on the grade between him and DJ offered visual obscurity in the dull morning light, but it was no shield from the bullets striking all around. He placed his hand over his left breast pocket and drew strength from his fiancée's tear-stained letter. Covering his heart, the hope birthed on that one page fit like impenetrable armor.

With his rifle resting in the crooks of his arms, in a flurry of elbows and knees digging into the carpet of decaying leaves and grass, he crawled down the slope, wriggling to the right side of the remains of the twenty-year-old's days on Earth.

He turned toward DJ. His helmet lay next to him upside down like a turtle on its back. Nyte picked up the headgear. A bullet had pierced it and then burrowed into

DJ's brain leaving a moist stream of blood across his forehead just above the "what-the-hell-just-happened" stare in his eyes.

"Sorry, kid," he said as he reached across DJ's body to slip the radio from his lifeless left hand. Nyte rolled to his right side and triggered the switch. A hiss of static hit his ears and impulse shot his fingers to the knob to silence the volume. Once adjusted, as he lifted the instrument to speak, like a small tree branch with the whack of a machete, his left arm fell useless. He gapped at the flaccid limb twisted across his chest at an incongruous angle, and clenched his teeth as if that would take the bite from the sharp ache already radiating from the bone-fragging wound.

He took the device in his right hand, and growled into the mouthpiece, "Taking heavy fire. At least five down. Request an airstrike now!"

"Negative, Sarge," the voice through the speaker crackled. "Pilots are on holiday."

"There *is* no holiday, soldier. Half the damn Cong army's on my doorstep."

"It'll be at least forty-five before I can find one who ain't hung over and get him suited up."

"Damn it…! We'll all be *dead* by then. Find that pilot…and get me a chopper, now!"

Since they were twenty klicks from base, Nyte knew the timing of the retreat was crucial. He looked to his left. The closest man, O'Leary, swapped magazines. Nicknamed after the infamous Catherine O'Leary of the 1871 Great Chicago Fire, if he had toted his flamethrower on this patrol, they might have faced a different outcome. Nyte yelled, "O'Leary, Dead run. One klick. Five minutes." O'Leary nodded and Nyte knew he'd carry the order to the others on the left flank.

While Charlie's hail of lead continued to strafe around him, Nyte dragged himself to the right under the brush with his weapon slung over his back and his useless arm in tow. Tarzan, so name because during battle he hopped from tree to tree firing into oncoming bullets, was pinned down reloading under heavy fire. Over the battle fray, Nyte repeated the order.

"Five minutes," Tarzan called back while Nyte crawled the five feet to Hal. He wanted to be angry with him for causing this catastrophe, but Hal was just a boy under extreme stress who, like most teenagers, thought he was invincible and didn't consider consequences.

From Hal's web belt Nyte pulled a roll of white gauze and bound it around his own arm. The blood flowed with such a heavy surge that it took several layers of wrap to stop the injury from soaking through red. Then he moved to where Boomer lay. The blood-drenched olive-drab blouse was convincing enough, but Nyte placed a confirming finger to the silent man's neck. No throb greeted his fingertips. *Such a waste. A damn stupid waste.* He looked around the ground near Boomer and picked up several triggers.

Looking passed Boomer to Boa who took cover between two thick tree trunks, Nyte said, "Dead run." Boa whose moniker derived from the night he slid into the enemy's camp and put several soldiers into choke holds, stopped shooting and turned toward Nyte, waiting.

As the rest of Nyte's squad ceased fire, he rolled toward Boa and scooted until he could see across the clearing through the trees. In less than a minute, the enemy's bullets, too, stopped. In the growing morning light, he sensed movement. Raising his field glasses, he watched a small group of about two dozen, not nearly the entire force, emerge from the tree line. They crouched low with their weapons at ready as they crossed the open field, but each step came slow and watchful as if they were walking through dead men's bones.

When they were within twenty meters, Nyte squeezed the detonators setting off the remaining Claymores.

The fire, smoke, and dust kicked up by the massive detonation hid the advancing guerillas, but the deafening explosion and the shrieks of the dying as the pellets tore through their flesh was the signal. Only seconds remained before the enemy waiting in the trees, disoriented by the blood and horror, and thanking their god that it wasn't them, ascertained that the blast wasn't another accidental discharge but a diversion.

Nyte jumped to his feet. After taking two steps, he realized Boa hadn't followed. He turned and forced a whispered order. "Retreat, now."

"At the rear, Sarge."

Minutes later, Nyte, his left arm swaying without purpose at his side, broke through the trees. He had lost his men in the retreat but as he made the clearing, he was relieved to see two of the others in front of him racing for the chopper just touching down twenty meters ahead. Behind him he could hear the blast of an occasional hand grenade and Charlie tramping through the jungle like a panicked sounder of wild boar, firing random automatic AK47 bursts.

When the two men in front of him reached the helicopter, they fell to the ground just below the door and pointed their weapons to the tree line. Seconds later,

Nyte swung onto the deck of the Huey and flattened prone. He pulled his fractured arm around in front of him to rest the barrel. But before he was in position, the two men on the ground resumed fire and chatter from two M60 machineguns erupted over his head. He looked up. Tarzan loped along with Lefty and one other man on his shoulders and behind him, dozens of Vietcong soldiers swarmed out of the jungle like ants racing from a fast spreading ground fire. No sooner did they appear, than they fell as they ran head-on into the wall of hot lead. But behind them more came. More than the guns could cut down. Nyte joined the fire fight but it still wasn't enough.

Tarzan, just a few meters ahead of the throng, took a hit to his leg and fell. Without hesitating, the two men at the door bolted for Tarzan. Each one took one of his burdens. The one with Lefty pulled Tarzan to his feet, and together they started to limp back.

It only took seconds, but it seemed like an eternity before the deafening sounds of the accelerating rotors hit Nyte's ears. As the bird took flight, the reduced frequency of *thunks* as rounds passed through the steel body of the chopper was a welcome resonance. Finally, out of range, Nyte found a place to sit on the deck to make an assessment. Not ten minutes before, he'd taken a mental roll call and knew which of his men were among the living and which would be left for dead. As expected Hal, Boomer and DJ were not present. One of the two men Tarzan had carried back was DOA. And Lefty didn't look so good. Tarzan was stuffing as much available gauze as he could into his belly.

Leaning back against the bulkhead, the ache in his left arm paled compared to what had happen to his men and what he had inflicted on the enemy. He took his helmet off to wipe the sweat from his brow with his forearm. Sad, weary eyes met his.

"You did good today," he said "But damn it, three unaccounteds."

Chapter 1

2010

The disturbance call being just a few blocks from her location on the Elliott Bay waterfront, Officer Kelsey Nyte flipped the emergency strobe lights and siren into action, and pressed the accelerator to the floor. As she changed lanes to veer around a slow moving cargo truck, she checked the time on her onboard computer, 11:47—just minutes before her shift *would have* ended at midnight.

She tapped the Bluetooth wireless device in her ear.

The halting voice answering yawned with a sleepy groan. "Hello?"

"It's Mom, Chrissie. Sorry I woke you?"

Kel had raised her thirteen year-old daughter off and on over the last eight years as a single parent. She hated leaving Chrissie alone for too many hours, but at times like this, the demands of the job required it.

Fortunately, the Neighborhood Watch program she had helped start in their townhome community gave Kel some confidence that her only child was safe.

"Hey…Mom. It's okay." With the grunts Chrissie uttered, Kel pictured her stretching the sleep out of her body. "Saul and I fell asleep on the couch waiting for you…Is that your siren?"

"That's why I called. I just got called out and it may be a long one. Sweetheart, I probably won't see you 'til morning.

"Uh…alright."

"You best get to bed. Take Saul with you, okay?" Saul, Chrissie's Rottweiler, had been a good companion for her. Even more than the neighbors, Kel trusted him to protect her daughter while she served the city. "We'll have breakfast together."

"Yeah…'kay."

As Kel reached the intersection at South Washington and made a hard right, she said, "Love you."

"Love you more."

"Love you mo—"

Chrissie's click ending the call cut Kel off. "—most," she said out loud to herself. Chrissie, it seemed overnight, had started maturing into a young woman. Sadness weighted Kel's heart at the thought that another ritual, like evenings with "Candy Land" or dressing and redressing one of Chrissie's many dolls, might disappear forever.

As she approached First Avenue South, two homeless men caught in her headlight beams, stumbled in the crosswalk. She slammed the brakes and tugged the steering wheel to the left, putting the light blue Seattle police cruiser into a skid. The squeal of rubber biting asphalt sobered the men enough to shoot her a panic-filled glare while they lurched to the safety of the sidewalk beyond.

Seconds later, Kel parked diagonally between the median and the cars along the curb, blocking the northbound traffic. She stepped out into the warm night air, slipped her baton into her belt and stepped onto the sidewalk near a bike racked at the curb. Her boots hammered against the concrete as she made her way to the street-level bar. The Pioneer Squarer watering hole had been a fixture in the community for more than twenty years and thrived during summer baseball season. It stood at the foot of a four-story terracotta structure built at the end of the nineteenth century.

Kel opened the door to the Wishing Well and saw that the raucous crowd required an officer-needs-assistance call, but with the sound of approaching sirens, she didn't trigger her radio's shoulder-mike. She took a single step inside, and as the door closed behind her, the air passing over a bottle's mouth whistled inches from her left ear.

The glass shattered against the door behind her, showering her back with icy beer. She couldn't control the sudden shiver, or the surprised gasp that poured the taste and smell of flat beer—both leaching from the old paneled walls and spilled on the hardwood floor—over her tongue and through her nose. The suggestion of something else caught her by surprise. It was burned and stale, but even the whiff of coffee brought a craving for the half-drunk latte she had to leave in her cruiser.

She shook it all off and focused her eyes in the direction the bottle had come, daring the pitcher to meet her glare. When no one turned her way, she pulled her nightstick and scanned the room. Except for the missing piano player hammering out a lively tune on a tinny upright, the overturned tables and the sight of doubled fists launching into faces reminded her of the classic western saloon fights she and her dad used to watch in black and white. *At least no one's toting a six shooter— my God, I hope not.*

"SPD," she shouted over Pino Palladino's lyric base line driving Melissa Etheridge's "I'm the Only One." "Everyone hit the floor!"

No one noticed.

Kel pivoted to a man with a Grizzly Adams's beard standing behind the dark oak bar. Frustration and rage converged on his face. Staring back at Kel, he shook his head and threw his hands up.

"Shut that music down!" Kel shouted to him with over articulated lips in case he, too, couldn't hear her.

When the music went silent, turning to the spectators and cheerleaders on the periphery, she said, "Leave your drinks on the table, and wait outside."

Most stood shaking their heads and started a slow trudge toward the door. But two men at a ringside table held their seats. One with red-hair glared back at Kel and without flinching lifted his glass to take a defiant swallow.

The color and the way his auburn hair rested limp on his shoulders wrenched a familiar yet disturbing memory to the surface. "*Lance,*" it whispered. The ethereal presence always showed up without warning and most often, like this, at an inconvenient time. She needed to close her eyes to banish the manifestation, but with the wreckage still falling around her, she couldn't take the luxury. She shifted her five-foot-five, muscular-frame toward him and fixed her eyes on the insolent man. With a sharp snap, she brought the nightstick down on the palm of her hand.

Slamming the glass down, beer splashed on the table top, and he stood. "Free drinks," he bellowed. He stood and then skirted the table to join his buddy already near the exit.

With the bystanders cleared, she glanced toward the fray. On the far right to the rear of the scuffle, one man gripped another's shirt. The razor-wire tattoo wrapped around his right forearm seemed to snap back and forth like a Slinky while he punched the face of someone she recognized.

The white greasepaint smeared across his visage and the bicycle she had noticed as she entered the Wishing Well proved Marcel was on the receiving end. No one knew his true identity, but over the last year or two he had imprinted his eccentricity in the downtown culture with his bike and a red tipped cane for the sight impaired. Since he never spoke, he had been dubbed Marcel Marceau.

With the brawl between them, Kel couldn't get to him—yet.

"Everyone hit the floor, now!" Kel said and slapped the nearest table with her nightstick.

Two women in their twenties scrapped five feet away, pulling hair and ripping at each other's clothes. The other brawlers turned toward Kel's voice and began to take the position, but the two women didn't go down.

To Kel, being ignored felt like itching powder sprinkled on a weeping rash. She stepped forward and grabbed the shoulder of closest one ready to slap the knees out from under the woman with her stick. The woman spun toward Kel. Her right breast fell out from her torn shirt and braless raised her fists.

"Really?" Kel asked and couldn't resist a smirk.

Braless paused, shot Kel a look of contempt and after several seconds went to her knees. The second woman followed. Kel's eyes drew down as the pair lay to their bellies and passed hateful stares between them. She glanced at the other bodies on the wooden floor. A dozen panting and wheezing people were sprawled at her feet.

But razor-wire still stood statuesque. He had dropped Marcel to the floor like a duffel bag of baseball bats. With the sweat glistening off his face and arms, he looked ready for the next round. He connected a menacing glower eye to eye with Kel.

She stepped around the two women toward him and shouted, "What part of 'hit the floor' didn't you get?"

Razor-wire bolted toward the door. The pathway cluttered with prone bodies, he jumped and stumbled around them. Kel stood between him and the door. She hardly had to reach to plunge her nightstick into his belly. The sudden impact lifted razor-wire off the floor and he fell on top of braless.

"Get the hell off me you son-of-a-bitch," she screamed, and springing to her hands and knees, she bucked him to the floor. He landed face up at Kel's feet.

Kel looked at him. He seemed small now, and anything but threatening. His eyes darted back and forth as if they were trying to find something solid on which to focus.

She placed the business end of her stick on his chest and barked, "On your face. Now!" But before he could move, his eyes turned to glass and rolled back in their sockets.

With a shake of her head, Kel jammed the toe of her boot under him, and forced him to his stomach. She drove her knee into his back and wrested his arms free. Pulling a plastic zip tie from a belt-pouch, she secured his hands behind his back.

"Hands behind your heads," she shouted to the others on the floor.

She glanced over the crowd to make sure they were complying and then looked back to the bar. Behind Grizzly, through the twin portholes in the swinging doors leading to the kitchen, two female servers looked out onto the scene. They stepped from their hiding place and joined the barkeep.

"What set this off?" Kel asked.

"The guy you're kneeling on," said the brunette with a nod, "asked Marcel what he thought about the Mariners losing four of their last six home games. When Marcel shrugged, that guy grabbed him and started throwing punches. Then the whole place just went to Hell."

As she finished, the barmaid's eyes darted toward the door. The shards from the shattered bottle scraped the plank floor as it swung open. Kel looked over her shoulder and watched two officers enter.

"Looks like everything's under control here," Scott Nillson said and gave Kel a wink.

Scott had been her mentor when she was a rookie cop. They had ridden together as partners for her first two years on the force while she learned her way around the streets.

"You guys might want to start hooking people up," Kel said, returning a smile. She stood, and nodded toward the two women hugging the floor. "Start with them."

Leaving the two officers to clear the rioters, she stepped over to the motionless heap known as Marcel. She kneeled and reached to his neck.

Chapter 2

Susanne Lowen turned the key in the front door lock of the Georgetown condo she shared with her partner and stepped inside. Trisha, visiting her sister in Colorado, with the exception of the cat had left Susanne with the house to herself for the weekend. Because the crime lab had been slow, her Sunday night shift dragged. A hot salted bath beckoned.

In the kitchen, she dropped her purse and keys on the countertop and took an opened bottle of Oregon Pinot Gris from the refrigerator. "Freda," she said. It wasn't unusual for the cat not to greet her at the front door, as most days, like today when she had been left alone for hours, Freda made her need for companionship known in any number of indifferent ways.

Retrieving a wine glass from the cupboard, Susanne favored herself with a generous pour, and took both the glass and the rest of the bottle with her. Outside, Amtrak's Coast Starlight running a couple hours late on its final approach to Seattle's King Street Station, rumbled by. As the clack of steel wheels faded in the distance, her grandfather's Swiss mantel-clock chimed a quarter after midnight—*always five minutes slow*.

She reached the bathroom door and called again. "Freda?" Freda still didn't appear.

Placing the glass and bottle on the vanity, she leaned to turn the tap and sprinkled scented bath salts where the water splashed onto the tub's floor. With the water drumming into the tub, she walked down the hall to the bedroom she shared with Trisha. Dropping her scrubs into the hamper, she covered herself with a lavender floral-print bathrobe and then flipped the light switch off as she left the room.

"Freda, where are you, girl?" she asked as she entered the hallway.

Across the hall from the bath, the door to Freda's room—the second bedroom—stood open. She peeked in to see if the cat was napping.

"Sweetie, you in here?"

In the darkness, her eyes pulled to the computer. Positive she had turned the system off after checking email earlier this afternoon, now the monitor was lit and Microsoft Word open. Trisha used the word processing application regularly but she had been gone for days and Susanne hadn't touched it in weeks.

No lonely feline brushed against her bare leg, so, without turning on the light, she entered the room and sat at the desk. Her eyes fixed on the text. An unfamiliar four-line poem cast its shadow on the backlit screen.

First the one who owes so much

Final payment by my touch

Breath of life fails to draw in

Pillow talk, my secret sin

As she read the lines a second time, the verse twisted her bowels tight as a braided rope. Her hands in reflex drew to her face and slipped over a halting breath, but her eyes stayed fixed on the lyrics. At first she couldn't tear away from the sing-song rhyme prophesying a future she couldn't accept. But then a dark dread, icy and resolute, slithered into her mind—*My God, is he's here!*

She sprang from the chair and turned to face the hall door knowing the implication of the two couplets meant she was intended to be the next victim under the medical examiner's knife. No one waited there. Senses peaked, she listened for any sound that didn't belong— the low hum of the refrigerator, water flowing into the tub, the computer's fan whirring. Nothing unusual.

In two steps she was at the doorway. She peered around the jamb searching the hall in both directions. *No one*. Susanne hurried toward the master bedroom and the nightstand.

When she reached the table, she fumbled with the lamp until she located the elusive switch. She pulled the top drawer open, withdrew her Browning 9 millimeter from beneath her cotton panties and picked up the phone. The bed next to her, she sat on the edge, placed the telephone in her lap and hazarded one last glance down the hallway before she dialed.

Halfway between the bathroom door and the bedroom, Freda sauntered toward her. Reaching Susanne's feet, she jumped onto the bed and crawled into Susanne's lap. Susanne wrapped one arm around the midnight-black cat and whispered into Freda's ear, "Where you been girl?"

She dialed 9-1-1. As the phone rang, she took deep breaths. Her pulse still raged against her temples but she felt control beginning to return. The police would be here in minutes. They would make a thorough search of her home and once they finished, she would initiate a forensic investigation into the computer. Until then, she had the Browning. Freda purred, and Susanne blew the fear from her lungs.

"9-1-1, what is your emergency?"

The sonorous voice in her ear jarred her. Susanne looked up and pointed the gun toward the hallway. In her haste, she hadn't noticed it before, but now the pistol felt light—*too light*. She released the ten-round magazine and found it empty.

The acid in her stomach began to reflux. Her mouth turned to ash and she couldn't swallow the acrid taste. It seared her throat. She fought the terror with a jerk, and twisted her eyes toward the hall. Still no one lurked there.

"Susanne, do you have an emergency?" the voice erupted again.

The last question confirmed her dread. The unseen voice speaking through the phone pressed to her ear also spewed into the hallway.

The sound of the water surging into the bathtub stopped.

Her lips quivered to find an answer, but words took no form. Susanne jumped to her feet. The phone tumbled to the floor and Freda shot away. *You traitor.*

You were cuddling with him., weren't you? She swung behind her and toppled the lamp off the bedside table so he couldn't see her silhouette.

Standing in the darkness, she continued her frantic stare in the direction of the voice. He had steered her into a trap. The only escape from her condo was through the narrow corridor the monster now controlled.

Chapter 3

Kel slammed the back door on the paramedic's rig and pounded on the side. After the clash, she'd been happy to find Marcel's carotid still throbbing. Unconscious when she got to him, if God *was* merciful, he didn't feel much of the beating. She knew that would change when he awoke, but hoped a couple days of medical observation would prove him fit to carry on being Marcel.

"Quite a shift-ender," Scott said as he walked up behind her, having loaded the last of the rioters onto the police bus. He threw his arm around her shoulder and pulled her close with a gentle hug.

She hadn't seen much of him the last few years as he'd been reassigned to South Precinct. Those years added a few pounds around his middle, and the gray strands of hair poking out from under a police issue ball cap replaced the black hair she remembered.

She looked at her watch. Under the street lamp she made the time as 12:58 a.m. She shook her head.

"'Fraid this one isn't over yet. Paperwork, booking…" A breeze blowing off the Puget Sound pressed against the back of her shirt still damp from the beer spattered on it, and she added, "And maybe a fresh uni before that. I'll be half the night."

"First responders have all the fun," he said with a chuckle. "But I'll help."

"Right." Her sarcasm snapped the word off.

One of the police bus's tires clattered through a pothole as it passed by them. Kel looked toward the portable holding cell. "What say we get this done?"

Turning away from Scott, she walked back to her cruiser waiting with lights flashing in the middle of First Avenue South. After she dropped into the front seat, a sharp rap on driver's side window jerked her head to the left. With her cruiser still cordoning off the street, she expected to find a frustrated citizen.

Instead, the blue flame of a lighter igniting the tip of a cigar illuminated a resolute face. His presence alone indicated this meeting was not an accident.

"Good evening, Officer Nyte."

Kel powered down the window and looked into the face of the man she hoped to work for soon. Even in the dim light she recognized the familiar circles of gray flesh sagging beneath Nathaniel Ballesteros's sixty-plus year-old eyes. She felt they gave witness to firsthand knowledge of the base brutality only human beings could inflict on their own kind. As he peered through the open window, they narrowed as if his well-groomed black eyebrows and his will conspired to constrain some darkness from finding the light.

She opened the car door. He stood aside while she got out and pulled the cigar from his lips.

"Chief Ballesteros," she said, surprised to see the head of detectives on the scene of a bar disturbance. "Not much detective work here. Kind of a slam dunk."

"Heard it on the police scanner as I was leaving Benaroya Hall," he said, the tension in his brow retreating for a moment. "The Summer Festival—Schumann, Mendelssohn, and Brahms chamber music. Always centers me. You responded to the call, and since I was close by, wanted to see you in action." He lifted the cigar to his mouth again. "What happened in there?"

"Just a fight over a ballgame. Left one guy unconscious and a baker's dozen packed up to dry out."

His thin lips wrapped around the Dutch Master, he took two puffs. A cloud of blue smoke hid his face while he asked, "You were first on scene?"

"Yes, sir." Kel had never cared for the smell of cigar smoke, and this one had a particularly offensive odor, but she didn't allow for face to reveal her disgust.

"And you went in without backup?"

"The situation warranted immediate action, sir. I could hear the sirens approaching, so I knew I didn't need to call the cavalry. The important thing was to gain control of the situation and stop the fight before someone got hurt bad or maybe even worse."

"And you accomplished all that by yourself?"

"In less than five minutes, sir."

"Well, then," he said, his voice relaxing, "good work, Officer. I'll look forward to your after-action report."

"It'll be in the system by morning, but I must say it seems odd, Chief, that you'd have interest in a report of barroom scuffle."

"I have interests in many things," he said, hooking his right index finger around the smoke and removing it from his mouth. "You might just be surprised. Reports on routine brawls are not necessarily on my must-read list, but seeing your reports are. How else can I judge your fitness for my department?"

Kel had taken the detective's exam several months earlier, and, even though she had passed it, where others had moved forward, there had been no promotion for her.

"I didn't realize you were watching," she said, allowing a smile but controlling a chortle.

"Oh, I've been watching, and I know you face odds."

Nepotism and politics both came to play in her career. Being the daughter of the Chief of Police made advancement difficult. She knew this was a risk when she joined the SPD, but she had believed in the ideal—work hard, perform well and progression in rank would be the natural outcome. But her commander, Lieutenant Louis Martinez, stood in the way. Promotion required a referral from her boss, and he was adamant not to give it. Her dad could have overruled him, but he didn't offer and she didn't ask.

"You may not realize it," he continued, "but your dad taking retirement last month puts a new dynamic in place. I wouldn't be surprised to see a change in your near future."

"Sir, I appreciate your interest in me," she said, realizing this might be the opening she had been looking for. "Believe me, it's unexpected. But if you're thinking I might have potential as a detective, then there's one thing I'd like to ask."

"Please." He nodded.

"I realize this may seem like it's coming out of left field, but Willie Jenkins's death is still unsolved."

Chief Ballesteros's biggest career embarrassment had been the SPD detective's unsolved murder. Willie and his partner had been assisting the Port of Seattle Police to infiltrate a smuggling ring at the docks. When he didn't return home after his shift one night, everyone knew something was wrong. Then a month later, his decomposing body turned up in a shipping container in Kuala Lumpur. Despite the Chief's trip to Malaysia with the grieving widow to bring his body home and a vow to find and punish the killer, sixteen months later, there were no suspects and the trail had grown cold.

"His wife and I were classmates at the UDub," she said. "It's been a real source of angst for my dad and frustrating for me."

"What's your point, Kel?"

"I don't mean to pick at a sore, sir," she replied, recognizing his sudden tone change, "but I wouldn't mind spending some of my off-duty hours digging around. Could you use an extra hand?"

"Look, your intentions are good, I'm sure, but my people are investigating every lead. We haven't given up—we'll find his killer." He paused. "I'll be watching for that brawl report, and don't leave anything out."

"With the scrupulous detail I'll provide," she said, masking her disappointment with a grin, "you'll think you're reading a Greg Isles novel, sir."

He switched the cigar to his left hand. "That's what I want to hear."

"Well, Chief, if there's nothing else, I have a bus load of perps to book, a mountain of paperwork ahead of me, and a daughter whose mom's already late getting home from work."

"Of course, by all means." Before turning to walk away, he took her hand, shaking it. "Again, good work tonight."

Kel watched him for a few seconds until he reached the intersection and disappeared around the corner. Slipping back into the driver's seat, she had just engaged the ignition when a vibration on her left hip pulled her attention to her Blackberry. She retrieved the smartphone from its holster and found a text message indicator on the screen. She tapped into the text.

"DK: Hear the wail from the cage

Lifting its clamor in a rage

From the grave forever sealed

Secret things will be revealed

Witnesses   their stories tell

Mine to teach the lesson well

Recompense   is
yours to pay

Mine to reap for
Hell each day"

The message screamed trouble but she knew no one with the initials DK, so she reasoned it could just as well have been a joke. She touched the reply key.

"Wrong number?" Kel typed the question and pressed Send.

She dropped the phone on the seat next to her, put the cruiser into drive, and eased northbound toward Cherry Street. With hope that a promotion might be coming, she gave her thoughts to the report she had promised Chief Ballesteros. He would be watching, so it needed to be lucid and precise.

As she pulled up the hill, the traffic signal at Fourth Avenue showed red. While she waited, the phone vibrated against her leg. Picking up the device, she read the backlit text.

"DK: Right Nyte, Kel"

Chapter 4

Kel made the final edit to the incident report and consulted the watch strapped to her wrist. Minnie Mouse had never lied to her—3:07 a.m. As she predicted, it had taken half the night at the King County Jail to book the tavern brawlers.

She slid the mouse over the Submit button on the monitor and clicked.

She had promised Chief Ballesteros a page turner, but this one wasn't up to her usual standard. Not long after she started writing, two more messages hit her phone from the same out-of-state number. They pulled her thoughts back to the poem. When that text first arrived, since it carried no specific timeline or threat to any specific person, she had parked it as the ramblings of a frantic mind. Not so with the new texts.

Her instinct said that whatever this DK planned to do, he had done, so the prudent thing would have been to report the messages as soon as they came in. Then, when she finished in Booking, she would have been free to go home to her daughter, and to shower off the beer still sticking to her back from the unchanged uniform shirt.

But he made it personal. *He knows my name*. As she walked to the garage elevator, she brought the messages up on her phone's display and found the first of the two texts. The address was only a short ten-minute detour from her route home.

The original poem's last line read, "Mine to reap for Hell each day," Did that suggest serial murder? He also had written, "Recompense is yours to pay." A*m I the prey or has the UNSUB already killed his first victim*?

Descending the shaft to the first-level parking, she scrolled to the second message—an invitation—"door's open." Despite what Chief Ballesteros had said about her potential a couple hours before, investigating without reporting in, even as an off-duty officer, could be career suicide, or at least result in disciplinary action. Being a patrol officer assigned to protect the streets from jaywalkers, illegal U-turns, and the drunk 'n disorderly, she had no authority to investigate a hangnail, let alone a violent crime. But with two generations of cop forming her DNA, the pull was too powerful to resist.

When the elevator door opened, she stepped into the garage and retrieved her keys from a clip on her belt. As she located the transponder for her cruiser, a thought that had been nagging at the back of her mind returned. *DK could have found my name anywhere, but my phone number?* He had chosen her SPD issued phone to be the communication link, yet all department cell phone numbers were unlisted. It seemed DK had a connection inside the department.

As she merged onto Interstate 5 South, she knew she shouldn't proceed without laying some ground work. She needed help with the phone number sending the texts. To do that, she would have to take someone into her confidence, someone she probably didn't know. Risky, but she picked up her phone and dialed the number.

"Crime lab, Bimal," a perky fresh-from-college-on-his-first-real-job male voice said with more than a hint of Hindi accenting it.

"This is Officer Kel Nyte, Bimal. I'm wondering if you could do me a small favor."

"Sounds like you're talking off the record."

"With your resources it should only take five minutes. Would you mind?"

"Well, it's been a slow night, sure why not? Anything for the SPD. What do you need?"

Minutes later, Kel stood aside her cruiser and stared up at the converted warehouse. Nestled under Interstate 5, the three-story building stood a few hundred yards from the runway of Boeing Field between the old Burlington Northern railroad tracks on the east and Airport Way South on the west. A developer during the inflation of the dotcom bubble despite the surround sound of trains, planes and automobiles had transformed this abandoned edifice into a trendy condo project.

She looked across the parking lot to the red brick structure. A sour taste rose to the back of her tongue. She swallowed hard, but an uneasy bitterness lingered on her palate. Pulling her weapon from its holster, she released the magazine to verify it was fully loaded. The weight in her hand gave witness to its lethal contents, and the click as she slapped it back in place gave her confidence. She moved forward, crossing the weathered asphalt to what appeared to be the main entrance.

With a tug, the glass door opened wide enough for her to slip into the small lobby. She followed the sign to the elevator and pushed the call button. The door parted immediately as if it anticipated her arrival. Once inside the cab, she pressed the 3 button and stood facing the door. She kept the gun angled toward the floor with her knees flexed and feet shoulder-width apart. When the lighted display flickered from 2 to 3, she took a deep breath. An anxious chill rippled over her as the door slid left. The hallway stood empty.

Peering around the exit in both directions, she blew her lungs empty and stepped into the corridor. The door nearest her read 301. She slunk down the hall, taking slow, cautious steps toward the door marked 304. Every few feet she looked behind her to ensure no one followed. No one did.

At the door, she slipped black leather gloves over her hands, reached for the door handle, and turning it, with no surprise found it unlocked—*door's open*. The anxiousness she had tried to swallow in the parking lot now manifest as fear. Not the paralyzing fear of an acrophobic on the brink of a precipice, but enough to heighten her senses—sight, sound, scent—to keep her at ready.

She knew she wasn't bulletproof but she believed she had been summoned to this address not to take *her* last breath. DK hadn't sent the incoherent text just to execute her; at least not yet. What she did understand from that message suggested that he had a plan—*mine to teach the lesson well.* The most likely conclusion was that he invited her here to expand her understanding of his mission.

Armed with the belief that if anyone was to die behind that door, they were already dead, she raised her pistol, and thrust the door with her foot. With the light of a single table lamp on the far side, she peered into the living room and searched for an indication that someone expected her. No one stirred.

The Glock in her right hand and her finger on the trigger, she pulled a flashlight from her belt with her left. After entering the apartment, she swung the front door closed behind her. The presence of the killer lingered in the room like the chill of a cloudless winter's night—unseen but unmistakably evident.

She pressed forward. Across the room, a photo took center stage on the lamp table. Her chest grew heavy as she looked at the two women leaning against the trunk of a palm tree captured in a loving embrace. *Victims?*

Behind the living room, the kitchen opened on the backside of a bar. Except for the clock on the microwave and the light streaming from the living room, it was dark. She slipped through the opening at the end of the bar and flashed her beam into the shadows. Other than a woman's purse and a set of keys on the counter, the room offered no other sign of human life.

She made her way down the hallway to the bathroom. On the sink, a solitary glass of white wine stood next to an uncorked bottle. The condensation from the two glass containers had created merging puddles on the countertop. Moving toward the bathtub, she gripped the flashlight between her teeth and slipped one glove off. The water was clean and tepid, and a baby powder scent rose to greet her. With the lack of soap residue on the surface and the towels dry and hung in place, she sensed the bath had been abandoned—or more likely interrupted.

Pulling her glove over her hand again, she embraced the flashlight with the gun and moved back into the hallway. From a room on the left she saw a dim glow pouring out of the darkness. Peering around the doorframe, she found nothing but the light of a computer monitor. She turned quickly toward the otherwise darkened room and swept it with the flashlight. *Clear*.

One room remained. She confronted the opening, feeling the hairs on her arms stand erect. The beam from her flashlight, trained toward the doorway, was absorbed by the darkness beyond. A dense gloom spilled out of the chasm. It eclipsed her despair over the expected victim with the evil of the unknown assassin. Yet it drew her from the void.

Behind her, from somewhere she had already cleared, a sound resonated off the walls—a distinct metallic click. A surge of panic filled her ears with the sudden hammering of blood as she sensed the muzzle of a cocked pistol pointed at her back. He had a clean shot; could drop her before she took her next breath.

It's said that in unexpected life-threatening moments, a disjointed newsreel of memory flashes through the mind. The good, bad, and ugly fly by in a fast-forward display of pride, disappointment and regret. Joy over accomplishments, sadness over loved ones left behind, remorse over unfulfilled dreams, guilt over fractured relationships.

But none of that distracted Kel from her duty—not this time. Her only thought? *"How'd I miss him?"*

As quick as the sound touched her ears, she twisted with a jerk to face DK down and dropped to one knee, making a smaller target. Sweeping the hallway with her handgun, she was surprised to find no one there. Nothing threatened.

Then a second click from the living room brought with it the familiar Big Ben chime. The carillon from an old clock rang the three-quarter hour and she recognized the clicks now as the clock's works slipping into action. She caught her breath, stood and turned back.

With only three steps, she reached the doorway to the master bedroom. She thrust her hands inside and followed the swath of light as it severed the murk from right to left. When the shaft swept over the bed, it fell on the form of a woman. Kel stood frozen for several seconds waiting for signs of life—a breath, a twitch, a sigh—but nothing stirred. The figure looked like she had lain down on top of the bedspread, perhaps waiting for the tub to fill, and fell asleep.

Shaking her head, Kel continued to sweep the room until she was certain she was the only other soul in the bedroom. Next to the bed, the only things out of place—a bedside lamp and a telephone—had tumbled to the floor, and adjacent to them, laid a Browning nine millimeter pistol.

Turning her beacon back toward the motionless body, she found the mid-fortyish face of one of the two women in the photo on the living room table. For the second time tonight, she felt for a pulse. Though the skin warmed to the touch, unlike Marcel, this time no throb greeted her fingertips.

She holstered her weapon and walked back to the second bedroom. Pulling her phone from its sheath, she called dispatch to report a suspicious death. With officers now on the way, and the medical examiner alerted, she turned to the glowing monitor and sat before the desk. A four-line verse, the same rhyme and iambic meter as the one she had received earlier, was on the screen. But where the original poem had been vague, this one confirmed with the first line that what she discovered in the bedroom was the beginning of a planned series of murders.

First the one who owes so much

Final payment by my touch

Breath of life fails to draw in

Pillow talk, my secret sin

She pulled a notepad from her shirt pocket and copied down the text of the poem. As she slipped it back into her pocket, her phone rang.

"Officer Nyte? Bimal from the crime lab. I think you'll want to hear this."

"Go."

"As you suspected, the number's untraceable. You can buy a prepaid phone like it just about anywhere."

"So there's no lead?"

"I didn't say that, but it took me more than the five minutes allowed."

"Okay, I owe you, but you're on the clock now."

"No longer off the record? Cool. Well, I've found some interesting things about it. It was bought online and drop shipped to Seattle from Taipei, Taiwan."

"Taipei? How was it paid for?"

"Still working on that."

"Do you know where it was shipped?"

"Of course, but the trail gets cold at this point. The address is a shop in the Roxbury neighborhood that been closed for a while. The tracking shows that the package didn't require a signature and it was left at the rear door, so there's no record of who received it."

"What about activity?"

"The last activity, almost an hour ago, came from the same tower that's pinging your call right now."

"That's no surprise. The perp sent a text directing me to this address. What about GPS?"

"Well, it gets even more interesting there."

"Why? Where's the phone now?" she asked, her mind a sudden whirl of apprehension.

"Give or take...within 300 feet of you."

Chapter 5

"Bimal," Kel screamed as she yanked her Glock from its holster. She bolted toward the doorway. "You think that might have been the first thing you told me? Call dispatch, get back up, and then come back on the line. " She switched the phone to speaker and slipped it into the holster on her belt.

At the doorway, she pushed the pistol out in front of her and peered around the opening. Alone in the hallway, she turned toward the master bedroom. Minutes before, distracted by finding the victim's body, she had not cleared the whole room, a neglect proving a mortal failure to rookies. Now she had to confront it again, knowing DK likely lurked in the darkness beyond.

Moving forward, she again pierced the darkness with the flashlight beam. As she neared the entrance, something stirred on the fringe, below the shaft of light. So transient, she doubted she had seen anything at all. In her heightened sentience, it could have been a shifting shadow caused by the nervous tremble of her hand as she focused the light into the gulf of uncertainty. Then, with a will of its own, her hand drew down, and the beacon fell on the glow of a pair of eyes. A cat whose coat was as black as the murk in which it had hidden whisked passed her down the hall.

Her heart had been pounding before, but now it rattled her rib cage. She paused, took a couple of deep, silent breaths, and held the last one. *Get to the living room and wait for back up.* There she'd have the advantage of light and space. But, exhaling with slow purpose, she pressed on, unwilling to give the murderer another moment's freedom.

She followed the light into the bedroom and swept as before from right to left. With her back to the wall, she skirted the armoire toward the only space left in the bedroom to hide. As she walked, her eyes continued to scan the periphery of the room for movement. When she reached the back side of the bed, she flicked the light momentarily into the void between the queen-sized bed with its lifeless burden and the wall. *Clear*.

Her eyes followed the beam as it rose toward the closet, and she crept to the opening. Before entering, she paused, listening for breath or the stir of someone beyond. If they had taken refuge inside, she envied their capacity for calm. She struggled for it now.

The light, married with her Glock, sliced the darkness, and she left the last bastion of safety behind and entered the closet. She found herself in a narrow hallway. On the left, double mirrored sliding-doors concealed the wardrobe of the woman on the bed. *The next time she's dressed it'll be by a mortician with a frock from behind that door*. On the right, a bathroom door stood ajar.

The master bath made more sense as a hiding place—it was larger and gave the perp more room to maneuver—but the closed doors of the closet stole her attention first. She reached with her left hand to the nearest of the two doors and, with a quick thrust, pushed it open. The wheels sent it sideways until a thump indicated it had come to rest at the end of the track. Diverting her flashlight to the nook, she peered into the space behind the double doors. An upright vacuum stood on the carpet below boxes on the shelf, clothes on the pole and shoes in a rack. *Clear.*

She turned the beam away and aimed it at the bathroom door. Knowing this was the last recess DK could hide she stepped to the side and raised her gun.

"Hands behind your head," she shouted, "and step out slowly."

She waited for the door to swing, the rustle of clothes or gunfire, but heard nothing. She raised her voice, "Now."

Still nothing stirred within. She pushed the door open and entered the bathroom. It, too, was clear.

Taking her phone, she said, "Bimal."

"Yes, Officer Nyte. Dispatch is sending a squad your way."

"Well, there doesn't seem to be a rush. Except for me and a cat, there's nothing alive in this apartment. I'm hanging up now."

As she walked back into the master bedroom her muscles were suddenly controlled by an electric discharge behind her. Her hands gave an involuntary jerk. The pistol and flashlight tumbled away. Still conscious, she saw the floor coming up fast to meet her. Once prone, unable to move, she lay sprawled.

"Face to face, Kel," a male voice whispered behind her. "Are you listening?"

Kel, paralyzed in body from the two electrodes grabbing her back, was still able to think. *A stun gun? He could have killed me instead.* That meant she had been right earlier when she reasoned he wanted her to learn more about his purpose. She pushed the embarrassment of being captured and the pain to the back of her consciousness—*damn it, I didn't clear the second bedroom closet*—and focused her attention on the tobacco-scented voice murmuring above her.

"I've only lost one quest in my life, Kel, and that one bound me for years. Now I'm inviting you to the pursuit of your life. Only one of us may survive. If you're the fortunate one, it's because you have learned from the teacher and passed my test. Failure is to your peril. I look forward to the final revelation."

In her mind, words formed without the ability to take voice. The cop bravado in her exclaimed, *I'll nail you bastard*, but if she could have asked just one question, it would have been, "Why me?" To her knowledge she didn't have enemies, at least none who would stoop to murder as a source of revenge, and certainly no one who would be willing to die to prove his point. *Is his demented lesson mine to learn, or mine to convey?*

When the faint whisper of a siren in the distance seeped into the bedroom, DK kicked Kel's pistol under the dead woman's bed.

"This isn't our last meeting. Be careful, though, as, just like tonight, you'll never know what rock I'll slither out from under, and next time I may not be so nice."

He gave her another jolt, chuckled. "Good hunting, Kel."

The stun gun fell next to Kel's head. The vibration of the floor beneath her gave indication that DK had run toward the living room door and the subtle click as it closed verified it. It took several seconds for her mind to regain control of her body, and once her muscles responded to her commands, she reached for the flashlight and then crawled toward the bed. She lifted the dust ruffle. Next to the wall on the other side of the bed lay her gun.

After circling behind the bed to pick up the .357, she sprinted to the common hallway. The electric hum of the elevator at the far end caught her ear. She knew he wouldn't take that way down and had probably engaged it as a diversion, but next to it, the green glow of an exit sign hung from the ceiling over a door. She sprinted for it.

Once inside the stairwell, she heard a door slam several floors below. She reached for her phone and started down the three flights, taking two steps at a time. As she ran, she pressed and held the shortcut key for Dispatch.

"Where's my backup?" she screamed when they answered.

"Identify, please."

"Badge five-zero-niner, location five-seven-one-four Airport Way South, unit three-zero-four. Perp has left the building, officer in ground pursuit."

"Five-zero-niner, officers are on the way. Do you have a visual?"

"Negative."

She reached the ground floor, exited the building, and found herself in the parking lot. She ran away from the structure to the center of the lot and searched for movement. Turning back toward the condos, in her peripheral vision, she saw a man, revealed under a streetlight. He ran on the sidewalk a hundred yards away on the far side of the street.

"Got him," she shouted into the phone and turned to sprint in his direction. "Send units to South Lucile and Airport Way."

"Copy," the woman's voice acknowledged.

"Going silent," Kel said and slid the phone into its sheath.

The man turned west on South Lucile and disappeared behind a building. Kel continued her charge toward the intersection. She had recovered from the Taser, and all five senses in her body converged into a solitary pursuit, now putting action to the words she couldn't utter moments before, "Nail the bastard."

As she reached the curb and leapt into the street, air horn blasted to her left. The sound of rubber screeching against the pavement robbed her thoughts of the task at hand. On reflex, she twisted away and hurled herself back toward the sidewalk.

Chapter 6

"What the hell do you think you're doing, Officer Nyte?" Lieutenant Louis Martinez shouted.

It had taken over two hours before the first crime scene investigators made their way to the scene. Martinez, her boss, and Chief of Detectives, Nathanial Ballesteros followed close on their heels, entering the building together.

After releasing the crime scene to a South Precinct officer, she had stayed out of the way in her cruiser, as ordered. While she waited, the paramedics on the scene cleansed the superficial scrapes ground into the heels of her hands she had used to break her fall to the sidewalk after jumping out the path of the eighteen-wheeler. They also offered two—she insisted on three—aspirin which had helped dissipate the ache in her knees. But they had nothing to offer for the earful she knew was imminent.

She had rehearsed the conversation. She hoped it would be after a morning double shot espresso or two, but seeing the stern look on Martinez's face when he exited the building after fifteen minutes inside, she realized no amount of caffeine could prepare her for what was about to explode. A civil conversation wasn't likely, judging by the deep furrow on his brow and the embers glowing in the eyes glaring at her through the window. To make matters worse, the scowl on Chief Ballesteros's face gave no confidence that the next few minutes would be anything other than grueling.

The way Lieutenant Martinez had called her by her title rather than his usual address, "Kel," brought back memories of her dad when she had done something stupid as a teenager—a frequent occurrence. Then, she'd expect the immediate outcome of being sent to her room. But now there was no room to go to, and Lou seemed in no mood to send her away, yet.

"Without backup?" he continued.

She stepped out of the car, hoping to subdue his wrath, and addressed him as she would in the squad room. "I'm sorry, Lou."

"'Lou' my ass. It's Lieutenant Martinez."

"Yes, sir."

"It's five-thirty in the goddamn morning. My captain woke me from a dead sleep to tell me to get my ass over here because one of my people is wandering around a crime scene, alone. Do you have any idea how pissed I am?"

"I'm beginning to understand, Lieutenant Martinez. But I…"

"But what, Officer Nyte?" Chief Ballesteros asked. "What compelled you to walk into *this* crime scene?"

Kel was surprised at the disparity between the kindness the chief had shown her after the bar scuffle only hours before and his agitation now. He didn't seem as full of rage as Lou, but there was nevertheless a succinct quality in his tone. She sensed something was wrong with the situation—more than just her discovering a murder.

"I didn't know it was a crime scene, sir."

"So what brought you here?"

"I received a message on my phone with this address," she said. She was willing to let them in on the latest two texts, but she needed to quiet their ire before she revealed the mysterious poem she had received earlier. "So I came to see why."

"Let me see it," Lieutenant Martinez said.

Kel took her phone from its holster on her service belt and thumbed to the right message. She held it up for both men to read.

"So whoever sent this," Ballesteros said, "told you to expect an open door. Did you think the suspect might have been waiting on the other side of that door?"

"I certainly gave it some thought, sir, and I was prepared."

"But you entered without back up," Lieutenant Martinez said, and Kel could see anger's flames crawling up his neck.

"Yes, sir. I didn't think I would need back up."

"And yet he was lying in wait for you. Maybe he wanted to kill you."

"Perhaps, but not tonight. He had a chance but didn't take it. Somehow in his mind I'm connected to this. Sir, he knows my name. He dared me to chase him."

"So what are you saying?" Ballesteros asked.

"Sirs, I need to work this case."

"You're not a detective," Lieutenant Martinez shouted.

"I've passed the exam," she said and paused, considering whether this was the time to express her derision. Deciding she might not get an opportunity like this again with Ballesteros already seeming to side with her earlier, she continued. "But you've been holding me back."

"If you're saying I've held you back for any reason other than there's no opening or you're not qualified, then this conversation is over."

"That I *am* qualified speaks for itself, Lieutenant," she said, glancing toward Chief Ballesteros, "but I'm not asking for a promotion, just a chance to work this case."

"For all I know, you did this."

"Me?" she said and her eyelids pulled back in astonishment. "What motive would I have to kill her?"

"Let's try to turn the volume down here," Ballesteros said, nodding toward the edge of the parking lot.

"You don't know, do you?" Lieutenant Martinez continued at the same volume, as if the chief hadn't spoken.

"Know what?" Kel asked, looking in the direction the chief indicated. A couple of news crews were pointing their cameras toward them. "What's going on?"

"The victim is Susanne Lowen."

"Susanne Lowen...from the crime lab? So that's why *you're* here, Chief. I've never met her. I had no idea."

"With Susanne having single handedly destroyed your dad's biggest case, would it surprise anyone if he wanted her dead?"

"So that's it? You think my dad put me up to this. Well, if I killed her, why would I hang around here to implicate myself? And why would I have these Taser burns on my back? Sir, this is only the beginning. You saw the poem he left up there. "First...'"

"That's enough, and that's an order," Ballesteros said, raising his voice again.

"Look, Chief, Lieutenant," she said, calming her tone and reaching for her phone. "He speaks in poems like the one he left Susanne. He sent me one just a few hours ago. Listen to this, 'Recompense is yours to pay, mine to reap for Hell each day.'"

"Sounds like he *is* after you," the Chief said.

"Maybe, but isn't it obvious Susanne's murder is the first of several he's planning? Why he's chosen to communicate through me, I don't know. But if I'm on his list, who better to investigate? I have motivation, and with this…," she shook the phone toward them, "a road map to this mind. I'm just asking for a chance. I'm due some vacation, let me take a week and see where it takes me. I'll keep you informed."

"Forty-eight hours," Lieutenant Martinez interjected, "but you're on the clock."

"Two days isn't much time to generate leads. How about four?"

"You're just a Temp-D, so two, and if you're making progress, we'll talk."

"You'll need a partner," Ballesteros said.

He turned toward a uniformed officer who was manning the crime scene taped barricade a few yards away and said, "Go find Jake deLaurenti. He's probably with the body."

"Jake?" she said. "You've assigned Jake to investigate a cop killer?"

Chapter 7

After leaving Susanne Lowen's crime scene, Kel stopped by her house. Saul challenged her at the living room door with a four-footed protective stance and a deep growl, but once he recognized her, he trotted over and nuzzled his snout into her hand.

"Let's find Chrissie."

As Saul ran toward the stairs, Kel stopped in the kitchen to drop two slices of whole wheat bread into the toaster.

When she reached the top of the stairs, Kel stuck her head into Chrissie's room. Saul stood next to the bed and looked eagerly back and forth between the two women in his life. Chrissie rose to her elbows, blinked the sleep from her eyes and stared at her mother.

"What time is it?" Chrissie asked.

"Seven-twenty. Breakfast, five minutes."

Kel walked down the hall to her own room to change out of her beer spattered uniform. By the time she arrived back in the kitchen, Chrissie had buttered the toast and poured a couple bowls of cereal—Wheaties for Kel and Coco Puffs for herself.

"Morning, sweetie," Kel said and slipped her arm around her daughter's shoulders.

"You look tired, Mom."

"Been a long night, but I'm fine."

"Hey, do I still get my phone back on Sunday?"

So Kel could spend most of the day with Chrissie, she had volunteered to take swing shift during the summer months. Chrissie's job during her summer vacation was to keep up with the chores around the house in the evenings so they could spend the daytime hours together. But she had gotten distracted with texting her friends, and after numerous reminders of the dirty dishes and laundry scattered around the house, and the bedroom that resembled the path of a Midwestern twister, she went on restriction.

"Do you think two weeks is enough to learn about privilege?" Kel asked, with a spoonful of the last scrapings of flakes on the way to her mouth.

Swallowing a bite of toast, Chrissie grunted, "Uh huh, I learned my lesson."

Kel gave her a wary look. "Well…you continue to keep up with your chores this week and you'll have your phone on Sunday.

"By the way, I'll be working days this week. I got a reassignment I'll tell you about later. So, you need anything, give me a call, okay?"

"'Kay, Mom."

"Now give me a kiss, I've got to run."

Even though the thermometer read the low 60s, in an attitude born in the Northwest—the sun is for basking no matter what the temperature—Kel decided the get acquainted cup of coffee with Jake would be best outside. She secured the last unoccupied sidewalk table at Starbucks from a young woman dressed in a dark blue business suit. The woman had been packing her laptop into a satchel as Kel approached and, shooting her a "don't rush me" glare, took her time gathering her things. Then she joined the Monday morning pedestrian parade of frown etched faces inching their way toward another work week.

Alone under the broad green canopy of maple trees lining the avenue, Kel unlatched the citadel protecting the painful yet pleasing memory the shoulder-length auburn-haired man evoked last night just around the corner at the Wishing Well. It transported her to a summer vacation when Chrissie was five and Lance, her partner, had yet to leave for the Middle East the first time. She could almost hear the hoof beats clomping on pavement as a draft horse drew a creaking street car down steel tracks, and it took her to a safe place the forces of circumstance could never breach.

Kel and Lance, exhausted after a long day, had stopped to rest for a few minutes inside the ice cream parlor on Main Street, Disneyland. Chrissie, who should have been whining and out of gas like normal five-year-olds, pranced around the table, pointing out the window, jabbering.

As Lance returned to the table, holding Chrissie's cone out, he asked, "Ice cream?"

"Goofy, Daddy," she said, grabbing the treat and pointing again out the window to the center of Main Street where, surrounded by kids and parents, the over-sized, floppy-eared character posed for pictures. "See Goofy?"

"You've got it, punkin," he said and picked her up in his arms. "Goofy it is."

Kel took her cone from Lance and, as the other two left the parlor, she pulled a camera from her purse. "This is what life's about," she thought as she watched Chrissie's arm slip around her daddy's neck and disappear under his shoulder-length auburn hair.

"Three simple rules," Jake said after he placed two recyclable cups on the table. He pulled out a chair and sat down.

Kel had never met Jake deLaurenti but with the word around the department she wondered why he hadn't been forced to trade his unmarked sedan for a three-wheeled Cushman, SPD parking enforcement's typical mode of transportation. He had a good closing ratio, but partnering with Jake wasn't for the risk averse. Of his last two partners, one lay in the hospital hooked to feeding and oxygen tubes. The other, Willie Jenkins, ended up dead.

"Only three?" Kel asked, picking up her cup.

Steam from the latte floated up through the drinking hole like a wisp of white papal-smoke. She raised it to her lips and turned her eyes away from the slender forty-five-year-old man. Across the street in Pioneer Park, a male guide led a group of two dozen tourists under the wrought iron Victorian Pergola and between the flanks of homeless who sat on benches for their morning social.

"First, stay the hell out of my way," Jake said following her eyes to the scene in the park. "My closing ratio's high, and I plan to keep it that way. No rookie slows me down, got it?"

She slurped the steamed-milk foam on the surface of her beverage, nodded an acknowledgement, and turned back toward him.

"Next, if you forget rule number one, I'll squash you like a cockroach no matter who your dad is or was."

"And number three?" she asked.

"Ah, yes, number three." He shifted his whole body toward her. "Rookies are a boil on my ass, and female rookies are the infected core. Any questions?"

"Just one?"

"And what the hell is that, plebe?"

"Are you always this sweet on a first date?"

"I don't have first dates, just conquests." He scanned her body from head to toe. "Interested?"

She recognized in his eyes the same leer she saw in so many men on a first encounter. She still piqued that she wasn't seen as a person but rather a desirable possession. Other women might use their appearance as a tool, but for her, the natural olive-toned skin, fine bone structure and eyes the color of spring growth on fir trees were a curse.

"You're such a charmer. I hate to say no, but," she paused and rubbed her chin, "I'll pass. However, now that we have the rules established, we have a serial killer with a tight timeline. We should swap notes."

"I'll go first so you can see how this works."

"By your leave," she agreed and shot him a sneer.

He turned his gaze back toward the park. "Well, for starters, *my* victim worked for the police department in the crime lab. That makes this personal. Judging from the two sizes of women's clothes and shoes in the closet, and mail addressed to two different women, she likely has a live in partner who is female. At the moment we don't know where she is, so she'll be a person of interest. I'll do some background on her today."

"I hate to disagree with you so soon, but…"

"Rule one!" he shouted and a couple at the next table broke off their conversation to stare at him.

While the two stood and left, he continued as if there had been no interruption, "See how this works? There was no forced entry, so either it was the partner or someone else with a key or someone she knew and let in."

"Or someone jimmied the lock," Kel added.

"No tool marks on the lock," he said, raising his voice over hers, "so if there's the remote possibility that's true, the perp has access to professional lock picking tools.

"Except for a few things out of place in the bedroom, there didn't seem to be much of a struggle, which would lead me to believe that she either knew her assailant or was somehow incapacitated very quickly—"

"He did stun me—"

"We'll get to that," he interrupted and faced her again. "Are you following me? Am I going too fast?"

"Not at all," she said. "So far it sounds cliché, by the book, but when you're ready for facts and not assumptions, you'll let me know, right?"

He rolled his eyes and shook his head, pausing to take a swallow of his coffee. "The lab guys will go over the computer to see if any leads can be generated from the poem. Once they've finished, I may have other doors to knock on. And then there's you."

"I thought I covered that with Martinez."

"Why do you think he wants you to ride shotgun with me?"

"I had hoped it was so I could learn something from a seasoned professional, but I see now it's so you can keep an eye on me."

"Right," he said, nodding. "You've passed your first test in deductive reasoning. Stick around and you just might learn something yet. For now I have a short suspect list, a lesbian lover and a green-eyed boil acting on behalf of her dad. What astute words of wisdom can *you* offer?"

"If the ME's time of death is accurate, around one a.m.," she said, placing her cup on the table grate, glaring at him, "you'll be able to corroborate my story because I was in Central Booking at the time, waist deep in drunks. And then there's the gender of the perp. I have doubts that the killer's female."

"Based on what?"

"I did have a personal encounter and as you already know, I have the Taser burns to prove it."

"So you say. Anybody could have put those there."

"My God, you're thick."

"Just doing my job. So this person who stunned you—"

"You mean the man who stunned me."

"Okay, the man. You saw him and can give a description?"

"Not exactly. Being pinned to the floor with 50,000 volts hammering you kind of puts a person's observation skills at a disadvantage. He stayed out of my line of sight. But when I gave chase, he passed under a streetlight and I could see he was pressing six feet in height and wore a red baseball cap."

"Look around, plebe. See any suspects?"

Kel scanned the square. A man and a woman with the tour guide wore matching red ball caps. She shook her head.

"What you meant to say is that you saw someone running. You have no way of knowing it was him. It could just as easily have been some guy with a red hat out for a jog."

"At three-thirty in the morning?"

"There could be a hundred reasons why he was out running. Point is, that may have been the perp, but you have no way of knowing for certain."

"I suppose you're right, but my gut says the coincidence of him running on that street at the very moment I'm giving chase—"

"Coincidence is usable but not enough. That's called circumstantial. It can be used to build a case, but there has to be more. What else you got? Did he speak to you with a distinctive male tone?"

"No, he whispered, but it was a man's whisper."

"Really." Jake gave her a noncommittal shoulder shrug and tipped his cup for another drag of caffeine.

Kel's eyes drifted toward the tourists again who had moved down the street another half block toward an alley entrance to Seattle's underground tour of the remnants of the great fire of 1889. Another block and a half away to the west, the sun glanced off the dark-tinted side window of a black sedan as it turned from Elliott Avenue on the waterfront and crawled up Yesler Way.

"The suspect is most likely not the victim's partner," she continued. "Susanne is an unfortunate part of a much larger plan, but not the endgame. This victim was probably not known to the suspect, but not a random choice, either."

"Humph."

"Lieutenant Martinez told you about the text I received last night. It's a poem just like what we saw on Susanne's computer." She held it up for him. "You can see there's a line that gives indication to motive, 'Mine to teach the lesson well.' He feels self-appointed to impart some knowledge to a specific pupil."

"And who's the pupil?"

"He hasn't given enough to know that yet, but it seems personal."

"As in 'you're the pupil.'"

"Maybe, but I'm not sure. You see that line, 'Recompense is yours to pay?' I just don't know if 'yours' is in reference to me, or if the pupil is something even bigger like the SPD or the city. As I said, I don't know enough yet, but there are other clues."

"Like?"

"For example, he uses the singular form of 'lesson' so it appears there's only one lesson, but he goes on to say, 'Witnesses their stories tell.' 'Witnesses' and 'stories' being plural. I believe he intends to bring multiple witnesses, each telling some story about the pupil to confirm the evidence of whatever truth he intends to reveal. Susanne's investigation, then, must center on finding the intersection between her and the pupil. So, yes, we should dig into her past, and let's look for old lovers, snubbed girlfriends, and since she was SPD, closed cases, but let's also keep an open mind. She may have been coincidental to her own death, not the subject of it. The deeper we dig into her history, we might begin to understand who the pupil is, and when we know that, there is a good chance he or she'll lead us to DK."

"DK? You're so convinced it's a serial you've already named him. Just like dear old dad. Let's see, what did he call his serial, the one Susanne set free? Oh, yeah, the Rat City Exterminator."

Kel glared at him. The mention of Rat City, a local colloquial reference to a part of southern West Seattle, and the district where the Exterminator disposed of his victims, stirred a thought. The Roxbury

60

neighborhood where DK had his phone delivered sat in the middle of Rat City.

"What, no sharp retort?" Jake asked.

"The press dubbed him with that moniker," Kel snapped. "Dad hated it. Now, may I go on?"

"Of course, I'm so enjoying your spin on this."

"'DK' is the tag on the texts, so until we know more, for me, 'DK' rather than perp.

"I don't think we have much time," she continued. "The opening word of the poem on Susanne's monitor is, 'First.' Susanne is the first witness and was the first victim, but more will soon follow. The final line of the poem right here," she said, shaking her phone, "is 'Mine to reap for Hell *each* day.' There's urgency here. If he's literal, then tomorrow there'll be another murder. That may give us more clues about the pupil, but the murders continue until either he teaches his lesson or we stop him."

Jake started clapping his hands, the sound echoing off the storefront behind them. "Daughter of the Chief, aspiring Nancy Drew, and pop psychologist all rolled into one slick chick. You need to leave the psychoanalyzing to the pros. Take your phone to the lab and, like I said, stay the hell out of my way. I'll start with Susanne's partner."

Taking another swallow from the cup, Kel noticed the black sedan she had seen a couple of minutes before had pulled to a stop and double parked in the street opposite their table. In her peripheral vision, she noticed Jake sit erect. She turned. His facial muscles twitched as his jaw clenched. He released his cup and slipped his hands below the table, unzipping his windbreaker. Then, he pushed the jacket aside and his hand fell on the butt of his service weapon.

Kel slowly reached to release the strap of her Glock.

She turned back to the Audi. The tint on the rear window was too dark to reveal anyone inside. After a few seconds, the window powered down, and the face of an Asian man in his early thirties peered out. He nodded towards her with a polite gesture and then turned to Jake and forced a smile. The leathery texture of his skin seemed to crack as it folded in an unnatural way. One hand appeared above the window frame. He formed a pistol with this finger and thumb, and aimed at Jake. Dropping his thumb as if the hammer had just fallen on the chamber, he jerked his hand back and pretended to blow the smoke away from the barrel. His smile dissolved into a scowl, and, after a long glare, he turned toward the driver and powered the window closed.

Kel looked back at Jake and noticed he had released his pistol and had wrapped his hands around the cup again. Although she felt the man's gesture a threat, it was as if Jake, seeing who was behind the window, knew it wasn't. She stood, walked to the curb, and watched the car amble up the street toward the next signal.

"Who the hell was that?" she asked as she returned to the table.

"Nothing for your pretty little head to worry about. He's my concern."

"You reached for your gun," she said as she found her chair again, "like you were expecting trouble."

"Trouble is something there's always plenty of, plebe. You best stick to the case and out of my business, or…" He paused.

She leaned forward with her elbows on the table. "That sounds like a warning, Jake."

"It is what it is. You just keep rule one in your head, and you'll be fine."

"Did Willie forget rule one?"

"Damn it," he said, every muscle in this face tightening. "Willie got himself killed."

"And the case is still unsolved, even though the PD has spared no expense or resource."

Without answering, he got up from the table. Stepping off the curb to jaywalk to his waiting car, he shouted, "We're done here."

"And what should I do, partner?" Kel shouted after him.

From the middle of the street, he barked without losing stride or looking back, "Stop trying so hard to be a boil on my ass."

"Just the infected core," she yelled. "The most painful part."

Chapter 8

When last she had seen him, he had been strapped to a gurney unconscious, but now as Kel approached the side of his bed in the Harborview Medical Center ward, his eyes followed her from behind a raccoon's mask.

"Marcel?" she asked taking the hand not connected to an IV tube. "May I call you Marcel?"

He nodded.

"I'm glad to see you're awake. I'm Officer Kel Nyte. I broke up the fight last night that put you here."

Again he nodded.

"I need to ask you some questions, would that be all right?"

He grinned. It was only then she realized one of his front teeth had been broken, leaving a jagged hole in his smile.

"Did you know the man who hit you?"

He shook his head.

"Would you be able to identify the man? I have a picture." She pulled out her phone and scrolled to a booking photo of razor-wire, the man she had witnessed punching Marcel. "Is this him?"

Marcel reached for the phone and brought it close to his face as if nearsighted. After a few seconds, in an exaggerated motion, he shrugged his shoulders and pouted his lower lip.

"I'm sure it all happened so fast. That's okay for now. We can talk about it later."

Behind her, Kel heard someone approach.

"Officer?"

Kel turned to see a young woman at the foot of the bed wearing green scrubs and holding a chart.

"Yes, Officer Nyte. Can we speak?"

"Certainly."

"I'll be right back, Marcel," Kel said with a smile, then squeezed and released his hand. She followed the nurse out the door.

"I know you can't divulge much about his condition, but we arrested the man on the scene who did this. He's in jail now. He's due to be arraigned later today, which means bail will likely be set. I just need to know if Marcel, besides a broken nose and tooth, is going to suffer any long term affects from this beating. Any reason that might affect bail?"

"The damage to his face is all superficial, and except what you've observed, he isn't busted up in any other way. We've done X-rays and taken an MRI which showed some brain swelling, but that's to be expected. Your assailant was probably too stoned to do any real harm. I wouldn't be surprised to see Marcel... is that his real name?"

"No one knows his real name."

"Well, I wouldn't be surprised to see him walk out of here after another day or two. He doesn't talk much—"

"Much, has he spoken to you?"

"No, just a few moans and groans. He was unconscious until a couple hours ago, but he seems alert now."

"That puts me more at ease."

Reaching into her wallet, she pulled out two SPD business cards. Handing one to the nurse, she continued. "I don't know if he has any next of kin, so if anything changes or he's ready to check out, would you please see that I'm called?"

The nurse nodded and clipped the card to the chart.

"Thanks," Kel said and stepped back into the ward. She held out the second card to Marcel.

"The nurse says you're doing fine and should be able to get out of here in a day or so. SPD impounded your bike, so when you're ready, you call me, and I'll deliver it to you."

Besides the mime paint, one of Marcel's idiosyncrasies was to peddle his bike down the city streets with a red-tipped folding cane for the sight impaired. He would rap it against the cars parked along the street as if using it to find his way.

Marcel took the card and pointed at the phone number. He started to smile but gave up when a painful look passed over his face. He held up the card, shook his head, and wagged his finger back and forth over the card.

"I don't get it, what are you trying to tell me?"

He extended his thumb and pinkie finger, forming an imaginary telephone receiver, and lifted it to his ear. With his other hand, he dialed an invisible rotary phone and mouthed, "Hello." Then, like he was telling someone to be silent, he put one finger to his lips and looked at Kel.

"Got it. You could call but couldn't speak."

Marcel began to act like he was typing on a computer keyboard. When he finished, he circled his index finger in the air and pressed an fictional Enter key. Then pointing to Kel, he pretended to have a cell phone and receive a message.

"I see. You can send a message to my phone from a computer."

He tried to smile again, but a grimace caught it short.

She took the business card from him and wrote her smartphone number in the back. Handing it back, she said, "Okay, I'll wait for your text."

Chapter 9

Kel parked in the underground garage of the West Precinct on Virginia Street and pressed the elevator call button. She made her way to the third floor. The clock on the far wall showed the time at three minutes after nine a.m. as she entered the detective's bullpen—a place she dreamed of serving, yet an honor still to be earned. The room went silent as she passed through the doors, and she realized she was not alone in that opinion.

She felt the weight of eight pairs of eyes glaring at her and said, "Good morning."

Her voice expressed enthusiasm and willingness to be part of the team, but when all heads turned away to find some way to look busy, she reminded herself that the gap between her experience and their trust would take a while to close.

The office of the precinct's captain of detectives was on the wall to the left, and she could see though the open blinds that he was in. She made her way to the door of the small space, and even though it stood ajar, she knocked and waited in the doorway.

"Nyte." Captain Marcos Silva looked up from the papers on his desk and stood. "I heard you'd be joining us. Chief Ballesteros gave me a call and told me to expect you."

Stepping out from behind his desk, he walked to the doorway. Kel, who still stood in the opening, backed out of the way and let him pass.

"Okay, guys, back to work. Show's over."

He turned to Kel and continued. "They're a curious bunch, you know, boss's kid and all, but curiosity is a good thing for a detective. I've read some of your arrest reports. You have a probing quality to your work. That should serve you and the department well. This'll be a big case, Kel. Cop killings always are. I can't pretend to understand why the chief assigned you to it, but I'm sure he has good reason, so I'm here to assist in any way I can."

"Thank you, Captain. Since you mention it, it may be temporary, but I could use a place to work."

"Of course. The desk opposite Jake's is presently unoccupied."

The desk belonged to Jake's current partner—the last to fall victim to his curse. The official story read that Eddy had gone rogue on a case without Jake's or his superior's knowledge and that one night he had taken three bullets, one of those to the head, putting him in a coma. But the gossip within the department spun a different story. Jake knew what Eddy was up to on the night in question, but he was too busy flashing Franklins around a Belltown pub, looking to get laid, and had turned his phone off.

As Silva led her to Eddy's desk, he said, "You can sit here for now. As you've said, it's not permanent. Just until this case is solved or Eddy walks out of that hospital."

"Of course, sir," she said with a smile.

"You look pretty rough if you don't mind me saying."

"It's been a long night, sir, and not much sleep before it all started."

"If you'd like, there's a shower down the hallway where you can freshen up."

"Thanks, but I'm not going to be long. Just want to lay out the case and do some research. Then I'll get a few hours' sleep."

"Suit yourself. You can log into the computer with your own credentials. I think you'll find everything you need." Reaching out his hand, he concluded, "Good to have you aboard."

She took the offered hand. "Thank you, sir. This'll be perfect."

After the captain ambled back toward his office, Kel sat down and hit the switch on the computer monitor. The screen came to life, the blinking cursor awaiting her command. She savored the moment like a first kiss, knowing that her next action would begin the first chapter in her new life. Her user name and password flowed from her fingers and she pressed the Enter key. Pride swept over her like a wisp of warm breeze as the Seattle Police Department intranet painted the monitor in front of her. The dream of serving her community by solving crime rather than busting speeders was reality.

She guided the mouse with a few clicks until she navigated to a digitized photo of Susanne Lowen and printed the color representation of her in life. A whiteboard on wheels stood in the corner, so she pulled it over near the desk. With a blue marker, she wrote "DK" at the top, and six inches below the title she drew the spine and first two ribs of a fishbone chart. Starting at the left end, she wrote, "Sunday night—first text" and filled in the rest of the known events in a similar manner. Under "Monday morning-first victim killed," she taped the printed image and wrote Susanne's name below it.

Satisfied that she had documented the facts in chronological order, she slipped behind the desk again and steered the web browser to the Department of Licensing.

Chapter 10

"Damn it," Kel shouted, "he shouldn't be out on bail, ADA Johnson."

After catching three hours sleep in the SPD quiet room—out so dead she didn't notice the mattress lumps pressing against her ribs—Kel had made her way to the courthouse where razor-wire's arraignment over Marcel Marceau's beating Sunday night was scheduled. After the hearing, she confronted the assistant district attorney, a man in his mid-thirties, about her age, wearing a suit jacket two sizes too small to cover his corpulent belly. They stood in the hallway just outside the courtroom.

Kel glared into Johnson's eyes. "Marcel's going to spend more time in the hospital and recovery than that piece-of-shit will behind bars."

"You testified yourself, under oath, Officer Nyte," Johnson said, holding his brief case in front of his groin like an ancient Roman shield, "that Mr. Marceau's injuries weren't life threatening."

"Well, a broken nose and tooth may not be life threatening, but they deserve more than a slap on the wrist."

"Remember, I'm on your side, Officer. That 'piece-of-shit,' as you describe him, will get his day in court, and—"

"And I'll be a witness for the prosecution. Count on it."

Twenty minutes after leaving the ADA behind, Kel stood in the crime lab behind a man hovering over a table. He stood facing a large, wall-mounted monitor with his back to her.

"Excuse me." Kel said.

The young man turned toward her. His tousled hair, dark circles under his even darker eyes, and wrinkled clothes gave the appearance that five minutes earlier he had been comatose.

"Yes?"

"Bimal?" she asked, recognizing his Indian accent. As she had suspected from his voice on the phone, he was fresh enough that he probably hadn't yet had enough time with the department to find a wall to hang his diploma.

"Yes, and you are…"

"Kel Nyte."

"Officer Nyte," he said and thrust his hand out.

Taking his hand, she said, "It's detective now, at least temporarily, but Kel will do fine. You look exhausted."

"I haven't been home since my shift started at midnight last night, but cop killings mean all hands. I don't suppose most of us here'll get much sleep until we nail this perp."

He sliced the tip of a cotton swab and dropped it into a small tube.

"Bimal, what do you know about Susanne's personal life?"

"Nothing, I just started with the SPD last month. We worked different shifts. Her friend Georgia, though, said that she liked cats and lived with a partner."

"I met the cat, but we'll need to clear the partner."

"I think Georgia said she's out of town this weekend."

"I saw a photo in Susanne condo. She was with a woman. You can't always tell from a picture but they looked happy together."

Bimal pointed across the room to another photo of Susanne Lowen. With notes fixed to the wall around it expressing people's prayers and memories. Even though it was the same picture she had hung on the crime board in the detectives' bullpen just a few hours ago, this one spoke of her life, not her death.

"It seems her coworker's want to remember her like that," Bimal said, "not as a body on a slab."

An inscription painted on the wall above the photo pulled Kel's attention upward. A quote from the New Testament Book of Hebrews read, "Though he is dead, he still speaks."

"That's our calling," Bimal said. "It's taken out of context, of course, but it says what we feel about our mission. We try to let our unwilling guests tell the story of their life…and death."

"Is Susanne speaking?"

"We know a few things that might help build your profile, but nothing definitive. The CSI swept Susanne's home with all the forensic gear and tricks in their bag, but so far there's no trace the perp had ever been inside the condo—no prints, no hairs, no skin, no fluids—not even the lingering scent of bad breath. He's a ghost, Kel."

"Well, that phantom left Taser burns on my back. He had to buy it somewhere."

"To be honest, trying to track its origin may not give us any more help than the phone he used to text you. We have the stun gun and we're tracing the serial number, but don't expect it to lead anywhere."

"There was a pistol at the scene on the floor."

"Yes, a nine mill. Registered to Susanne. Only her prints on it. No bullets or spent rounds in it."

"She tried to hold him off with an empty gun?"

"Our theory is he had removed the bullets before she got home," Bimal said. "Let her think she had a chance."

"Playing with her like an old tomcat does a mouse. Bastard. You said you found something, though."

"It's not much. Toxicology found succinylcholine in Susanne's blood." He clicked the computer mouse and a folder opened on the screen with a series of photos overlaid in a stack. He selected two and dragged them out of the folder. Each focused on separate small flesh wounds. "It was probably delivered by one or both of these needle sticks we found on her body."

"This guy has access to drugs and medical supplies. Could be some kind of medical professional."

"Possibly but not necessarily, we all have access if we know where to look."

"How's that?"

"The Internet, Kel. Everything's there, where to buy it, dosage, even how to use a syringe. It's probably where he got the Taser and we already know the phone came from there."

"He's not making this easy."

"His point, you think?" He winked at Kel. "You know what's sad? Succinylcholine is generally used to immobilize patients during surgical procedures, but it can also be used as a fast acting paralytic. You see that wound here at the base of the neck?" He moved the pointer of the mouse until is rested on the wound, "It presents with a lot of bruising around it."

"So you think it was the first blow, to stop her from fighting. Was she awake after that?"

"Probably. Our theory is that he immobilized her for some reason. Then, when he was ready, he gave her a second dose. That one was a more skillful penetration of the median cubital vein right here in the elbow joint." He tapped the vein of his left arm with his right forefinger.

"Did that kill her?"

"It could have induced death, but in her case, the dosage was enough to put her to sleep, not stop her heart."

"There were no signs of rape or trauma at the scene. What was he doing with her?"

"Convincing her why *she* had to die? Terrorizing her? We may never know, Kel. All we know is he kept her powerless and awake until he was ready to finish her."

"He used the phrase 'Pillow talk' in the poem he left on her computer. When I found her she was lying on her bed with a pillow under her head. I suppose he could have been trying to absolving his guilt or something like that. So, if the drug didn't kill her, what did?"

Bimal pulled another photo from the folder onto the monitor's desktop. Susanne's face appeared. "Asphyxiation. Do you see the tiny specks in her eyes? That's petechial hemorrhaging. When the airway is obstructed through manual strangulation, it puts a lot of pressure on the tiny blood vessels in the eyes. They'll burst leaving this bruising."

"That's consistent with the poem then. 'Breath of life fails to draw in, pillow talk, my secret sin.' He smothered her with a pillow didn't he?"

"That's correct. There's trace of her saliva and mucus on a pillow. That's not uncommon for a bed pillow, but the placement puts the stains in the exact location of her mouth and nose. What's interesting is that the fluids were on the underside of the pillow—against the bed not her head. We believe he held it over her face, and once she expired, he slipped it under her head as if she was asleep, almost as if he cared about her."

"He put her to sleep so she wouldn't have to endure the further panic of suffocation?"

"It looks that way."

"Who intentionally kills someone but doesn't want them to suffer?"

"Someone very sick, detective, but not getting off on their struggle or pain."

"Wait, what if killing *her* was not the point? Obviously it wasn't random. She was intentionally selected. He could have put her to sleep permanently but he chose to suffocate her instead. Cause of death is a piece of the puzzle."

"Isn't COD always a part of the killer's signature?"

"Of course, but he's made a point of reaching out to me. He knows who I am. He waited for me at Susanne's to lure me into the chase. The poem on her computer was specific and he left it where I was sure to see it. No, in this case I'm not convinced COD is as much a signature as it is part of the message—part of his lesson plan.

"Speaking of his lesson plan, you should download the messages DK sent me so we can get them into evidence? They need to be analyzed."

"Of course, just need your phone," Bimal said.

Kel watched as Bimal located a cable to fit her Blackberry and plugged it in. He clicked the mouse on a popup bubble that appeared at the bottom of the large monitor.

"Haven't learned anything new yet about the *perp's* phone," he said as he clicked a folder inside her smartphone's hard drive. "We have inquiries out to the manufacturer. Hoping to hear soon…There they are. This'll only take a few seconds."

She watched the green progress bar speed across the screen.

"Has anyone been working on Susanne's computer?" Kel asked.

Bimal disconnected the cable on the phone and handed it back to Kel.

"Yeah, I've taken a peek. Just like everything else, no leads. He could have typed the poem while he sat in front of the monitor, or delivered it via some kind of portable media like a memory stick. There's no external metadata to lead us anywhere. I'm still digging, but it looks like another dead end."

She slipped the phone into the holster on her belt. "I want you to keep me informed of any developments, got it?"

"Got it. You're my first call."

Having confirmed that Susanne lived with a same-sex partner, and that she was probably out of town, as she walked away from Bimal, she called Jake.

"Spoke to Trish this afternoon, plebe," he said, and even through the poor connection, Kel heard his condescension. "She was in Denver at the time and is on her way back now. Like I said, stay the hell out of my investigation."

She felt the warm flush of outrage crawl up her neck. "I'm supposed to ride shotgun. If you don't let me in, I'll solve this solo."

"Like hell," he said, laughing.

"What do you know about Tribune Investments?"

Before she left her new desk in the bullpen, she had searched the Department of Licensing database for the plate number of the black Audi that stopped on the street next to her and Jake at Starbucks. The record showed the vehicle registered to Tribune Investments.

"Stay out of it or suffer the consequences," he said.

"Now that sounds like threat."

"It can sound like whatever you want it to. Just remember rule one."

"Stay the hell out of your way," Kel said then realized she was speaking to dead air.

Chapter 11

Built after World War II, except for fresh coats of paint, the two-story, three-dormer Cape Cod home Dirk and Clarissa Nyte had owned on Queen Anne Hill for thirty-seven years hadn't changed. They had struggled in the early days. The combined income of a rookie cop and third grade teacher weren't enough to afford the spacious home, so five years after they recited their marriage vows, Dirk took a second job as a security guard, and they moved in. Only when the family began to come along did the house transform into a haven, and the Nytes knew they would spend the remainder of their days under this roof.

The evening had been perfect for a barbecue, but as the day's shadows grew long, clouds draped the sky with dappled gray sheets, threatening rain before morning. When the wind shifted and a cool breeze from the Puget Sound crept across the yard, everyone retreated into the family home to continue Danny's, Dirk's four-year-old grandson's, birthday party.

Exhausted from the day, Dirk had settled into his favorite place—an overstuffed, brown leather chair. As he gazed around the study, echoes of laughter and tears leached from the hidden recesses in the lath and plaster where they lived in reserve waiting to form memories as vivid as the Kodachrome prints in his family photo albums.

Some of the tales were happy, like when Clarissa sat on the raised red-brick hearth and announced that Dirk was going to be a first-time daddy or the day he told her he had quit his extra job, having been promoted to sergeant with the Seattle Police Department. Others weren't so kind, like when he got the phone call from his now deceased dad, also a retired cop, that his mother had been diagnosed with Alzheimer's disease, or when Clarissa broke the news that she had an inoperable brain tumor.

The familiar moan of a loose board in the hallway's hardwood floor brought his mind back to the present. His two daughters had finished cleaning the kitchen, and judging from the sound, one of them was about ten feet from the doorway. He looked up as Shelia, his youngest daughter, Danny's mother, entered and walked across the room. She sat next to him on the hearth, took his hand, and caressed it. A ruthless litigator with an unquenchable desire to win, she was still daddy's little girl. Her tender smile warmed him.

"You look awfully comfortable there, Dad. You feeling okay?"

He massaged his left humerus. From time to time the old battle wound ached when the weather suddenly turned cool and damp. "I was getting kind of tired, but I'm better now...Can't believe Jackson would miss Danny's party."

Jackson Savell was Shelia's husband. Long before they had exchanged vows, however, he had worked his way into fabric of the Nyte family. Even more than Kel's Lance, for Dirk, Jackson filled a void. The vice-president of a local pharmaceutical research company, frequent travel was part of the job.

"He's in the other Washington this week. Meetings with the FDA. Couldn't be avoided."

Kel, who had been a few steps behind Shelia, entered the room and stopped inside the doorway. Taking a heart-shaped, framed picture of her mother from a shelf in the bookcase, she looked at the image taken the year before her mom's health had begun to fail.

"You know, I still miss her," she said, catching a tear with the back of her hand before it ran down her cheek. "It's been over a year and a half, and I miss her like it was yesterday."

Looking between the photo and Kel, Dirk felt it could have been Clarissa's reincarnation standing in the doorway. Her skin tone and deep brown hair, even when pulled back into a bristly ponytail like today, were genetic gifts from Clarissa's Sicilian heritage. Like her mother, when walking into a room, Kel brought the radiance reserved a solitary crimson rose. Without any pretense or knowledge of her effect, everything else diminished by comparison.

"I know, girls," Dirk said, nodding. "I still feel her, too." He looked beyond the room and through the years like he was reaching for a favorite comforter. Then, without warning, as if the blanket had become a leaden cloak, his eyesight blurred, his shoulders bowed and his head became too heavy to hold up. He forced his eyes closed and shook his head to clear the despair. "I know you'll think I'm losing it, but…I talk to her."

"About?" Shelia asked.

"Mostly you two."

Kel placed the picture back on the shelf and turned toward him. "What else, Daddy? You said, 'mostly,' what else do you talk about?"

He turned his eyes to the floor.

"Judging from that pained look a moment ago there's something else." Kel paused and smiled. "It's okay, Daddy. We're big girls. We can take it."

"Well, it's not like I'm depressed or morose. I know you won't get this, but I'm okay with it. So I talk to your mom about what it's like…afterwards…you know."

"After death, of course," her tone turning serious, "that's got to be on your mind. But there's more, I sense it. Something in the living is eating you."

Turning to look each of his daughters in the eye, he said, "Six months isn't enough time to say all the goodbyes, give all the hugs, and put everything right. I have a death sentence, and I'm okay with it now. I've had a good life—not as long as I would've liked, mind you—but I promised your mother I'd keep an eye on you and hopefully keep you out of trouble." Raising his eyebrows and winking, he added, "Not that you've made that easy."

Everyone laughed, and Dirk absorbed the airy lightness it offered for the moment. He didn't want his final days to be shrouded with grief. The family's reprieve had been short after Clarissa's death when three months ago the doctor had given him a six-month life expectancy.

Kel walked across the room and took her mom's matching leather chair next to Dirk. She reached for his hand.

"The truth is," he continued, "I miss your mom every day. God knows I tried to move on, but I just can't do it. So, on the plus side,"—his cop instinct surfaced as he slipped into making a list like the pros and cons of a suspect—"being terminal means I know the loneliness of missing my best friend will soon be over. But on the other hand, knowing the day doesn't mean you stop thinking about the others you love or wondering if your life had purpose."

"You *have* purpose, Dad," Shelia said, "and right now the important thing is that you know people care. Look at what the mayor's done to show appreciation."

A month ago, no longer able to give full vigor to the office, Dirk gave in to the pancreatic cancer ravaging his body and stepped down as Police Chief. The mayor held him in such high regard that he had declared Dirk the Grand Marshall in the Torchlight Parade, Seattle's annual celebration of the return of summer, on the following Friday.

"I know but there are regrets. Things your mother and I worked through. But…" He turned his eyes back to the floor. "Dying with the knowledge that someday these things may come to light is an unbearable weight. I can't go in peace wondering if someday you'll return to my grave for the last time and ask, 'who was this man, anyway?'"

"Dad as scary and as utterly absurd as that sounds, we all have secrets," Shelia said, leaning forward and slipping her arm around his shoulder.

"I know, Angel," Dirk said and met her gaze. "But every day they seem to invade my present more and more. I so fear you'll be hurt, it's keeping me awake these days."

"I understand, Dad," Shelia said. "Kel?"

"Got it, but unless you want to open the confessional now, how 'bout we keep the lid on Pandora's Box for another week, maybe longer. Then," she said, crinkling the corners of her mouth and winking, "when you're ready, you can tell us where the bodies are buried, okay?"

Dirk shook his head at the daughter who always tried to joke her way through even the heaviest matters. His years and position had given him insight into human nature. He knew Kel's sarcastic wit put off an "I don't take myself too seriously" attitude. But he feared it was really defensive posturing to camouflage her secret torments.

"This week, though," she continued, "as the mayor declared, it's 'Dirk Nyte Week,' and Friday you're the guest of honor. Can you live with that?"

"Probably, but I still worry that when the day comes—

"Don't even say it, Daddy. One thing you and Mom always taught us, despite the seriousness of our actions or the embarrassment we caused the family, forgiveness always followed. Punishment first, but then forgiveness. Whatever's haunting you, when you're ready for the exorcist, we'll be here, and we'll still love you. Don't lose another minute's sleep over it."

"Mom," Chrissie Nyte-Thorsen interrupted, her subtle contempt indicating an urgency only known to thirteen-year-old girls.

Seeing his only granddaughter, a smile returned to Dirk's face. "There's my sweet cherry pie, and where's that Danny boy?"

"He thinks it's time for birthday cake, but I got him busy watching Steamboat Willie *again*," she said and cocked her eyebrows, "for the first time."

"Ah, yes, Mickey Mouse, one of our favorites."

"What is it Chrissie?" Kel asked and shot a grin toward her daughter.

Holding up a newspaper and pointing to a front page headline, she said, "You're in the paper."

Chapter 12

"The news said you were an off duty officer who happened on Susanne Lowen's crime scene," Dirk said. "But there's more to it, isn't there? Why were you there?"

"This can't leave the room," Kel said, looking at Chrissie. "This wasn't released to the press yet, so it's important."

Chrissie, who sat on a leather hassock in front of Dirk, nodded in agreement.

Kel pulled her cellular from its belt holster and searched her messages. She stood. "I got a text, a poem, on my phone last night. Comparing its timestamp to the ME's approximate time of Susanne's death, it was sent about the time of the murder. The first part seems like a blathering rant and is hard to make sense of, but the last four lines seem pretty clear."

"Read it all," Dirk said.

She read. "Hear the wail from the cage, lifting its clamor in a rage. From the grave forever sealed, secret things will be revealed. Witnesses their stories tell, mine to teach the lesson well. Recompense is yours to pay, mine to reap for Hell each day."

When she finished, except for the distinguishable falsetto of Mickey Mouse's voice drifting down the hall from the television in the living room and the innocent laughter of a four-year-old, the study was silent.

After a few moments, Dirk spoke. "May I see that?"

He read it again to himself. "Rant or not, this is a manifesto. The first couple of lines give clues to his identity. A cage could mean many things. It could be literal, like a prison cell or, perhaps, something intangible—a psychological cage. Whatever it is, he's angered by it. 'Clamor in rage' seems to indicate the cage is unfair. The grave is interesting, but I can't tell from this if the secret it holds is from the past or future. Whatever it is, it's the key to his main purpose—to teach someone a lesson—and, obviously, he's going to keep killing until his target learns it."

"He wants me to pursue him. He made that clear while he pinned me to the floor."

"Mom?" Chrissie shouted. She jumped up from the hassock and threw her arms around Kel's waist. "Are you okay?"

"I'm fine, sweetie," she said, stroking her hair. "He just wanted my attention.

"I can pull some strings," Dirk said, "and get you assigned to Captain Silva."

"No need. Chief Ballesteros already saw to it."

"Really? Fill me in."

"Not much to tell. I convinced Chief Ballesteros and Lou Martinez that since DK choose to communicate through me, I should be part of the investigation."

"And they agreed?"

"Martinez not so much, but the Chief seemed convinced. Anyway, they put me on a short leash—two days."

"That's not much time."

"No, but Martinez has a theory," she said and sat down in her mother's chair again. "Your name has been thrown into the suspect pool."

"Pops?" Chrissie asked, and looked toward Dirk. "They think you killed that woman?"

"I'm not surprised," Dirk said. "If there's a chance Lou can smear my name, he'll take it without blinking twice."

"Why, dad?" Shelia asked.

"I'm not going there. Maybe someday but not now. You were saying, Princess?"

"His motive's as weak as you've been lately, Daddy. Just because Susanne did her job with your Exterminator case doesn't turn you into a murderer."

"Vince Buckley's guilty," Dirk said. "He may have gotten released from prison, but it's where he belongs."

"Careful, Dad," Shelia cut in. "The court freed him. Besides, he works at my firm."

"Neither of which makes him innocent. He slaughtered nineteen women before we nailed him in '92. How many victims have there been since I locked him up? None. Taking him off the street stopped the slaughter."

"Dad, I know how you feel, but to make accusations with nothing to back them is no different than what got him kicked a few months ago. I don't mean to be cruel, but he's free today because the only physical evidence you produced is the same evidence that overturned his conviction."

"What was that?" Chrissie asked.

"The Rat City Exterminator," Dirk said to his granddaughter, "whether it was Buckley or not, was ruthless. The victims were prosti…" He stopped short and shot a glance between Chrissie and Kel.

"Pops, I know what a hooker is."

Dirk looked back at her and shook his head.

"Well, after he finished with the…hooker business, he took each of the victims to an alley near where he had picked them up. Ligature marks on the victims' necks pointed to strangulation, but we never found the garrote. But from the smoke in their lungs, we determined that once they lost consciousness, he poured gas on them and then lit them on fire."

"They were still alive?" Chrissie asked.

"I told you he was ruthless. At one of the scenes, we found a cigarette underneath the girl. It was the same brand found in the ashtray of Buckley's truck. Our theory had been that he used a lit cigarette to ignite the gasoline. In all but one case, though, the cigarettes were completely consumed in the fire. But in this one, it appeared she rolled on top of the cigarette and smothered whatever flames might have burned it up."

"So, Chrissie," Kel interjected, "the woman who was murdered this morning was ordered by the court on a motion from Buckley's court-appointed attorney to retest the butt, and she found that the only DNA came from the victim herself. She had smoked the cigarette."

"It didn't prove Buckley's innocence," Dirk said. "He could have offered the girl a smoke before he killed her, but it was enough to convince the judge that there was reasonable doubt and rather than declare a new trial, he threw the case out. After serving a decade and a half, he just walked right out of prison. Tainted evidence!"

While Chrissie returned to the hassock, Kel laid her hand on Dirk's arm.

"That was *The Seattle Globe's* headline," he continued. "Susanne's report never used that word, but once the story broke, the public never heard anything else. There was nothing manufactured about the evidence, but the *Globe* editor used the column to launch an attack on me. He fixated on how a detective on a slow rise through the ranks was suddenly lifted, as it were, on the wings of the Exterminator's conviction, ultimately becoming police chief, and how Susanne's report threatened to undermine my credibility."

"But the district attorney exonerated you, Dad," Shelia said. "If you were going to kill Susanne, why now and not then? Martinez's theory doesn't make sense."

"I didn't kill her, but if this is Buckley's work, it wasn't because she set him free."

"Why then, Pops? Why would he murder her when she got him out?"

"Because her testimony put him away in the first place."

Chapter 13

DK had turned east off Interstate 5. His commander, the sterile voice of a GPS tracking device, guided him to the country road he now drove along. As if he willed it, the moon had taken cover behind a heavy blanket of clouds which left the landscape cloaked in darkness. As he passed through a rural neighborhood, an occasional stake-mounted mailbox and random security light gave evidence to the sparse population. That suited his purpose, the fewer prying eyes, the better the likelihood of success.

After another three quarters of a mile, he drove under a covering of tall fir trees. Just as the voice intoned, "Turn right in fifty feet on Balados Road," his headlights caught a green street marker. He made the turn, and as he pressed the accelerator to the floor, his eyes drifted toward the dashboard clock's amber digital display. It recorded 2:17.

Before the voice could announce his arrival, a hundred feet ahead on the right he saw what had to be his destination. Like a beacon to an approaching airplane, three red reflectors attached to a post caught his high beams.

"Destination on your right," the simulated female commanded.

He took heed and rolled to the edge of the road, verifying the address on the mailbox caught in his headlamps was his target. Powering down the GPS, he drove ahead until he found the wide spot he scouted last week. He looked into the distance both to the front and in the rearview mirror. His nerves settled a degree when he saw no headlights in either direction. He switched his headlamps off, made a U-turn, and pulled his car under an evergreen tree.

A shoulder bag with everything he needed lay on the passenger seat. He grabbed the handle, eased the driver's door open, and stepped out on the soil dampened by an earlier rain shower. With a nudge of his hip, the door clicked shut. He glanced up and down the road again for signs of life. When none appeared, he started jogging the seventy-five yards back to the mailbox.

Distant gunfire and exploding mortar rounds were familiar companions on his last night mission. It had been hotter then, much hotter than this cool night, and rather than fir trees, the surrounding flora had been jungle.

As each second passed, the blue glow on the horizon grew brighter. Even though darkness still prevailed, Wolf knew it wouldn't be long before Charlie, on the other side of the clearing, would swarm like the Biblical plague of locusts from their cover. Despite the human costs, they wouldn't relent until every GI was dead.

"Hell, you're a long ways over here," O'Leary said as he rolled in behind the tree where Wolf had made cover for the last twenty-five minutes. "Nearly got my ass shot off."

O'Leary and Wolf had served together on the Vietnam battle front for the four months since Wolf had been assigned to Sergeant Dirk Nyte's squad.

"Why'd you bother?" Wolf asked, shouting over the sound of bullets tearing into the trunk providing them cover. "We're all dead, anyway."

Wolf looked around the left side of the tree and took aim at an automatic muzzle flash, pulling off three rounds in quick succession. To his satisfaction, the AK-47 on the other side of the clearing went silent.

"Sarge ordered a dead run. One klick," O'Leary said, pointing to the rear of their position. "I've got to get back to Lefty. He took a hit to the gut and can't get out without help."

"Dead run?" Wolf dared to hope he might yet get out of this one alive. He rolled to his back and exposed a shoulder wound caked with blood and dirt.

"You're hit."

"It's just a damn nick. My shooting shoulder's still fine. Go on. Get the hell out of here. I'll see you at the LZ."

Nodding, O'Leary rolled to his stomach and crawled away to the right under the jungle vegetation.

As he left, Wolf drew to his knees, keeping his body against the tree trunk in preparation to run on the signal and his eyes on O'Leary. The gloom of the slowly approaching dawn hadn't yet covered O'Leary when

96

Wolf saw his body jerk and then go limp. Slinging his M-16 over his back, he crawled on all fours to O'Leary's side and dropped to his stomach beside him. O'Leary no longer took breath.

Logic said he should go back to the relative safety of the tree trunk until the claymores went off, but he couldn't rely on logic alone. All the gunfire had stopped on his side of the field, and he knew in just moments the enemy should ceasefire, too, thinking the Americans either all dead or retreated.

He couldn't wait for the lead to stop flying, though. Not knowing how far away Lefty lay wounded, he stooped low and ran through the brush. In the relative darkness, he thought himself invisible, but after taking a half dozen steps, a bullet found him.

Now, as he crossed the distance in a crouched trot, he welcomed the throb in his chest pounding harder with each step and the dry, gritty taste on his tongue. He had lived through not only that mission but the years of hell following it. And now he had a lesson to teach, one that would outlive them all.

His ears, alert to any sound disrupting the silence, picked up the frantic yelp of a pack of coyotes closing in on a kill in an adjacent field. *They'll be busy feasting for a while.* He pressed on and found the opening to the driveway.

Paved with gravel, it headed off the road through a stand of trees. He stepped to the side of the rock bed to silence his footsteps on the moist weed-choked earth, careful not to alert his target. Fifty feet from the road, a clearing opened before him. A dim porch light marked the front door of a double-wide manufactured home another hundred feet away and gave enough light to expose the silhouette of his objective. At the edge of the lawn next to the tree line, the black Kenworth tractor stood stalwart.

He moved to the driver's side of the rig, the side facing away from the home. Stooped behind it, he ran his hand along the cool steel until he passed the cab. He dropped to his knees and felt along the chassis until his hand bumped into the 120-gallon diesel fuel tank in front of the rear tires.

As he slid underneath the truck, the ground felt cool to his back, and although the moisture from the grass seeped through his windbreaker, he didn't shiver; his mission took precedence. Setting the bag next to him, he reached into the outside pocket, and pulled out a flashlight.

He flipped the switch on, clamped the light between his teeth and began his inspection. Before he finished, nothing more than blades of grass parting under a gentle force, caused him to freeze. Turning his ears to the night sounds, he realized the coyotes had gone silent. If one tore into his flesh, the others would follow and his entire operation, not just tonight's mission, would fail. But fear of pain—of death—was an emotion he had long ago expelled from his mind. From the opposite side of the rig, a low growl rolled across the lawn. He doused the flashlight and twisted his head to look behind him toward the house. The porch light revealed the shadowed figure of a single four-legged beast creeping up on him near the other side of the truck.

In a silent by swift movement, he slipped his hand into the bag and searched by feel until he located a sealed baggie. He unzipped the top, removed a T-bone steak and tossed it to the rear of the truck near the animal. Lying still, he waited.

When the creature's jaw chomped into the meat, he switched the flashlight back on and pointed the beam in the direction of the sound. Relieved, he found a black and white Border-Collie. The dog turned its head toward the source of the light, but more interested in the unexpected meal than alarmed by the intruder, it lay down and continued gnawing.

Chapter 14

The bedside clock buzzed at 3:02 a.m. Tuesday morning, and Kel rolled toward it.

While she had studied psychology at the University of Washington sixteen years earlier, one night without sleep was exhausting. Now she felt like she had pulled two back-to-back all-nighters cramming for college midterms. Her mind threatened to congeal into a gelatinous pool of incoherence.

She opened her eyes, and a smile crept onto her lips. Saul, Chrissie's Rottweiler, laid snout to nose, inches away.

Over her ardent objections, Kel had sent Chrissie to spend the night with Shelia. Believing she had unwittingly become the epicenter of DK's plot, Kel felt Chrissie would be safer with family. If DK did act on his "each day" threat, she wouldn't have to leave her daughter at home alone again like last night.

Saul snorted.

Kel reached to slap the snooze button on the clock and then realized the annoyance had come from her SPD smartphone vibrating against the wooden nightstand. She glanced at the phone's display.

"Okay, let's see who it is, Saul," she said. She engaged the call, thrusting a finger and thumb of her free hand into her swollen eyes.

"This better be good."

"Better than good."

She recognized the voice of the fresh-from-college lab tech. "Why are you calling at this god-awful hour, Bimal?"

"It wasn't god-awful when you called me about this time last night."

"Touché," she said, raised her torso to one elbow, and yawned. "So, what's up?"

"You remember the phone number you gave me last night?"

"Yeah, it's a burner. We've been over that."

"You asked me to track the shipment."

"I asked you to track the payment."

"Right," Bimal said and paused. "Okay, we spoke to the manufacturer today. They said the payment arrived by mail in a money order."

"So another dead end?"

"Yeah, but we can track the pings. Your text buddy didn't just buy one disposable phone, he bought four."

"Four?" she shouted and sat up on the edge of the bed. "So he really is serial."

"Could be, but I have great news. I just found an email from the manufacturer's warehouse as a result of our query, and I have the subscriber identity module num—"

"Subscriber what?" She shook her head.

"The SIM card numbers. I know all four phone numbers. I'm about to put a trace on the other three."

"Has there been any activity on the first one?"

"Not since after we talked last, but—"

"You mean not since you almost got me killed."

"Yeah, well I'm real sorry 'bout that. Anyway, with this new data I can follow his movements and maybe get a step ahead of him."

"But only when the phone is on, right?"

"Yeah, but with a trace on all the phones, the moment any one hits the BTS—"

"Hey, stop showing off. I may still be sleepy, but I do carry a gun and know where you are *right now*."

"Point taken, enough techno speak. BTS, base transceiver station, you'd know it better as a cell tower or cell site."

"See, that wasn't so hard. So what you're saying is that when the cellular is turned on it'll ping a cell site and then you'll have a location. What's the range?"

"That's the tricky part. Depending on a lot of factors, it could be anywhere from a quarter mile to 50 miles. Quarter mile if the phone is downtown, 50 miles it's out in some—"

"Got it, density and terrain. So, is anything pinging?"

"I just got the SIMs, and I'm setting up the tracking as we speak, so how 'bout I keep you informed?"

"Do that, Bimal, but I need more than pings on towers. I need activity. I need to know what numbers he's calling and texting."

"That means a warrant."

"Of course, do it legal. Whose side you on, anyway?"

"Yours, detective. You said before I'm on the clock, so let's do it right. Don't leave him a crack to slip through."

Kel knew he was right but it meant she would have to play nice with someone she had possibly burned a bridge with twelve hours before.

"Did you check out that address?" Bimal asked.

Kel paused for a moment working out what he meant by "that address." Exhaustion was already taking its toll and she had just started the investigation. She looked to Saul for inspiration, but with his head still resting on the edge of the bed, his sleepy eyes gave nothing away. She stroked his snout.

"Ah, you mean the Roxbury address where the phones where shipped? I dropped by yesterday after I left you and spoke to the neighboring shop owners. No one remembers a delivery truck on that day or anyone snooping about the deserted shop. It wouldn't take much for DK to see that the store had been closed for a while. There's another thing I want to check out about that address."

"What's that, can I help?"

"Let's just call it a hunch, I'll let you know if it leads somewhere. You keep working on the phones."

Disengaging the call, she placed the phone back on the nightstand and switched on the table lamp. She lay back, stared at Saul, who now sat on his haunches panting, and patted the edge of the bed. He moved next to it. She stroked his head and then turned her attention to the oscillating ceiling fan.

The townhome had been stuffy when she arrived home, so she had opened the upstairs windows for ventilation despite the patter of rain on the porch roof below. Before hitting the bed, she switched on the fan. Now, the click of the gold pull chain tapping a constant rhythm on the glass light cover and the breaths of warm air wafting over her body lulled her thoughts.

It had been too long since she felt Lance's breath on her neck. She took her personal cell phone from the lamp table. The closest she could come to him now was the digital photo she used as a background for her phone. Taken the morning he boarded that 747 to fly to the Middle East, he sat in the kitchen in his Army uniform looking up from a bowl of dry cereal like it was any other day.

She flipped to the photo gallery app. Until the day he went missing, there were few days he didn't text or email. Often he sent photos, and without realizing their significance, she stored every one—*another connection*. Going through them now she felt the painful fusion of desire and dread she suffered each day. But with Saul's head in her hand, today her heart ruptured and the tears flowed.

Kel met Lance Thorson at a fraternity party at the end of her junior year at the University of Washington. Joining the U.S. Army and serving a tour of duty which included a role in the ground force freeing Kuwait in the first Gulf War, Lance was four years ahead of Kel in age, but just one year ahead of her in college. After graduating and starting a career in the field of business intelligence, while Kel finished her BA in psychology, they fell in love and moved in together. Before two years had passed, Chrissie came along and life for Kel felt perfect.

A few months after Chrissie's fourth birthday, the World Trade Center towers fell. The recession that followed cost Lance his job in the spring of 2002. He had been among the many patriots who felt that after freeing Kuwait in 1991, the coalition forces should have turned north and marched on Iraq. So, despite his young family, just after their trip to Disneyland, he reenlisted in the Army and within months, headed for his first mission to the Middle East.

Saul jerked his head away from Kel's hand and turned toward the nightstand. The phone vibrated again. "Easy boy," she said, swallowing her tears and reaching for the phone.

Seeing the text icon on the screen, she scrolled to it, but when a phone call came in, she punched the "Answer" button on the touch screen.

"Got a ping, well, two pings," Bimal said and was so excited, gasping for air, he sounded like he had just finished running a 100 yard dash.

"One was to me, right? I just got a text."

"One is the phone he texted you from last night, but the other is from one of the other phones."

"Where are they?"

"One is pinging a tower north of Bellingham near Lynden."

"Lynden? That's near the Canadian border. A couple hours north of here."

"The first one's still pinging, but the one he's been using to communicate with you came on just a couple minutes ago."

"Just long enough to send me another text."

"Right, what does it say?"

Kel scrolled to the message. "'Boom.'"

Chapter 15

"I've got to go," Kel said, rising from the bed and swinging her legs over the edge.

Saul, at the word "go," trotted to the doorway and then looked back.

"Not you, Saul," she said. "Come here, boy."

Saul hesitated, looking from her to the hallway. When Kel dropped to her knees with her arms outstretched, he made his way to her.

"That's a good boy." She put her arms around him, stroking his short black coat. "We both have our jobs to do. You keep the house safe, and I make the streets safe."

Saul whined.

"I know you want to go, but not this time, okay?"

As if realizing this was an argument he wasn't going to win, Saul lay down on the floor next to her.

"Good boy. Now I've got to get dressed.

Believing DK could strike at any minute, she had tossed her jeans and T-shirt across a chair last night before lying down. Within five minutes of settling Saul, after binding her hair in a ponytail, and taking the Glock from the gun safe in her closet, she backed her silver-metallic Jeep Liberty out of the garage.

As she made her way down the residential street lined with vacant vehicles awaiting the morning light to rise and engage the commute, her headlights illuminated the trees in adjacent yards. The shifting shadows on both sides crept like silent ninja warriors silhouetted against the facades of the house fronts. The still gloom brought with it an inky foreboding that she had felt last night before discovering Susanne's body. It seeped through her pores with a near paralyzing dread, yet forced her to move toward the event to which she had become unwillingly conscripted.

The smell of fresh drip coffee drifted into Terry Graham's bedroom and nudged him out of sleep like the gentle caress of a snuggling woman. Rising, he disregarded the sweatpants lying in a heap on the floor by the edge of the bed and padded his way to the kitchen wearing nothing but boxers.

"Smoky?" he called as he reached for a cup.

After filling a mug with the steaming brew and a bowl with dry cereal, he slipped a cigarette behind his ear and stepped onto the front porch. The sun had not yet made an appearance and the air was cool on his bare skin. Holding back a shiver, he sat down on the porch step. Before resting the coffee next to him on the cedar planking, he took a swallow.

"Smoky, where are you boy? Chasin' rabbits? Come here boy."

Spooning a bite of cereal into his mouth, he scanned the front yard looking for signs of movement. There were none.

Over the last decade, Terry had exiled himself to the obscurity of a small town and the hard life of an independent short haul trucker. His only consistent companion had been his border collie, Smoky. Raised from a pup on his spread, with few fences to dampen his spirit, he knew the freedom of exploration and thrived on romping through the fields looking for sport. He also knew Terry's voice and never failed to respond.

Having finished the cereal, Terry lit the cigarette, picked up the mug and walked toward his rig, continuing to scan the yard for his companion. Worried because of the coyotes in the area, he did not feel the wet grass sliding in and out between his toes. Approaching the tractor, he saw Smoky lying on the ground under the truck, just inside the rear tires.

"Hey, boy," he said as he stooped, placing his right hand on the dog's long black and white coat. "You okay?"

Smoky lifted his head and whined, and then dropped it back to the ground again.

"Come here, boy. Let's go into the house.

Tossing the rest of the coffee out of the cup, he slid his arms under the dog, scooped him up in his arms and carried him into the kitchen. Laying him on the tile floor, he ran his hands over his coat to see if the dog had been injured in a fight. When his fingers found nothing obvious, he poured fresh water into his dish and then placed it next to him.

"Here boy, drink."

Smoky looked at Terry again and then rolling to his belly, kneeled. Dropping his face into the bowl, he began to lap at the water like he was parched.

"I think you'll stay in today, buddy, but Daddy's got to go to work."

Smoky looked up from the bowl and whined.

"Be a good boy. Don't fuss. You rest today, and tomorrow we'll go to work together."

Smoky cocked his head as if he understood but still had a question.

"No arguments, okay? While I get ready for work you eat your breakfast and if you do that, I'll give you a treat before I head out."

More than an hour passed as Kel travelled northbound on Interstate 5. She turned her eyes to the east of the highway. Minutes before, Arlington had passed by, and now the valley floor rose toward Whitehorse Mountain. Across the sky, she saw that the sun, not yet above the horizon, painted the scattered clouds with the striking hues of a school of koi.

Her phone rang, and she pulled her attention back to the road ahead. She lifted her hand to the Bluetooth device in her ear and engaged the call.

"Nyte."

"Bimal here. About five minutes ago my tracker showed that we have movement."

"What direction."

"It's heading west. No wait," he said and paused, "it just hit another tower. It could be heading south now."

"Can you ID the tower enough to know what road it's on?"

"Of course. It's on State Highway 539. If it keeps heading in that direction, in a few minutes it'll be in Bellingham. It should be easier to pin an actual location there."

"Keep tracking, I'm still an hour out. Let me know if the other phone goes live."

"Refill?" the high school-aged girl asked as she slid a breakfast platter in front of DK and hovered over his mug with a glass carafe.

Her interruption pulled his thoughts back to the clatter of silverware on ceramic plates and the low conversational din of the nondescript 24-hour café. He sucked in the fragrance of bacon fried crisp, smiled and nodded toward the cup.

"Sun'll be peeking through that window in a few minutes," she said when she finished pouring. "Want me to close the blinds?"

"No thanks, dear. I'm enjoying the view."

"Looks like it's gonna be a nice day."

"Yep, a real scorcher."

As she turned back to the kitchen, he heard the throb of a powerful diesel engine heading south on the highway. He lifted his eyes to the window. The black Kenworth passed by.

Another twenty-five minutes passed, and Kel's phone rang again.

"It stopped moving just north of Bellingham," Bimal said. "The signal hasn't changed in over ten minutes. I gave it a few minutes before calling to make sure it wasn't just a traffic signal or bagel stop, but it's been still now for a while."

"Is he still on five-three-nine?"

"Or somewhere real close."

"Have any of the perp's other phones powered on?"

"No, all's quiet there."

"Keep an eye on it. I'm still a ways out, but there's no traffic, so I'm making good time. And Bimal?"

"Yes, ma'am."

"You're doing good work today, but I need you to do one more thing."

Chapter 16

DK knew the truck driver's routine. He had cased him for several days and was a patient man. *A damn cage will teach you the meaning of "wait for it."*

Wolf never felt the bullet enter his body and didn't know how long he had been out, but when he regained consciousness, his gut felt like someone had dug into it with a dull pocket knife and used chopsticks to extract a foreign object. The last thing he remembered, O'Leary told him Sarge had ordered a retreat, and as he was lying on his stomach, he knew only seconds had passed since he had been hit.

He listened for battle sounds and found it quiet. Not even a bird dared peep. The lull before the storm—a storm Charlie couldn't survive. Since the shooting had stopped, he pictured along their line that what remained of his squad waited for the Vietcong to creep from their cover to investigate. O'Leary was dead, and he needed to get to Lefty to help him to the chopper. One klick.

If Wolf had a buddy in this godforsaken place, it was Lefty. He was due to rotate home in two weeks. Can't let that goddamn short-timer die out here.

Opening his eyes, he felt as if he were just recovering from the effects of delirium. Yet, even though darkness surrounded him, he was hot. Remembering it was just the break of day, the cool before the dawn, he realized that the sweltering jungle hadn't caused the sensation but the burning radiated from inside his body. This disorientation blurred his vision, and he was unable to take in his surroundings, but knowing Lefty couldn't be far away, he tried to stand.

As he struggled to his hands and knees, something above him arrested his movement. Whether a tree limb extending just above the ground pressed against his back or the hand of God held him in place, he couldn't tell. He paused. That simple movement took every ounce of strength from his reserve. Gasping for air and feeling the retch of this stomach again, he couldn't move forward. He closed his eyes and tried to gather his essence. Lefty waited not far away, and he needed to save him. But with his mind swirling on the verge of catalepsy, he came to a new realization. He, too, needed to be rescued. Someone'll come for me.

An overpowering urge to lie back down swept through him like the torrent of a swollen river. He eased to his left side and reached to his belly, attempting to comfort the unrelenting fire tormenting him. He expected to find his olive green blouse dripping with his own blood. Rather, he discovered his shirt missing. The cloth wrapped around him felt like soiled rags from a kitchen spill. They were stiff and crusted with something dried— blood. My blood!

"Nurse," he yelled, thinking he was in a MASH unit, "my dressing needs changed."

"There's no nurse here."

The shock of the unfamiliar voice coming from somewhere behind him disoriented him further. Another wounded soldier in the next bed? He began a painful roll in the direction of the voice and found his back, again, encountering restriction. When he reached with his left hand to free himself from the constraint, it fell on a piece of steel pipe. Panic set in, and he grabbed the vertical tube and shook it. It wouldn't move. He slid his hand a few inches and confirmed another pipe, and another, and another.

Rolling back to his side, he extended his arm in all directions, finding himself encased. He stretched his legs only inches and with sudden clarity knew that the only way he'd fit in his new home was to stay in a fetal position. He was a long way from a medic unit.

"You'll just find gooks here, GI."

Always punctual, *the atomic clock is probably set to his comings and goings*. That served DK, a man of order and control, well. Knowing this, he didn't need to sit and observe. He could have pulled the trigger from his lounge chair while he watched the morning news. But this was too big and too personal to view in reruns on television or read about in the newspaper. He needed to see it happen.

He waved to the server who was chatting with a customer at the counter. When she approached, he said, "Dear, I'm ready for my bill, and I'll take the rest of the coffee to go."

115

As he waited for her return, he checked his watch again. Time was running short for witness two.

Chapter 17

Kel passed through Bellingham and from the freeway exit, took a right on State Highway 539, heading in a northbound direction. She dialed the crime lab.

"Where are the locals?" she asked as soon as Bimal picked up the call.

"They would be there, but I couldn't tell them exactly where to go, and they weren't inclined to go anywhere on my word."

"Has the signal moved yet?"

"No."

"Am I close?"

"You're pinging off the same tower. What do you see?"

"Just normal stuff," she said, scanning the buildings on either side of the highway. "When did I hit this tower?

"Just a few seconds ago. Maybe I should call the number. Then I could triangulate and get an exact position."

"But only if he answers, and then he'll know we're on to him."

"Good point."

"I'll keep driving north, and you tell me when I hit another tower."

"That's good. Then we'll have an idea of its north and south boundaries."

"Wait…," she said and paused.

"Kel? The other phone just powered up."

DK checked the digital clock on the dashboard as he drove south on Highway 539. It was time. He found the speed dial button on the keyboard and paused, allowing his soul to feed on the rush of retribution as it cascaded over the spillway.

Chapter 18

With Bimal still on the line, Kel pulled across the
street from a petroleum distribution terminal. Behind the
twelve-foot chain link fence, with a coil of barbed wire
running along the top, she could see numerous
cylindrical storage tanks. Parked in front of one of them,
fifty yards behind the galvanized barrier, stood a black
truck connected to two chrome tanker trailers. The sun
sent shafts of light reflecting off the containers, and a
man crouched on top of the rear trailer, rested his hand
on a large hose that disappeared into an opening.

Turning off the engine, she stepped from her car
and waited by the hood for the last car on the four-lane
to pass. A security shack stood outside of the gate
several dozen yards off the highway. A guard seated
inside looked out the open door in her direction. He
appeared to be a young man in his late teens or early
twenties. As he stood, behind him, the gates of Hell burst
wide open.

The powerful blowback from the blast pushed
Kel backward over the hood of her SUV. She landed

face down in the dirt on the passenger side and then pushed herself up to her elbows. Disoriented, she shook her head from side to side until her hearing returned and her head cleared.

She scrabbled to her feet and crouched behind the front fender. Peering over the hood, the flames and black smoke belching upward and outward reminded her of everything she had imagined as an adolescent girl when her priest preached about the follies of sin and Hell's fire and brimstone. Engulfed behind an orange and black wall, she couldn't see to the center of the firestorm where the truck had stood, but it was obvious the tankers had burst. Like molten lava racing in multiple tributaries down the sides of a volcano, flames spread across the concrete yard, consuming everything in their path.

Seconds ago a guard shack stood twenty-five yards from the highway. The flames now had overtaken the structure, their greedy orange fingers wrapping around it to feed its ravenous appetite.

Out of that inferno, like a scene from a horror movie, the guard ran into the sea of flames. His clothes afire, a wretched scream escaped from within the staggering blaze, followed by a shriek that could only be emitted by someone realizing the futility of their struggle. It wasn't a cry for help but a plea for mercy. The guard fell, and the fire feasted on his flesh.

Terror wrapped around her chest as she realized that if she hadn't waited for the car on the highway to pass a few seconds earlier, she would have walked into the direct path of the firestorm with no way to escape. She had sworn to protect, but, feeling her utter uselessness, she watched from behind the Liberty's fender. Her heart ached with regret for the souls she couldn't save. *What kind of maniacal rage could cause someone to do this to innocent people?*

Remembering Bimal, she reached to her ear for the Bluetooth. It was gone. She made a quick search on the ground around her and found it in pieces a few feet away. Reaching for the phone on her belt, she disengaged the wireless connection and heard Bimal's familiar Hindi accent.

"What the hell's going on, Kel?" Even over the roaring flames she could hear hysteria in his voice. "Are you all right? What's happening?"

"Call every emergency agency in Bellingham," she shouted, "and send them to my location. Armageddon just happened. Do it now!"

As she finished speaking, she felt the telling vibration of another text message and remembered the last one—*Boom.*

DK pulled to a stop in the middle of the highway behind several morning commuters. He had seen the effects of napalm dropped on an enemy, but what he witnessed now as the plant erupted was far worse than the white heat of those attacks. He lit a cigarette and took the final swallow from the cup of coffee he had taken from the diner. Unlike witness two, it was lukewarm.

Chapter 19

Kel looked up from reading the text—"Quite a sight. Rain of flames. I deliver"—and stared, aghast at the raging hellhole across the street. The intense heat, lashing against her face, chapping her lips and burning her eyes, made the air so searing it was painful to breathe.

Does he know I'm here? Is he tracking me?

"Kel, Kel," Bimal's voice exploded through the speaker phone.

"I thought you were getting help."

"Did that, but he's pinging the same tower as you."

"Does he seem to be moving?" She looked up from the phone. In the distance to the left she heard the blare of sirens approaching and saw a stream of pulsating emergency lights snake their way toward the scene.

"Hard to tell."

The phone vibrated again. Looking at it, she saw an address and a curious instruction. "Take care of the mutt."

Turning to the southbound lanes, she saw a vehicle stopped in the center of both lanes. The driver stood on the pavement next to the car's open door. Even with the distance between them, it looked like he was taking pictures with his cell phone. *Curious—or collecting trophies.*

Despite the scorching heat, she slipped the phone back into its holster and resting her right hand on the butt or her Glock, ran toward him. She had been unable to save anyone at the plant. If this *was* a bystander and not DK, maybe she could save his life.

When she was within fifty feet of the man, another blast came from inside the plant. She turned in the direction of the sound. Out of the whirling, snarling firestorm, a flaming missile was launched on an arc toward the highway. She stopped running and glanced toward the man who continued snapping photos. If he didn't move, he might be hit by the small tank, but she was too far away to help him.

"Watch out!" she screamed.

Above the roar of the fire she was certain he didn't hear her call, but when he looked up away from the camera, the jerk of his body indicated he recognized the imminent threat. The tank plummeted to the ground a few feet in front of his car, and he dove back into the driver's seat.

On impact, flames, sparks, and shards of steel sprayed out. A large section of the cylinder bounced onto the hood of the car and slammed into the windshield. Without breaking it, the projectile continued on its trajectory, sliding over the roof of the sedan. It fell to the asphalt next to the driver's door and skittered to a stop on the far side of the road.

Anxious, Kel had been prepared to dart any way she needed to avoid the same fate as the car, but when none of the fragments flew in her direction, she sprinted again toward the vehicle.

Grabbing the open door, she shouted, "Police." She flashed her badge fast enough he could see it but not long enough to notice she wasn't the Bellingham Police. "Are you all right?"

"Damn it, that thing almost got me. Yes, I'm all right."

She reached her right hand again to the Glock. "Please stay in the car. Give me your phone and then place both your hands on the steering wheel."

"Phone? What are you talking about? That thing almost killed me!"

"This was no accident, sir. Please do as I ask."

"You shitting me? You think I did this? I almost pissed myself when that thing hit."

"Your phone, now, and your hands on the wheel."

"Okay, okay, here," he said handing it over.

Kel kept her eye on his hands until he placed them at the ten and two position on the steering wheel. Locating the call log, she scrolled through the last few calls. Her number didn't appear. She retrieved her phone and dialed DK's number.

When the driver's phone didn't ring, Kel gave it back to him. Not convinced that the phone she sought wasn't somewhere silenced in the car but having nothing on which to hold him, she said, "It's not safe here. Turn around and find another way to your destination."

She stepped back from the door and closed it. The driver shot her a final glare through the windshield and powered his car into a U-turn. As she backed out of his path, she noticed several cars up the line a black sedan had already turned around and was moving away. She called Bimal.

"What's his location?" she asked, jogging back toward her car, staying as far away from the heat as possible.

"He just turned his cell off, but before that he was stationary."

"Damn," she said, realizing that by the time she'd reach her Jeep, she'd have no hope of finding him. "He was right here."

Kel looked past her SUV. Several fire and police vehicles had taken position and one police cruiser headed toward her. As she reached the Jeep, the officer came to a halt next to her.

"Kel Nyte, Seattle PD," she said through the passenger window, holding her shield up. "Badge 509."

"You need to get to safety, Officer Nyte."

According to the tag on his chest, his last name was Monroe.

"Just clearing some spectators, Sergeant Monroe," she said, seeing the chevron on his shirt sleeve.

"And we appreciate your assistance, Officer, but you're in danger here."

"Sergeant, you're right, this thing could blow again. I'll move my car and help clear citizens, but this was no accident. This is the perp's second lethal act in the last two days.

"By the way," she said, showing him the text displayed on her phone. "Will you be able to direct me to this address?"

Chapter 20

Kel turned into the driveway at a few minutes after 8:00 a.m. Parked nose in, a Whatcom County Sheriff's SUV sat idle on the gravel drive. She stopped behind the vehicle and stepped out.

The tan uniform on the young female deputy standing on the front porch of the manufactured home looked like it had just come from the cleaners—*heavy on starch.* Next to the slender woman, a long-haired black and white Border collie pranced, his tongue hanging from his mouth.

"Officer Nyte?" asked the woman with a bun of blond hair at the crown of her head.

"Yes," Kel said, her badge clipped to her belt for confirmation. She walked toward the cedar porch. The decomposed granite crunched under her feet.

"Deputy Carter," she said. "Sondra, if you like. Why are we here?"

"You heard about the fuel plant?" Kel asked, taking a quick glance around the front yard.

"Yes, how awful. I understand you were there?"

"When it blew. First on scene."

For the second time in so many days she could make that claim. She had been drawn to Susanne Lowen's. But this time the suspect couldn't have known she was tracking him. Yet, as if timed to perfection, she found herself outside the fuel terminal, almost caught in the blast.

"Do you know how many victims?" Sondra asked.

"At least two fatalities. We're at the home of who I suspect was the main target. Who's your friend?"

Walking up to the covered porch, Kel crouched down and let the dog greet her. Saul's scent lingered on her, and the collie became excited, jumping and lapping at her face.

"Don't know," Sondra said, stroking his coat. "Came from around the house when I arrived."

Kel remembered the last text. *Take care of the mutt.*

"He looks friendly enough," Kel said, rising to her full height. "Do you know who lives here?"

"The property's registered to a Terrance Graham."

"Terrance Graham," Kel repeated the name. Rubbing the back of her neck, she searched her memory.

"Do you know him?"

"Sounds familiar, but distant. Anyone home?"

"I rang the bell, but the only response was our new friend."

"Let's knock this time." Kel pounded on the front door.

When the dog growled, she crouched again, wrapping her arms around his neck, and dug her fingers into his coat, giving him a firm rub.

"It's okay. We're here to help," she said and wondered what would happen to the dog now that his owner was gone.

The collie responded with a bark of approval.

"Good boy," she said, patting his side.

Sondra smiled. "Looks like we both passed the sniff test."

Kel stood and reached for the knob, and the door swung open. The collie sauntered inside and then turned as if to welcome the two officers into his home. Kel gave the deputy a puzzled look.

"People don't lock their doors so much around here."

"I see," Kel said, facing the living room. DK's invitation yesterday—*door's open*—still resonated. With the Taser burns still stinging her back, even with the dog being so friendly, she was unprepared to accept the deputy's explanation. She drew her weapon and entered.

"Do you think that's necessary?" Sondra asked.

"Precaution," Kel replied and scanned the room. "You take the left, I'll take the right." Remembering where DK had hidden in Susanne's condo, she added, "Don't forget closets."

"Closets?"

"Long story, just do it," she said and then realized her tone was sharp, making it sound like an order in a county where she had no jurisdiction. "Please," she added.

When they finished clearing the small home, they met in the kitchen. Kel glanced at the counter. Next to the coffee pot, yesterday's newspaper lay with a stack of mail piled on top. Picking up one of the envelopes, she read the name, Terry Graham. That brought it back. *But there could be hundreds of Terry Grahams.* She needed confirmation.

Back in the living room, on a table next to the large plasma television, a picture drew her attention. She lifted the frame and recognized the face of one of the three men holding sockeye-salmons by the gills. His features were older, and the hair thinner than her recollection.

Witnesses their stories tell. She knew what this witness would say. Her stomach clenched as she placed the picture back on the table and tucked the memory, and the conversation soon to come, away.

"Did you find a computer?" she asked the deputy.

"No, didn't see one. Why?"

"Look, Sondra, I'm on the trail of a murderer. I believe Terry's his second victim. At the first vic's house, he left a message on her computer."

"If Graham had one, it must be a laptop, and he took it with him."

"You okay with your friend there? I'm going to have a look around outside."

"I'll freshen his water. We'll be fine."

Kel nodded and left them. From the porch she noticed the tire tracks of Terry's rig in the grass. She marched over to the depressions. At the rear of the indentations, on what would have been the passenger side, the remains of a T-bone steak lay on the lawn. The grass next to it was matted as if the collie had lain here. She moved around the tracks and stooped to examine the remnants. Little meat remained on the bone, but from what she could see, canine teeth had ripped and gnawed at it.

Leaving the bone lie, she stood and surveyed the rest of the area where the truck had been parked. In the middle of the tracks on the driver's side, a much larger depression, about the size of man's torso, matted the damp grass in front of where the other set of rear tires would have rested.

"What you got?" Sondra asked, having come up next to Kel with the dog at her heal.

"That bone is evidence, deputy. You should collect it before he has a chance at it again. Could be the perp spiked it to put the dog to sleep."

Sondra shook her head, pulled gloves from her pocket and picked up the bone.

"I think our suspect," Kel continued, pointing to the larger depression in the lawn, "lay over there in the night to place a bomb under Terry's truck. There could

131

be other evidence here, Sondra. You need to get your investigators on the scene."

"I'll make the call now." She turned toward her SUV.

Awakened by Bimal, with only five hours sleep, Kel rubbed her tired eyes. Something had been nagging at her about DK's last text. As she watched Sondra and the Border collie cross the lawn, the annoyance returned. Like trying to focus on eye floaters exposed against the blue afternoon sky, she hadn't been able to get an absolute fix on the object. The closer she got, the further it drifted, never quite lining up.

She pulled her phone from the belt holster. Thumbing through the messages, she found the source of the harassment and read it again.

"Quite a sight. Rain of flames. I deliver."

She had read the first two lines to mean the massive explosion and interpreted the last to mean he had delivered on his earlier promise, "Boom." But now the last phrase didn't fit. The first two were like lines of the same verse. They had rhyme, rhythm, and their context was obvious. But the last line didn't mesh. It was more like "door's open" or "boom," meant specifically for her.

But what did he deliver? The bomb, obviously, but, if he stayed true to his MO, there had to be something else. With no computer, was he telling her where the victim's poem waited with the explanation of the lesson?

I deliver.

Who delivers? Truckers, like Terry, deliver. Fed Ex delivers, speeches are delivered, but what would a poet deliver? A poem, of course, but where?

Then, as if a whisper echoed off a canyon wall, she remembered a slogan she often repeated as a child when she waited for the mail on a snow day. *Neither snow nor rain nor heat nor gloom of night stays these couriers from the swift completion of their appointed rounds.*

The US Post Office delivers mail.

She had seen Terry's mail on the kitchen counter, but nothing seemed out of place there. Then, remembering the address on the mailbox as she turned into the driveway, she darted across the lawn. As she hurried through the gavel, her phone vibrated. Checking the number, she recognized her partner's, Jake deLaurenti, and let it go to voicemail.

"What is it, Officer Nyte? Sondra said, catching up to Kel as she reached the mailbox.

"I think I know where the message is."

"But tampering with mail is a federal crime."

"Well, murdering a truck driver may not be a *federal* crime but if I'm right, there's a letter waiting for me, which means our suspect tampered first."

Chapter 21

Standing in the kitchen measuring coffee grounds, Dirk Nyte had heard the voice in his ear before. Jared Collins, a newspaper columnist of national merit, called when the story broke about the Rat City Exterminator's release. He wanted an interview.

"One of the victims," Jared said, "was Terry Graham, your former partner, and according to your daughter, this may be related to the death of Susanne Lowen last night."

Despair's swift fist knocked the air from Dirk's lungs. He grabbed for the counter with his free hand, almost dropping the phone, to fight the illusion that he had been pushed from the brink of an abyss.

"Chief Nyte?"

The concerned voice in his ear centered his thoughts, and he found breath. "Terry is one of the victims?"

"Yes, I thought you would have known by now."

"No. My God, Terry."

"Yes, I'm sorry. It sounds like you were close."

"At one time we were like bothers, but, still…" Dirk didn't finish the thought.

"So, as I was saying—"

"Yes, as you were saying. You think, Terry Graham was killed by the same person who killed Susanne Lowen?"

"No, your daughter stated that."

"And you're calling me because you want an exclusive due to my connection with both victims?"

"That, and you're an expert in solving serial cases. I'm particularly interested in the minds of mass murderers."

"Look, Mr. Collins, with all due respect, there are two detectives assigned to the case. One of them happens to be my daughter, and I'm only saying this because you already know it. The SPD doesn't comment on ongoing investigations, and, even though I'm retired, I still honor the code. Until your call, I didn't know about Terry's death, so with no offense intended, I just can't talk about this right now."

"No offense taken, Chief, and I understand completely. If and when you're ready to talk, you'll give me a call?"

"I have your number," Dirk said and then placed the receiver in the telephone cradle.

Chapter 22

Peter McCabe found a parking stall near the back entrance of the store. He looked to the envelope on the passenger seat. The instructions had arrived Sunday.

"Sir." The hostess had approached the table, sweeping her long black hair away from her face as she leaned over his shoulder with the envelope.

The tall, stunning Malaysian woman always called him sir—in public. She was one of the lucky ones—and smart. McCabe recognized it in her eyes the moment he first saw her. And for that, he rescued her from a life destined for drugs, prostitution, and likely an early, unmarked grave. She still prostituted herself, but that was what made her smart. She only had one client; the one who arranged the day job at the Highlands Country Club and the one who paid for the downtown Seattle waterfront condo.

"This just came for you by courier," she whispered in his ear and placed an envelope in his hand.

The scent of her perfume drifted past his nose, and he took a greedy drink.

"Thank you, honey," he said and slipped a twenty dollar bill into the same hand she used in the evenings to massage him in just the right places.

Looking at the three men around the table who had made up the rest of the foursome for this morning's golf round, he smiled, folded the envelope, and tucked it into this hip pocket. "This'll wait, I'm sure."

Now he looked at the envelope again. Since Sunday he had personally tested it for any trace of the sender. The courier company stated the job had been sent to them via the internet, and they kept no records of IP addresses transmitting orders. Only the accounts of individuals or companies paying the bill interested them. But in this case, along with the envelope, there had been cash.

The envelope itself had been left on the front porch of a house in the Blue Ridge community, an exclusive neighborhood not far from the Highlands Golf Course. The owner and his family had been out of town the entire weekend and had no idea how the note ended up on their porch. Even a telephone canvass of the neighbors didn't yield a clue. No one noticed any strangers on the sidewalks or suspicious vehicles on the street.

The note disturbed him, but what made it worse was that someone knew his routine. During the summer, he golfed every Sunday, even in the rain, and finished the round with a martini lunch with his associates. That explained why he had waited nearly forty-eight hours before following the instructions. If anyone had been tracking him, he wanted to be sure they wearied of the wait.

He looked at the note again. Its message shook him.

"Open if you dare."

He removed the key stamped 37 resting in the bottom of the envelope, looked around the parking lot, and, finding himself alone, stepped from his Lexis.

Inside the unfamiliar private mailbox and shipping store, he found the box among the dozens of other similar sized mailboxes on the third row from the top. He slid the key into the slot, and, reaching in, found one letter-sized parcel, addressed to "the Don."

Locally, a mythical mobster known in the press as the Don of the Docks had risen to the level of legend. No one knew who he was or if he really existed. But whoever sent him this message was making a statement.

"Ludicrous," he mumbled under his breath and then looked to see if anyone heard.

At the desk twenty-five feet away, a lone clerk wrestled a large box from the counter to a cart. He didn't pay any attention.

McCabe took out a pocket knife and slid the blade along the fold, opening the top of the number ten white envelope. A single sheet of paper inside waited for his eyes. He removed it and unfolded the two creases. The brief note had been printed on recycled copy paper common in any office supply store by an inkjet printer— *impossible to trace*. As he read the short message, his heart skipped a beat and then pounded against his ribs.

Above a Hotmail email account name, the words screamed from the page. "My blood's on your hands."

Twenty-five minutes after leaving Deputy Carter in charge of the investigation at Terry Graham's home, Kel had turned her car into a Bellingham parking lot. As she passed through town on the way to Interstate 5, two shops at the mini mall beckoned her like a compass dial drawn to magnetic north—Starbucks and Radio Shack. Now with a triple shot latte resting in the Jeep's cup holder, a raspberry scone on the console beside her, and a new Bluetooth earpiece, she was ready to face the rest of the morning.

As she reached the parking lot's driveway, she remembered letting her temporary partner's call go to voicemail. Listening to his, "Where the hell are you," message, she placed the call.

"Plebe," he said as he picked up. "Been lookin' for you."

"I've been busy, and so has our perp."

"What are you talking about?"

"Have you seen the news?"

"Been busy."

"With who?"

"That's between me and the sheets. What's your DK up to?"

Kel filled him in on her morning, bringing him abreast of the suspect's activity over the last several hours.

"Damn it, why didn't you call me before you headed north?" Jake said.

From his tone, Kel knew he was angry. He couldn't let a rookie get ahead of him or, worse, solve the case without him. How would that look on his closing record? He'd get credit for it, but the word would get out that he didn't do much, if anything, to crack the case.

"Rule number one, remember?" she said and felt justified as the sarcasm spirited through wireless connection straight into his ear.

"We've got to work together. I'm the primary here, so if you have a lead, I'm your next call. Got it?"

"That cuts both ways, so why don't you tell me about your leads."

"My leads?"

"Yeah, you mean you've got nothing?"

"Well…" He paused. "Do you know who Terry Graham is?"

"That's all you've got? Something I told you? Of course I know who he is, and that's one of my next calls."

Peter McCabe approached the counter where the clerk had finished with the large box.

"I'd like to close my account," he said.

"Certainly, sir. What's the number?"

McCabe handed him the key.

140

The clerk reached under the counter for a file box, and while he thumbed through three by five cards, McCabe waited, quelling the urge to drum his fingers on the countertop.

When the clerk pulled a card from the wooden box, he said, "Here it is, Mr. Jenkins. Are you sure you want to close this? You just opened it two weeks ago."

Taking the card, he looked for the owner's name on the mailbox. Again, his heart shook his rib cage, and he felt the blood drain from his face.

"Are you all right?" the clerk asked.

"Fine, yes, fine, young man. I know I just opened it, but I got the parcel I was expecting."

Studying the name, he knew someone was toying with him. They had set a dangerous game in motion, one they couldn't possibly win with his resources. *This pile of shit's just showing off and making me pissed.* Before he slid the index card across the counter, he took another look at the box owner's name.

Willie Jenkins.

Kel tapped the Bluetooth and navigated her way through the telephone tree until an actual live human voice entered her ear.

"ADA Johnson."

Shit, of all the lawyers in the DA's office, why did I draw him? Kel thought.

"Detective Kel Nyte," she said. "I need to pull a warrant to trap several cell phone numbers."

"Is this the same Nyte who tried to rip me a new one just yesterday?"

She remembered standing in the hallway outside the courtroom were razor-wire had just been released on a small bond. ADA Johnson had thrown his briefcase up between them as if she was about to knee him in the crotch.

She smiled at that thought and said, "'Fraid so, and I apologize. I was coming off an all-nighter with just three hours of sleep."

"I told you then we're on the same side, detective. So build me a case, why do you need a warrant?"

After she explained how DK was using cell phones to communicate his messages to her, she concluded by saying, "Bimal at the crime lab has all the numbers. I'll have him call you."

"I'll get your warrant, detective."

"Thanks Johnson, now there's just one more thing I'd like to ask. My new partner is Jake deLaurenti. I seem to be having trouble connecting with him. Have you worked with him in the DA's office?"

Dirk leaned over to the stove. Routine had always been his way to ward off emotional distractions. An act as simple as scrambling an egg gave his mind the room needed to distill information. With his cancer, routine had kept him grounded. The daily rhythm was a stay of execution. But this week, instead of feeling his life ebb away one heartbeat at a time, his mind was absorbed by others whose lives were being sacrificed in a demented plan to posit a message—*but to whom and why?*

He took an egg from the carton. Following mundane habits seemed pointless when Terry and Susanne would never eat another breakfast, but he held the oval in the palm of his hand. The rough, protective exterior gave the impression of durability, but, just like the illusion of immortality, its fate would render to the will of the one who held it.

He was about to crack the egg on the edge of the skillet when the phone rang.

"Daddy, DK struck again." Kel said, before he could speak.

"I know. I saw it on the news."

"I was there when it happened."

"Are you okay?"

"I may need to pencil in eyebrows for a while, but otherwise I'm fine. Mad as hell but fine. I think Terry was one of the victims."

"I just got off the phone with *The Globe*. I know about Terry."

"How'd they find out?"

"They must have released his name."

"I suppose that possible, but it seems premature. Anyway, I always liked Terry. I still remember him and his wife coming to the house for barbecues. "

"I know, Princess. I can't believe it myself."

"This is the second victim in two days."

"He's making good on his promise, isn't he?" He remembered the line read in his study last night—*Mine to reap for Hell each day*. "Who would do this? What's behind it?"

"I've got some thoughts, Daddy," she said. "I'll stop by this afternoon. We can talk then."

Chapter 23

At noon Kel entered into the lobby of *The Seattle Globe*, the Puget Sound's regional newspaper. A uniformed guard, standing behind a chest-high marble counter, greeted her.

"May I help you, ma'am?" he said as the glass entrance door closed behind her.

"Detective Kel Nyte," she said, approaching the man and raising her shield. Even though she wasn't officially a detective—as her boss Lou Martinez said, "A Temp-D,"—in the eyes of the man behind the counter, she was more than a plebe. With confidence, she continued, "I'm in the middle of an investigation, and I'd like to use *The Globe's* archives."

Five minutes passed while the guard made a call and then a woman in her early fifties with stringy, shoulder-length gray hair appeared and walked across the marble floor.

"May I help you, Detective?" The woman removed her half-frame glasses, letting them dangle on a chain.

"Yes, I'd like to use the newspaper's archive to do some research."

"You can get most of the same information online these days."

"I'm sure I can, but I thought I might be able to focus my search if I used your archives. Then I can weed out all the other hits a web search'll return."

"Very well, then. If you'll follow me."

The woman made an abrupt turn toward the glass door by which she had entered the lobby, and Kel followed, making one final glance toward the guard to thank him. Already absorbed in the newspaper, he didn't notice. Entering the hive of frantic activity behind the transparent wall, she followed the woman to a darkened office.

"I believe this is available," the woman said as she entered the windowless room. She walked around the desk, found the knob on the solitary lamp, and turned it on. "I'll sign you in to the computer with a guest login and then point you to the archive."

"Thank you." Kel looked around at the sterile furnishings—a dark green steel desk and a matching pair of ladder-backed chairs were the most formidable pieces in the office. Obviously *The Globe* felt no need to tempt the current occupant with plush surroundings. In direct contrast to the stale setting, several writing awards, represented in polished wooden plaques of mahogany and walnut, donned the back wall.

"Jared Collins," she read aloud. "Why do I know that name?"

"New York Times bestselling author," the woman said as she tore her eyes from the keyboard and searched for Kel's. "He's a nationally syndicated columnist."

Kel looked toward the voice and found a look of contempt. Behind it, though, her eyes revealed something else—scorn—but not aimed at Kel. The woman had been rejected. She sensed they were in Mr. Collins's office because she had been smitten by him. Yet, either he had outright rejected her or had just ignored her like the rest of the plain furnishings in his world.

"Of course, I'm sorry. I wasn't aware he lived in Seattle."

"Just the last year or so. Moved here to start winding down his career.

"I think that's about got it," she said, the disdain having crawled back into the dark recess from which it crept. "If you'll step over here."

A few minutes later, Kel found her way around *The Globe's* intranet. She had a vague recollection of when her dad and Terry's partnership collapsed, but at the time her life had taken such a dramatic twist, reading it now was like digesting fresh copy. The article on the screen, dated February 23, 2000, outlined the details.

Terry Graham, a detective with the Seattle Police Department, was suspended from duty today pending investigation into allegations of driving while intoxicated and battery.

A neighbor, who asked not to be identified, stated that Graham arrived home just after two a.m. He and his wife were awakened when Graham's car crashed into a metal garbage can and ran up onto the Graham's front lawn.

"That's when the shouting started," the neighbor said. "It's become such a common thing over the last several months we hardly pay attention any more. But this time it was different. Mrs. Graham was screaming for him to stop."

The neighbor went on to report that the noise died down after a second car pulled up and another man, reported to be Detective Dirk Nyte, Graham's partner, went inside.

The SPD has refused comment other than a written statement. "Terry Graham is a highly decorated member of the Settle Police Department. No charges have been filed at this time, but Graham has been placed on paid administrative leave until the internal investigation is concluded."

Kel looked away from the monitor and rubbed her eyes. She had been staring at it for over an hour, and her mind grew weary.

The breakup had been bad, that much she knew, but she had never considered her dad to be a whistle blower. Now here it was. A domestic dispute between two of Mom and Dad's friends had become the catalyst for Terry's dismissal. But whether he felt mandated or duty bound, she couldn't see him intentionally ruining his partner's career.

She turned her thoughts to Tribune Investments. Jake warned her to stay clear, but she typed the company name into *The Globe's* internal search engine anyway. Not many hits resulted. One reporter had posted his research notes. According to what she read, Tribune was a shell company that had never filed a Federal Tax return and had no substantial assets. The reporter hadn't been able to link Tribune to a parent company, but he located the names of the principals of the company—Toshio Aoki, Yoshi Kobayashi, and Peter McCabe. Not only was Yoshi Kobayashi associated with Tribune, he was also listed as CFO for Saito Global, a shipping company doing overseas transport out of the Port of Seattle.

She opened a new tab on the web browser and searched for information on the names. Peter McCabe seemed out of place with the other two of Japanese origin, so she investigated him first. When no useful results were found, she began looking for the other two. Only one of the names yielded anything helpful, Toshio Aoki. A picture appeared on the screen, and she recognized the man being led from a courtroom as the same leathery face peering out the rear window of the black Audi yesterday in Pioneer Square. According to the newspaper archives, Aoki had done time for racketeering, and until three months ago, had been in prison. The arresting officer was Willie Jenkins.

Kel looked up from the monitor and drove her knuckles into her eyes. Too little sleep and too much adrenaline were on a collision course with the caffeine withdrawal in her head. She leaned back in the chair, laced her fingers behind her head, and closed her eyes for just a few seconds to relieve the burn.

"May I help you?"

Tipping the chair forward and forcing her eyes open, Kel jumped to her feet. The familiar face of a man she had seen in photos took shape on the opposite side of the desk. She rarely read his weekly column, which was why she hadn't immediately recognized the name earlier on the wall plaques. But it all came together now. Aged by at least ten years since the last time he updated the photo running next to his byline, the man before her, without doubt, was Jared Collins.

"No, I mean, yes. Well, I mean…sorry, I'm Kel Nyte, SPD, and someone out there," she said, waving toward the fortress of cubicles beyond the office, "said you would be out the rest of the afternoon. Half frame glasses on a neck chain?"

"That would be Millicent the Magnificent," he said. A smile broke the stern look of a high school principal from this face, and he ran his fingers through the bristling hair of his more salt than pepper shaded beard.

"Mid-fifties, shoulder-length gray hair?"

"By your careful observation, I'd say you're a detective."

"Yes, detective, plebe grade according to my partner."

"That's our Millie. She's one of our better proofreaders."

"It's none of my business, sir, but I think she has a thing for you."

"Comes with the territory," Jared said and waved his hand at the trophies of his success hanging on the back wall. "Happens so often I just ignore it."

"As I said, it's none of my business. I'll leave you to your desk."

"Don't leave on my account. If Millie said you could use my desk, you can use my desk."

"I do need to get going." She glanced at the Minnie Mouse watch she always kept strapped to her arm with a leather band. The animated face reminded her not to take life too seriously. "Oh my God, I had no idea it was so late. I just closed my eyes for a few seconds, at least I thought. I must have napped for over an hour. I have to go. Thank you for the use of your computer."

She stepped out from behind the desk, picking up her notepad and a couple of news reports she had printed.

"Plebe grade, huh? Who's your partner?

"Jake deLaurenti. My first week on the job"

"I see. Doesn't he have trouble keeping a partner around?

"Shouldn't comment on that."

"It's public knowledge, Detective. Seems he has one in the hospital and one in the grave."

"You've been tracking him?"

"It's my business to keep an ear to the ground. Mr. deLaurenti has the makings of a good story."

"You won't learn much from me. We just met yesterday."

"I see. Well, you best be careful. I'd hate to see you meet the same fate as your predecessors."

"I'll keep that in mind," she said, heading for the door.

"You said your name was Nyte, didn't you?" Jared asked as she walked by him.

"Yes, Kelsey Nyte." She stopped, placing her hand on the door jamb.

Few people used her birth name and then it was generally people who didn't know her well. When she had started high school, she decided to shorten her name to Kel—Kelsey was too girly. Even though her mother never quite accepted it as Kel had been named for a favorite aunt, high school and eventually college branded her for life.

"You've been in the news today."

"I suppose I have."

"Talked to your father, this morning."

"So that was you. Dad said a reporter called, but why? You're a columnist, not a staff writer,"

"Even a columnist is interested in the plight of the human condition. If I didn't care about humanity, I wouldn't have many readers."

"I suppose that's true. So, on the heels of this tragedy, why's my dad suddenly a human interest story?"

"He and I share something. Your father, Dirk, and I both have an interest in depraved minds. He's become somewhat of a local celebrity, what with his success in catching the Rat City Exterminator and then the recent overturn of the convict's verdict. I thought he

152

might have an opinion on the series of murders you're investigating."

"What series is that, sir?"

"Don't be cagey. You said so yourself."

"I said there was a series of murders?"

"You said that to a sergeant on the scene from the Bellingham police just this morning. He let it slip to a reporter."

"Of course," she said and turned her eyes away from his. She had thought the information safe behind the blue veil, but apparently Sergeant Monroe felt otherwise. "I didn't realize the press had that information yet."

"Oh, we're pretty good at ferreting."

"Like Terry Graham's name?"

"Okay, that was an educated guess."

"Go on."

"The officer also said you asked about an address, and shortly thereafter the local sheriff was called to it. Apparently, you showed up. It doesn't take too much digging to find out that Terry Graham lived there and drove fuel for the terminal that exploded."

"All right, you've demonstrated that you're perhaps a superior detective and that I need to keep my mouth shut. Lesson learned, now I need to get moving."

"Wouldn't dare stand in your way, Detective Nyte."

Chapter 24

Dirk had taken a carafe of coffee with him when he retired to the study after breakfast. From the dark walnut bookshelf, he pulled Ken Follett's *Pillars of the Earth*. Even though he had read the novel several times, it always took him to a place where his own trials didn't bear as much weight. Over the next several hours, he lost himself in the vivid characters, attempting to push Terry Graham's death out of his consciousness.

Reading had always been something he took pleasure in, even as a kid. Once Kel and Shelia were old enough not be under foot all the time, he and Clarissa spent many hours reading in this very room. But in the last six years, the demands on the office of police chief made reading a luxury for which he had little time and even less energy. Now, though, it brought a comforting means of escape from the pain of his disease, and, whenever he picked up a hardbound edition, it seemed to invite his wife's spirit to join him.

As midafternoon crept in and the sun continued to heat the house, he found it difficult to concentrate despite the intriguing plot developing on the page. Something more evil than Follett's antagonist wove a spider's web of brutality on his city, and Dirk saw no end in sight.

The news of Susan Lowen's murder had been as difficult to take as any cop's death. But she was more than just a cop. Although they hadn't worked together side by side, she had analyzed in her lab the evidence he uncovered on the street. Together they had brought a number of criminals to justice.

But nothing compared to a good partner, and Terry Graham had been a great one. To say they had each other's back was cliché. Even when they fought like brothers, that being a frequent disruption in the bullpen, their passion for the victims and commitment to closing the case gave them an unstoppable edge.

From the moment Jared Collins told him about Terry, Dirk felt like he'd been hit with a doubling punch to the gut and an upper cut to the jaw. Not only was the sudden loss of his old friend shattering, but it came with a hostile reminder that the breech between them had never been restored. Time, distance, and a decade of life dulled the ache, but with all the fences he could have mended in his last days, Terry's was one that mattered most. Now it was too late.

Getting up from the chair where he had sat for several hours, he made his way to the refrigerator. *Pillars* always put him in the mood for courser fare, so he pulled some summer sausage and block of sharp cheddar to slice a snack.

His thoughts drifted back over the more than twenty years of their association. Terry had been closer to Dirk than his own brother for more than ten of those years. Although the friendship failed in 2000, during the decade of the nineties, Dirk and Terry had been inseparable, closing more cases leading to conviction than any other two detectives in the city.

Their streak started when they became the primaries on the Exterminator case in 1990. While every spare resource worked the case, two seasoned detectives managed the taskforce. When they both retired the same year, Dirk and Terry took the lead, seeing it all the way from suspect to conviction. On the day Vince Buckley stepped off the bus for what they thought was his last breath of free air, they waited outside the gate of the Washington State Penitentiary in Walla Walla until they were sure the gate slammed behind him for good.

Finished with the knife, he piled the snack on a small plate, refilled his carafe, and grabbed a box of crackers on his way back to the study. Easing into his leather chair, he balanced the plate in his lap, reached for his cup and took a deep swallow. Like the bitterness of he and Terry's war, the taste of the cold coffee lingered on his palate. He placed the half-filled mug back on the reading table.

A ten-minute drive from *The Globe* put Kel on her dad's narrow street. She pulled her Liberty from under the tree-lined awning into the driveway and walked up the concrete steps to the covered porch. She let herself into the living room through the front door. The handmade Turkish rug under her feet, and the familiar scents of furniture polish and hardwood floors welcomed her.

No matter how many years she had been on her own, this was always home. What would happen to it after Dirk's passing hadn't been a topic of discussion in the last few months, but she knew he'd have it covered in his will. Without Dad and Mom, though, the home would lose its comforting significance. Even if she or her sister moved in, the nostalgic memories wouldn't replay without their parents' presence, but then the thought of putting it on the market and seeing strangers move in left an awful void.

"Daddy?" she called.

"In the study, Princess. Bring a couple of cups."

Moments later, Kel entered the study and went straight to Dirk. Wrapping her arms around him, she said, "I love you, Daddy. I'm so sorry about Terry."

"We both are, Princess," he said and gave her a kiss on the cheek.

Spying the carafe on the lamp table, Kel released her hug and began to fill the two mugs.

"How are you and Jake getting on?" Dirk asked.

"He calls me plebe," she replied handing him one of the cups.

"Plebe, huh? I guess you've got to start somewhere."

"May as well be at the bottom, right?" she asked after settling into her mom's chair.

"So he's working you?"

"No, we're stuck on rule one." Seeing the cheese and sausage on the edge of the table, her stomach rumbled reminding her that her last meal had been a raspberry scone this morning, she asked, "Hey, you eating those?"

Dirk offered her the plate. "Rule one, what's that?"

"'Stay the hell out of my way,'" she said and placed her cup on the table to take the plate.

"He's a bit of a loner, but he does have a good closing ratio."

"So I've been told."

"And a little ego."

"Now there I must disagree categorically." A grin passed over her lips. "He has enough ego for the entire department. So I'm running my investigation, and he's running his. He's going to be by shortly."

"I'm still on the list?"

"As far as I know, Daddy, from his perspective, you are the list. It's still early, but the only thing we can find in common between Susanne Lowen and Terry Graham is you. So Jake's coming by to ask some questions."

"I'd rather hear them from you."

"I'd rather ask them, but due to the circumstances…well, you understand."

Dirk nodded his head and shifted to face her.

"It seems," she continued, picking up a bite of sausage and cracker, "like Jake works one lead at a time. Not so much into multitasking as far as I've seen. I can't figure out how he closes so many cases. But right now, since you're the main attraction, I think he just needs to get it out of his system."

"Do you think I'm guilty?"

The leather grunted against her blue jeans as she shifted, leaning forward to look straight into his eyes.

"Everything inside me screams no, but the evidence says maybe. Daddy, I have this recurring thought. If the daughter of a serial killer was asked before her father was arrested if he would senselessly take someone's life, she'd say, 'No damn way.' And now I'm that girl."

"Kel, you wouldn't be doing your job if you didn't look to me as a suspect, especially now with the second death so close to me, even closer than Susanne."

"It's not right, though."

"Be that as it may, search in every nook and cluttered closet. Just keep an open mind." He tilted his head, forced a smirk to his lips, and continued, "I could have hired a hit man, you know."

"Daddy!" she shouted.

"Think like a detective, not a daughter. There *is* a murderer out there. You keep following the evidence, and you'll bust this perp. Have you thought any more about Vince Buckley?"

"I put a BOLO out last night, but he's off the grid. Once I find him, we'll have a little chat about his whereabouts the last few days. Then I can escalate or eliminate him."

"No telling if Buckley's taking out everyone who was a part of his conviction and through you giving me a firsthand view of his master plan."

"It's possible," she said, "but until I find him, I can't ask the questions." She placed the plate on the table, picked up the cup, and leaned back into the leather, crossing her legs. "Daddy, there's something about the case I haven't told you."

"If I'm a suspect, you shouldn't tell me anything else."

"If you're the doer, you already know what I'm about to tell you. If you're not, you might be able to help."

When he didn't object further, she continued. "You know about the poem DK sent me, but there're more. To date, he's left a poem at every scene. Each one is in a very structured seven beat, iambic style. Did you ever study or write poetry?"

"Never even tried. Does that take me off the list?"

"Not necessarily. They're pretty simple, but that's good to know. There are some things in each poem that give an indication of his point. The first line in each one, for example, seems to show a relationship between the victim and DK's target."

Opening her notebook, she continued, "Last night you said Susanne worked in the lab in the 90s. That made me wonder who the first line was written about. Listen, 'First the one who owes so much.' Can you make sense of it?"

Dirk leaned into the chair and sipped from his cup. Then, looking across the room toward the bookcase without focusing on anything animate, he nodded his head. "Me…Maybe I'm his student."

"Why, what did Susanne owe you?" Kel asked.

Meeting her eyes, he said, "After Buckley's arrest, Terry and I gained a lot of notoriety, not just departmental but in the press. We had brought an end to a crime spree that had the whole town on edge. Even though we were a long way from conviction, the press painted us as heroes. This naturally found its way to the police chief who was always eager to shine a positive spotlight on the department, so commendations were handed out.

"At the time I had a friend who was a detective in South Precinct. His friend's niece had recently graduated with a double major in biology and criminology and was looking for work in the public sector. I knew of her, and since I had the ear of the police chief, I put her name in front of him. Susanne owed her career to me. What does Terry's poem say?"

She placed the mug back on the table without taking a drink and pulled gloves from her hip pocket, slipping them over her hands. From her notebook she withdrew a white envelope with her name hand printed in block letters on the outside. Extracting a single piece of white paper, she unfolded it and began to read.

"Two is he who joined your cause

Now must suffer from my laws

Tissues scorched, torn asunder

Victim of my hurled thunder"

"What do your make of the first couple of lines, Daddy?" she asked and stood. "The phrase 'joined *your* cause,' if Susanne's poem is directed to you, then knowing this was written with Terry in mind, could it also be a reference to you?"

"My partner. Makes sense."

"So if that's true then," she said and paced the floor, "and you're the target, you need to look past Buckley. Make a list of people with the means, motive, and mindset to commit these acts."

"Pretty long list, I'd think."

"Regardless, it's the place to start. Look for any reference to someone with the initials DK. Now," she continued, looking back at the paper, "he uses the word 'laws.' I think that could be a play on words."

"Possibly. Terry and I both being cops at the time of Buckley's arrest."

"You're still fixated on him," she said, looking up from the paper and into Dirk's eyes. "Broaden the pool, Daddy."

"Of course, you just said that."

"Are you feeling okay?"

It wasn't like her dad to lose focus. He had always been the first to put things together, but over the last several weeks, she noticed his mind didn't process as fast as it used to. She felt pressure behind her eyes and walked away to the window where he wouldn't notice if she cried. She hated what was happening to him, and in moments where it became obvious he was failing, her heart grieved.

162

"I'm fine, just get tired in the afternoon, even when I haven't done anything all day. Damn this disease."

"Why don't you rest? We can continue this later?"

"No, please go on. I want to hear your thoughts."

Feeling composure return, she turned her head toward him. "Okay, if you're sure."

"Please, in some ways this is cathartic. I spend most of the day killing time just waiting to die. This is at least a break in that dreadful deathwatch."

She turned to face the window. "It seems to me that DK has his own set of laws. He calls them 'my laws.' I think he believes something in his life gave him the authority to throw out one of our most basic human rights, the right to life. He's replaced it with something he feels trumps, and I fear that until we figure out what's driving him, we're going to be powerless to stop him."

Dirk lifted his cup to his lips and took a swallow. "But, if I'm the object, why doesn't he just come after me? Why do others have to be hurt?"

She stared blankly out the window. "Because he claims to be a teacher. Remember he said, 'Mine to teach the lesson well.' If my theory's true and you're the object, you have to learn the lesson. He's giving you hints, but it's up to you to search for the answer. Ultimately, since whatever it is you need to learn revolves around him, I think he plans to reveal himself once you figure it out. He wants to he caught, but not before you know at what crossroads you two intersected." Turning back to him, she continued, "And I hate to say it, but so far he's been punctual. Remember his first message to me, 'Mine to reap for Hell *each day*'? There's no time to waste, Daddy. I need your help."

"I kept personal journals. I'll read through them. Maybe there's a DK lurking in there, if those are his real initials."

"I think they are. Probably another clue."

"What I don't understand," he said, placing his cup on the table, "is why you? Why is he communicating with you and not me?"

"It's more *through* me rather than *with* me. Obviously he knows I'm your daughter. So, in essence, he's using me as your tutor. Maybe he knows you're ill, so he's giving me enough information so I can be the witness to his acts and pass on to you what I've seen.

"But," she said, folding the letter and tucking it back into the envelope, "we've found a way to track him."

"How's that?"

She walked back toward the chair and told him about the four burner phones DK had purchased.

"That's how I knew something was about to happen up north. A second of the four phones became active. Unfortunately, I was unable to get to it in time to stop *this* tragedy, but maybe the next time I will."

"Do you think he knows?"

"We can't be sure of anything, Daddy, but if he's watching the news, it's pretty obvious I knew enough to be on scene when the plant exploded. He could be tracking me like I am him. He could know I'm here with you right now."

"Which could mean you're in danger."

"We could both be in danger," she said, sitting back down in the leather chair, "but you've taught me to face threats head on, not run from them."

"That sounded a lot better when I was talking about me."

"Comes with the territory, Daddy. You know that."

"I've stared down the barrel of a lot of guns before and survived them all. As if it weren't enough that I sit here day after day with an unseen enemy killing me from the inside, if I'm the true target, now I have to worry about what this damned DK has planned for those I care about."

"I'm going to catch him, Daddy. You can count on that."

"I know you will, Princess, I have no doubt."

"Now, before Jake gets here, there's something else I'd like to ask." She picked up a slice of cheese and poked into her mouth. "Do you know the name Toshio Aoki?"

"Aoki, of course. What does he have to do with DK?"

"Probably nothing, but he seems to know Jake, and I'm trying to run down how."

"That's interesting. How'd you make that connection?"

"Yesterday, Jake and I were having coffee, and Aoki drove by. He had his driver stop long enough to make eye contact with Jake. Something definitely passed between them, but Jake denies it and as much told me to stay out of it."

"But of course you couldn't do that."

"I'm just naturally inquisitive, Daddy," she said and grinned. "Comes with the Nyte blood in my veins. Anyway, I ran across his name when I searched for the owner of the Audi. It led me to Tribune Investments."

"That's a shell."

"I know, but for who or what? I did some research this afternoon and found that one of the principles of Tribune, Yoshi Kobayashi, is also the CFO of Saito Global, which seems to be a legitimate shipping company."

"We've never been able to nail Aoki for much, but we're pretty sure he's part of a crime syndicate. As for Kobayashi, he's like Teflon."

"There's a third name associated with Tribune, Peter McCabe. I can't find anything on him."

"And you won't. I'm sure you've heard of the Don of the Docks."

"Is McCabe the Don?"

"No one knows. We can't even confirm that the Don exists. What we do know is that the syndicate Aoki is part of has a very long and very tight-lipped reach into the longshoreman's local at the Port. We've suspected that it goes all the way up to my counterpart at the Port Police."

"The port police chief?"

"Possibly. Even though the docks are within the Seattle city limits, they have jurisdiction. We've tried forging cooperation between the SPD and the Port Police, but it's been difficult. Jake and your friend Willie Jenkins were the first."

"And then Willie ended up dead in a shipping container nearly half way around the world, just about the time Aoki went to prison."

"Coincidence or retribution?" Dirk asked. "But no one's talking."

"Code of silence."

"And within the police community, that's more sacrosanct than a novice monk's vow."

Chapter 25

DK wept.

Deep in the bowels of the Emerald City, he could hear the muted bustle of the burgeoning evening commute—the whine of a hybrid articulated-bus, the hollow rumble of an SUV passing over a steel grate, and the thunder of a motorcycle's glass-pack exhaust pipe. Submerged so deep in his subterranean sanctuary, he could only imagine the feet on sidewalks shuffling on every course to their daily escape from making a living to having a life—secretaries transforming into soccer moms, Harvard grads turning into homework dads— each one exploiting God's ultimate gift, freedom of choice.

The beam of the battery-powered flashlight resting next to him on the floor rose like a beacon to the low ceiling and radiated off the exposed pipes and rafters overhead. The small abandoned room had escaped the eyes of all despite the frantic activity of the courts and the contractors.

On his knees in this condemned hovel, he looked to the shrine he had erected rising above a wooden altar made of short lengths of wall studs. Over the collage of photos and artwork, a paper banner with a Biblical quote from the Book of Deuteronomy stretched across the wall before him.

"The secret things belong to God, but the things revealed belong to us."

Displayed in a montage of faded photos of people to whom he had been forced to estrange, the only life DK truly lived spread before him on the memorial wall. In the center, the purest, immortalized in a white wedding gown.

His hands drew instinctively to the invisible scars of the facial reconstruction surgery he self-imposed so many years ago—necessary to save those he loved and now even more important as he walked near the enemy. They had become a silent testimony to the man he unwillingly had to become.

He looked to the altar. He had placed photos of five victims, each with a two-inch white pillar candle concealing the subject's face. Susanne Lowen's likeness was on his far left. The candle had burned once, but now rested cold, extinguished like her breath. Turning his thoughts to the next, he leaned forward and blew on the flame dancing on Terry Graham's wick. It sputtered into darkness and sent a thin, white ribbon of smoke in a spiraling ascent like Terry's soul. Mingling in the confined space with the dust particles floating in the stagnant air, except for the lingering waxy scent, its distinction dissipated.

Before him the third victim's photo rested on the altar. He removed the candle from her face for one final look. As he did, tears flowed again down his cheeks, and he sobbed without embarrassment in deep remorse. He didn't mourn for the victim who soon would die. She didn't matter to him. He understood that to those who loved her, she would attain a state she couldn't reach in this life—omnipresent immortality—as they memorialized her memory. It was the only gift he could bequeath as her death was necessary, a payment on a long owed debt—deserted, imprisoned, hunted like a beast, and then forced to forsake everything.

The scent of cold rice roused him from sleep. Like the gentle touch of his wife when she rolled over in bed to slip her arm around his chest, it brought a welcomed comfort. Arriving every morning before dawn, it had become his only luxury. Like breathing in and breathing out, the bowl tethered him to a fragile thread of sanity. It embodied his daily quest.

When the imprisonment began, he had used his fingernail to memorialize each sunrise with a hash-mark on the wooden floor of his prison, but after tracking two years, it just didn't matter. He had become like a circus animal. Chained by day and caged by night, he performed his mindless tasks from daylight to nightfall.

Nine years of exposure in the sweltering jungle had baked his mind to an anesthetized numbness. The macabre screams of the innocent lives he had slaughtered and the thrashing visions of his buddies' last breathes vanished from his nightmares. The image of the three-year-old son he left crying on the front porch had long faded like an echo in a secret crevasse, yet there remained a child-sized breach in his memory that yearned to be filled.

Even though his own name retreated so far into the past it seemed of no importance to his daily existence—not worth the effort to recall— the phantom with sergeant stripes stalked day and night. The questions he asked in the beginning—intentionality, cowardice, misinformation, dereliction—had faded with the other bits of his life. But in the void, the face symbolized all his loss and gave sustenance to his present reality.

Sold and resold, stolen and re-stolen, beaten only to revive to be beaten again, if he had ever been a prisoner of war, those days were long past. He was now a slave and gave willing assent to whoever held the key to his coop— the faceless men who delivered the rice.

So why eat?

Reduced to the most basic human precedence, even pain by whip no longer gave witness to life. It would have been easier to acquiesce to the evidence. Release, rescue, or escape could never be attained. He should have forsaken the thought that the next marauding gang would be someone sent from home to rescue him, and not another warring tribe to seize his servitude. Death offered an almost uncontrollable appeal, yet he fought the longing with each breath. He purposed to stall its coming because there remained one thing, one leash, one hope— the end of the cage.

He sat up, leaned his back against the familiar bars—his home—and caressed the bowl. Around him, the familiar sounds of the jungle waking for a new day— chattering vernal hanging-parrots and a couple of black crested gibbons singing their morning breeding song— filled his ears.

In his hand the only meal he would see today writhed like a bucket of snakes. He reached in with two fingers, scooped the white rice and maggots into his mouth, and savored the insipid pleasure.

The bride in the collection earned DK's longsuffering lament, his wife, the mother of his children, who to this day thought he was dead. Such joy she had given to him before the end. When departing, he pledged that if his life ran its course before he returned, her love would have been enough. But then the single action of one man caused him to lose it all to a living death. That act could have been forgiven, but when his recklessness reared again, the only means of atonement required the ultimate price.

Returning the candle to cover the smiling image of the middle victim, he reached to his breast pocket. He tore a paper match from the book, slid the head across the striker, and listened as it crackled into its transitory existence. Then, holding the match to the center candle, he watched as the flame passed its life to the candle wick resting over his next sacrifice.

Chapter 26

Dirk heard voices and the clanking of dishes in the kitchen. He wasn't worried about the meeting to take place in his study, but he didn't look forward to it, either. Since Lou Martinez threw his name into the suspect pool, more out of vengeance than any rational police work, and now with two dead cops both connected to him, he knew he had to be eliminated from the list.

"Daddy," Kel, who had left the study when the doorbell rang, reentered the room. "You know Jake deLaurenti."

"Of course," Dirk said, pushing himself to his feet, using the arms of the leather chair for support. He offered his hand in greeting. "Good to see you again."

"Not the best circumstances," Jake said as he took Dirk's hand. He shook it with a single jerk.

"No, I think not. Please sit." Dirk waved to a rocker opposite his chair on the other end of the red-brick hearth.

While Dirk eased himself back into the soft leather, Kel poured coffee from the carafe into a fresh cup she had brought from the kitchen and handed it to Jake. Then, as she repeated the action, warming her father's and her brew, she said, "Jake has some questions we need to ask." After handing him his mug, she patted his leg and then sat down on the edge of her mom's old chair.

"Are you having much pain these days?" Jake rested the cup on the arm of the rocker.

"It's my body's way of talking back to the disease. Pancreatic cancer is no picnic, son."

"I can't imagine. Not only the pain but the knowledge there's no cure. My God, Chief, it's awful. I'm so sorry."

"Thank you Jake. Now, I don't mean to be rude, but today's been a difficult day, and I'm already beat. Before I fade further, you better go for it."

"Of course." Jake placed the mug on the hearth and unzipped a notebook-sized portfolio. From an inside pocket he pulled a pen, and raised it, poised to take notes. "You knew Susanne Lowen, correct?"

"Yes."

"How did you first meet?"

"We had an opening in the crime lab, and I put her name in front of the police chief."

"And?"

"She was hired," he said, crossing his legs and placing the steaming cup on the lamp table, "and helped me solve any number of cases. Her lab skills are legendary. It's such a tremendous loss."

"I agree." Jake leaned forward. "Then, fast forward, she undermined the Vince Buckley serial murder case."

"It's true, but not her fault. The evidence was weak. The whole case was a house of circumstantial cards, but we knew that going in. When his lawyer petitioned for a new trial, Susanne pulled on the right one and the whole thing crumbled. I bear her no ill. She was doing what we paid her to do, process evidence. If we would have had the right technology in the 90s, he might have never been convicted. At least we got him off the street for a while."

"You said 'we.' Who helped you build that case?"

"You already know it was Terry."

"Terry Graham," he said and leaned back in the rocker, taking the cup from the hearth. "And you know he was killed this morning?"

"Yes, a reporter from *The Globe* broke the news."

"Interesting." He made a note. "What reporter?"

"Jared Collins."

"I know of Collins. Columnist, right?" Before Dirk could answer, he continued, "So how long was Terry your partner?"

"More than a decade."

"Were you close outside of work?"

175

"Extremely. We did family things together. Back then the Grahams and the Nytes were inseparable."

Jake raised the mug to his lips, looked over the edge, and asked, "Then you know why he left the SPD?"

"Of course. It's in the record. He and his wife were having personal issues."

Lowering the cup and swallowing, he asked, "Personal issues, can you elaborate?"

"What does this have to do with his murder? That's ancient history."

"Background."

"Background?" Dirk paused. He recognized the tactic. Jake was on a fishing expedition. Toss in the bait, feel for a nibble, and then set the hook. With a sigh, he continued, "Something had been gnawing at Terry for a long time. He had lost most of their life's savings on an investment."

Kel stood and walked to the front window. The questions were taking the conversation in a direction that made her wince, and she didn't want her dad to shade any answers, attempting to protect her. In the final years of the 90s, she had used her psychology degree to help an up-and-coming dotcom find a market. They were in the IPO process and one of her benefits was pre-IPO stock. Confident of its success, she had boasted about it to her parents, and they chose to buy in with a small amount. But Terry, hearing about it from Dirk, poured in everything.

176

"He always liked to stop for a drink before heading home," Dirk continued, "trying to wash the day's debris out of his mind. You can understand that, son, I'm sure."

"Comes with the territory."

"About the time he lost his investment, the drinking became heavier. He didn't try to hide the tension building between him and his wife. We trusted each other and kept each other's confidences, so he told me that she had been complaining about the late nights. At the same time, a captain's position came open in the detective's squad at West Precinct. When he didn't make the cut, it was like pissing gasoline on a fire."

Dirk's face went ashen. "Oh my God, how inappropriate." A vision of Terry being consumed in the flames at the fuel terminal played through his mind. He planted both feet on the floor, leaned forward, and threw his head into his hands.

Kel turned from the window and rushed to him. "It's all right Daddy," she said. Placing her hand on his shoulders, she began massaging them. "You meant no disrespect."

"Damn it. None of this is right. While we're sitting here drinking coffee, Terry and Susanne's murderer is plotting his next move."

"We're going to get him, Daddy," Kel said.

"But this just seems like such a waste of time. I have no motive now and didn't then. Besides, I'm too sick to have committed these atrocities. "

"I know these questions seem pointless, Chief," Jake said, "but you know it's necessary. If you're all right, can we go on?"

"Of course." Dirk leaned back into the chair, lifting his legs one at a time to rest them on the hassock. "I'm sorry."

"No apology needed. So, when Terry didn't make the cut, it angered him and made matters worse?"

"Yes, and it didn't help that I was on the short list."

"Did he confront you?"

"Yes, one night we were on our way to arrest a man we suspected of heading a car heist ring, and he brought the subject up. 'Hell,' he shouted, 'this is bullshit. We've both worked our balls to a nub and have damn good records.'"

"I see. Then what happened?"

"Well, it was the evening of Valentine's Day. Terry should have been home with his wife, but he was at the bar again. He was in terrible shape. I tried to get him to let me drive him home. But he wouldn't hear of it. Clarissa, Kel's mom, and I had plans, so I made arrangements with the barkeep that if Terry got out of control he was to call me.

"After several hours, I got the call. By the time I arrived, Terry's vocabulary had disintegrated into halting phrases with one syllable words. He wasn't making much sense and wouldn't listen to reason. I tried again to get him to let me take him home, but he was livid, spewing out trash about his marriage. He was embarrassing himself but had no intention of leaving until they kicked him out on the street. So this time I left enough cash with the proprietor for a cab and headed home.

"It was about 2:30 a.m. when I got the next call. Clarissa answered and immediately handed me the receiver. It was Terry's wife. He had driven himself home, and, once there, his words turned into fists, and she became the target. After quite a beating, she managed to lock herself in the bathroom and called me."

"Why not call 9-1-1?"

"Cops code, you know. She didn't want it on the record."

"Yet it did get on the record, didn't it? How'd that happen?"

Dirk glared at him and shook his head. "A couple days later, her neighbor spoke to her. All the makeup and sunglasses in the world couldn't cover up the bruising. The neighbor called it in."

"So then you had attempted a cover up?"

"We were off duty at the time so, yes, I wanted to protect my partner—my friend—and the SPD from unnecessary embarrassment. In retrospect, that wasn't the best decision because truth has a way of bubbling to the surface. As I said, we spent a lot of time together. The neighbor recognized my car at the curb."

"And somehow you came out of it without a stink."

"I was told to file an official report, Jake. 'Get it in his jacket,' they said."

"And how did that go?"

"Now that the truth was out, my first duty was to the people I serve and the department. Even though I knew it would be damaging for Terry, I had no option but to tell the truth."

"And there is no other reason you hung him out to dry?"

Dirk dropped his legs from the hassock and using his hands on the chair arms to pull his torso forward, he focused his eyes on Jake's. "First of all, son," he said, trying to control the building vehemence by keeping his words clipped and terse, "I didn't hang him out to dry. I followed orders. Second, are you implying something?"

"Not implying anything, Chief, just getting background. If there's something else, just tell me the whole truth, as you said, before it bubbles to the surface."

Dirk shot Kel, who had stepped behind her mother's chair, an apprehensive glance. Last night, she joked about Pandora's Box, but he wasn't ready to take the lid off. Not like this. Not in front of Jake.

"Jake, maybe you should give him a break," Kel said. "He's exhausted."

"Like Hell," Dirk said, giving full voice to the rage he had checked. "If you think there's something else, spill it out."

Dirk paused, giving Jake time to speak. When Jake lifted his cup and smiled, Dirk relaxed back into the chair. "Just as I thought, innuendo, nothing else. Once it all came out, the department had no choice. They couldn't tolerate the bad press, and he was dismissed."

"And who did the dismissing?"

"That's a matter of public record, too. You know already or you wouldn't ask."

"Just to tickle my ears, tell me anyway."

"Damn it, Jake, I feel bad enough that we never patched things up. Why are you dredging this up now?" Dirk sighed and shook his head. "By the time Terry came clean, I had been promoted to captain and was now Terry's boss. So, since Terry had pled guilty to physically abusing his wife and then refused to see the department psychiatrist, I had no choice. I had to let him go. Hardest thing I ever did, but by the book."

"How did he feel about that?"

"How do you think he felt? He had just lost his career, and his marriage was a shambles. He lost his life savings, including as much of his 401k he could borrow, and then his best friend sent him packing to the unemployment line at a time when unemployment was skyrocketing. So he probably wasn't very happy about it or me."

Jake placed his cup back on the hearth and then stood. "Do you mind if I use the restroom? That coffee seems to have gone right through me."

"Of course not," Dirk said, surprised by the abrupt shift. He nodded towards the door. "There's one just off the kitchen by the back door."

Jake took his notepad and left the room.

"What do you think, Daddy?" She turned her eyes to him as she stepped around and took a seat.

"I know he's just collecting background, but I thought he'd be more interested in my whereabouts this week."

181

"Maybe he's just getting warmed up. You still okay? This could go on a while longer."

"I'll be fine."

While they sat in silence, Kel took hold of Dirk's arm, gave it gentle squeeze, and passed him a smile. Dirk felt her hand but couldn't look her way. Jake had stirred a monster that he thought had been buried a decade ago.

When Jake reappeared he didn't move to the rocker but stopped in the study's doorway. "Well, Chief Nyte, I think I have enough for now."

"What? You're not going to ask me where I was at the times in question?"

"Not right now. Besides, I'm not sure you have the strength to overpower someone like Susanne Lowen. By the way, do you own a cell phone?"

"Don't use it much now but yes."

"When was the last time?"

"I don't know, maybe a couple of weeks. I take it with me when I go out."

"Do you mind if I pull your records?"

"Whatever you need—my land line, cell phone, computer, I have nothing to hide. And I just want to make one last statement, Jake. I've built my career on prosecuting criminals. With three months to live, do you really think I'm going to suddenly become one?"

"Ever hear of going out in a blaze of glory, Chief?"

Chapter 27

Kel pressed the button on the remote, engaging the automatic door opener to her single-car garage. She was relieved to finally be home. The day had started without enough sleep at 3:00 a.m. and with the clock on the dashboard now registering 7:58 p.m., she let her eyelids slide shut as the garage door slid open. The smell of pizza coming from the box on Chrissie's lap reminded her stomach that except for the small snack she ate at her dad's, it had been neglected since she devoured a raspberry scone in Bellingham ten hours earlier.

Once the door ground to a halt, she opened her eyes and guided the Jeep into the dimly lit cavern. Lined with boxes of Lance's things, things too painful to encounter around the house on a daily basis but too sentimental to donate, the narrow passage left just enough room on each side to squeeze through the SUV's open doors.

As Chrissie stepped from the car, Kel's phone rang. "Nyte," she said, tapping the Bluetooth.

"Detective Nyte?" The voice of the desk sergeant filled her ear. "We picked up Vince Buckley."

Inquiries with Buckley's neighbors and at his place of employment, Shelia's law firm, yielded no clues to his location. His supervisor stated that he had requested a couple days off but gave no indication as to his plans. With the malicious gossip mill circulating stories about his past, he made no friends in the time he had worked there, so no one could account for him. "He keeps to himself," his supervisor concluded. With the knowledge that he was due to report to work on Wednesday morning, the SPD doubled the stakeout at his home.

Before leaving the SUV, she called Jake. "Got Buckley in the box?"

"Why?" he asked. "Your dad put you onto him?"

"He has motive, Jake, both for Terry and Susanne's murders. More than my dad has. If you'd get your head out of your ass, you'd see that."

"Where I put my head is my business, plebe. And I'll interview people I have a feel for when I have a feel for them. He's on my list, but he hasn't warmed up to me yet, so if you're going to interview him, it'll be without me."

"Hot date, huh?"

"Again, that's my damn business. Tonight, I'm otherwise engaged."

Otherwise engaged. Jake deLaurenti was an enigma. Around the precinct, people talked about Jake's company of women as if he were a Greek god. Some of them so exotic, reconciling his plain face and stunted personality with their stunning bodies was as likely as tanning to a golden brown in a Siberian blizzard. He relished being seen in public with them on his arm, but how he met these beauties or why they clung to him so attentively, he wasn't talking—gloating by their mere presence, yes, but not talking. That they were escorts was the most obvious answer, but on a detective's pay he should have only been able to afford sidewalk skanks.

Although just in its second day, to say he and Kel had formed a partnership would stretch even the most liberal definition of the word. No bridge had begun to take shape. In fact, to Kel, it felt more like the Great Wall of China had been dropped between them. He didn't take her seriously, and his track record proved that if things got rough, he wouldn't have her back.

Following the scent of the pizza, she eased between the storage boxes and the Liberty, and moved through the door into the passageway between the garage and townhome. Reaching the back door, which Chrissie had left ajar, an eager snout greeted her.

"Hey, Saul," she said as she squeezed through the door opening. She reached down and petted his head. "What's up, boy? Want some dinner?"

More than a watchdog and family friend, Saul had been Lance's dog. Lance had left him in Chrissie's charge when he mustered out for Afghanistan on that final mission. When he didn't return, Saul became a lingering ray of light in a passage that otherwise would have flickered out.

"How many slices?" Chrissie asked as she pulled two plates from the white particle board cabinet above the counter,

"Make it two." Kel took two napkins from the holder on the counter and placed them on the bar.

"Jessica invited me over to spend the night Friday. Would that be okay?"

"I don't know. Friday night's the Torchlight Parade. Pops is going to be in it, remember?"

"Yeah and Jessica's family is planning to go. I'll be there to see Pops." She slid two pieces on a plate and handed it to Kel.

"Thanks, Hon," Kel said and placed the plate on the laminate counter top. "We're all planning to sit together, to be his cheerleaders."

"Me and Jessica'll find you. Please?"

"Well, so long as you promise." She sat down on a barstool. "Aunt Shelia and Danny will be there. We should sit together. This'll probably be Pops last special night."

"That makes me so sad, Mom," Chrissie said as she came around the counter and sat next to Kel. "I promise I won't miss it."

"This smells so good. Say, I have to go back to work in a few minutes."

"Mom," Chrissie said in a sing-song whine.

"I know, sorry. How 'bout you ride along?"

"I don't know. Sounds pretty boring." Picking up the first slice, she aimed it for her mouth.

"I'm going to interview Vince Buckley."

"The Rat City Exterminator? Cool."

"I see you've been doing your internet research?"

"Yeah, since you and Pops were talking about him last night."

"We've been looking for him, and he just turned up. I need to ask him a few questions. You're welcome to come with, but you probably won't get to see him. It could be late, but I'd love to know you're just in the next room."

"I don't know," she said, her mouth full of pizza.

"You can see my new desk."

"Oh," she said, rolling her eyes, "now that's real cool, Mom."

"So that's no?"

"No," she said and paused, "that's a yes," and then took another bite.

Chapter 28

Kel logged into her computer and turned the mouse over to Chrissie. She looked toward the DK crime board and noticed a lot of empty space. The last thing she had written was the timeline leading up to Susanne's death. More than a day passed since then, and three more victims had given their lives for DK's cause—*whatever the hell that was*—Terry, a man who assisted Terry as he filled his tankers at the fuel terminal, and the young guard she watched burn to death. *Collateral damage.*

Beyond the white board, a beige cinderblock wall separated her from the main suspect in her investigation. She placed her hand on Chrissie's shoulder, leaned down, and kissed her on the cheek and then began a deliberate walk that would lead her into the presence of the once convicted serial killer.

Kel had seen photos of Vince Buckley, newspaper clippings at the time of his arrest and trial. She remembered one in particular, shot as he was leaving the courtroom moments after his conviction. In the photo, he struggled against the shackles on his hands, throwing one of his shoulders back to thwart the deputy's grip. His eyes, the lids pulled back and his tiny pupils protruding from their sclera, looked like Charlie Manson's on a bad day. The veins popping in his neck gave life to the rage gripping his face, and on his lips formed a silent shout captured under the photo, "I'm innocent."

The years in Walla Walla had changed him. A maximum security prison in eastern Washington, there he kept company with the Green River Killer, Gary Ridgway, and one of the Hillside Stranglers, Kenneth Bianchi. The man Kel found sitting at the table in Interview 1, "the box," bore no resemblance to the convicted murderer she anticipated meeting. He had lost the majority of his hair, and what remained formed a gray fringe trimmed close to the scalp. The wild eyes she expected to see were now covered with dark-rimmed glasses, giving him a surprising look of normal. Except for several days' beard growth, he could have passed for an accountant.

"Vince Buckley?" she asked as she pushed the door closed behind her and locked on his eyes. She watched intently for something she knew would only have a second or two of life before it expired. If Buckley had been the man who attacked her with the Taser in Susanne Lowen's condo, she'd see it on his face, but a stoic stare met her eyes, revealing nothing.

"What am I doing here, Detective?" Buckley said.

Kel could tell from his tone that he fought to hold back his wrath. He flicked his eyes to the tabletop.

"You've kept me here behind a guarded door for what must have been a couple hours, and no one has offered me a glass of cold water or told me anything. Am I being charged with something?"

Kel walked across the room, pulled a steel-framed chair from the table, and sat down. "You're here so we can have a talk. Would you like some water?"

"No, and I've already invoked," he said, turning his eyes up to hers and placing the palms of his hands on the laminate top. "My lawyer should be here any minute."

"That's your right, of course." She opened her notebook and rested it on the table. "But unnecessary since you haven't been charged with anything. I just have a few questions."

"I'm not talking without my attorney."

"Then I'll start while we wait, if that's okay?"

"Fine, but expect it to be a one-sided conversation," he said and looked at his hands. He interlaced his fingers.

"Perfect, and excuse my rudeness. I didn't introduce myself. I'm Detective Kel Nyte."

As she said her name, she paused and watched again for his reaction. His eyes rolled up, connecting with hers, and she saw the flash of name recognition pass over them. When he didn't comment, she continued.

"The man who charged you and saw you through to conviction is my father, Dirk Nyte."

Again, she hesitated before continuing, waiting to measure his reaction.

A smirk curved across his lips. "So now there's a new generation of Nytes to roust me? What is it about my overturned conviction you people don't understand? Without new evidence, you have no right to hold me."

"That's true Mr. Buckley, but you're not here as a direct result of evidence on the Rat City case. You're here so I can eliminate you as a suspect in another string of murders."

Kel heard the door open behind her, and before she could turn toward the new arrival, a familiar voice spoke.

"I do hope you're not questioning my client without counsel."

"Except to verify his name and to see if he needed some water, I haven't asked Mr. Buckley a single question. We're just getting acquainted."

Kel stood and followed the lawyer with her eyes as she walked around the end of the table to take a seat next to her client.

"I'm surprised to see *you*." Kel shook her head. "How'd you pull this case?"

"We'll talk later," Shelia said. Moving the chair a couple of feet from her client, she took a seat.

"You *know* each other?" Buckley asked.

"It's a small community, Mr. Buckley," Kel said, returning to her chair, "and it gets even more convoluted. We're both Nytes. Shelia's my sister."

"Hell," he said and turned toward his lawyer, "is that the best our firm can do, send the kid of the man who trumped up charges against me?"

"Snelling sent me to represent you," Shelia said, pulling a yellow legal pad from her briefcase, "not because of my dad, but because they knew I'd be unbiased and give you the best counsel." Then to Kel, she continued, "Whatever questions you have for Mr. Buckley, I'm here to make sure he doesn't implicate or perjure himself."

"Of course." Kel turned to Buckley. "It's your call. Snelling, Hardcastle, and Purdin have plenty of other lawyers. We can wait until they send another, or we can proceed with the counsel at hand. I've known Shelia all her life, and she's always been above reproach."

"Why should I trust either one of you?"

"You have no reason to, but allow me to ask a few questions, and if at any time you want to stop, just say so."

He looked from Kel to Shelia and then back at Kel. "Go ahead, but if I so much as hear the distant whistle of a goddamn train, I'm the hell out of here."

"Sounds fair, no railroad job. Now, if I may, according to the police report you live on 17th SW. Is this true?"

"That's where your boys in blue picked me up?"

"So, that's a 'yes?'"

"Yes, what about it?"

"According to your address, your house is only a couple blocks off Roxbury St. Is this also true?"

"What of it?"

"Well, it may be just me, but it seems awfully coincidental that the trail I'm following begins about three blocks from your house."

"What trail's that?" he said and leaned toward the table.

"Are you familiar with Susanne Lowen?"

"Yeah, she's the lab rat that overturned my conviction."

"And the one who sent you up in the first place."

"True enough."

"What about Terry Graham?"

"Just another cum-filled cop trying to make his mark. Along with your daddy, he put me away."

"Would you be surprised to learn that both of these police officers were murdered?"

"You think I killed them?" He jumped to his feet. His chair flew back slamming hard into the wall. "That's why I'm here? This trail just happens to start near my house and two people who had something to do with my imprisonment are dead? And now you accuse me?"

"Please sit back down, Mr. Buckley. I'm not making any accusations. But now that you bring it up, did you murder them?

"Don't be ridiculous. I've never murdered anyone. "

"I'll ask you again to take your seat."

Buckley glared at Kel, shot a glance at Shelia, then reached back for the chair and eased into it.

"So, can you account for yourself since yesterday morning?"

He looked at Shelia again. She leaned in toward him and he turn to whisper into the ear facing away from Kel. Nodding her head, she said, "Go ahead and answer."

He bent forward toward Kel. "I've been in Yakima since Friday night with my kid sister and her family. You see, they never lost faith in me. They believed me innocent, and they still do." Relaxing into the chair, he said, "My nephew plays second base in the senior little league division, and this was the state play offs. His team kept winning right up through this morning. Little shit struck out in the last inning of the final game, and they lost."

"And your family can vouch for you twenty-four hours a day?"

"I had a separate hotel room, so not while I slept, but from breakfast through dinner, we were together."

"What time was breakfast yesterday?"

"The hotel served a continental breakfast, so we met in the dining room. Let's see, that would've been about…eight."

"What about this morning?"

"'Bout the same time. No, wait, not this morning."

"Why not today?"

Shelia took hold of Buckley's arm and leaned toward his ear. After several exchanges of whispered secrets, Shelia sat back in the chair. "Against my advice, my client wishes to continue."

"Perfect," Kel said. She leaned forward and locked her eyes on his. "So what time will your sister say you met up with her?"

"That would have been around eleven this morning, before my nephew's final game."

Kel knew his timeline gave Buckley ample opportunity to commit both murders. Yakima being two hours' driving time southeast of Seattle, he could have killed Susanne Monday morning, waited around to attack her, and still returned with time to spare for an 8 o'clock breakfast. Bellingham was about five hours from Yakima, but since he had missed breakfast today, he had plenty of time to plant the bomb on Terry's truck and then set it off while still at the fuel terminal.

"What made you late this morning?"

"It's kind of personal, but since you need an alibi. I split up from my sister's family after dinner last night and made my way to an alcoholic beverage establishment."

"We'll just say a bar, right?"

"Let's call it a lounge, the hotel lounge. I met a woman there and, well, one thing led to another and…Ah hell, let's just say that this morning we were kind of tied up in the sheets. I didn't make breakfast."

Damn it, she thought but said, "And you have this woman's name, of course?"

"Damn if I know." He laughed. "All those years out of circulation in Walla Walla, who cares about names? I'll say this, though. If you find her, you'll be

195

able to verify my story because my DNA will be inside her—several times."

Disappointment clouded Kel's mind. Day two had been brutally long, and only a few hours remained to find a suspect before the deadline her boss, Lou Martinez, had given her. She had hoped Buckley would escalate to a viable suspect, but with this alibi, though flimsy, he was beginning to look less attractive. She turned her notepad around and slid it toward his side of the table.

"I need a description of the woman," she said, her tone reflecting her irritation, "and, since you've included your sister and the hotel in your story, I need their names and numbers."

Buckley glared at Kel for several seconds. "I shouldn't have to provide a goddamn alibi. I'm not a felon any longer. This has the stink of profiling."

"Stink or not," Kel said, glancing at Shelia, "from my point of view, you've been unaccounted for during the time of both crimes and have motive. On that I could hold you, but if you wish to cooperate, you'll give me the information. The more detailed the better."

He looked at Shelia again. She didn't object, so he took the pen and began to write.

Kel knew he was right. The only reason he was sitting across the table from her was because of what he *had* been convicted of doing—a conviction that no longer stood. But until she verified his story, she planned to keep him in her sights.

After he finished writing, he pushed the pad toward Kel. "Can I go now?"

She scanned over what he had written and then stood. Walking to the door, she opened it with a jerk. "The officer outside will see that you get a ride home."

Kel gave her sister a stay-put stare as he walked around behind Shelia and exited the room. Stepping back to the table, she gripped the back of the chair until her knuckles turned white.

"What the hell, Shelia? You're defending him?"

"It's what they call the law, sis. The suspect provides an account, and the police try to shake it."

"I like him for this, Shelia, but going up against you isn't my idea of fun. What if I break his alibi?"

"Then do it right this time," she said and stood. "He walked out of that prison because Dad didn't seal the deal. You want him, work for it."

As she finished speaking, Chrissie's voice erupted from outside the door. "Don't touch me."

Kel turned and ran for the room's exit. Tearing through the opening, she could see Chrissie leaning back against the edge of the desk and Buckley leaning in toward her. An officer grabbed Buckley's left arm and attempted to lead him toward the door.

"Lovely girl, Detective," Buckley said without moving his eyes from the teenager. "You should be cautious about bringing her into a place like this. There are unsavory types lurking."

"Get him the hell out of here," Kel shouted to the officer, "before I find reason to hold him overnight."

"Sorry, Kel," the officer said, tugging at Buckley's arm. "Come on."

"Okay, okay." Buckley threw his palms up toward Chrissie. "I meant her no harm, Kel, just admiring your beautiful handwork. Takes after you, don't you think?"

Chapter 29

Marilyn Winston rolled over in bed and looked at the clock. She hadn't slept well through the night, and now the clock's white digital beacon warned her that in five minutes what little rest she had taken would have to be sufficient for the day.

While she tossed and turned in the night, she had cried silent tears, being unable to shake the image of her ex-husband, Terry Graham, burning to death. Logic told her that he never felt a thing. Likely the explosion itself had produced such a concussion that he probably was unconscious before he knew what happened. But the image of someone running out of a burning building with hair and clothes ablaze kept playing in her mind on an endless recorded loop.

Though they hadn't spoken in years and their marriage ended in a terrible disaster, she could imagine no reason he should fall victim to such an absurd overkill. She didn't still love him—not like before—but at one time she committed her whole life to him. They had enjoyed such pleasurable intimacy that the thought of him being destroyed by such violence made her angry.

Even in divorce, Terry had been honorable. He took more blame than he should have for the failure, and, shamed by the way he treated her in the last few months of the marriage, he signed over the house they shared and what little remained of his 401k. She objected, but he could be obstinate. In the end she couldn't convince him otherwise, and as he drove away for the last time in his little beater sedan, she forced her eyes closed to dam the tears from racing down her face. Many were the days she wanted to call him to put things back together, but she knew if she did, she would have to keep one thing from him—a secret she planned to take to the grave, a betrayal he must never know.

The chorus of Rick Springfield's 1980s classic "Jesse's Girl" started low on the radio alarm, and Marilyn reached over to shut it off before it stirred her husband, Paul.

Paul had landed a telecommuting job a few years back, and since his clients were in Europe, he often worked through the night and spent much of the day asleep. She knew her boss would understand if she took a mental day due to Terry's death, but staying home with Paul asleep would mean she'd be alone with her thoughts and unable to get the ugly vision of Terry's death out of her mind. She needed to work. Work would distract her, give her purpose. Work would fill the void she knew would plague her mind if she allowed it to be idle.

She slipped from between the linens and sat on the edge of the bed. The light of the morning sun brightened a glow behind the pale aqua drapes. A sudden breath of wind filled the curtain's folds like a hot air balloon, and then they exhaled, flattening against the window screen as the breeze shifted. Beyond the window a bird cried, *chick-a-dee-dee-dee*, and the painful images evaporated like a bad dream. Taking her robe from the floor, she made her way to the bathroom.

Marilyn stopped at the door and turned back to Paul. He had given her a second chance at love, and although he wasn't as attentive to her physical needs as Terry, he loved her, and she knew it. He inhaled a deep breath, letting it out like a sigh. If the clock had disturbed him, he had no knowledge of it now. Closing the bathroom door behind her, she prepared for work.

Twenty-five minutes later, Marilyn reopened the bathroom door and saw that Paul hadn't moved. She kissed two of her fingers, placed them on his cheek, and turned toward the stairs.

In the kitchen, she reached for the freezer door to select a frozen Weight Watchers. With lunch in hand, she moved to the counter and saw that Paul had done one of his thoughtful things. Snipping a solitary red rose from her garden, he had placed it in a crystal bud vase before he turned in. She didn't recognize the container, but that was like Paul—"Just to say 'I love you.'" A computer printout beside the rose read, "There are more like these in the garden."

She lifted the flower to her nose, smelled the fresh aroma, and smiled at Paul's thoughtfulness. With lunch in her bag, she went out the back door and locked it behind her.

On the way to the garage, she saw the rose bed. As Paul had said, the garden had a colorful palette of fresh blooms. She drifted across the lawn, feeling the cool morning air from the threatening clouds brush against her bare arms. Bending at the waist, she lifted a fresh bud. She sensed it would burst into full aperture when the sun peaked over the roof top. Stroking its velvety satin texture between her fingers and the palm of her hand, from her core a latent memory arose with such power she trembled, yet felt no shame. Terry, a passionate lover, would blossom so before he entered her that all her senses would unite in her arousal. And then, once their bodies had come together, the thread binding her to reality would snap and a tsunami of satiation would wash over her, cleansing her soul with ecstasy and understanding. She released the rose, stood, and dabbed a tear from her cheek.

Movement behind her as sudden and silent as a dandelion's parachute drifting on a gust of summer breeze caught her breath in a gasp. She sensed the presence and warmth of a man's body close to her. Ready to fall into Paul's arms, she started to turn, but stopped short when from behind a hand clasped over her mouth. It pulled her head into a shoulder as if it were an intimate caress.

Her mind froze in terror when in front of her, her own fear-filled eyes reflected back in a chrome blade extended before her. The knife slicing deep into the tissues of her neck felt more like a razor nick on her leg than the fatal wound she knew she had been given. She reached to find the unseen face, but feeling the cool morning air again as it whispered against the warm blood flowing down her throat, her mind faded fast. Her hands dropped and no awareness remained.

Chapter 30

Kel crouched next to a woman she hadn't seen in years. More than a decade passed since this same woman stood in her daddy's backyard with a plate of potato salad in one hand and a hamburger in the other. Chrissie, who had always thought of her as another aunt, had thrown her arms around Marilyn's neck, hugging her so tight, Marilyn had lost her balance and fell backwards on the grass laughing, spilling her plate.

Now she was on the lawn again, but what had spilled didn't bring laughter this time, and there was no way to clean up this mess. Her blanched face set in stark contrast to the scarlet stain on her blouse, and the red of the rose on Marilyn's breast. Her fingers were wrapped around it like a funeral pose. Although the blood had stopped flowing, it was clear Marilyn's life had poured from the wound and soaked into the soil.

When Kel received the text, she had just risen for the day, glad to have slept through the night. She had thought she would find sleep evasive, that her mind would replay the interview with Buckley or the last two

203

days of murder and suspicion, but as soon as her head caressed the pillow, she drifted to sleep.

Seeing the address on her phone and knowing without looking to the phone number that sent the text, she called her partner, Jake. When he didn't answer, she left a message. Then, not wanting to make the same error in judgment she had made Monday morning at Susanne Lowen's condo, she called dispatch.

By the time she arrived at the address, a patrol officer had awakened the husband and discovered the body. Minutes later a full complement of uniformed officers and crime scene investigators were dispatched to the scene.

"COD is exsanguination due to a severed carotid artery," the medical examiner said, looking toward Kel, "as if that's not obvious." He pointed to a ceramic-handled kitchen knife with a six-inch blade, bloody and lying next to the victim. "This looks to be the smoking gun. It appears that the perp killed her then snipped the rose with it." He pointed to the rose bush. "If you look close at the stem, you'll see traces of blood."

Kel placed her hand on the victim's thigh and looked to her face. "I'm so sorry, Marilyn," she said and, without turning away from her, asked the ME, "Where's the husband?"

"House," he replied and raised his eyebrows as if pointing her in the right direction.

She paused a moment and thought of her dad. This was going to hit him hard, first Terry and then Marilyn. As she started to stand, a sudden sense of relief washed over her with such power it startled her. And, just as fast as it came, shame followed like a flashflood.

She shook her head, pushed the emotions aside, and headed for the backdoor of the house. A short man, a few inches taller than Kel and wearing a bathrobe occupied the doorway. On his face, a pained look of disbelief, anger, and sorrow mixed together.

"Mr. Winston?" she asked as she reached the patio.

"Yes," he said. The strain of grief made his voice crack.

"My name is Detective Kel Nyte." She showed him her shield. "May I ask you a few questions?"

"I already gave a statement."

"I know you did, but if you could tolerate just a little more. Why don't we step inside?"

"Does he have to…" he started to say to Kel. Then, raising his voice, he looked past her and shouted, "Do you have to do that? My God!"

Looking back to the crime scene, she realized he reacted to the photographer snapping pictures of his wife's body.

"Mr. Winston," Kel said, keeping her tone calm, "he's just doing his job. It may help to find her killer. Please, let's go inside so you don't have to watch this."

Paul rotated his face to hers and stared for a few seconds then made an abrupt turn, leading the way through the kitchen to the living room.

"I can't believe this," he said, lowering his head and shaking it back and forth. "Yesterday it's her ex and today her. What's happening?"

"I'm sorry for your loss, Mr. Winston. I wish—"

"Paul, please."

"Of course. Paul, I wish I had answers, but at this time we don't know. Please, let's sit. Could I get you a glass of water or something?"

"Glasses are in the cupboard to the right of the sink."

Kel placed her hand on his forearm and squeezed it. "I'll only be a moment."

Walking back to the kitchen, she found the glasses behind the cherry finished cupboard door. Filling one with ice water at the refrigerator, she noticed the note lying next to a cut rose in crystal vase.

She read it to herself, "There's more like these in the garden."

Stepping back into the living room, Paul had found his way to the couch on the other side of the room and sat with his head resting in his hands.

"Here, Paul." Kel extended the glass.

Lifting his head, he took it and drank.

She slipped around a mahogany coffee table and sat beside him on the couch. "I noticed a rose in a vase in the kitchen. Did you leave that for Marilyn?"

"No, it must have been her killer. He was in my house—oh God, and I was just sleeping without a care."

"Is it your habit to sleep in?"

"I work from home. My clients are abroad, so I'm usually up all night. Generally, I'm still up when she leaves for the office, but last night I finished early and was tired, so I went to bed. I never heard her get up.

"It wasn't until your officer rang the doorbell that I saw she was gone. You never know when you've spoken your last word or given the last kiss, do you?"

"I know what you're feeling, Paul. I lost my closest friend and my daughter's dad in Afghanistan. As painful as that was, and truthfully it still aches today, even though every nerve feels raw right now, it'll get easier. The important thing is to find your wife's killer."

"But how did one of your officers know she might have been hurt?"

"We didn't know who was hurt. I can't discuss how, but I *can* say that I had reason to believe something bad happened, so I sent a squad to investigate. Earlier you mentioned Marilyn's ex-husband's murder. There was another victim earlier his week. Evidence indicates it's the same person who took all three lives. I'm sorry I have to ask this, but did you know Susanne Lowen or Terry Graham?"

"You think I did this?" Paul shouted, slamming the water glass down hard on the table in front of him.

"What I think is not the issue," Kel said, keeping her tone even, "and you didn't answer my question."

"No, I've never heard of this Susanne woman and I never met Terry. And before you ask, no I *did not* kill either of them or my wife."

"I'm sorry, but I have to ask."

"My God, this is unbelievable!" He rested his forehead on his hands and shook his head. "One minute you're taking each other for granted, and before you can

207

start planning their funeral, you have to start mounting a defense."

"To be honest, Paul," Kel said and placed her hand on his shoulder, "I have no reason at this time to believe you had anything to do with this, but it's my job to eliminate those with proximity so I can focus on the real suspects. I do need to ask some other questions, though, if you're up to it."

"Look, I already told you I was asleep. I didn't hear or see anything, so I'm not sure I'm going to be much help."

"You must have a computer."

"Yes, of course, that's how I communicate with Europe. Why?"

"The killer always leaves a specific message for me somewhere near his victim. Have you checked your computer since you were awakened?"

"No," he said as he stood, gathering his bathrobe and cinching the belt around his waist. Without speaking further, he stepped around the coffee table and led the way to the downstairs office not far from the living room.

"What are we looking for?" he asked as he sat down behind the keyboard.

"Please don't touch anything."

"Oh course, fingerprints." Standing, he gave a wave of his hand toward the chair.

Kel pulled a pair of latex gloves over her hands and moved to face the laptop. Except for what appeared to be a company logo floating on the monitor, the screen was black. Shaking the mouse, it came to life. They both saw the words at the same time. Kel leaned forward and read them aloud.

"Three's indulgence now plain view

No escape the sickle's hew

River red that will not heal

My death blade the soul to steal"

"What does it mean?" Paul asked.

"I don't know, Paul. For now it's another piece of evidence. I'm going to need to take the computer to our lab for analysis."

"You can't take my computer. That's my bread and butter."

"It'll only be for the day," Kel said with hesitation, wondering if what he had said wasn't a tell, "and you already claimed you sleep during the day."

The first people to be cleared were the people closest to the victim, the spouse and other family members. She didn't know the Winstons or anything about their marital relationship. It was possible there was discord in the home. Paul could have set up his wife's murder from the beginning. After all, every victim to date had at one time been in the news, as had she. Research wouldn't have been too difficult, especially for someone who appeared to be as computer savvy as Paul. He could have easily gathered enough information to connect the victims to her dad and somehow located her phone number.

"But I...I have people I need to contact," he said, and a tear began to course down his unshaven face. "My contacts are all in there."

"I'm sorry, but we need to take it. There could be other clues to your wife's killer's identity. If you like, however, you can come with me to the station. Then, as soon as we're done with our investigation, you can take it with you."

"No, I'm sorry." He stared at the floor, shaking his head. "That won't be necessary. Of course you need to take it. It's just that I'm closing on a big deal in Belgium at the moment, but my boss will understand. I'll give him a call."

An hour later, Kel walked back to her car parked in the Winstons' driveway, and left the scene for the investigators to process. As an officer herded the onlookers back by moving a barricade to open the way for her Jeep to pass, the euphoric feeling she experienced as she stood over Marilyn's body returned. This time the guilt restrained itself. Following Jake's logic, since her dad would have no reason to kill Marilyn, she was sure this would take him off the short list.

Chapter 31

The clock read 3:00 when Kel pushed the bullpen door open. Jake sat on the edge of his desk facing the crime board. He turned toward her as she entered the room.

"Afternoon, Plebe," he said. "Sent a squad to pick up your dad."

A flush rushed to her cheeks, and she couldn't disguise her irritation. "Why? He's too sick to be rustled from his house on such short notice. If you have more questions, we could have done it there where he's more comfortable."

She looked beyond Jake's desk to the crime board she had begun. Jake had made some changes since she saw it last—before Vince Buckley's interview. On the right edge, he wrote DK in quotes and below it taped a copy of the "manifesto" as her dad had called it—the first poem he sent to her. On the other side, under a hand written "#1," the picture she printed of Susanne Lowen, wearing a white lab coat draped over pink scrubs, smiled at the room. Her eyes followed Kel as she stepped closer. The poem she discovered at the scene was printed and taped beneath the picture. Below the "#2," Terry Graham's picture, the way she remembered him from more than a decade ago, grimaced from the newspaper photo of him pointing his gun at a suspect on the ground. Below it, the faces of the two men's who died with Terry mocked her. A photocopy of the poem she found in his mailbox was secured to the board below the pictures. Next, "#3" was written above a picture of Marilyn Winston lying lifeless on the grass.

As she took the printout of the poem taken from Paul Winston's computer to tape it below her picture, Jake stood. "Because the three main victims have one thing in common."

Removing a fourth photo from a manila folder, he taped the image of the former police chief, Dirk Nyte, to the center of the board and, with a black marker, drew a connecting line from each victim to Kel's dad.

"My dad has nothing to do with this. What motive could he possibly have to kill Marilyn? In my worst nightmares I can't believe he'd do any of this."

"Which makes you prejudicial," Lieutenant Martinez said from behind her.

A shudder coursed its way down Kel's spine. She knew since this morning this meeting was imminent as Martinez had called her phone when she left the Winston's home. Letting it go to voicemail, she stalled the confrontation as long as possible, hoping a new lead would surface. She believed the breadcrumbs DK dropped would lead her to him. But she needed more time.

From the beginning her service in the detective squad was bound by a tenuous thread Martinez could sever without hesitation. He had given her forty-eight hours to generate a suspect from the evidence, and now it was just short of fifty-eight since the countdown started in the parking lot of Susanne Lowen's condo. Then, the Chief of Ds, Nathaniel Ballesteros, had been her advocate, but she hadn't seen or heard from him since. He couldn't protect her now.

The man taking pictures of the explosion at the fuel terminal with his cell phone was the only real lead she produced. But she had run his vehicle plate through the Department of Licensing and pulled his phone history. Both brought her up empty. Other than Vince Buckley, and with his incomplete alibi, she had nothing solid. She looked at the crime board again and saw the black lines pointing to the man she loved more than life and shook her head.

"I'm still objective," she said, not turning toward Lou's voice.

"Easy to say now," Martinez said, as he walked up next to Kel and stared at the white board, "but when you see the evidence piling up against him, your instinct will be to defend him despite the facts."

"He's not guilty."

"Of course he's not in the eyes of the law—until proven otherwise. But somehow evidence implicating him is coming out, and you, with more than two days, haven't given us anything but hindsight."

"What evidence?" She swallowed hard to mollify the queasy stirring in her stomach. "If I'm working this case, why am I not being informed of developments?"

"You're not going to like it," Jake said, standing beside his desk and glaring at Kel. "You'll just have to watch and lea—"

"Where have you been since this morning, following leads?" Martinez asked. "I've been trying to reach you."

Not long after leaving Marilyn's crime scene, another text hit her phone following Lou's unanswered call. Thinking it was DK with another riddle, she glanced at it.

"Where is my bike?" it read.

That reminded her of the promise she made to the mime, Marcel, while he was in the hospital.

"I was running an errand."

"And when was the last time you met with your partner?"

"Don't even go there."

"I assigned you to work with Jake."

Looking at her partner, she saw Jake's crooked smirk, and said, "And he told me in so many words to piss off. Rule one, right Jake?"

Jake's smile faded, and he picked up the now empty manila folder.

Kel shot a quick glance from him to the room and realized their confrontation was drawing an audience. Other detectives in the bullpen stopped their work and chatter to observe the sparring match in the center of the room. Even Captain Silva stepped from his office and now stood at the right side of the DK crime board with his arms folded across his chest.

"Rule one? What does that mean?" Martinez asked.

"You should ask him. They're his rules." When Jake made no indication he'd offer an explanation, she shouted, "Stay the hell out of my way."

Turning to Martinez, she continued. "That's rule one. As soon as Marilyn's address came across my phone this morning, I called Jake. But when the call went to voicemail I left him the address and called dispatch. I was on the scene for nearly two hours, but Jake never called or made an appearance. One has to wonder if he's too busy with other commitments or if he is so convinced that my dad is the only suspect, he's looking nowhere else. Who's not being objective here? As much as I don't want it to be my dad, at least I'm working the case. Except for Monday at Susanne's, I can't put Jake on scene one time. We're now five dead into this, two of them cops, and he's not even phoning it in. He's just an absentee."

"If you have a complaint against your partner, take it up with the chief of detectives, that's his problem. But I'm yours, and I say you can't be objective. I want your phone."

"What?" she roared and dropped forward, placing her hands on the top of the desk to keep from falling over. "That's how the perp's communicating. Without that you're crippling the investigation."

"You're being benched, Nyte, get it? Off the case. Give me your damn phone, or I'll take it from you myself."

She felt like a barracuda caught in a school of hungry sharks. She needed an ally and looked back at Captain Silva. He shook his head, unfolded his arms, and drove them into his pockets.

"How can you do this?" Kel asked, turning back to Martinez.

"I gave you two days, and you've turned up nothing. Your phone!"

"What about Vince Buckley?"

"Buckley? Why don't you Nytes get off his case? He's got nothing to do with this."

She knew this was a long shot. Before Marilyn's death she could see a connection. But as far as she knew now, Buckley had never met her. Still, it was something that might buy her another day or two.

On her way to the impound lot to pick up Marcel's bicycle, she made several calls to verify Buckley's alibi. His sister stated that he had been with them the whole weekend, but she admitted they parted company each evening. The hotel said they would turn their security tapes over to the Yakima Police Department but went on to say that if the woman in the hotel lounge wasn't a registered guest, there wasn't much they could do. And then, after she met Marcel, her cellular rang with the Yakima Police.

"We're coming up empty," the detective had said. "A hotel clerk reported she may have seen a woman matching the description you gave eating the hotel's complimentary breakfast Tuesday morning, but she doesn't appear on any security tape. We're processing the room, but housekeeping has cleaned it

twice since yesterday, so evidence would have likely been destroyed."

"Is there a way for him to leave the hotel and return without being detected?" she asked.

"The only cameras running are in the lobby," the detective concluded, "so if he took the elevator to the garage or a side door, yes."

Now, knowing his story was still uncorroborated gave her hope.

"He has motive for the first four murders, and his alibi has holes big enough to drive suspicion."

"Like?"

"For starters, no verified witnesses to his whereabouts for the twelve to fifteen hour periods when the first two crimes were committed. And then there's Paul Winston—"

"Winston?"

"He could be copycatting."

"You're stretching it now and trying my patience. Your phone, and that's an order."

Kel glared at Lou. She could see by the swollen and throbbing veins in his neck, and his clenched jaw bringing a wooden character to the muscles in his face, that his rage was beyond consoling at the moment. Resigned to being officially sidelined, she reached to her belt and retrieved the smartphone.

As she did, motion in her peripheral vision caught her attention, and she looked past Lieutenant Martinez toward the doorway. Two uniformed officers led her dad into the room. They stood on either side of their former chief and held his arms, not like they were restraining a suspect, but, rather, supporting a frail man too weak to depend on his own strength.

A proud smile lit up Dirk's face as he looked toward her. Not arrogance, but a special pride reserved for someone he loved.

"Go write more tickets," Martinez shouted as he grabbed the phone out of her hand.

Her heart skipped the next beat, and she felt a heavy lump in her throat beginning to apply pressure to her tears. Without turning away from her dad, she said, "Respectfully, sir, I would like to ask to observe Jake's interview."

Lieutenant Martinez followed her gaze and met Dirk's eyes.

"Observation, not participation," he said, his tone flat.

"Agreed."

Next to her she heard Jake raise his voice and say, "Interview 2." She rotated toward him and noticed a satisfied smirk cross his lips. As her dad and the officers walked across the bullpen to the glassed holding room, she turned her eyes back toward her boss.

"After Dad is done here, I need to take some personal time."

Martinez stared into her light green eyes for several seconds before responding. "Perhaps that'll be best, *Officer* Nyte. And while you're taking a break, maybe you could focus on learning respect."

"I'll make it a priority, sir."

Chapter 32

Kel stood in the observation room, watching her dad from behind a one-way mirror.

It could have been worse. The look in Lieutenant Martinez's eyes had told her that if the disagreement continued much longer, she might have been suspended for insubordination, resulting in more than the loss of her police-issued phone. Her gun and badge would have been surrendered. But taking personal time, she could continue to keep DK in her sites without the constraints of the department or an absentee partner.

Before walking to observation, she left the bullpen to collect her personal phone from the locker in the women's washroom. Now, while she waited, she sent DK a message. "New number."

Her dad had been in Interview 2 for half an hour waiting for Jake to begin his inquisition. Through the glass, she could see him grimace and shift his position every few seconds as if searching for comfort. But the hard chair he was confined to wasn't the source of his distress. The discomfort and weakness of his cancer played havoc on every tissue in his body. While he waited, she watched his face grow pallid and his body start trembling. She was certain the sudden interruption in his daily routine and the knowledge that another friend had fallen victim to DK's lesson plan exacerbated his pain. She wanted to be in the room with him, to hold his hand and tell him she believed in him, but, with her proximity to the case and their relationship, she knew this would look wrong. She could hear Jake say, "You could have been making up an alibi." So she hadn't broached the subject. She hoped her father understood.

The door opening to Interview 2 caught Kel's eye. Her sister entered the room. Kel had called Shelia at her office from the desk phone as soon as Lou Martinez left the bullpen. Shelia had been in a deposition at the time, and when Kel put Jake on the phone, Shelia asked him to wait until she arrived before proceeding with any questions.

Kel watched as Shelia walked around to the back side of the table and, taking the seat next to her dad, put her arm around his shoulders, kissing him on the cheek. Jake, who followed Shelia into Interview 2, grabbed the chair on the opposite side of the table, turned it backwards, and sat with his arms folded across the ladder back for support.

"Now that your attorney's here, can we begin?" Jake asked, his voice coming through the speaker on Kel's side of the wall. "Dirk or Chief, which would you prefer."

"Suit yourself," Dirk said and folded his arms in front of him, resting them on his stomach. With Kel's psychology training, she recognized the silent barrier this action formed between her dad and his accuser.

"Three victims of violent murder," Jake said, placing his zippered notebook on the laminated Mediterranean oak top of the table, "and two collateral damage. Cleaning house?"

"Do I really look like I'm physically capable of these horrific acts? I can hardly sit here in this uncomfortable chair, let alone fight with someone."

"Well, our suspect, which for now is you, seems to be perfectly capable of disabling a person very quickly. Did you kill Susanne Lowen?"

"Don't answer that, Dad," Shelia said.

"Over my counsel's advice," Dirk said, placing his hand on Shelia's thigh, "I *will* answer that absurd question. What you're accusing me of is lying in wait for Susanne, subduing her in my weak state, holding a pillow over her face until she suffocated and then waiting for my own daughter so I could attack her with a stun gun. I retract, that's not an absurd question. It's preposterous."

"Well, you did dose Susanne first."

"But wouldn't that require me to subdue her enough to inject the paralytic?"

"Is that how you did it? You injected her?"

"Dad, stop. Don't answer."

"You seem to have forgotten," Dirk said as if Shelia hadn't spoken, "that my other daughter has intimate knowledge of this case."

"Dad, shut up now."

"Hum." Jake rubbed his chin. "Knowledge she shouldn't have passed along to a civilian, someone not involved with the case."

"In my opinion, I *am* involved in this case. Not as the suspect, though. As the target."

"So you think the perp is really after you. Why doesn't he just kill you and get it over with?"

"Maybe I'm the end game. He said he wants to teach a lesson. So maybe after he's done, I'm last on his list."

"I guess we'll just have to take your word on that. So you and Terry Graham were partners."

"Is that a question?" Shelia asked.

"Statement of fact, counselor. Matter of record." Turning back to Dirk, he said, "Now, Chief, let's go back to the domestic incident that occurred in the early morning hours of February 15, 2000."

"We've been over this. I've nothing to add."

"We'll see about that."

"Dad, what's he driving at?" Shelia asked.

Kel watched as her dad looked first at Shelia and then to the one-way mirror. Pain registered on his face, but it wasn't physical any longer. The memory of something long ago rising out of the secret place and into the knowing clouded his eyes. She remembered sitting next to him Monday evening when he said, "…there are regrets. Things your mother and I worked through." Was this that furtive event he had sheltered away? Was this Pandora's Box?

Dirk turned back to Jake, uncrossed his arms and, leaning forward, grabbed the table with both hands to shift his position in the chair.

"Marilyn called me at home at about 2:30 a.m. She said that Terry had come home drunk and was beating her. She locked herself in the bathroom, but Terry pounded on the door with something harder than his fist. She thought it was his gun."

"Why did she call you and not 9-1-1?"

"As I said yesterday, she was trying to protect him."

"Is that it? Is that the only reason she called *you*?"

"Yes, why else?"

"Where are you going with this?" Shelia asked.

"If you'll permit me, Counselor?" he said to Shelia and directed his eyes back to Dirk. "You have two daughters, isn't that correct, Chief?"

"You know the answer to that and you're wandering way off course."

"Am I? I only ask because I'm trying to give you a point of reference."

"For what?"

"Would you say your daughters are close?"

Kel wanted to smash the window separating her from the people she loved and throttle Jake. Shelia turned toward her and shrugged her shoulders with a look of confusion across her face.

"Yes, I believe they're very close."

"Do you think there are things they might tell each other that no one else knows?"

"I'll ask you again, Detective," Shelia said, glaring at Jake, "where are you going with this?"

"Patience, Shelia."

Kel understood that Jake was grinding a point into her sister. Shelia was no longer in Interview 2 as her dad's lawyer. She had slipped into the protective daughter role.

Turning back to Dirk, Jake cocked his head to the side. "Chief, I'm waiting for an answer."

After a brief pause, Dirk said, "The bond existing between sisters, especially sisters as close as my two daughters, is something no two men will ever understand. So, yes, it's true, they might tell each other their secrets and seal the vault."

"Would it surprise you to learn that Marilyn Winston had a sister?"

"I don't know much about Marilyn's family. I think she may have mentioned a sister at some point. So yes, she has a sister."

"*Had* a sister, you mean. Marilyn's dead."

"Obviously," Shelia said, "you don't know sisters well, Detective deLaurenti. Sisters are forever, in this life or the next. Death doesn't break that bond."

"In any case, Chief, Marilyn *has* a sister." He glanced at Shelia and then to the mirror on the wall. "You're so fond of talking about our conversation yesterday, Dirk, do you remember when you mentioned that truth has a way of bubbling to the surface?"

"Of course I do."

"I spoke to Marilyn's sister a couple of hours ago, and she told me something you already know but have tried to conceal from everyone for more than a decade."

"And you revealing it now only has one goal, doesn't it? It has no bearing on this case. Your only motives are to catch me in an omission if you can and embarrass me in front of two people I love. Not a great strategy, Detective."

Shelia stood, walked behind Dirk's chair, and hugged her arms around his shoulders. Leaning down to his ear, she said, "What's this about, Dad?"

Kel bolted for the separating door and burst into the interrogation room, placing her hands on the end of the table. "What's going on, Jake? What are you talking about?"

Dirk patted Shelia's hand and looked into Kel's eyes. Leaning forward, he said, "I told you the other day, girls, there were secrets. Things Mom and I worked through. This is one of them, and it's a big one. I didn't want it to come out this way, but…"

Turning toward Jake, he continued, "It's true. Marilyn called me and not the police that night in part because she didn't want it on Terry's record, but there was another reason. I'm sorry, girls. For several months, Marilyn and I had been having an affair."

Kel released the table, took a step back, and threw her arms up in front of her as if she were fending off an attacker. Her breath caught in her throat and only a whisper escaped her lips. "Daddy?" He looked away, unable to bear eye contact with him. Then, finding her voice, she rolled her eyes toward Jake. "My God, you bastard, I *won't* believe this."

Shelia slid her hand away from her dad's. Dirk doubled his fist, slammed it to the table and rotated his head to face Kel. "Terry had been suspicious and accused me that night at the bar. I denied it, of course, but realized Marilyn and I had to call it off. I told Mom the next morning. To this day I don't know why, she, a much better soul than I ever will be, forgave me."

Of all the secrets to come out, an affair was the last thing Kel would have considered. She had always believed her dad a man of honor, infallible, and her mother the personification of truth. If there had ever been discord in their marriage they had masterfully shielded it from her *and* the world. Now, her heart sagged heavy with bereavement as she saw the long years of innocence gasping without hope for life. Tears began to form, but something more powerful held them back.

A new reaction emerged unexpected like of a bolt of lightning before the clap of thunder—betrayal. A traitorous collusion between her parents to hide this unspeakable fact now threatened to drive a breach too wide to ever heal. An understandable secret between *them,* but once revealed, trust so cherished was crushed by the utterance of that one ugly word—affair.

Kel was angry. She glared at Jake but saw DK. How dare he force this confession to the surface? How dare he expose such an embarrassing family secret? Her dad indicated Monday night that he intended to step into the confessional before his death, but then it would have been on *his* terms. Even though wretched and raw, it could have been worked through. Now DK through Jake had exposed the most intimate failure of her dad's life as a matter of public record.

Finally able to face him, Kel turned back to Dirk. Their eyes met. The sadness he expressed grasped for her heart and begged for understanding. She had to avert again before he could gauge the cauldron of anger seething inside her. Almost impossible to thread the difference between them, the revulsion was not toward him directly, but for the concealment of the act. And for the way it came to light—once exposed it could never be extinguished.

Shelia shifted and drew Kel's attention. She retreated as far away from her dad as possible, leaning against the wall. Her eyes had become moist pools and the first trickle now overflowed down her cheeks. By the stunned look on her face, Kel knew she no longer wanted to be in the room. The burden of this new knowledge was too much for even this powerful litigator to bear, but she had a client and had no choice but to remain there.

Directing his eyes back to Jake, Dirk asked, "Are you satisfied? Is this the affect you wanted? You want my daughters to hate me in my last days? Why, a decade after it's over and everyone's moved on, would I start a killing spree? Is this the best you can do?"

Kel struggled against the loathsome news to change the subject in her mind. The first line of DK's poem on Marilyn's death drifted by and she grabbed it. "Three's indulgence now plain view." It was clear DK was referring to the affair, but Jake had no prior knowledge of it, at least as she could tell. Yesterday at Dad's he was on a fishing expedition looking for some other reason for Marilyn not to call 9-1-1. But today, armed with her sister's statement, he could make the connection to motive.

But how did DK know? It seemed to have been a closely guarded secret, known only, with the exception of Marilyn's sister, to the four people involved. Dad and Mom would never speak of it, so unless DK got to the sister, which was unlikely, Marilyn or Terry must have confided it to someone—someone who could be trusted. Someone with an ax to grind. So did Terry know DK?

Jake's voice interrupted her thoughts.

"Maybe adultery *did* lead to this. Maybe you're taking out old memories before your passing. I can't speak to motive at this point, only evidence.

"Kel." Jake focused on his newest ex-partner, "I'm not done yet. Get your ass back to observation, or I'll have you escorted from the building."

Chapter 33

"What evidence?" Dirk asked after Kel left Interview 2.

Kel reached for the volume switch in the dark room and increased it. She didn't want to miss anything Jake threw at her dad.

"Hard to hear, isn't it, Officer Nyte?"

The voice coming out of the darkness made her flinch. Her eyes had adjusted to the light while in Interview 2, so she didn't notice that Lieutenant Martinez had entered and now stood against the back wall in the shadows.

"Someday I'd like to understand what you have against my dad," Kel said without turning to the voice.

She kept her eyes on the three people in the room beyond. "He is a good man, was a good cop, and he's been good for Seattle. I don't know why you can't see it and why you hold me responsible for whatever it is. But right now, with all respect, sir, I'd like to hear what Jake is about to say."

She shoved her hands in her pants pockets and prepared for his terse response. She was surprised when, without retort, the side door opened and the swish of his jacket gave indication of his exit.

After standing to turn his chair round, sitting in it properly, Jake leaned toward Dirk. He placed his elbows on the table and stared at the chief. "Physical evidence, Chief."

Dirk broke the stare and looked toward the opposite wall. Jake smiled and drew a report from his zippered notebook and, laying it on the table, shoved it to where Shelia had been sitting.

Shelia wiped residual moister from her eyes with the back of her hand and walked toward her chair. Picking up the paper, she sat down and said, "This seems to be a DNA report. You found a hair at the scene?"

"Actually, we found a hair resting on the keyboard of Paul Winston's laptop computer."

"And from this report you're concluding what?"

"The hair is a positive match to the chief, so my question is, how did your dad's hair come to be on Paul's computer?"

Kel's mouth dropped open. If she hadn't insisted the computer be brought to the lab, it was likely the hair would have gone undiscovered. The euphoric feeling she had while leaving the Winston's house this morning that Jake would be forced to take her dad off his list, quickly ebbed away. Now there existed a connection she could not have anticipated. Without knowing it, she had moved her dad up another notch on Jake's suspect list.

Shelia faced Dirk. He sat stoically as if the question wasn't meant for him and continued staring across the room.

"Are you okay, Dad?" she asked.

"I'm fine, Angel, just thinking." He focused on Jake again. "At the moment, I have no explanation for the hair. As you can see, I don't have much on my head to leave lying around. Though I do have reason to believe it could be mine, let's wait until all the evidence is on the table. What else do you have?"

Jake paused without speaking for a few seconds and then retrieved a photograph from his notebook. He laid it on the table and spun it 180 degrees so Dirk and Shelia could see it.

"Is this the murder weapon?" Shelia asked.

"It was collected right next to the victim's body. The wound track is consistent with the blade, and the blood has been found to be hers. So, yes, we're sure the killer left this knife after slashing her throat."

Pulling another photo from his folder, he placed it in front of the couple on the opposite side of the table.

"This is the same knife after we got it back to the lab. As you can see, there is a clear print on the handle."

"And whose print is it?" Shelia asked.

"Whose do you think, Counselor?"

"It's mine, isn't it?" Dirk asked, turning toward his daughter.

"I think you've said enough, Dad. This interview's over."

"No, I want to hear this."

"Yes," Jake said, "it's your print. Can you explain it?"

Dirk took a second look at the knife in the photo. "I would like a private word with my lawyer."

Jake smiled and rose to his feet without speaking, looked up to the camera suspended from the ceiling in the corner of Interview 2 and motioned "cut" with his right hand, as if slashing his own throat with his fingertips. He walked to the adjoining door and passed through the opening to where Kel stood on the other side of the glass.

So he couldn't hear their privileged communication, she turned the volume switch hard to the left in one swift movement.

"Do you see what I'm saying?" Jake asked, staring through the one way mirror. "Evidence. That's how you build a case, plebe."

The wound Jake had caused by exposing her dad's affair still stung. She couldn't look in his direction so she stood next to him and watched her dad and Shelia. "I'm sure there's a perfectly sound explanation for his prints being on the murder weapon."

"Sure, like he did the deed."

"Or something else."

"Yeah, like the story they're fabricating right now."

Interview rooms at West Precinct weren't really for interviews at all. They were interrogation cells and as such were bugged. There was no expectation of privacy in the room. Even though Jake had made a show of indicating the recording devices were to be shut down, somewhere out of sight, an analyst had a pair of headphones over his ears while he watched a monitor, capturing the entire conversation, both audio and video. The ruse often worked, and lesser suspects revealed their guilt when they thought no one was listening. But behind the glass her dad and sister were making use of the only hope of privacy, whispered tones behind cupped hands.

"Do you really think he's stupid enough to leave his prints at a crime scene? Whoever the killer is planted those prints to implicate him."

"Could be," Jake said and pivoted his body toward Kel, "but we'll have to see what angle they come up with."

"They're not making up anything, Jake. He's conferring with his counsel, just like the Miranda Rights state."

"He's not under arrest."

"Yet," she said and turned to face him, her light green eyes turning dark as her anger peaked. "You had him brought in here like a common thug. You and Martinez have jumped to a conclusion that he must be guilty, even though he's physically incapable of doing the things you're accusing him of. You've twisted a poor decision he made ten years ago to make it fit this case. Tell me, what evidence have you found on his phone or computer which ties him in any way to this?" She paused, but he didn't answer. "As I suspected, nothing. You don't care about the truth. Find a suspect, hook him up, and close the case. Guilty until proven innocent. You want the truth? Here it is."

When Kel had asked ADA Johnson about Jake yesterday, Johnson had been honest about Jake's record and courthouse reputation, saying, "Beyond my better judgment, I like you. I don't want to see you end up like either one of his last two partners."

Kel faced Jake. "I've done my research, and while it's true you have a high closing ratio, it's also true you have a low conviction rate. Talk around the courthouse is that defense attorneys love to take cases when you've been the primary 'cause they know that more than fifty percent of the time, your evidence is contrived and easily kicked. You're just a dumpster diver looking for easy pickin's on which to build circumstantial cases."

"Pretty smug, aren't you, police chief's kid. So damn self-righteous."

"What I can't understand is why Chief Ballesteros hasn't kicked you to the curb long ago. No one wants to partner up with you 'cause of your curse. Let's talk about Toshio Aoki."

Even in the darkened room, Kel sensed Jake stiffen.

Jake turned back to face the window. "What *about* him? I locked him up, he served his time, and then he got out. Happens every day."

"So you were the arresting officer?"

"Willie Jenkins and I took him down."

"And right after that Willie disappeared and ended up dead."

"Aoki's connected. If you'd have done your research you'd know that."

Ignoring him, she continued. "So if you both took him down, why didn't they come after you, too?"

"Maybe they did."

"If they did, there'd be a record somewhere, but there's no trace of it."

"I told you before to leave this alone. If you know what's good for your health, you'll get the hell out of my business and leave Aoki alone. This is way over your head."

"That sounds like another threat."

Jake suddenly stood taller and lifted his head. Kel shifted her eyes to the window as Shelia waved an invitation for Jake to reenter.

"Guess our little discussion's over," Jake said. "Looks like they're ready to confess. Make sure you turn the volume up. You won't want you to miss this."

While Kel advanced the volume knob, Jake tore the door open and whisked back to the lighted room, taking his seat at the table.

"The reason my print is on that knife handle," Dirk said, pointing to the photo, "is because it came from my kitchen."

"Is that a confession?"

"Only that the knife belongs to me, not that I took it to the murder scene."

"Then who do you suppose took it to Marilyn Winston's?"

"Obviously, the murderer with the intent of framing me."

"When was the last time you saw the knife?"

"Yesterday, about an hour before you came to my house."

"So, now I'm the killer?"

"Is *that* a confession?"

"Hardly, I have no motive."

"Neither do I. Yet it seems the UNSUB has information about me that's not common knowledge."

"Are you implying that's me?"

"No! Unlike you and Lou Martinez, I don't jump to conclusions. I weigh the facts. And the fact is, that's my knife," he said, tapping his finger on the photo. "But there are more facts. You see, after you abruptly left last night without finishing my rudimentary interview I was too tired to clean up the kitchen, so I went straight to my bedroom. It wasn't until I went to fix breakfast this morning that I noticed the knife missing, another fact. When you left to use the bathroom last evening, you took your notebook, and it was unzipped. When you returned, it was zipped—more facts. You had to pass right through my kitchen, right by that knife, and it could have easily fit inside your notebook.

"Not only that, the bathroom you used is the one I use every day, all day. So, it's likely a stray hair of mine might be lying around that room. You could have easily picked one up and then transferred it to the laptop.

237

Since you're the primary detective on this case, no one would question you about checking out the laptop from the evidence locker.

"Do you see how facts work, son? If I was the conclusion-jumping type, I'd say it's just as likely you're the murderer as it is me."

"Are you accusing me of something?"

"Doesn't feel good, does it, son? Now, besides my hair and the prints on my knife, is there any other evidence?"

Jake stared at him expressionless and didn't answer.

"Well, Detective?" Shelia asked, leaning in toward the table.

Jake looked at each of them and gave an almost imperceptible shake of his head. Then, without speaking, he gathered the photos and reports strewn across the table, dropped them in his notebook, and stood. As he opened the door, he said, "You're free to go," and then slammed it behind him.

Chapter 34

After Shelia and their dad left the West Precinct, Kel stepped into Captain Marcos Silva's office. The knife and hair coming from her dad's house meant that if Jake hadn't taken them, DK had while her dad slept upstairs. She asked Silva if he would send a team of investigators to the Nyte family home and set a protective patrol at the curb until the case closed.

Now, as she sat at her desk, she felt as violated as if an intruder had rummaged through her underwear drawer touching her personal things. To think of DK being inside the house in which she grew up brought a knot of anger to her chest. Their home had always been a shelter of safety with nothing but fond memories. Now it had been desecrated by a man, a stranger, a murderer who could have killed her dad last night if not for his own restraint. Just as he waited for her at Susanne Lowen's, rather than take her life, he had chosen to draw her into his game. Now he was doing the same thing with her dad, like he was saying, "I can get to you anytime I choose. But first, watch and learn."

She studied the crime board with the photos of the dead. The lines Jake had drawn connecting her dad to the three crime scenes gave her an idea. Her dad said that someone had information about him that wasn't common knowledge. So, as much as there was a common suspect, could there also be a common source of this information? And if that were true, and she could locate the source, that might lead to the suspect.

She considered that DK and Terry Graham could have spoken. If that had happened, she was sure DK initiated the dialog. And Terry, eager to vent years of frustration for the life he sacrificed, didn't foresee his own fate—*tissues scorched, torn asunder*—or Marilyn's—*river red that will not heal*. So DK had to come across to Terry as sympathetic. Someone Terry could entrust the demons troubling his soul; someone he'd pour out information about his own personal failures without fear of judgment. If Terry saw this as a means to bring disgrace on her dad, he would have believed DK embodied the influence required to bring down someone as powerful and well-loved as Dirk Nyte.

But who?

Doubtless her father had enemies, but since he resigned his post, he lost his power, so political opponents would have nothing to gain in pursuing him now. But convicted felons like Vince Buckley would. Yet as much as she wanted him to be DK, seeing Terry connected to that man as the source was flawed. First, she couldn't imagine Terry volunteering to him any sordid details of his life. And then, despite the reversal of Buckley's conviction, he wasn't a popular man, so he didn't have the influence.

But what if her dad's enemies were internal? If a conspiracy existed, it would involve people within the

SPD. This had occurred to her before when she realized that somehow DK got her SPD issued phone number. Now it seemed even more plausible.

Besides Terry, she let her thoughts drift to other possible sources. Lou Martinez was a possibility. He and her dad had gone through police academy together. With his longevity in the department, there would be few doors restricted to him, and he had access to internal court-sealed files. Once the murders started, he went right after her dad. Was he so blinded by rage that even though he hadn't anticipated murder would be the outcome, he twisted it into an opportunity to point a finger at an old adversary? Did he agree to her assuming a part in the investigation because he believed she'd fail? Was he relying on her insistence that DK was anyone other than her dad part of his plan to discredit her as well?

Jake, on the other hand, had been assigned to the DK case as the primary right after Susanne Lowen's murder. She remembered that Martinez and Chief Ballesteros had arrived together at Susanne's condo. They, too, went back a long ways in the department. Had Lou influenced the chief to put Jake on the case, putting him in the perfect position to manufacture and manage the evidence? A single focus to the exclusion of any other suspects was on Lou's lips from the beginning of the investigation. Now it seemed to bind Jake and Lou together. Over the last two and a half days, they shared the same tunnel vision toward Dirk.

But where's the proof? She needed help, someone she could confide in, someone who knew the turf.

241

A voice interrupted Shelia's thoughts.

"Excuse me, Counselor."

"Yes?" She glanced at the time on the computer clock—6:17 p.m.—and looked up from the email she was writing into Vince Buckley's eyes.

While incarcerated for his conviction as the Rat City Exterminator, Buckley filled his free hours studying computer technology. Because one of the named partners of Snelling, Hardcastle, and Purdin had turned the defense of Buckley's serial case over to a second year associate who mismanaged the case, when his conviction had been overturned a few months ago, the partners of Snelling decided it was in the best interest of the firm to hire him for their Helpdesk team. Shelia hadn't favored the move since her dad put him away nearly a decade and a half earlier, but being an associate attorney, she held no status.

"Just a verbal," he said. "Friday evening we'll be shutting down all systems for a global refresh. You'll get an email reminder Friday afternoon."

"Thank you, Vince," Shelia said and turned back to the monitor.

"Since I've interrupted you, I also wanted to thank you for standing up for me yesterday during that interrogation. A complex situation, what with your dad and sister."

Shelia wanted to say, "Just doing my job," but said, "The firm fully supports you, Vince. The partnership believes in you and is ready to stand behind you."

"Well, I appreciate it... Hey, who's your friend?" he asked.

"My son, Danny." She smiled at the towheaded boy sitting on the floor drawing a picture. "Say good night to Mr. Buckley."

"'Night Mr. Buckley," Danny said.

"Good night, son."

Turning her attention back to the figure in her doorway, she said, "Thanks."

She followed him with her eyes until he passed. Not until she heard his voice speak to the person in the next occupied office did she turn to Danny.

"Almost done," she said.

"Then McDonalds?"

"Then McDonalds."

As Kel stepped through the elevator doorway into the secure parking garage at West Precinct, the light fell on Chief of Detectives, Nathaniel Ballesteros.

"Good evening, Chief," she said as he made way for her to pass.

"Detective," he said with a nod.

Rotating back, she asked, "Do you have a moment?"

He entered the cab, turned and held the door.

As the elevator motor engaged, and she felt the first tug of the lift, a growing apprehension tightened her stomach. Some of what she had to say had a direct bearing on his role as Chief, but the first thing out of her mouth didn't. And she was certain that part of the conversation would not go well.

"There're a few things I wanted to clear up if you don't mind."

He didn't answer but looked straight ahead at the door.

The throb of her increased heart rate pounded in her temple, but she pressed on. "First, Monday morning at the Wishing Well, you told me you'd just come from Benaroya Hall." She noticed a subtle upturn of his head. When he didn't respond, she continued. "You remember, of course, that I'm a patrol officer. I had passed by Benaroya just a few hours earlier, about 9:30, and it was dark. So I checked—"

"You're investigating me," he said without turning toward her voice.

Kel knew it wasn't a question and she was about to traverse a deep murky bog where one misstep could get her buried alive.

"Well sir, I'm sure it's just a simple mistake, "she said, although she couldn't see how he could have forgotten where he had been just an hour before meeting her. "The Summer Festival was on Saturday night and got over about ten-thirty."

"And your point is, I couldn't have been there. Is that correct?"

"Begging your pardon, sir, but yes."

He turned his head slowly to face her. The tension in his brow was as taught has the skin on a snare drum. "Perhaps I misspoke. Being in Pioneer Square brought back memories of a quite pleasant evening. As you can imagine, the demands of my job are many. I'm sure I was just confused. But it goes without saying, Nyte, my comings and goings are police business and not yours. You don't need to be investigating me."

That wasn't a satisfactory answer. She knew that someone within the department had given her SPD issued cell phone number to DK. For all she knew the *Chief* was DK and *he* hit her with the stun gun in Susanne Lowen's condo. But he out ranked her and the rumors in the locker room had him in a dead heat with the acting chief as the next police chief. It probably *was* nothing more than a mistake. So as a matter of preservation and respect, she decided to let it go.

"Of course, sir. I'll say no more about it."

"Now then, you said there was something else?"

"Yes. Lou kicked me from the case you assigned me right in the middle of the bullpen."

"I see." He flicked his eyes back to the door. "And why do you think he did that?"

"He said it was because he gave me two days to find a suspect. I gave him several options, but he didn't like my list."

He pulled at one of his eyebrows and stood silent until the elevator came to a stop. When the door opened, he said, "Go on," and led the way into the hall.

"Well, sir, I've begun to have concerns about both Lou and Jake. First of all, in my opinion, they've focused all their attention toward my dad on the DK case. They don't talk about any other suspects. They've prejudiced themselves, and rather than look at the field, they're trying to build a case against the most convenient suspect. I concede to their theory, but I don't believe they welcome another. Jake shut me out from day one, and now being fired from the case makes it appear like Jake and Lou are colluding."

"That's a serious accusation, Officer Nyte. It implies something illegal. We better take this in my office."

Kel followed the chief down the hall, and after he entered his office, she filed in behind him and pushed the door closed. As the motion sensor brought up the lights, through his window she could see the high rise across the street. The night crew was busy cleaning one of the offices, and she wondered what it would be like to work a job where the biggest issue was whether her wipe-down rag had enough moisture to clean the desktop of someone else's coffee rings. She turned her attention back to the chief. He had walked behind his desk but didn't sit down. She took this as a sign the meeting would be brief and rested her hands on the back of a side chair.

"I didn't mean to imply they're doing anything illegal but—"

"I sense," Ballesteros said, "there's more angst with Jake than just a rough start."

It surprised her that he cut Lou out of the conversation and zeroed in on Jake. He had done something similar when she brought up Willie Jenkins' death after the bar brawl Monday morning. True, she had issues with Jake reaching far beyond DK, but she couldn't put her finger on what she might have said to indicate such.

"What's really bothering you about him?" Ballesteros asked.

"Sir, I don't know that I can trust him. I know he works for you, and that makes him your concern, I get that, but he's come up short in a couple of things and then…" She paused.

"What do you mean 'come up short'?" he asked, his tone turning inquisitional.

"Perhaps I've said too much, sir." She backed her way to the door. "I should leave you to your desk."

"You'll do no such thing. You're making an accusation about one of my men, and I'll hear it now."

She hesitated. "If I may be permitted to make a couple of observations, sir, then you can judge if they warrant further inquiry." She paused again until he acknowledged. When he nodded, she continued. "Jake stated that he and Willie Jenkins took Toshio Aoki down and then right after Aoki went to prison, Willie was found dead. Yet I find it curious, sir, that there's no record of anyone ever coming after Jake, and he offers no evidence that anyone did. And then, what makes my instincts flare even more is he reported being indisposed at the Belltown Pump the night his last partner, Eddy, was shot. Sir, the bar was closed that night and had been for a week while the health department identified the source of an outbreak of salmonella."

"I see," he said, again not registering any emotion under his black brows. "I believe you indicated there's something else, Detective? What else is on your mind? Let's get it all out into the open."

She exhaled like she was blowing out all thirty-six candles on her birthday cake with a single breath. "I hesitate to bring this up, Chief, but an incident happened Monday morning that made me curious. I did some background, and when I asked him about it, he got very defensive."

"What kind of background?"

"Sir, he seems to have some connection to Toshio Aoki, more than just as his arresting officer. I'm just wondering if…" She shook her head.

"Spell it out for me, Detective. Are you saying he has ties to organized crime? That's a serious charge."

"No sir, I haven't any basis to make such an accusation, but as I said, something just doesn't add up. Tribune Investments, a company where Aoki is a principle, might be a shell for Saito Global. They owned the cargo container in which Willie was found. Is it possible Jake is involved with Tribune? Is that why no one ever came after him like they did Willie? Does Jake know who killed Willie and is covering?"

Ballesteros leaned forward. He placed his clenched fist knuckles down on the top of his desk and drew his eyebrows into one.

Kel saw an expression she didn't expect. Aggravation hovered on the surface but beneath, uneasiness threatened.

"Kel, I think I've heard quite enough. As you said, your assumptions are baseless, and that's all they are, assumptions. Rather than try to solve Willie's death, and I do remember you telling me he was your friend, you should leave this to the seasoned detectives. As I told you the other day, we have resources dedicated to solving his murder. You flailing around with these kinds of allegations only muddies the water. Now, if there's nothing else, I'll bid you good night."

Chapter 35

DK arrived early at his Sanctuary long before the buses and the bustle of the Thursday morning commuters could interrupt his tranquility. On his knees before the two by four altar, he lifted his eyes and read again the words stretched above the photos and artwork of the memorial collage.

"The secret things belong to God, but the things revealed belong to us."

Yesterday's revelation had been the most fulfilling thus far and brought atonement for his wife's abandonment into another man's arms. Today, another surreptitious journey into the past would bring expiation for a long-held debt. Among his collection, taped to the wall, a picture of his son on his third birthday ripping the wrapping paper off a Tonka dump truck took prominence.

Extinguishing with a silent breath the candle resting on the photo of Marilyn Winston, he watched the smoke rise like the bouquet of a Biblical sacrifice, but there was no redemption. God had forsaken him, and his offerings now would never appease the wrath of the One who would punish him for his actions. Wounds too deep to be seen but mercilessly felt couldn't be absolved by the passage of time. Mark Twain had written, "Forgiveness is the fragrance that the violet sheds on the heel that has crushed it," but time had transmuted the aroma into the stench of retribution. He could no more turn away from the path he had elected than a vulture could stop circling the dead. Vengeance was his lone reward.

Wolf didn't know what year it was or how many he had passed stooped in this remedial task, but he straightened from his position once more to take a brief respite. The shade from the scorching sun thrown on his back and the relief of the spinal aches was only temporary but savored. With his feet shackled by a three-foot chain, he sidestepped to the left. He bent forward again and as he finished planting another hand full of rice seedlings into the ankle-deep paddy, two gunshots rumbled through the clearing and into the forest behind him.

Raiding bands of Asian paramilitary were common, and he had been stolen so many times he no longer feared for his life. He stood erect again and looked in the direction of his guard. When last he had seen him, he had been sitting on a tree stump ten feet away, taking a toke from a hand-rolled marijuana cigarette. He wasn't surprised to see him lying crumpled on the ground, the smoke from the joint curling around his face. Turning toward the direction of the weapon fire, he saw four men in camouflage uniforms stomping through the field about twenty meters away.

He dropped the seedlings from his hands like discarded trash. It wasn't another troop of gooks vying to take him by force. Although an updated version, the uniforms had a familiar American appearance and the M-16 rifles they carried across their bodies confirmed his hope. After all this time someone back home had remembered and sent a rescue squad. It was over— finally over. No more nights in the cage. No more bowls of rice. No more blistering sun. Her face had all but blurred from recognition, but he could almost see his wife racing to him as he stepped off the airplane. His son would be there, too, to wrap his arms around him again.

The soldiers split up. One walked toward him and the other three turned toward his buddies in the field. These few men—captured, left behind, forgotten—had shared a common threat and had bonded them in a way people in comfort could never fathom. In disbelief he saw their salvation slogging through the field to embrace them. To take them home.

Then another shot echoed deep into the surrounding trees, coming from his right. He thought it must have been one of his other captor's rifles. They would've heard the initial report and come running to protect their property. He twisted toward the sound. He had too much at stake to watch the murdering bastards take his final chance at freedom away.

Even in his world without hope, what he saw was worse than he could imagine. He often had visions of someday outliving his usefulness in the paddies. That image had him shot or knifed, and buried in an unmarked grave. But, as if in slow motion, one of his friends fell backward into the swamp. Then another shot exploded, and another, until, in just seconds, he was the only POW still standing.

He turned back to the soldier who approached him. He was now on a run crossing the paddy, his boots splashing through the water. Ten meters away, he raised his weapon.

Not taking time to think, Wolf's body acted on impulse as if the infantry training he had drafted into at Fort Bragg had been yesterday. A bullet from another explosion behind him buzzed passed his ear.

He dove toward the dead sentry and fell to the ground, putting the stump between him and the oncoming soldier. After rolling his lifeless captor to his side to increase his cover, he seized the guard's automatic rifle. He lay on his stomach and placed the gun cross the deceased man's torso. On the other end of the barrel, the rogue combatant continued to fire random blasts. Wolf squeezed off his first round, and the projectile made a direct hit to the soldier's chest. A burst of blood blossomed on his shirt as he fell backwards.

Realizing now this was no rescue but rather an assassination, he searched the field for the other armed men. The three had taken defensive positions on their knees in the paddy, firing at their new target. Still prone, he used the stump and the guard for cover. He took aim at one of the men and fired a round. It went wild.

He needed to focus, breathe, and remember.

The bullets flying around him, striking the stump, tunneling into the ground, and ripping into the flesh of the dead guard brought it all back. Years before, more time than his mind could process, he had lain behind a downed tree and faced odds worse than this. The suddenness of the memory was like the surprise eruption of a long dormant volcano. He had been a marksman. He could take out an enemy soldier with a single shot.

Even though the AK-47 in his hands was unfamiliar, the embrace of the handgrips and the site on the barrel felt familiar. He brought the second man down. By the time he turned to the others, they had cut and run toward the opposite side of the swamp. With the sights set now on surrogates for those with complete disregard for his right to life, his blood ran cold. They, too, fell.

Lifting the fourth candle, DK lit its wick and placed it over the photo of the next to die.

Chapter 36

Kel's body jerked to a sitting position. She raised the cell phone she had been grasping in her sleep and saw that a new text announced itself. The clock at the top of the screen showed 6:08 a.m.

After being fired from the case and then finding Chief Ballesteros unsympathetic to her suspicions, she needed time to think. Lance had always been good at listening without needing to interject his opinion or advice. But in the last couple of hours before she left West Precinct, she had witnessed all her support vanish. Her partner, her boss, the Chief of Detectives and Captain Silva abandoned her like a bad idea. The perfidy of her dad's affair had sent Shelia scurrying back to her office, presumably to bury herself in work—Shelia's preferred coping mechanism. Unable to look at her dad without wanting to punch something or someone, left Kel exposed and alone. There was no one to turn to.

Knowing her dad's house would be safe with police presence at his curb, she convinced Chrissie that Pops needed his only granddaughter to comfort him in the loss of his two close friends. Chrissie, unlike Monday night, went willingly. Kel dropped her at the curb and then made her way to the townhome she had shared with Lance. Rather than find comfort in his lingering presence, though, she collapsed into a deep sleep on the couch.

Twenty-five minutes after being awakened, Kel looked again at the Rainier Valley address on the phone's display. She drove her Liberty south on Rainier Avenue, what the locals called "the valley of stray bullets." Strip clubs, seedy bars, abandoned store fronts, and mini-markets passed on either side of the road where drug deals and prostitution went down in the parking lots and shadows without fear of arrest.

She turned left on the street DK texted to her phone and made her way down a narrow street lined with seventy-year-old ramshackle homes with steel bars over the windows and chain link-fenced yards. In the morning light, they seemed disconnected to the polished, newer vehicles parked along the street. Apparently, pride in this neighborhood was best expressed in the car you drove, not in the house you slept.

Arriving at the address, she found herself in front of a fortress. Instead of chain link, an eight-foot cinderblock fence, topped with a four-foot steel, spike-tipped railing loomed like the curtain wall of a medieval castle. Its duty clear; keep the riff-raff out and give the occupants a sense of security. To Kel it looked like a dare. Some enterprising youth on a gang initiation challenge would score big points by breaking into the house to steal the blue-ray DVD player or plasma TV.

A single SPD cruiser, parked in the driveway, waited for Kel. Two officers sat inside. As Kel pulled up behind them, the officer behind the wheel stepped from the blue cruiser and approached her silver Jeep.

Bending at the waist and placing his hands on the window opening, Scott Nillson, Kel's former mentor, asked, "What do we *have* here, Kel?"

"Don't know for sure. Have you spoken with the occupants?"

"No, waiting for you."

"Then let's do it."

Scott walked back to the car. Before dropping inside, he pushed a speaker button on a post next to the ten-foot steel gate. Moments later, it swung open, and once the gap was large enough, Kel followed the cruiser through.

Behind the gate, Kel was confronted with an anomaly. The short driveway rose up a steep incline, and the house erected on top of it was a small, two-story mansion. Overbuilt for the neighborhood, she deduced that the owner must be the drug lord of some of the dealers she had passed on the street. But why DK had brought her here she couldn't reconcile.

She knocked on the front door. When an overweight Caucasian woman in her late forties answered, the contrast between the appearance of the figure before her and her assumptions moments before struck her dumb. With bed hair and a crumpled, ankle-length nightgown under an untied bathrobe, the woman didn't appear to be the wife of a wealthy drug kingpin.

She looked first to Kel and then to the two uniformed officers behind Kel. She asked, "May I help you?"

"Tracy Kinnear?" Kel asked, having gained the name of the home owners from dispatch. "I'm Detective Kel Nyte."

"Yes, what do the police want with me at this hour?"

"Do you live alone?"

"No, with my husband, but he left for work about six. Why?"

"Could we come in, please? I have a few questions."

"You're frightening me. Is Roger okay?

"As far as we know he's fine. If we could just speak for a few minutes?"

Tracy moved aside, opening the door wider, and Kel, followed by Scott and his new trainee, Valerie, passed into the entryway. Over the east-facing door, the arched windows allowed the ascending sun to penetrate its warming rays, and as Tracy turned toward the living room, the swirl of her robe caused dust particles caught in the light to shimmer like the glitter of a snow globe.

"Mrs. Kinnear," Kel said after they were all in the living room, "where does your husband work?"

"Why? What's happening?" her questions revealing her irritation.

"Ma'am, your husband may be in danger. Where does he work?"

"Danger? Oh my God," she said, her tone changing to despair. "We own a home furnishings store in Ballard. He gets there early to do paperwork and tidy the store before it opens."

"Where's the store located?" Kel asked, unable to mask the urgency she felt.

Taking down the Market Street address on her notepad, and after sending Valerie outside to make the call dispatching SPD, she turned back to Mrs. Kinnear. The expression on her visage and the terror in her eyes both spoke of the fear that what she was about to be told would include the fate of having to face the rest of her life without the security of her husband.

"We have officers on the way," Kel said, trying to assure the woman, and herself, that tragedy was certain to be averted.

"My God," she pleaded, "what's happening?"

"I'll explain everything, but every second that passes increases his risk. Please help me."

"Oh my God, this can't be happening. What do you need?"

"Two things. First, do you have a computer in the house?"

"Of course, he keeps it in his office, down to hall to the left." She pointed toward the doorway. "What else?"

As Scott left the room to locate the computer, Kel asked, "Can you reach Roger right now?"

"I can't believe this is happening." She dabbed at tears with the sleeve of her robe.

"Tracy, this is important."

"Sure, I'll try," she said through sobs and went to a lamp table at the end of the couch. Picking up a telephone, she pressed a speed dial number and held the receiver to her ear.

"Come on Roger, pick up, pick up. Please!"

She disconnected the call and looked up toward Kel.

"Voicemail," she said. Her eyes pleaded for mercy. She looked back toward the instrument in her hand and pressed another speed dial number.

"He always carries his cell phone. He's sure to answer."

Kel heard in her tone an attempt to build confidence that all would be well. She knew it wouldn't.

"Roger," she shouted into the phone. "Ro...Roger?"

Kel watched as the woman listened, pressing the receiver against her ear as if the voice on the other end was almost inaudible. Then her expression changed as the blood drained from her face, turning hope into despair. Her knees buckled, and she collapsed onto the couch.

"Oh my God," she said. Looking up toward Kel, she held the phone out, and through anguishing sobs, asked, "Did you say...name...Kel?"

Chapter 37

DK had sat in his car on the street for more than thirty minutes. From his place at the curb, he watched the alley behind the Kinnears' home furnishings store. While he waited, he smoked a stream of cigarettes and filled the ashtray.

Right on time, Roger Kinnear pulled into the alley, slipping his Mercedes into his parking space next to the rear entrance. After stepping from the car, he entered the shop through a man-sized door next to the ground-level cargo rollup.

DK gave him five minutes alone, enough time to fill his lungs with the scent of fine furnishings and to relish for the last time the successful empire he had built over the last two decades. Then, he drove his car into the alley and parked next to the Mercedes. After he closed the car's door, he flipped the safety off his pistol and tucked it into his belt at the small of his back. Opening the alley door, he stepped inside to a small warehouse. He listened for the sounds of life. After two silent minutes, he heard the squeak of a desk chair's dry spring and moved toward the mournful squawk.

Between the racks of couches and chairs draped with clear plastic dust covers, he saw a light coming from a small interior office. Inside, his target, the one for whom the candle burned beneath the condemned façade of a previous era, sat bent over a desk filled with papers.

As quiet as a winged owl at midnight, DK moved down the cavernous row of towering shelves toward his objective. Another secret to reveal. Arriving at the end of the row, he paused. Roger stood and then exited the office. The cup in Roger's hand, led DK to believe the interruption would only be temporary, and once Roger was out of sight, having stepped into another room, DK slipped into the office and took cover behind the door.

He waited.

Moments after Roger entered the room with coffee and a napkin-wrapped apple fritter, the phone on the desk rang. He let the automated attendant take the call while he took a bite of the pastry. A swallow from the cup followed, and he placed the cup and treat on the desk. Still standing, he looked down at a stack of paperwork arranged in a neat pile.

"Roger," DK said as he stepped from his hiding place.

Roger turned quickly to the voice. His face flushed, his mouth gaped, and his eyelids drew back as he stared down at the barrel of DK's pistol.

DK didn't want to prolong Roger's terror, but he knew for the next few moments it would be unavoidable. Like Susanne Lowen, powerless to stop what was about to happen, he could see Roger searching for his voice.

"Wh...who are you?" he said, his voice straining to remain calm. "If it's cash, there's some in the safe. I'll open it for you."

"What I want you can't give. I must take it."

DK pulled the trigger and watched as Roger staggered backwards, falling over his chair and then onto the cement floor. He landed on his back. A trickle of red flowed from the black hole in Roger's forehead and pooled around the casters of the chair. Death had come mercifully quick.

Placing the pistol on the desk, he turned to leave before any employees arrived. As he reached the door, from Roger's hip, his cell phone began to ring. *It's probably her.*

He reached for the phone, saw a name on the display, and smiled. He pressed the button on the screen labeled, "Answer."

"Roger, Roger," a woman's voice screamed in his ear.

"He can't come to the phone, Mrs. Kinnear. Is Kel with you?"

Chapter 38

"Detective Nyte," Kel said into the mouthpiece after she took the phone from Mrs. Kinnear. She turned to face the entryway.

"Kel."

The woman's voice on the other end jarred her.

"DK?" she asked.

"Yes. You give me that name?"

The last time he had spoken to her he whispered. He wasn't whispering now. She realized he was modulating his voice with a voice changer, which meant he knew she would recognize his voice.

Ignoring his last question she said, "Let me speak to Roger."

"I'm afraid he's taken his last call."

Since Tracy was still within earshot, she forced the words into a calm tone. "I see."

Valerie walked back into the living room and gave Kel a "follow me" wave.

Kel, keeping the wireless phone to her ear, fell in behind the officer as she led the way. They left Mrs. Kinnear alone in the living room in her uncertainty.

"What's this about?" Kel asked, once out in the hallway.

"I'm sure your daddy will soon figure it out. I've left a gift."

"The best gift would be for you to stop this and give yourself up."

"Can't see that happening. Not until he understands what he did to me."

"There has to be another way."

Valerie led her to where Scott stood in a small office. On the desk, a computer monitor displayed four lines of type. Kel didn't need to read it to know what they contained.

"Why don't you tell *me* about it? Maybe I can help."

"You're doing enough already."

"We're going to find you."

"Of that I have no doubt, and I look forward to it. That's why I picked you. But I've not yet completed your daddy's curriculum. So for now it seems I must take my leave since I hear the siren's wail of Seattle's finest. Keep up the hunt, Kel."

"Why Roger?" Kel shouted, but the question went unanswered as the call disconnected.

"What happened to Roger?"

The despair filled voice behind Kel spoke with such passion it was all she could do to keep her own emotions from pouring over the spillway. She looked from Scott to Valerie, who faced her on either side, and then turned to the woman with red, swollen eyes and tear stains still wet on her cheeks.

"Please." Kel motioned for Tracy to sit down on a wing-backed chair in the corner of the office. Glancing back at Scott, she pointed to the monitor and said, "Print a copy of that."

Scott, who already had a glove on his hand, manipulated the mouse. Kel walked across the room and knelt in front of the widow.

"Officers will be on the scene in a few moments, and we'll know for certain—"

"That my Roger's dead?"

"If Roger's okay, is what I was going to say."

"I still don't understand how you knew he might be in trouble."

Kel pulled her phone from the holster on her belt and searched for the latest message.

"A man sends me a text with an address." Holding the phone so Tracy could see the screen, she said, "At six this morning, your address appeared on my phone. Have you followed the news this week about the man the press is calling 'DK?'"

"Oh my God and now he's killed Roger, too."

"As I said, we won't know for certain until our officers arrive at your store, but if this man follows the same pattern…"

"Roger's dead, I can feel it."

"Believe me, I understand the horror of uncertainty you're going through at the moment. My best friend, the father of my daughter, left for the war a year and a half ago. I lived for months not knowing if he'd ever come home again."

The crackle of a garbled radio message broke the conversation, and Valerie shot a glance at Kel. As she walked for the door, she raised her hand to squeeze the trigger on the microphone attached to the shoulder of her blouse. Valarie said, "One moment," and then stepped into the hallway to take the call.

"Did he come home?" Tracy asked.

"He left three times but only returned twice. They say he was killed in action, but they never found him."

"And my future lies in the message that kind officer is taking right now."

"It's possible, but despite all you're feeling, I need to ask you a question. May I?"

When she answered with a slight nod, Kel continued. "DK's other victims all have a common thread. They all have a connection to Chief Dirk Nyte. What connection do you or Roger have to the him?"

Kel could feel what the woman's face said. The anguish between knowing the actual truth and praying for it to be a nightmare was a weight too heavy to bear.

But Kel needed an answer before the death knell lost Tracy in grief.

"Tracy, stay with me. I need you to think."

"Uh, nothing."

"Neither you nor Roger have any relationship to Dirk Nyte, now or in the past? What about family history?"

"I only know the chief's name from the papers, but *my* family has no relationship with him. I don't think Roger's does either. Chief Nyte being such a public figure, Roger would have said something."

Kel heard the rustle of Valerie's uniform as she reentered the room and followed Tracy's eyes as they rose to meet the officer's.

Walking over to the woman in the chair, Valarie squatted in front of her and took her hand.

"I'm so sorry," she said.

Tracy stared at the messenger. The shock of certainty had cloaked whatever was left of her emotions in merciful numbness.

"Why would he want to kill Roger and Susanne?" she asked, staring through Valerie as if she were a crystal figurine. "What did *they* do?"

Kel leaned forward and wrapped her arms around Tracy. Resting her face against Tracy's cheek, she felt hot tears flow again. Kel wept, too. When Tracy's chest convulsed into heaves, she held on until they slowed.

Once Tracy found control, Kel pushed back and asked, "Did you know Susanne Lowen?"

While she had held her, Kel wondered why Tracy mentioned Susanne and none of the other victims. There had been more press coverage over Terry's death due to the spectacular explosion, and then with the connection to Terry's ex-wife, Marilyn, the local press and news media hadn't been able to put the story down.

"Yes, we were very close. Her memorial's today. Roger was going to the shop to get things ready for the day, and then we were taking the rest of the day with his family."

"Family? Are you somehow related to Susanne?"

"Susanne? Yes, she's Roger's younger sister."

Chapter 39

On the way to the Kinnear residence forty-five minutes earlier, Kel had placed a call to Jake deLaurenti. Though Lieutenant Martinez had taken her off the case yesterday, she had reason to keep Jake abreast of new developments in the case. He was the lead detective, and each victim, at least until Roger, seemed to draw closer to her dad. Having been ordered to surrender her phone, it might have come as a surprise to Jake that she was still in contact with DK, but that didn't worry her. *What can they do, order me to turn over my own phone?*

As expected, her call had gone to voicemail. She hadn't given him her number, so it was a number he wouldn't recognize. He had been known to turn his cell off when not on duty, which, under normal conditions, would have been puzzling for a detective, but in his case, it wasn't out of character at all.

Now standing on the Kinnear's front porch, leaning against the wooden railing, she punched his number into the phone's keypad again. When she reached voicemail, she said, "Get your ass out of the sheets, Jake. We have another victim."

Disconnecting the call, Kel looked over the security fence surrounding the Kinnear home. Across the street behind a steel-barred window, backlit silhouettes stood, peering through the open blinds. She knew their thoughts as they stared toward the fortress they had come to know and probably despise. *If their neighbors could fall victim behind a 12-foot fence, what could save them from the absurdities of their own fate?* The irony was that even with the stronghold Roger had built to keep predators out, his armor was not without flaw. A secret marauder plundered the most priceless possession Roger had—his own life.

Footsteps behind her on the wooden planking pulled Kel from her reverie. Officer Scott Nillson stepped onto the front porch and joined her at the railing.

"Thought you'd want this," he said, handing her the printout from Roger's computer.

She took it and read each line, attempting to digest the meaning. Despite the wrench ratcheting her heart, she tried to distance her feelings from the words. Only then might she find clarity.

"Four the sowing of wild fruit

Guilty now there's no dispute

Armor cracks, it cannot shield

My jacket's load, death will wield"

The last two lines were clear. She had confirmed with the first responder at the crime scene that a single gunshot wound to the head was the most likely cause of death. "Armor cracks"—his skull, the helmet, "jacket's load" a reference to a lead-filled bullet known as a full metal jacket. The second line—"Guilty now"—contained the obvious verdict. *But what's Daddy guilty of?*

She read the poem again, hoping, like the optical illusion of the old hag and beautiful young woman she had been introduced to in Psychology 101, the riddle of the first line would snap into focus. Each of the previous verse's coded lines hadn't been difficult to decipher, pointing to the relationship between the murdered victim and her dad. Without knowing who Roger was, however, and if being Susanne Lowen's brother held any meaning, this new addition to the demented collection gave no obvious clue. It set off a mental itch, though, she couldn't scratch.

"I need to get to the scene, Scott," Kel said, "but we can't leave Tracy alone."

Before Scott could answer, a voice behind her interrupted.

"I'm going with you," Tracy said.

By the tone of her voice, Kel recognized she wasn't making a request. She turned to look into the face that a few minutes before had been ravaged with horror. Only the dark gray skin sagging around her eyes and her whites, now webbed with red, gave indication of grief. Her resolute expression indicated that "no" wasn't an option.

"I tried to tell her that's not a good idea," Valerie said, having followed her out to the door.

"I insist," Tracy said, "I want to see my husband."

"You don't want to see him like this, Mrs. Kinnear." Kel put her hands on Tracy's shoulders. "If you do, it's an image you may never forget. There'll be time for viewing later, but right now is the time for grieving. Is there someone we should call, children, your mother, your pastor?"

"I just won't believe it until I see him."

"Tracy, you know I understand how hard this is for you right now. You've been so brave this morning. But we're closing in on the man who did this, and we'll be able to work much faster, maybe even stop him before he hurts someone else, if you let us do our job."

Jake deLaurenti disconnected from voicemail. "Get your ass out of the sheets," he said out loud to the two men facing him in the back of the limousine. "Who does that goddamn bitch think she is?"

"That bitch may be the one who sticks a needle in your arm," Peter McCabe said, staring out the window at a reach stacker dropping an intermodal container onto a flatbed trailer. "That one ours, Tosh?"

Toshio Aoki turned a pair of binoculars on the end of the blue Saito Global cargo box.

"What are you saying, she knows?" Jake asked.

"She's smarter than you've been crediting," Peter said. "She saw you two together the other day, and she's been sniffing up your ass ever since. She's close to making the connection."

"She don't know shit, and even if she did, she can't prove nothing."

"That's ours," Toshio said, resting the binoculars on the unoccupied seat between himself and Peter. "The container number matches." Looking across the passenger compartment to Jake, he added, "Shit or not, you're in it to your waist and sinking like quicksand. You keep treating her like horseshit and she's going to get stink all over you. Lighten up, asshole, or you're a loose end."

"Loose end? Now I'm expendable?"

"Maybe expendable's a little extreme, but before she ties the knot between us, we've got to take *her* out."

"Is that always your solution?" Peter asked. He withdrew a cigar from his thin lips and sent a smoke ring floating toward Jake. "Think about it, shithead, two dead cops?"

"Do you always have to pollute the air with those foul smelling things?" Jake asked.

Peter cocked his head, furrowed his dark eyebrows, and blew the rest of the smoke in his lungs across to Jake.

Toshio looked first at Jake and then back at Peter. "People die. Cost of doing business, and like Willie, if she's getting too close...Anyway, how many shallow graves you got out in that goddamn desert from cargo that didn't survive the crossing?"

"That's different. They begged us to bring them here."

"For jobs and a better life. We make promises and then herd them into an untenable container under subhuman conditions we wouldn't expose a stray dog to."

"Exotic Malaysian pussy fetches a far better price than stray dogs. I don't see you complaining on the way to the bank. You having regrets, Tosh?"

"Hell no, we're providing a service. I'm just reminding you that whether it's a cop or a cunt, dead is dead."

"We could make it look like DK pulled the trigger," Jake said, "whoever the hell he is."

"Whoever *he* is," Peter said, "that may not be enough."

"Why, what do you mean?" Jake asked.

"Someone else thinks he knows."

Jake glared at Peter and tried to mask the fear he felt building in his chest. "Who?"

"Damned if I know, but someone left me a note. It claimed to have been written by *him* and said, 'My blood's on your hands.'"

"Willie!" Jake shouted, leaning forward in the bench seat, the new leather talking back to his chinos. "The note came from Willie?"

"Of course not, asshole. He's dead, but someone put it together."

"And not Nyte?" Jake asked.

"No. I was tipped off about the note on Sunday, and Kel didn't see you two together 'til Monday. It has to be someone else who either has deep resources or a very long fishing pole."

"Katana rattling," Toshio said.

Jake missed the samurai sword reference and ignored Toshio with a glare. To Peter he said, "Hell, I'm not going down for this. It was your damn call. You set it up."

"Piss off," Peter said, taking another draw from the cigar and looking toward the window again. "We've been able to contain this up to now. Nothing's changed."

"Up to now it's been our little secret," Jake said, "but if we've got an unknown shooting off his goddamn mouth, I'd say something's changed."

"Look, he gave a Hotmail address. I'll set up a meet."

"That's validation," Toshio said, his tone a warning.

"Validation or not," Jake said, "we've got to find out what, if anything, he knows."

"You don't get it. Just showing up confirms guilt."

"And what do you suggest?" Jake asked. "Ignore him? If we do nothing, what's his next move? The cops? Face it, he's got us by the balls."

"Leave me out of 'us,'" Toshio said. "Remember putting me in prison, shithead? He must think it's one or the both of you, and we all know who pulled the rug out from under Willie. Set up the meet in a public place. He'll demand it. I'll have my men staking it out, and once we know who it is, we'll discretely show him the gates of Hell."

"There it is again," Peter said. "Kill the bastard. And what if he's wired and his last words utter my name into some cop's ear?"

"Then you're in even deeper shit than your protégé, here. I thought you said you could contain it, Chief."

Chapter 40

Kel pulled into the single-row, street-front parking lot just before 7:30 a.m. Three SPD cruisers had beaten her to the scene, and their red and blue strobe lights danced a syncopated rhythm in the Kinnear's store window. She approached the front glass door and a uniformed officer reached to open it for her.

"Good morning, Zek," Kel said as she paused, waiting for the opening to appear.

"Morning, Kel," he said and let her pass through. "Body's in the back office."

Damn shame. An hour ago Roger was a living soul. Now he's just a body, a piece of a puzzle.

Once inside, she took a moment to scan the showroom. She could tell at a glance the Kinnear's had good taste. The high-quality furniture looked more fitting a Ballard or Blue Ridge home than the Rainier Valley neighborhood Roger and Tracy lived. The smell of death hadn't spilled out from the back room yet, so she teased her sense with the fragrance of fine leather and hand-polished walnut.

Despite the fact that the showroom had more uniformed officers in it than it probably did customers at any one time, the scene demanded the respect of silence. They stood in three scattered groups. Two officers with their arms folded across their chests took their station just inside the front door, protecting the scene from unauthorized entry. Three others gathered around a bar-height counter, resting their elbows on it while they drank coffee from biodegradable cups. One lone figure stood with her hand resting on the facing of a door in the back of the showroom, and peered through the opening.

Kel walked to the backdoor and drew next to the officer.

"Hey, Nancy."

"The ME's with the vic now," Nancy said, not looking away from the view behind the door but pulling it open enough so Kel could slip past her.

Kel entered the warehouse, and as she walked by a small kitchen on her left, she glanced in. The coffee in the glass pot had nearly been drained, but the lid was still secure on a distinctive aqua-colored box with the name "Flaky's" printed in white letters on the side. Despite his grief over his sister's death, Roger had bought pastries for his staff. It might have been the one thing grounding him to the constant ebb and flow of life—birth, donuts, death—and as long as there were donuts, death could be forestalled.

"One shot, dead center."

She peered through the open doorway to a small office. The medical examiner kneeled next to a man in his late forties or early fifties. The guest of honor, Roger Kinnear, lay on his back. Gravity had drawn what blood hadn't spilled onto the cool concrete floor toward the corpse's backside, leaving his face a pallid mask. Despite this, there was something familiar about him. She had seen him before, perhaps at a fundraiser. Her dad, since her mom's death, had dragged her to a few of those. Even though socializing wasn't her strength, to support him as the chief of police, she tagged along, making polite talk.

A slender man, standing six foot three inches, pointed a digital camera toward the victim, shooting off several frames. He was the same man Paul Winston yelled at the morning before while he photographed Marilyn's lifeless body.

"Detective Nyte," Kel said, announcing her presence.

"I'll wait outside," the man with the camera said and backed out of the cramped office. Bumping into Kel, he said, "Excuse me, ma'am" and jerked to his right as if to avoid further physical contact. "Small quarters, but I'm done for now."

"Thanks." Kel moved inside, filling the space he vacated.

".45 caliber to the forehead," the medical examiner said, looking up only high enough to see Kel's boots. "Probably came from that Remington on the desk. We'll test it to make sure. Your doer military?"

"Could be. Why?" Kel bent at the waist to examine the gun. *I've left a gift,* she remembered DK saying less than an hour before. This scene was no different than the others. With each victim, in addition to their poem, he left the instrument of their demise

280

behind—a pillow, fragments of the bomb's detonator, and her dad's kitchen knife.

"Standard issue sidearm for US military from before World War I until after Vietnam," the ME said. "But he could have bought it at a secondhand gun store."

Kel turned from the desk and squatted next to the body, eye level with the medical examiner. Looking across the lifeless form, she said, "I have no doubt he left it. That's been his MO. He likes leaving clues, so it probably has significance. Anything else seem out of place?"

Pointing to a cigarette butt lying on the floor next to him, he said, "What about that? No ashtray in here."

"That's got to be it."

"Be what?" he asked, reaching into his kit for a plastic evidence bag.

Before she could answer, a voice behind her said "Hey, plebe, thanks for the wakeup call, but what the Hell are you doing in my crime scene?"

Kel chose not to turn toward the voice as she examined the cigarette the ME dropped into the bag. "You only know about this crime scene 'cause I called you—twice."

"And you knew about it how?"

"DK texted me the Kinnear's home address."

"Lieutenant Martinez threw you off the case and confiscated your phone."

"More than one phone receives text messages, and a good cop is never really off duty. Do you think I'm going to sit by if I have a chance to stop a murder?"

"Point taken," Jake said, joining them in the crowded office. He leaned over the body. "So what's up with the butt?"

"It seems out of place. There's no ashtray in the office, and I was in his home. There was no trace of tobacco there, either. Take a deep breath, Jake. What do you smell?"

Jake crinkled his brow. "Okay, I'll play along." Inhaling a deep exaggerated breath through his nose, then exhaling, he said, "Let's see. Leather, stale coffee, and the glaze of that apple fritter on the desk."

"Exactly, no burnt tobacco, right? DK left it. I spoke to him on the phone and—"

"You spoke to him?"

"I asked Mrs. Kinnear to call Roger so I could warn him, but DK answered and asked for me—by name—and said he was going to leave a gift. I've felt all along he wants me to figure out who he is, and when we process this, we'll find a clue to his identity."

Turning to the ME and holding up the evidence bag, she said, "This is top priority. We need to get this to the lab for processing immediately. I'm going to send it with one of the uniforms. Any objections?"

"None from me."

She stood and looked at Jake.

"I agree. Good idea."

Turning back to the ME, she asked, "Are we good here?"

"Yep, the investigators are waiting outside to process the room when you're finished."

"Good. Now," she said to Jake, "could we step outside?"

As they left the office, Jake took the lead. They made their way toward the back door down a row of high shelving stacked with furniture.

Once they were outside and away from the emergency vehicles blocking the alley, Kel said, "Look, I think we got off on the wrong foot."

"I know what you're going to say, and it's not necessary," Jake said. "I tried my damn level best to get you kicked from this case and out of my way. As far as I was concerned, I wanted a chasm between us big enough to float a fully-loaded aircraft carrier. But you've done all right. Despite my efforts, you've not only kept up, but in some ways you're ahead of me.

"So here's the deal. Until we've solved the case, you're my speed dial number one. No more voicemail. I'm still not going to appreciate the finer things like getting my ass out of the sheets especially when someone else's ass is keeping me company. But we've got to figure this out. We need to start fresh now."

"You kidding me?" She felt as if he had poured ice water on her fury. "Why the sudden conversion?"

"Do you want to work together or not?"

"No more rule one?"

"Of course."

"No more plebe?"

"Granted."

"Okay, then, on a trial basis. And," she said, averting her eyes, "what I said the other day about your conviction ratio was below the belt."

"No apologies. It's true, and I know it. Besides, with two partners either dead or disabled, I have this constant reminder that my rule one may be the problem."

"Well, on the record, I don't want to be signing up to be another casualty in the line of duty, but if we *could* work together to bust this UNSUB..."

"Okay, then. Who's the victim, and what does he have to do with your dad?"

"According to his wife, nothing, but there's another twist. Roger Kinnear and Susanne Lowen are siblings."

"So, all the victims are connected in some way. This has to be more than coincidence."

"I know, and even though we don't know if Mr. Kinnear's connection to my dad, until we unravel that knot, we've still got nothing but a ticking clock."

Mine to reap for Hell each day.

"That leaves us only one person who can fill in this piece," Jake said.

"And even though you and I have this new bond of collaboration, I'll take this interview without you."

Chapter 41

Shelia Savell pushed her chair back from the desk, stood, and walked to the window. From the fifteenth floor of the Mangorn Building, her eyes drifted across the cityscape. Despite the recession of the last couple of years, newly built and renovated office towers cast their shadows across the city. With the vistas of the Puget Sound and the Olympic Mountain Range concealed behind the high-rise veil, the shrieking wail of a gull or occasional Washington State Ferry's air horn drifting through the skyline served as evidence that Seattle still thrived on the waterfront.

Directly across the street, a seventeen-story, terra cotta-style tower built in 1922 and damaged by the Nisqually Earthquake nine years earlier, stood stripped of its former dignity. With her near flawless court record, the structure had become a reminder of one of her only failures.

Shelia, with the backing of the firm, had taken on the city and the developers who wanted to level the building to make way for a fifty-two-story, soda cracker box, steel and glass atrocity. The architect, from the looks of the elevation drawings, was a third grader with a small set of broken crayons. In the end, she lost her bid to have it declared an historic landmark.

Now, the former edifice gaped like a bombed-out Bagdad shell. Most of the window glass had been removed in preparation for the demolition soon to commence. By the end of August, an implosion would reduce the artifact to a pile of rubble. She could already imagine its last whimper—the rumble of heavy equipment hauling away its broken remains.

One case she wouldn't have minded losing worked at the Snelling Helpdesk three floors below her office. The criminal practice group chair, knowing of her dad's relationship to the Rat City Exterminator case, had so much as said the full circle of justice would be served if he assigned her as Vince Buckley's lawyer. "Besides," he said, "if it comes to trial and you win, your partnership's a lock." She argued that she was a corporate litigator, not a defense lawyer, but she lost that argument, too.

Complicating her emotions, she wanted to buy her dad and Kel's theory—Buckley was DK. She had little doubt that he was in fact the Exterminator, so seeing him sentenced to death for the DK murders would also restore justice for the nineteen known Exterminator victims. But now, being his lawyer, if Kel busted his alibi, she had an ethical obligation to provide him a proper defense.

A light knock on the open door turned Shelia from the window.

"Hey, sis," Kel said as she walked into the office. "Interrupting something?"

"No, how'd you get to this floor? It's locked off."

"Isn't it obvious?"

Off Kel's left pocket, a shaft of light reflected off her gold shield. Covered in her dress blue uniform, Shelia realized her sister had come prepared to go directly to Susanne Lowen's funeral. She had never quite understood what drove Kel to follow after her dad and grandpa's career, but seeing her decorated so, reminded her of the pride she felt when, in a similar uniform, Kel graduated from the police academy nine years earlier.

"Opens all kinds of doors," Kel said and a smile lit her face, deepening the twin dimples on her cheeks.

"Apparently." Shelia walked to the desk.

"Brought you a little something, Sis." Kel held up a Grande Cappuccino in a disposable cup. In her other hand, she held her own latte.

"You're such a cop-cliché, Kel. Always with the coffee. You just need is donut to complete the picture. Here, give me that and take a seat." Shelia waved to a chair. "We still have a couple of minutes."

As Kel reached to swing the door closed with her foot, a medium-built man with black hair appeared in the doorway.

Kel noticed Shelia's eyes lock on his.

"I need that file," he said.

Shelia reached forward and lifted a thick manila folder from the top of a stack on her desk. Entering the office, he reached and slipped the file from Shelia's hand.

"Ryung, I don't think you've met my sister. Kel Nyte...Ryung Kim."

"Obviously, you're a police officer," Ryung said to Kel and extended his hand.

Kel stepped to Shelia's desk, placed the Cappuccino on the nearest corner and then took his warm hand.

"Ryung's an associate attorney here at SHP," Shelia said. "We're working a case together and have a motion due in court on Monday. Since I'll be out all afternoon, he's going to help me with some research on precedence."

"Nice to meet you, Ryung." Kel gave his hand a firm shake.

With a polite smile, he left the office, and closed the door behind him. Kel sat down in a side chair across the desk from her sister. Shelia took her seat, spinning it around to face Kel.

"He's really smart," Shelia said, and leaning forward, rested her elbows on the desktop. "And single."

"Here we go. Not with the match maker again."

"I'm just saying, you're alone, Chrissie needs a dad—"

"Oh, and now it's the dad card. You know how I feel about this. It's too soon. I'm not ready to even think about dating."

Eighteen months earlier, Lance had left for Afghanistan for a twelve-month deployment. Four months in, the caravan of armored vehicles he rode with came under attack. In the fight, he disappeared and his body was never recovered.

"I just worry about my big sister living like a nun without that special person in her life."

"Even nuns have someone special; they're married to Jesus Christ, for God's sake."

"You know what I mean."

"Shelia, you know I miss Lance every day. There may come a point when I feel certain he's not coming home. But it's the *not* knowing that has my heart bound. Am I holding on to the memory of a dead man or just keeping the spark of hope alive that at the very worst he's in some prison thousands of miles away?"

"I'm sorry. I don't mean to press you."

"Then, can we change the subject?"

"Sure. The news says DK struck again."

"Roger Kinnear. The name mean anything to you?"

"Nothing. Who's he?"

"When I first saw him at the scene, I had an odd feeling there was something familiar about him. Still haven't put it together, but I have a hunch. Curiously, he and the first victim, the one we're burying today, were brother and sister."

"That can't be a coincidence."

"Not likely. All DK's main targets up to now have been killed presumably because they had something in common—Daddy—but so far I can't put him and

Kinnear together. At first, my theory on the murders centered on the victim's relationship to the Exterminator case, but, unless Marilyn had some connection to it, and there doesn't seem to be one, her death yesterday turned that notion upside down."

Kel had learned from the Yakima Police that even though the woman Buckley used as his alibi hadn't been found, a jailed prostitute claimed she overheard a woman boasting that she spent Monday night with the man who had been accused of being the Rat City Exterminator. According to her, Buckley bragged over drinks that he knew one of the Hillside Stranglers and the Green River Killer. She stated that she gave him enough mind-blowing sex to make up for his years of drought in prison—on the house.

"Buckley's not off my list yet," Kel continued. "He could have paid that hooker for his alibi. The police have yet to locate the woman he was supposed to be with, so she may not even exist."

"Remember this is my client you're talking about."

"So, I'm discussing a new theory with my sister and holes in Buckley's alibi with his lawyer. You can keep that straight, right? I'm not asking you to comment or divulge any privileged communications, just hear me talk this through.

"If I'm correct and Buckley did this, he planned a little misdirection. Susanne and Terry's murders were designed to confuse the investigation; Daddy and Buckley both being implicated. But Marilyn's murder should take him out of the pool because she had nothing to do with Buckley's conviction. It's brilliant. What better way to absolve yourself, but by pointing the finger right at yourself?"

"If I may speak candidly as his lawyer, I think you're missing something. How would he know about Dad and Marilyn?"

"I've been thinking about that. If DK is the Exterminator, he must have connections. For one, he must know someone in the SPD. Otherwise, how did he get my unlisted department cell phone number? And then, how did he learn about Daddy's affair? But he certainly wouldn't have any friends within the SPD and Terry wouldn't give him the time of day let alone information about his suspicions about Marilyn. He has to have an accomplice."

"That may be true, detective, but if it's not my client, and you're giving me lots of reasonable doubt here, DK may not need an accomplice. I'd say your new theory is a stretch and a long one at that."

"Well, either way, we may not have long to wait. Shelia, DK intentionally left a clue to his identity at Roger's crime scene. Once the lab finishes, we should know who he is."

"That should put a stop to him."

"I'm not so sure. I have this gut feeling that even if we have his name, we still may not know who he is, at least not 'til he's ready. He's still in control and making it personal."

"What do you mean?" Shelia leaned forward, resting her forearms on the desk.

"Sorry I have to be so clinical about Daddy, but right now it's the only way I can handle it. Daddy had sex with Marilyn. Not just once but apparently several times. What if DK had wanted to kill Mom, but since she's already dead, he went for the next best, someone Daddy had been intimate with."

"Assuming Marilyn was killed because Dad slept with her."

"True, but why else? Certainly not just because she was Terry's wife. That just doesn't fit."

"It doesn't fit your theory, you mean, but if we make that assumption, then why Kinnear? What does he have to do with Dad?"

"I don't have that answer yet, but look at this." From her notebook, Kel pulled the printout of the poem found on Roger Kinnear's home computer.

Shelia read it over and then her eyes drift up, meeting Kel's.

"It's a similar style to one he texted to you before."

"Yes, the same seven beat rhythm and feet. We've not released the poetry angle to the press so there's no doubt it's DK. What do you make of the first line?"

"'Four the sowing of wild fruit?'" Shelia asked. "It's not clear."

"Not clear or you don't want to accept it? Shelia, I've had some time to think about it, and I think I know what it means. If I'm right, there's only one person who can confirm it."

"Dad?" Shelia said, her eyes drifting back to the page.

"Yes, so far it's all about him, and if my instinct's right, we're not going to like this answer any more than we did learning that Daddy was unfaithful to Mom."

Chapter 42

Until the organist fingered a natural instead of a flat, Kel couldn't tell if the background music was recorded or live. The aroma of fresh-cut daisies, roses, and begonias filled the small chapel at Vincent's Funeral Home. Their natural fragrances lost distinction as they conflated to cover the scent of death skulking in the corners. Around the room lining the walls, uniformed police and fire personnel stood frozen like wooden soldier decorations, staring at the floor, each other, and the closed pink and gray coffin bearing the remains of a colleague most didn't know. The stoic features on their faces intoned what Kel's heart prayed, "But for the grace of God go I."

To allow family and close friends to crowd forward near their loved one, Kel had stayed with Shelia at the back of the chapel near the exit. Her dad, weak from his disease and the stress of the last several days, had been taken to a seat near the front. On his left, the acting chief of police sat with his head bowed as if entreating his god for the safety of his people and the soul of the departed. On his right, his escort, Chrissie, sat fidgeting, looking over her shoulder trying to find a familiar face in a sea of identically dressed warriors of the street. Kel could see by her expression that she didn't like being that close to Susanne Lowen's casket and was desperate for it to be over soon.

"Even though I walk through the valley of the shadow of death," the priest read from Psalms 23, the New American Bible version, "I will fear no evil, for you are with me."

Kel listened as the homily began. The well-meaning man with the clerical collar had designed the sermon to give comfort to those who suffered sudden loss. She knew from her mom's service, it would fall short. No one's grief would be eased in the next few minutes.

She couldn't see to the front pews, but she could hear sniffling and an occasional heaving sob. Someone, perhaps Susanne's partner or her parents, grieved. Kel mourned with them, and for the families of the other victims of DK's recompense. They, too, were headed for morose gatherings of their own.

When the service ended, the two sisters were some of the first to exit the chapel, leaving Chrissie to help Pops navigate the crowd. Out on the sidewalk, a warm sun had eluded the cumulus clouds, and dressed in her blues, Kel's skin began to break out in prickly sweat. She led the way to a shade tree on the front lawn.

"Afternoon, Detective."

Kel turned to the voice and found Bimal had separated from the crowd on the sidewalk. He walked toward her and Shelia, looking a little less like an unmade bed than the first time Kel met him. His hair today was combed back and the three-day-old beard shaved.

"Shelia, this is Bimal. He's the lab analyst I've been working with on this case. Bimal, my little sister here is a lawyer."

"Nice to meet you, Shelia," Bimal said, taking her hand. "But what she was too kind to add was that I almost got her killed twice this week." He smiled and released her hand.

"So that was *you*," Shelia said, pouted her lips and placed her hands on her hips.

"So, she did tell you."

"No, I read it in the newspaper. You best be careful with my sister, she's the only one I've got."

"I'll make it my purpose to work on that skill set, but you must know she threatened to shoot me. Isn't there a law about that, counselor?" His face brightened into a smile.

"I'm sure I could find one, but it sounds more like self-defense." Shelia winked.

Bimal grinned and then turned his face to Kel. "I had hoped to catch you. I was still on duty when word came in about the Kinnear murder. I processed the gun found at the scene, and there's something interesting. A match to a slug pulled from a DB two months ago."

"Let me guess, an unsolved?"

"The body was found," he continued, nodding his head, "in a house fire. At first it looked like he fell asleep smoking, but the autopsy found a bullet lodged in his frontal lobe, much like Mr. Kinnear. If there was any trace evidence, though, it went up in smoke, so the case is still open."

"I remember seeing the story on the evening news," Shelia said. "High school teacher and freelance writer as I recall."

"DK's *first* victim?" Kel stroked her chin. "What does a freelance writer have to do with this?"

While Bimal was speaking, behind him and Shelia, Kel noticed the flow of blue uniforms leaving the building by the double oak door had dwindled. She watched for her dad and Chrissie, but they hadn't yet appeared.

About thirty feet away, in the center of the sidewalk, Lieutenant Lou Martinez and Chief of Detectives, Nathanial Ballesteros, were deep in conversation. Lou was doing the majority of the speaking, his eyes flitting between Ballesteros, the ground, and the crowd. Although Kel couldn't hear his words, his tortured expression gave her the impression the source of his distress wasn't the victim whose memorial had just concluded. Ballesteros looked on, offered a hand on the shoulder, and a nod of sympathetic acknowledgement. When the Chief leaned in and spoke a quiet word in Lou's ear, the lieutenant looked up and scanned the crowd. The conversation abruptly ended.

Martinez turned away from Ballesteros and toward the parking lot behind Kel. Their eyes locked. A flash of anger crossed his countenance, and then guilt took its place. He dropped his eyes to the concrete at his feet. Then, with an abrupt shift, he found another route from the chapel.

"Kinnear's autopsy is still pending," Bimal was saying as Kel tuned her ears back to him, "but I'm sure we'll find a matching bullet."

"What about the cigarette butt?" Kel asked.

"No prints."

"DNA?"

"We did find skin follicles and we're running them, but that takes a while. Don't get your hopes up. Most people aren't in the database. I'll keep you posted, though, as soon as we learn anything."

Out of the corner of her eye, she saw Dirk exit the doors of the funeral chapel. With Chrissie's arm laced in his on one side and the acting chief on the other, they cut a swath like Moses parting the Red Sea through the retreating crowd. Kel waved. Chrissie nodded, whispered in Dirk's ear, and steered him with a gentle tug toward the trio under the tree.

As Dirk and his entourage approached, Bimal nodded an acknowledgment, turned and left.

"Good afternoon, Chief," Kel said, addressing the acting chief of police. She shook her head. "Tough day."

"They get no worse," he responded, then faced Dirk. "Looks like you found the best place to escape this hot sun. Just yesterday it was raining, and today it's a bake off. Now, if you're okay, Dirk, I have to lead the motorcade to the cemetery."

"Got my best people," he said and threw a wink to Chrissie. "I'll see you there."

As the chief walked away and Shelia moved close to take his place, supporting her dad by the arm,

Dirk said, "That service will be for me soon, and the way I feel this week, it won't be long now. I want a service like that, girls."

"We don't have to do this now," Shelia said.

"I know. I'm just saying I want to make arrangements while I still have strength."

"We will, Dad, but for now we should get you to the car."

"As long as I've got you and Chrissie, I'll make it just fine."

Kel looked beyond to the crowd on the sidewalk. A man she recognized was making his way to the family circle under the tree.

"Good afternoon, Chief, ladies," he said. "Jared Collins of *The Globe*. How goes the hunt, Detective?"

"We have leads," Kel said, "but you know I can't discuss them."

"Of course not. I wouldn't impose myself on an ongoing investigation. My apologies for poor timing, but I wonder if I might have a word with the chief?"

"Is that okay, Dad?" Shelia asked.

"I'll only be a moment. Just a quick question."

"It's all right, Angel," Dirk said. He turned to Collins. "What is it?"

"You remember our conversation the other day?"

In the frenzy of the week, Dirk had forgotten the telephone call Jared placed to him the morning of his former partner, Terry Graham's, death in the explosion. Now he remembered Jared asking for an interview.

"I know you want a story, and I have no good reason to disappoint you. But can it wait until this is over? With all that's happened this week, three people I knew and loved, dead, not to mention the others who were caught in the blast in Bellingham…"

"Four," Jared said, "a true serial killer."

"Four!" Dirk met Kel's eyes. "Who else, Princess? When did this happen?"

"You've had enough on your mind today with all this," Kel said, waving her hand to the crowd walking to their vehicles.

"Who?"

"From all we can tell, you don't know him. Maybe we're wrong, Daddy. Maybe this isn't about you at all."

"Who is it, damn it?"

"It's all over the news," Jared said. "Roger Kinnear."

"Roger? Roger! Oh my God," Dirk said. "I should have seen this coming."

His knees buckled, and he began to collapse on the grass. Chrissie and Shelia grabbed his arms tighter to keep him on his feet.

"This way," Kel said.

Together, Shelia and Chrissie led Dirk to a bench at the edge of the sidewalk.

Seeing there was no place to sit, Kel ran ahead. "My dad needs to sit down. Could you make room?"

An older woman wearing a powder blue pant suit sat on the bench with a wooden cane wedged between her thighs. Next to her sat a young man whose upraised brows and engaging eyes suggested he was engrossed in telling the woman a story. He turned, and jumped to his feet.

"Here, take my seat. I'll get some water."

"Thank you," Kel said to the back of the man as he ran toward chapel.

"I'm so sorry. I had no idea he'd react this way," Jared said, following the group to the bench.

"Perhaps it's best if you go now, Mr. Collins," Kel said. "There'll be no interview today."

"Of course, my apologies." He backed away.

Shelia and Chrissie settled Dirk on the bench next to the woman. With his elbows on his knees, he hunched forward and massaged his temples with his fingers.

"Everything okay, dear?" the woman asked.

"He'll be all right now," Kel said. "He's not well and has had a very stressful week."

"So that's why," Dirk said.

"What do you mean, Daddy?" Kel asked.

"I kept looking for Roger at the service. He's Susanne's brother. Damn it! Who is this DK, anyway? Does he know all my secrets?"

301

Chapter 43

Dirk Nyte sat under a green canvas awning in a plastic folding chair. Seated in the second row at Susanne Lowen's graveside service behind Trisha, Susanne's partner, and Susanne's parents, he couldn't focus his attention on the priest's discourse. His heart had been racked by grief this week, as if some monster reached into his chest, ripping at his pulsating heart with a dull blade. So many had died due to him—*and now Roger.*

Just yesterday in Interview 2, he sensed both his daughters distance themselves from him emotionally at the revelation of his affair with Marilyn. Since then, neither one of them had been able to voice with him their feelings. He looked around the cemetery. The dried and decaying flowers that once graced a headstone two rows away brought back the fear he had expunged only Monday night—"I can't go in peace wondering if someday you'll return to my grave for the last time and ask, 'who was this man, anyway?'" Now as the week wore on and the lessons DK claimed he had to teach kept mounting, the confidences were out of "Pandora's Box," as Kel had put it. And with Roger's death, a secret thought buried almost fifty years ago would now be revealed.

A bond existed between them of which even Roger had been unaware. Until today he thought it known to only a small number of people, who for the good of all, had chosen to keep it sealed. But whoever DK was, his reach and his resources had no end. The master teacher had forced him to be exposed, stark naked before the world and, more important, those he loved, with all his furtive past.

The priest's closing words pulled Dirk's thoughts back to the service.

"Ashes to ashes, dust to dust," he said, taking the Aspergillum and sprinkling holy water over Susanne's casket to consecrate her spirit back to God.

Dirk's eyes followed the priest as he made his way toward the friends and family seated in the row in front of him. Greeting each one, he gave them a blessing. He paused when he reached Trisha and wrapped both of his hands around hers. "God bless you, Trisha," he said and then turned to the woman next to her. The priest took Susanne's mother's hand and leaned forward, whispering into her ear. Dirk could feel her heartache. On the same day she was destined to bury her only daughter, something she thought she would never do, she also learned that her son had fallen victim to the same murderer—a murderer who was taking these innocent lives to settle a score with him.

When the priest finished with the family, two uniformed pallbearers stepped forward and took the corners of the American flag draping the coffin. As they folded it military style, the discordant wheeze of a lone

303

bagpipe filling with air broke the silence. In moments, its sonorous voice began to play "Amazing Grace."

Behind Dirk, a single voice began to sing the first line, "Amazing grace how sweet the sound," and then another joined in. "That saved a wretch like me," and then another. By the time the music reached the final line, the whole gathering sang in unison, "Was blind but now I see."

As he sang the last phrase, a revelation struck Dirk, and DK's motive became clear. A lump he couldn't swallow seized his throat and the more pressure it produced, the more unrestrained tears flowed down his cheeks.

Chapter 44

"Roger? Our brother?" Kel asked. She had sensed this was the only plausible answer to DK's riddle—*Four the sowing of wild fruit*—but now that the word was in the air, it seemed unreal.

Kel had driven Dirk, Shelia, and Chrissie back to the Queen Anne hill family home after the graveside service. Since it was nearing six o'clock in the evening and no one had eaten anything since breakfast, they left Chrissie in the kitchen to warm some canned soup and make grilled cheese sandwiches. The other three settled into the study to learn about Roger Kinnear.

"Half-brother, actually," Dirk said, adjusting himself in his brown leather chair.

"Mom's or yours, Dad?" Shelia asked as she took her mom's chair, each syllable clicking off her tongue in staccato.

"Mine, and before you ask, Mom knew all about him."

"And not us?" Shelia continued her inquisition as if her dad was a hostile witness. "Yesterday we learn that you had an affair with your partner's wife, one of mom's friends, and today we hear for the first time that we have a brother. I didn't know we had family secrets, Dad. I thought we were above all that."

"It was a delicate and discrete situation." He rested his hand on her leg and she jerked it away. "The girl was fourteen, and, at the time, I was sixteen.

"Fourteen?" Kel shouted and leaned forward from her seat on the rocking chair. The contempt for his actions rose in her throat with the bitterness of bile. Still angered from the concealment of his affair with Marilyn, this new knowledge threw added fuel on an already raging fire. "That's just a year older than Chrissie."

"When you put it that way, I'm so ashamed," he said and shifted his eyes away from Kel to the cold fireplace. "I was a child rapist by law. We never saw it that way, of course. We were two kids experimenting with raging hormones. By the time she figured out something was happening inside her body, she was in her second trimester.

"You have to remember," he continued and looked first to Kel then to Shelia, "that back in 1961 it was a different world. That was before the free love movement, the space race, hell, it was before the Beatles.

"Despite the voices calling her a slut, our parents felt it in the best interest of the baby that the child be allowed to come to term and be put up for adoption. Even before Roger was born, a couple said they would raise him as their own on two conditions. First, that the two families paid all the costs of the birth and adoption,

306

and second, that Roger would never know anything about it.

"Then, it must have been about ten years ago, I heard his name on television. Mom and I were watching Leno in bed one night, and a commercial came on. There was Roger pitching his furniture store. I had never seen him, not even as a baby. Mom saw the resemblance immediately. He had my chin, same as yours, Shelia."

"When I saw him this morning," Kel said, having brought her ire momentarily under control, "something seemed familiar about him, but I thought maybe I'd bumped into him somewhere. So when you saw him, did you tell Mom who he was?"

"She knew before we were married that I had a son out there. It was at the time I was fixing to head to Vietnam. Your mom had agreed to marry me as soon as I returned. So, I took some leave, and a couple of nights before I left, I told her about Roger."

"How did she take it?"

"I lost her. She had thought we were both coming into our marriage as virgins, and I had let her believe it. But somehow I knew if we started our life together with a lie, if the truth ever did come out, it'd ruin us. She was so wounded by my deception she couldn't speak to me. You have to remember we met at church. Were. both good Catholics, and even though it had been several years since I had been with the girl and before I knew your mom, it stung her deeply. Ultimately, I had orders to report to Travis Air Force Base in the Bay Area for transport to Saigon. I had to ship out without saying goodbye.

"After I left, I tried to write every day, yet it was weeks before I heard back. Receiving that letter was sheer torture. I was so afraid she had written just to tell me to stop bothering her that I couldn't open it for days. Then, when I did, it gutted like a fish, girls. Her handwriting had been blurred with tear-stains. She had wept her heart out finding forgiveness. That letter brought me home alive. It never left my breast pocket until I made my way back to her. I admit I failed her again with Marilyn, but after I got home we agreed to never keep secrets from each other."

"I guess we didn't warrant the same promise," Shelia said and stood, looking down on him.

Dirk turned his head up to her. "DK has done his damnedest to publically flog me. I know I can't un-ring any of these bells, and I know you're both hurting from all this. I can only apologize for the secrecy, but my actions hurt others not you. Not telling you two was for your protection."

"Let's at least be honest now," Kel said. "It was to protect our name from public scrutiny. From the stories you and Grandpa told us growing up, he was rising in rank at SPD at the time. His reputation couldn't bear being sullied by a son who, pardon my crudeness, couldn't keep his dick in his pants. I'll be the first to admit that I wasn't all that virtuous, but at least I owned it. I remember distinctly you chastising me for my promiscuity as a teenager and you weren't exactly thrilled that I chose to live with Lance outside of marriage.

"But with a brother we're just hearing about for the first time after more than three decades of life under this roof, an affair that lead to your partner's dismissal and possibly your own rise to chief on Terry's broken life...and now all three of them dead...There's a lot to think about."

"I know. I just hope I live to see the day when we can mend this."

"Dad," Shelia shouted, "that's not like you. You don't have to yank on the 'I'm dying card.' Give us some time, we'll get past it, just understand that even though these things happened years ago, in our minds they just happened. We need time to work through these raw emotions."

With a case to solve and her dad the focal point, Kel had to put her fury aside. She needed more information from him but she also needed a break from the emotional pressure in the room.

She stood and walked toward the doorway. "I'll see if Chrissie's needs help."

Chapter 45

"This smells and looks ridiculous, Chrissie," Shelia said, reaching for a sandwich.

Chrissie had placed a plate full of hot cheddar and Swiss cheese sandwiches stuffed with slices of tomato and green chilies in the center of the table. Bowls of steaming soup rested on royal blue placemats on each side of the dinette, and while Dirk took his usual chair at the end of the table, the others filled the remaining seats.

"Ridiculous?" Dirk asked. "I think it's magnificent."

"Magnificent *is* ridiculous when you're thirteen, Dad."

"Oh, there's that generation gap," Dirk said, lifting a spoon full of soup to his mouth. "When I was a teen, good was bad."

Chrissie laughed. "Good's still bad, Pops."

"Speaking of bad," Dirk said after swallowing the first bite, "I have a theory about our *bad* guy, DK. Look at his MO. It would seem to be all over the map. But I've begun to believe that in some way, this has to do with my tours in Nam. This DK may have been one of my men. Think about how people die in war and then correlate that with the cause of death for each of the victims."

"Suffocation, explosion, exsanguination, gunshot," Kel said. "You know, right after Susanne's death I thought that COD must be just as much a part of the puzzle as anything else. Now if this is true, it all begins to make sense."

"But what does this have to do with this guy?" Chrissie asked.

"Well, sweetie," Dirk said, "the modus operandi, or MO as we cops like to say, a serial killer chooses is generally the same act again and again. He attempts to absolve some heinous malformation in his psyche by reenacting the retribution he'd pay if the architect of his psychosis were present."

"The architect?"

"The person he feels has caused all his pain. Typical criminal investigative analysis might find it difficult to nail the MO since he chooses different forms of violence for each victim. Normal profiling has to be tweaked to understand this guy. As I see it now, each death symbolizes a different means of killing in war."

"Daddy," Kel said, "two days ago I asked you for a list of suspects from your past. You never gave it to me. People are dying. I need to know who's capable of doing this and has a severe enough grudge to carry it out."

"And just as important," Shelia added, "if this goes back over forty years, why now? Why not then? People die in war—how can that be your fault?"

"I haven't forgotten your list, Princess. As I said then, there's a lot to go through. I've been checking past cases, but nothing has popped. It was only at the graveside that the war connection came to me. I'll dig into that next.

"As to why now, though, that's a different story, Angel. There has to be a trigger. Something happened recently to push him over the edge of sanity. Look, culpability is the prerogative of the human mind. We blame who we want to blame whether truth or fiction. It doesn't have to be right or just. So, without understanding the trigger, it may make no sense to anyone else. But in the serial's mind, human rights have no bearing. Victims are only collateral damage. They just happened to fall in the path of the killer's endgame."

"So what's DK's endgame?" Chrissie asked.

"Me," he said and then turned to Kel. "You've ask *me* for a list but has your investigation turned up any clues to his identity?"

"Not yet," Kel said, placing a half-eaten sandwich on the plate next to her soup bowl, "but he intentionally left a cigarette butt in Roger's office."

"That may have his DNA," Dirk said.

"The labs working it, Daddy." Kel paused, holding a glass of water half way to her mouth. "I believe he left me that clue because he wants me to know who he is. But after his big reveal, what then? Does he plan to kill you next?"

"Maybe, but I don't think so. I think he wants me to…" He paused, digesting the thought coming to him. "…suffer…loss. Yes, that must be it. All these people in his mind may represent people he lost. Does he have children, a wife, a brother? Is he blaming me for losing them somehow? We already know each death this week strikes closer and closer to me. Just like family relationships vary in proximity. Cousins aren't as close as siblings, for example. It's like he's firing mortar rounds."

"What do you mean, Pops?"

Turning to Chrissie, he said, "Mortars are a bit unpredictable. It's all about angles and distances. So let's say you're trying to take out a machine gun. You make your best calculations and fire the first round. Once it explodes, you adjust, right, left, forward, back by changing the angle."

"So Susanne," Shelia said, "was associated to you, we thought, only because of her relationship to the Rat City Exterminator case."

"But there was more to it, I knew—"

"Because of Roger," Kel interrupted. "That makes sense. Then Terry was closer to you, because you were partners."

"And then there was Marilyn. My relationship with her was unknown to almost everyone. How DK found out is still a mystery, but he knew I'd know the significance. And with Roger related by blood—"

"Daddy," Kel said, "something's been gnawing at me since this afternoon. Bimal, one of SPD's lab analysts, said ballistics proved the gun that killed Roger also killed a high school teacher a couple of months ago. Do you remember that case?"

"Yes, our theory was that the house fire was an attempt to cover the true COD."

"Right. Since the same gun killed both Roger and the teacher, this makes DK the suspect in both murders. But why would he kill the teacher? What does he have to do with DK's lesson plan?"

"He was also a freelance writer," Shelia said. "Adam Cozens. He billed himself as an investigative journalist and had a popular blog. I followed it for a while. His mission was to expose corruption."

"That could be it," Kel said. "Sheila just this morning I said Buckley would have to have an accomplice, a common source of information. What if Cozens is the source?"

"Again, you're implicating my client."

"Okay," Kel said and shook her head, "but even if it's not Buckley, follow me a sec.

"He was killed shortly after the Rat City case was overturned. What if DK, who already hates you, Daddy, knows Cozens's penchant for exposé and approached him. What if he fed him some tidbits of information, some people to contact? All DK has to do is point him to two people with an ax to grind, Terry and someone within the SPD.

"You said the other day that Terry confronted you about his suspicion of your affair with Marilyn. What if Cozens approached Terry, and Terry told him about it? Then what if he found out about your relationship to Roger?"

Dirk shifted his weight on the dinette chair. "But those records were sealed nearly fifty years ago. Except for my mother, and with her Alzheimer's she doesn't remember any of that, and Roger's adopted parents who would have no reason to say anything, who would he contact?"

"One of your enemies, Daddy. What if DK knew of one and steered Cozens toward him? And what if that man used his authority in the SPD to dig around? And what if he ran into a fifty-year-old sealed record with the family name of his nemesis?"

"That's a lot of what ifs," Shelia said. "Do you have anyone in mind?"

Kel looked at Shelia and nodded. "I think I do." Turning back to Dirk, she said, "Daddy, what happened between you and Lou?"

"Martinez?" Dirk asked, shaking his head. "Do we really need to go into that? What could he have to do with this?"

"It's just a hunch, Daddy, but since it seems to be casting a shadow on my career, humor me, please, okay?"

"Well," he began with a deep sigh, "when I became captain of detectives at West Precinct, Lou's father came under my command. There was a lot of corruption in the squad at the time. I discovered that some of the detectives were skimming. For example, after a drug bust, they would confiscate the contraband and cash, and before they turned in the evidence, they'd take a cut. Seeing as I was new and needed to strengthen my platform, I suspended them all. The DA brought them up on charges.

315

"Lou's dad was not a part of the gang, but I found out that he knew about it and was being paid for his silence. So, I offered him a deal. No prosecution if he would resign and give up his pension. Trouble was, he was two years from retirement. He took the deal but couldn't take the dishonor. He swallowed his pistol, and Lou never forgave me. But what does this have to do with DK?"

"It may be nothing," Kel said. "But this afternoon, while Bimal was telling Shelia and me about the ballistics match on the bullet, I saw Lou and Chief Ballesteros talking outside the funeral chapel. Lou seemed very agitated. I'll swear in court that Ballesteros shut him down as if the sidewalk was not the place to have that conversation. Then right after that, Lou started to leave, and when his eyes fell on me, the look on his face was not his usual disdain. It was guilt. He couldn't look me eye to eye, and then he made an abrupt turn as if he needed to avoid me."

"So you think Lou's been digging into my past? But for what reason?"

"After what you just said, is it too far a reach to think he might want to destroy your reputation before you die? Think about it. If a noted blogger who was committed to expose corruption came to him looking for some secret in your past, do you think Lou could pass on that chance? Especially if the writer swore to keep his source's confidence. So when a positive link between Roger and the journalist showed up, Lou realized he was contributory to a serial murderer which makes him just a guilty as DK."

"If that's true, I'll have his badge."

"There'll be time for that, Daddy. If he's guilty, I'll see to it myself. By the way, how well do you know Chief Ballesteros?"

"I've known him for over twenty years, why?"

"It's probably nothing, but he either lied to me or made a mistake."

"In what context?"

"Early last Monday morning he showed up at the scene of a small riot. After we packed the perps on the bus, he came over to talk to me. He told me he had been at Benaroya for a concert. But there was no concert. He was a day off. I just wondered if it was like him to get things confused."

"I've seen it a couple of times over the last year or so, but nothing consequential. Do you think this has anything to do with the DK murders?"

"Oh, I doubt that. You know me—every i dotted and t crossed."

In fact, since speaking with Ballesteros last night, her suspicions had only intensified. Fabrications of fact gave her reasons to wonder. From the timeline of the first murder, Ballesteros could have killed Susanne Lowen on Monday morning, dropped by the Wishing Well to have their conversation about her future and then gotten back to Susanne's condo in plenty of time to Taser her. She had hardly noticed it then but she remembered now that both Ballesteros and DK had at least one thing in common. They both smoked. It was a long shot and nothing she could mention to anyone at this point. She needed facts. She needed the DNA from the cigarette butt.

"Enough of that," Kel said. "We have to figure out who DK is before he hits his next target."

"Do you think he's coming for one of us next?"

"Shelia," Kel shouted, nodding her head toward Chrissie.

"Sorry, but it's obvious, isn't it? Dad said a couple minutes ago that every victim is closer to him. It can't get much closer than his immediate family."

"It's okay, Aunt Shelia. I get it. We're all in danger," Chrissie said, and her eyes began to well. "Mom, I'm really scared."

"We're all scared, sweetheart." Kel stood, walked behind Chrissie's chair and put her arms around her neck. "But we'll be okay." She kissed her on the cheek. "We have the whole police department to protect us."

"What would you do, Dad," Shelia asked, "if the mortars were zeroing in on your position?"

"I'd give the 'dead run' order."

"What's that, Pops?" Chrissie asked and wiped a tear from her cheek.

"Dead run means everyone who can, grabs everyone who's wounded, and runs to the nearest chopper like winged scorpions were at their back."

"We seem to be short of choppers, Dad."

"I know, Shelia, but this may be exactly what he's thinking we'll do. A dead run is every man for himself. Everyone scatters with the predetermined point to regroup. In each case, so far, DK's waited until he had his victims alone, right?"

"Correct."

"Then none of us can be alone until we catch him. Alone makes you vulnerable."

"What about you, Dad? You're alone most of the time."

"We already know he's been in the house. I was alone then, and he didn't come after me. No, he wants me to live with the pain, not end my suffering by killing me. Besides, tomorrow is the Torchlight Parade. I'll have people around me most of the day."

"You'll be awfully exposed on the parade route," Kel said. "Are you sure you want to do this?"

"It's a once in a lifetime, Princess," he said, smiling, "and I can say that with assurance."

"Pops, let not start talking about you dying."

"Sorry, Chrissie, but honestly, I think I'll be fine."

"I've already set up round-the-clock police protection for you until this is over. Chrissie, you'll be with me tonight, and then tomorrow I'll have someone at the house until you go to Jessica's. What about you and Danny, Shelia?"

"Danny's with his au pair and will be tomorrow as well. I'll be working right up to the parade, so except for my drive to town, I'll be around people. I'm covered."

Chapter 46

"My blood's on your hands," he had written to the Don of the Docks and the plan worked. He now sat concealed in darkness in a street-level parking lot opposite the meeting place. The email the Don sent to his untraceable Hotmail account gave him time and place. But thirty minutes before the meet, they changed the site. That didn't matter to him. He had no intention of keeping this appointment.

He had cased the three men related to Tribune Investments for months. He knew their habits, their haunts, and this bar wasn't on their list. Though they could have sent any one of the three, he suspected Willie's murderer would be the one to show up. He'd have the most to lose if the truth surfaced and the most to gain by silencing the unknown witness. In reality he was just playing a hunch, an educated hunch, but when Jake deLaurenti walked up the sidewalk an hour ago and disappeared through the front door, all suspicions were confirmed.

Certain the Capital Hill tavern crawled with the syndicate's henchmen, he waited. By now deLaurenti would be convinced that his target was a no-show. He could picture him at a table, nursing his third scotch, despondent, having concluded that he had become the mark.

But the bar wasn't the place to take him.

Chapter 47

Chrissie lay on her bed with her pods stuffed in her ear canals listening to the latest download of the newest release by her favorite local band, Dead Toads. With the volume set at 7.0 on the Richter scale, she glanced around her room at the posters of the Toads, Taylor Swift and the boys of Twilight.

Saul, who had been absent when she awoke, nudged her arm with his cool, wet nose and then started for the door. Once at the doorway, he looked back at her.

"What is it, boy?" Chrissie asked as she removed the ear pods.

Saul whined and turned back to the door.

Chrissie followed Saul down the hall into her mom's bedroom. The Rottweiler put his paws on the ledge of the second story window and pressed his nose against the glass. Chrissie came up behind him and looked out.

"It's okay, boy," she said, kneeling on the floor and taking Saul's face in her hands, "just the police."

She figured the Seattle police cruiser parked at her curb had been there since her mom left for the day but Saul seemed anxious as he pranced around her, sniffing and panting.

Back in her bedroom she slipped out of her pajamas and threw on a pair of cotton shorts and a bulky black t-shirt. Saul trotted at her heals as she ran down the stairs and into the kitchen. While a small pot of coffee brewed, she found a single-serving container of creamed cheese and sliced a bagel. Once the coffee finished dripping, she filled a disposable cup and took the breakfast snack to the front yard. As she approached the curb, the driver's door opened, and a tall, slender man exited the car.

Saul jumped in front of Chrissie, bared his teeth, and gave a low growl.

"It's okay, Saul, heel. He's the police."

Saul held his position between Chrissie and the officer, riveted on the uniformed man.

"Heel, Saul!" Chrissie shouted. The Rottweiler then relaxed, turned about, and came up next to her.

"Is there a problem, miss?" the officer asked.

"No, everything's fine. For some reason Saul thinks men in uniform pose a threat. Mom thinks it has to do with my dad leaving for war and not coming home. Anyway, thought you might want a snack. Coffee and a bagel?"

Her path took her to the street in front of the police car, and she stepped off the curb.

"That'd be nice, thank you," he said and walked to meet her at the front of the cruiser.

"You know, Office Kent," Chrissie said, reading the last name off his badge and handing him the paper plate and cup, "I'm just fine here. As you can see, Saul's not going to let anything happen to me. I think you probably have better things to do than sit here watching the grass grow."

"That may be true, but I have a direct order to watch your house and make sure you're safe."

"I have a few chores, but after that my friend is coming over, and we're going back to her house."

"I'll be right here. You keep your doors locked." He lifted the plate. "And thanks for this."

Back in the house, Chrissie locked and bolted the front door. Then, walking through the kitchen, she unlocked and opened the back door to let Saul out into the yard.

"Play ball?" She picked up a tennis ball lying on the patio and threw it.

Saul ran across the small yard and retrieved it. After a few minutes, he tired of the game and lay down on the grass to gnaw on a bone he found. Chrissie walked back to the kitchen. Saul could come and go as he pleased through the doggie door, so she closed and locked the back door behind her, and went upstairs to pack for her sleepover with Jessica.

Chapter 48

Weeks ago Lieutenant Martinez had assigned Kel to traffic and crowd control duties during the Torchlight Parade, but, since she had taken a few personal days, she was relieved of her post. Police estimates indicated a crowd of 300,000 were expected, and now at half past five in the afternoon, as Kel pressed her Jeep through the crowd clogging the sidewalks and surface streets, she believed it.

A traffic officer with his palm stretched out toward her forced her to wait at an intersection until he waved her through. On the cross street in front of her, motorists anxious to escape the city for their Friday evening commute jostled into position for a freeway entrance a few blocks away. Despite police presence trying to keep order, the revelers meandered across the avenue and stopped the flow of traffic. The temperature in the 80s, the commuter's frustration mounted, and they took it out on their horns without effect.

She needed to make sure her dad was as comfortable as possible, and safe. In the advanced stage of his disease, he was prone to exhaustion, anyway, yet with the tension and grief he suffered this week, when she saw him yesterday, he showed such fatigue in his face she feared he'd be hospitalized before the end of the day. Dirk, a proud man, even if things were wearing on him, though, would soldier on without complaint.

She had not spoken to him after leaving his kitchen with Chrissie last night. She had parked her anger during dinner, but through the day, when her mind wasn't otherwise occupied with following leads, she tried to find a way to rationalize her dad's secret life. In the end, she could only come up with one solution. Despite the pedestal on which *she* had placed him—which was the biggest hurdle of them all—he was just as human as she was, prone to mistakes and errors in judgment.

Fifteen minutes later, she made her way to the Seattle Center where the parade would begin its annual pilgrimage down Fourth Avenue in about two hours. She left her Liberty at the curb and made slow progress walking through the mob of spectators. People in groups hustled to reserve their piece of sidewalk while street vendors hawked their wares.

As she neared the parking lot where her dad waited, white-faced Marcel Marceau rode past on his bicycle, tapping cars with his red-tipped cane. With all the chaos of the week and the dread of what was still to come, she smiled and shook her head with the knowledge that life went on anyway. Marcel's behavior was bizarre, but today his idiosyncrasy made the world eccentrically normal.

Sticking to the sidewalk, she made her way toward the convertible in which Dirk was to ride. Near it, on the edge of the lot, he sat dressed in his summer uniform, shaded under a white, plastic awning. Around him several uniformed officers stood watching the crowd—the human shield she had demanded to be put in place.

"Hey, Scott," she said, approaching her friend Scott Nillson, "have you seen Jake out here? He was supposed be part of Dad's protection."

"No, just me and the cycle cops over there."

"I haven't been able to reach him all day," Kel said.

"Well, your dad's in good hands," he said, waving toward the entourage of officers milling about.

"Princess," Dirk said.

"Daddy." She ducked under the awning and kissed him on the cheek.

Where it would often take weeks or even months for her to get over disappointment like she experienced over the terrible secrets in the last few days, she knew he didn't have that much time. Despite what she needed, he needed to know she didn't retain any bitterness. She spoke low into his ear. "Everything's alright now, I get it."

"We're okay?" Dirk asked and held her cheek to his.

She felt the wetness of his tears against her face. "We're good. Everything's going to be fine. Now, how're you feeling?"

"Couldn't be better now," he said and released her. "Stop worrying.

"Say," he continued, "after you left last night I thought about some of the men in my squad." He pulled a black and white photo from his breast pocket and extended it to her. "I had to go through some old photos to come up with it, but I found this picture from when I was stationed in Vietnam. Look at the one standing just to the right of the group. Everyone earned a handle in that squad. We called him Lone Wolf, but his given name was Darrell Klineman."

Kel examined the photo. Faded and scratched by age, the picture still captured several U.S. Army soldiers with hardened faces. Wolf, a cigarette hanging from his lips and holding his rifle by the muzzle slung like a putter over a golf caddy's shoulder, looked weary. His expression wasn't mere physical exhaustion, though; he manifested the weight of death as if it shrouded each breath he took.

"How does this man more than forty years later justify taking innocent lives just to prove some depraved point. Daddy, how did Darrell Klineman become DK?"

She lifted her eyes from the photo and looked back to her dad. He had drifted from the present into an unspoken memory.

Sergeant Dirk Nyte squinted against the debris kicked up by the chopper's decelerating blades, and surveyed the morgue patrol as they swung the first body bag from the deck to the dirt. He adjusted the sling supporting his left arm, just two days in a cast. The ache in his bicep dulled as a bitter metallic taste coated his tongue, and his stomach soured as he watched their perfunctory ritual. It lacked the solemn respect due those who had given up everything. But then he knew they weren't to blame. His job was to keep his men safe. He gave a remorseful sigh and stared as they continued to mop up his mess.

As soon as the first body was in place, Tarzan unzipped the black bag enough to reveal the face. Nyte knew what to expect. He had been here before, but some hope dared him to believe the exposed countenance would be one he didn't recognize, someone for whom he didn't have to prepare the "With your government's deepest regrets" letter. The first bag held Boomer. When Tarzan opened the second bag, O'Leary's empty expression glared back as if an accusation were being hurled from his silenced lips.

As the third bag opened, Tarzan gasped. Nyte, standing beside him, peered at the man, and grief rammed his throat. Holding back tears, he saw that Boa filled it.

"That one's a hero," said one of the men as he placed DJ's remains next to Boa. "The area around him was littered with grenade pins. Looks like he gave you boys a little insurance before they brought him down."

When the last man, Hal, came to rest at Nyte's feet, there were five bodies in the row.

"There's one more. You must've missed one?" he shouted, looking toward the empty helicopter bay.

"Where's Wolf?" Dirk said aloud.

"Daddy?" Kel squatted down in front of him and took his hands.

Dirk turned his eyes to Kel. "I left him behind, Princess. He was wounded and I left him."

"You said yesterday that a dead run means every man of himself."

"True, but as the team leader, it was my responsibility to make sure every man alive got out. When he didn't show up at the LZ, I thought he must have been killed during the run."

"And you haven't heard of him since that day?"

"No, after I returned to the States I kept up on the reports of MIAs and POWs. I followed every action taken during the 70s and 80s to bring the boys home, alive or dead. From time to time his name came up on a list, but as far as I knew, he never returned. Except for him, every other man who served with me was accounted for. I have recurring nightmares to this day about losing him."

"But he *is* alive, Daddy. The lab learned something new about him today. Vietnam may be part of the motive, but the trigger could be Willie Jenkins."

"Willie, how do you figure?"

"The DNA found on the cigarette at Roger's crime scene. It's a familial match to Willie Jenkins. DK isn't just Darrell Klineman. He's Willie's biological father."

"Oh my God," Dirk said, grabbing hold of his forehead. "Darrell's son worked for me and then became another casualty under my command. That must have been more than his psyche could withstand. That's got to be the trigger. No wonder he needs recompense."

"This may help us understand him," Kel said, looking first to her dad and then to Scott, "but we can't excuse him just because he's had a psychotic break.

Even though he didn't strike this morning, he's still out there—*Mine to reap for Hell each day.* We have no indication he's completed his lesson plan."

She still held the old photo and looked back to it focusing on Klineman's eyes. They showed the horrors of the senseless slaughter he had both witnessed and committed. But something else reached out from that picture despite its age and the distance in years. Klineman looked directly at her through the camera lens and she felt a tightening in her chest as she realized she had seen those same eyes this week.

She turned her eyes back to her dad's. "I know who DK is."

"Who?"

While she spoke, Kel felt the vibration from her cell phone. Now it rang. "Just a minute," she said as she stood and turned away from her dad and Scott. Taking the phone from her belt harness she connected the call.

"Detective Nyte, this is central dispatch. There may be a problem at your house."

Chapter 49

"What do you mean Kent didn't check in," Kel shouted into her phone.

As she had driven away from her townhome this morning, leaving Chrissie asleep, Kel pulled her Jeep up next to Officer Kent's cruiser. "She's my life, Kent. Don't let anything happen to her."

Now, she threaded her way through the parked cars in the lot, taking a shortcut to her Jeep. Anger had stopped her initial tears over panic for Chrissie's safety, and she mopped the remaining moisture from her face with the heel of her hand.

"It appears that Officer Kent was drugged after his last report," the dispatcher said. "The man claimed to be DK."

"Damn it! How'd this happen? DK was at my house? When?"

"The last time Kent checked in was eleven. With the parade, we're stretched. We didn't think to check on him until about a half hour ago when he was late for his next assignment. When Kent didn't respond after several tries, we sent another officer."

"Shit! Where's my daughter. Has anyone checked the house?"

"Pete Sanders is on the scene now, but no one's answering your door. Should he go inside?"

"Hell yes! There's a key to the backdoor hidden in the patio. Tell Pete to be careful of the dog. His name is Saul. If Pete calls him by name and gives him a sniff, he'll calm down and let him by."

The dispatcher let the phone go silent.

Winded from the anxiety and the short jog, Kel approached her Liberty. From ten feet away, she hit the transponder button, unlocking the door, and ran around the front end of the SUV. The press of passing motorists was heavy, so she waved her badge toward a man behind the wheel of an Acura and jumped into her Jeep. By the time the ignition fired the engine, the man had held the traffic back enough for her to pull away from the curb.

"Officer Sanders," the dispatcher said, "reports that Saul is lethargic. Maybe he was drugged, too, but he seems okay. The backdoor is unlocked. Sanders went inside."

"Stay with me until he's cleared the house." Even with the hole opened by the Acura, the congested streets around the Seattle Center made forward progress almost impossible. She slipped the Bluetooth into her ear and said "Dispatch, get me an escort out of this traffic."

Once headed east on Denny Way, she stayed in the left lane, following the workweek evacuation toward the freeway. Keeping one eye on the door mirror, at last she saw the flashing lights of a police cruiser traveling east in the westbound lane. The incoming traffic veered right, making way. Holding her badge out the window, to get the officer's attention, she pulled in behind him as he pressed forward.

Even with the cruiser acting like an icebreaker in a clogged harbor, progress crawled. Several minutes later, as the freeway entrance came into view a block ahead, the dispatcher came back on the phone.

"No one's inside, Kel, but there are signs of a struggle."

"Like what? I need his eyes."

"In your daughter's room several things seem to be upended, but there's nothing to indicate she was injured."

Kel could feel panic building in her chest. This was exactly how she had found Susanne Lowen's bedroom. At first glance an overturned table lamp, a dropped phone and then her dead body.

"My God, he has her," she said, forcing the hysteria from her voice. "Have Pete take a look at the computer in the kitchen. I need to hang up, but call back as soon as Pete is at the computer. "

Kel pulled the phone out and scrolled through the contacts until she found Jessica, Chrissie's friend's listing. She dialed. Voicemail answered.

"Jessica, this is Chrissie's mom. Call me as soon as you get this."

"Damn it," she muttered under her breath. With Chrissie still two days from having her cell phone restriction lifted, the phone lay hidden in the glove box of the Jeep.

Kel waved thanks to her escort as she slipped into a line of cars queued in the Interstate 5 onramp. Finally merging into traffic, she tried to change lanes heading south toward her West Seattle townhome, but the drivers on the four-lane were less forgiving than on the surface streets.

After a fruitless two minutes, dispatch called and she tapped the earpiece.

"There's a poem on the monitor."

"What does it say?" Kel asked, her mind in a sudden whirl of dread.

"Fifth   the   child
princess bore you

Now a part of my
plan too

Hard and stiff will
be as such

Hands   will   show
my final touch"

"Chrissie's poem," she whispered. Unable to slam her eyelids closed in the rush of commuters around her, she grit her teeth against new tears that formed.

"I'm sorry, Officer Nyte. Why a poem?"

"I don't know why, but DK always leaves a poem on the vic's computer."

Realizing she had leapt to depersonalizing Chrissie's fate like Nancy had at Roger Kinnear's crime scene—*The ME's with the vic now*—she slammed the heel of her hand against the steering wheel. She hadn't been at the cat and mouse game long enough to be insensitive to others' suffering, but the reflex action fit as natural as a foot in a sock. Tell a joke, make a wisecrack, refer to the person as a fatality—anything to strip them of their humanity, or else lose perspective and end up broken.

A chirp from her phone broke her thoughts. She pulled it from her belt and thumbed to the message screen.

"Snoqualmie Falls Lumber Mill," she read to the dispatcher and struck the steering wheel again. "Damn it! He has my daughter. Where the hell is this mill?"

Chapter 50

It had taken Kel over forty-five minutes to make the thirty mile drive southeast of Seattle. Once at the off ramp from Interstate 90 she fell in behind a King County Sherriff's SUV. Now at the crest of a small rise on a county road, the wall of evergreens on her left parted and the 211-foot brick smokestack of the Snoqualmie Falls Lumber Mill loomed into view. During the infancy of the twentieth century it was considered the second largest electric lumber mill in the world. Now, the abandoned plant seemed to kneel in silence like a humbled subject at the foot of Mount Si's jagged monolith erupting nearly four thousand feet out of the valley floor.

She brought her Jeep to a skidding stop in the gravel parking lot, causing a dust cloud to float toward a small cluster of county deputies. She tore open her door and stepped out. A man with sergeant's stripes on his chocolate brown shirt broke away and walked toward her.

"Sergeant Villa," he said without pronouncing either L. "Everything's secure, ma'am. We've torn the plant apart. No one's there."

"I need to see for myself." She started toward the bleached-brick building.

"I know it's your daughter. I understand. I have kids, too. So believe me when I say there's no sign of her or anyone else in the power plant. You might be better served, ma'am, to join the search over there."

Kel stopped and turned. She saw Sergeant Villa pointing to a building behind her some hundred yards away. The remains of the log-storage house rose to a height of thirty or forty feet and stretched at least a football field in length. Across the roof, the faded outline of the Weyerhaeuser brand stood out from the rusted tin like the embossed letters she remembered from her dad's original copy of The Beatles "White Album."

Her mother's protective instinct trumped her cautious cop's training, and she broke into a sprint. Crossing the clearing in seconds, she approached the central doorway. DK's whispered warning while he had her pinned with a Taser to Susanne Lowen's floor echoed in her mind—*next time I may not be so nice*. She pulled her Glock from its holster, embraced it with her flashlight, and entered the structure.

Shafts of light from deputies already searching the empty building looked to her like a lightsaber battle from a *Star Wars* movie, something Lance had loved. Since the effort was concentrated to her left, she moved right to the yet unexplored section. Sergeant Villa and two other deputies followed. The declining western sun penetrated through the breaches in the walls and made quick work of inspecting the dirt floor, so she focused a

338

search grid of each ceiling support and cross beam. Except for resident pigeons, nothing living or unexpected revealed itself.

As she approached the back of the building, a small enclosure built into the lumber warehouse took shape. Two right-angled walls, connected in the corner to the exterior siding, rose to a height of about ten feet. Unlike the outside of the building, they weathered the years with more dignity.

She trained her flashlight on a man-sized door at the end of what looked to have been a tool shed. The padlock hanging from a hasp seemed incongruous with the rest of the structure. *The building has been abandoned for decades. Why a lock?* She holstered her gun and pointed the flashlight beam on the lock. Lifting it, she realized the size of the lock and the scuff marked indentions on the wooden door beneath it didn't match.

"Chrissie," she screamed and banged on the door. When there was no answer, she turned toward Villa whom she heard come up to her side. "I need to get in here now." Turning back to the door, she pounded on it and shouted again, "Chrissie!"

Sergeant Villa dispatched a man with the name Tarza inscribed above the right pocket of his shirt and within two minutes he pulled up in his sheriff's SUV. Tarza jumped from the driver's seat with bolt cutters, slipped the blades over the lock's shaft, and, with a quick thrust, severed it. He tossed the lock to the ground.

Kel withdrew her pistol again and grabbed the door, swinging it open. She stepped into the room and penetrated the darkness with her flashlight. The beam traced the seams between the walls, floor, and ceiling until it rested on a tarp-covered mound in the furthest

339

corner. She didn't know whether to pray for some sign of life or that the heap had been abandoned decades ago.

"Chrissie, I'm here," she said and raced across the floor, keeping the stream of light fixed on the canvas. It didn't move.

Kneeling in front of it, she found the filthy oilcloth draped over a human-sized object. By the decreasing white circles of light on it, she knew the deputies were approaching, so she slid her gun into its holster and looked toward Sergeant Villa.

"No one shoot, please," she said and turned back to the tarp.

Taking the corner of the cover resting on the floor, she pulled it back.

When the lights behind her came to rest on a body propped up in the corner, she gasped—a lifeless nude adolescent female sat on the floor. Chrissie's still eyes stared back.

Chapter 51

DK knelt at the makeshift altar in his subterranean sanctuary. The sound of the construction workers had long silenced and been replaced by the cacophonous, muffled roar of the gathering throng echoing through the vacant building above. The time drew near.

Leaving for the war, he knew the risks of not seeing his wife and family again. Too many boys were coming home in a box. So, earning the moniker Lone Wolf by separating himself from his comrades wasn't a protection from the sorrow of losing friends to the enemy, rather, it grew out of the expectation that each sunrise would be his last. He had never been able to blame Agie for moving on with her life. The government led her to believe he was dead. But having been abandoned in the jungle, ripped from the heart of those he loved, Dirk Nyte's face had become the symbol of his tormentors during captivity. Once stateside, though, he realized that Dirk was not the enemy. Dirk was under orders. But when DK's son died, the disrespect that ensued fueled that latent rage.

A year of plotting strengthened the bastion of emptiness he had harbored in his soul for decades. The unrequited love of those pictured on the wall collage tormented him in captivity until he could no longer remember, but now they drove him to fill the void with forgiveness not granted. And finally, Dirk would pay.

The sun beat on Darrell Klineman's back as he sat in the cemetery. Compared to the jungle's humidity and temperature, he didn't feel the above-average, ninety-seven degree dry heat. The caretaker had pointed him to this row of headstones. "You'll find him there," he said, but before walking the row, he sat on a stone bench and thought about what brought him to this serene place.

To get stateside, he had taken the identification of one of the men who tried to kill him and found a halfway decent passport forger in Cambodia. When his plane did touch down in Spokane, Washington, the homecoming he dreamed of didn't materialize, and over the last few days, he learned that the life he knew before shipping over to Southeast Asia for his fourteen year odyssey had all but vanished.

He had stood on the wooden porch of the house he owned in 1967 and knocked on the front door. The clapboard needed a coat of paint then and even though the siding was a deeper shade of brown now, it needed the attention of another brush.

Remembering a loose plank on the decking, he stooped to see if it had been fixed. Willie had gotten a sliver in his finger playing with the board, and while he cried, his young wife, Agie, sat down on the porch cross legged with a pair of tweezers and eased it out, kissing it "all better."

Now, when the door opened, a young Mexican woman appeared with a little boy at her side. He was about the age of Willie the last time he had seen him.

"Senor, 1967 was a long time ago," she explained after Darrell asked if she knew about his family. "My husband and I bought this house six years ago. I don't remember the previous people's name or where they moved to, sorry."

That brief conversation led him to the county clerk's office at the Whitman County Courthouse on North Main Street in Colfax, Washington.

Handing a piece of paper to him, the high school-aged girl said from the opposite side of the counter, "There's a record of a Molly Klineman. She was born on February 21, 1968. Let me check on the other name for you."

He laid the birth certificate on the faded linoleum and rubbed his fingers over the name. Molly had been the name he and Agie had decided on if it was a girl. On the day he shipped over, he hadn't known his wife was pregnant, but after a couple months, she had written him with the news. He never received the letter confirming her birth, though, nor had he been able to pass out the cigars stored in his foot locker. Now he knew why. Molly, named for his mother, had been born eight months after his deployment to Vietnam, and three weeks after his confinement to the cage. She had fallen away from him as if he didn't exist.

"There's a record of a marriage," the girl said when she returned from the file room, "between Thomas

343

and Agnes Jenkins in 1975. She listed her former name as Klineman. Do you think that might be her?"

"Has to be," he said, taking the proffered document and turning away so she wouldn't see him weep.

After he left the courthouse, he stopped at a phone booth. Scanning the white page listing, he found nothing for Tom, Thomas, or T. Jenkins anywhere in the County. Agie had moved on, taking his past with her.

Before visiting the cemetery, he also scoured back newspaper issues at the Whitman County Gazette office. He discovered that the United States Congress had been frustrated with public sentiment over the unresolved Vietnam era POW/MIA "problem." Congressmen weren't being reelected, and a public outcry demanded resolution. Steps had been taken to open political discourse with Hanoi, but progress was slow and deniability high on both sides of the Pacific. A hometown boy, his name was among the missing.

Now, after sitting on the warm granite bench for a while, Darrell stood and looked down the row of headstones. He had come to the conclusion that the uniformed men in the field that day in Cambodia were a CIA sanctioned black ops hit team on a mission to end the rumors that American GIs were still being held. So, if Darrell Klineman suddenly reappeared on US soil with a story about operatives ordered to kill POWs, he believed he and his family would be in danger.

Darrell stepped onto the grass and began to read the names on the memorial stones. As he approached the last few in the row, he found the one he had expected.

"Born a beloved son 1947 Died a hero 1968"

With the grave to prove it, he turned to walk back to his rented car and left Darrell Klineman to rest in peace.

DK read his mantra aloud. "The secret things belong to God, but the things revealed belong to us."

He brought shame on Dirk with the secrets he had exposed—lust for power, lust for pleasure, lust for life—just to name a few. Now, one final lesson remained—one to teach Dirk the full burden of abandonment.

He touched a picture on the wall of Molly as an adult. Retrieving a match, he lit the final candle and placed it over the pretty smiling face representing his daughter on the altar. Then, he stood, and picked up a rifle and duffel bag from where they rested on the floor.

Chapter 52

At a few minutes before 8:00 p.m., the computer monitor flashed, and the image dissolved to black as if someone had tripped over the power cord.

"No," Shelia screamed, as she looked up from the hard copy of the transcript she had been reviewing and shifted her feet from the top of the oak desk to the mocha-colored carpet beneath it.

Yesterday, her coworker, Ryung Kim, had found some precedence that shed new light on the case they were trying. Despite her son's attempt to get her away from the office by telling his Columbian au pair to text her personal phone every fifteen minutes, the last one asking, "RU DUN," she had spent all Friday afternoon writing a brief due in Superior Court on Monday morning. She was just researching the final citation.

Now, she couldn't remember the last time she saved the document, and if she lost her work, she'd either have to cancel her trip tomorrow with Danny to the Woodland Park Zoo or return on Sunday, missing the barbecue at Dad's. Neither option had an acceptable outcome. She had little enough time with Danny as it was, and since Dad had only three months to live, missing one moment with him would be one moment too many.

She leaned forward, still seated in her desk chair, grabbed the mouse, and shook it attempting to wake the machine. Nothing changed. She knew pounding the Enter key was futile but did it anyway several times, punctuating each stroke with "Please!" But when the monitor's black eye reflected the despair on her face, it also seemed to release a sinister taunt.

Remembering she had been warned repeatedly that the IT department was to shut down all systems this evening for some kind of refresh, she punched the speaker button on the office phone. When the audible dial tone confirmed she could make a call, she jabbed the five-digit code for the firm's helpdesk into the keypad. While she waited for a voice, she turned toward the window and glanced out. The sun had yet to dip behind the distant mountain range across the Puget Sound. Boiling over them, a fringe of smoke-gray clouds threatened to cloak the otherwise pristine sky and shower the events on Fourth Avenue, 15 floors below.

Waiting there, Danny, whose impatience, doubtless seeded by an ample supply of sugared and caffeinated snacks, was only exceeded by the excitement of the sound she could hear in the near distance. The cadence of snare drums and the blare of the brass from an unseen marching band playing "Louie, Louie" echoed between the cavernous walls of the high rise structures lining the street, marking the beginning of the Torchlight Parade.

Before assistance came on the line, a familiar chirp indicated that another text had arrived on her cell phone. She turned back toward the desk. "Danny, sweetie, Mommy's almost done," she said aloud as if he was squirming just behind her, staring out the window, impatient to accost a street hawker for cotton candy or ice cream dots.

But when she realized that the display on her firm's smartphone had come to life, she disengaged the land line and reached for the Blackberry.

Her heart pounded heavy as she read the text, "Hows danny"

She grabbed the device from the desktop and swiveled her chair toward the window again. The window, a step away, she stood to type a message on the small keyboard. "Who RU," it read. While she waited for the reply, she searched the street below to locate her son. She knew the au pair had held seats all afternoon just outside the entrance to the Mangorn Building, but from her office, it was impossible to distinguish in the mob below one towhead from another.

The chirp and vibration seconds later indicted a second message arrived.

"No matter"

Frantic, she dialed the number, but after several rings with no answer, she disengaged the phone. Dropping it on the desk next to the computer, she picked up her personal cell phone and, skirting around the end of the desk, headed on a run toward the door. She hadn't taken two steps when the firm's smartphone vibrated against the desk.

Stopping with her hand on the door jamb, she looked back, stalled in indecision between running to Danny and wondering if this call would provide more information. She needed to protect him. With DK still at large—still threatening to teach her dad a lesson—she had to stop him before Danny became his next causality.

Turning back, she slipped her cell in to her pants' pocket and grabbed the smartphone.

"You called?"

The female voice in her ear took her by surprise, but then she remembered Kel saying she was sure DK disguised his voice with a voice changer. She jabbed her finger into the speakerphone button, ready to shout with the intensity warranted the interrogation a hostile witness. What she felt surging through her body, though, wasn't courtroom demeanor. The instinct to protect her young, whatever the cost, seethed.

She held the phone in front of her. "What the hell do you want?"

"You didn't answer my question. How's Danny?"

"Who are you? What do you want?"

When there was no answer, she raised her voice and repeated, "What do you want?" but still no response came. The connection died, and she knew this phase of the conversation had been terminated. She redialed, but when there was no answer, she tossed the Blackberry on the desk next to the computer again.

As she stood behind the desk waiting for further contact, her desk phone rang. Grabbing the handset, she screamed, "What do you want, you bastard?"

"I'm sorry, Ms. Savell? This is Vince at the helpdesk. Did you need something?"

Of all people to fix her computer, Vince Buckley was the last person she'd reach out to. He *was* her client, but with his alibi still not verified and with the threat now looming, she didn't know what to believe. Just yesterday in this same office she had told her sister, Kel, that her theory about Buckley was a long stretch. She still wanted to believe it was someone else, but now with his voice on the line, her professional resolve waivered.

"Huh, oh, ah, sorry," she said. "I thought it was someone else."

As she spoke, another text arrived on the firm's Blackberry.

"I see. You called. Did you need some help, Counselor?"

She sat down on the desk chair and stared at the message. It said, "IT'S YOUR CHOICE"

She lifted her fingers to her temples and massaged them with a circular motion. "Just leave us the hell alone."

Chapter 53

Only 10 minutes had passed since she found the lifeless body in the tool shed, but each tick of Minnie Mouse's second hand felt like hours. Her mission to rescue or recover Chrissie at the abandoned lumber camp had been DK's effective ploy to pull her away from the real target. The paper mask, made from a photo on Chrissie's Facebook page was wrapped around the head of a manikin—*Hard and stiff*—and the inscription on the note taped to the figure's plastic hand—*Hands will show*—confirmed it.

"False the lead that brings you here

Unspoiled still your one so dear

The messenger's last appeal

Reveals wounds that will not heal"

While she paced in the field awaiting a faster ride back to Seattle than she could navigate in her SUV, she called her partner, Jake. "Where the hell are you?" she shouted into the Bluetooth when he didn't pick up the call. "I thought we were done with voicemail."

The thump of distant rotors of the King County Sheriff's Bell 407 helicopter pulled her attention to a dot in the western sky, and she punched the code for Shelia's cell phone. Before it rang through, Jessica's number appeared across the screen.

She tapped the button on the ear piece. "Jessica?"

"Mom?"

"Chrissie, are you all right?" she asked. Hearing her daughter's voice, a weight like a wrecking ball lifted from her chest.

"Yeah. Me and Jessica are walking toward Aunt Shelia's building. Her phone was in her bag, and we just now realized you called."

"Chrissie, I want you to listen to me. Find some place you and Jessica can go inside where there are lots of people."

"We're just leaving Westlake Center."

"That's good. Go back inside, and stay there."

"Mom, you're scaring me. You said I'd be okay if I wasn't alone."

"And you will be if you do what I say. Go to the food court. I'll send someone to find you."

"What about Pops and the parade?"

"Pops is fine. Just go to the food court and watch for the police."

As she disengaged the call, the helicopter landed in the field thirty feet away. Running for the closest door, she climbed into the rear passenger compartment and leaned forward. "How fast does—"

The pilot pointed to a headset hanging next to the rear seat. After slipping it over her ears, she asked again. "How fast does this thing go?"

"It's rated at 256 kilometers per hour."

"Then Seattle and floor it," she said.

She took a seat on the left side behind the pilot and reached for a seatbelt. Beside her she heard voices and turned just as Sergeant Villa stepped into the compartment. He smiled and sat in the seat next to her. Behind him, Deputy Tarza tossed two shotguns and a case of shells on the floor. He jumped into the cabin and found a seat facing Villa.

"Sure you're up to this, guys?" she asked. "It could get messy."

"Sure." Deputy Tarza grinned. "Just another day at the office."

The drone of the blades filled her head as they pulled the aircraft into the evening sky. She took a deep breath and exhaled the mounting frustration in her chest. Her mind had been gnawing on any hidden message contained in the last poem that might reveal DK's next target. The word messenger—*The messenger's last appeal*—seemed to have a double meaning. All week DK had fashioned himself a type of messenger, conveying his lessons. "I deliver," he texted her Tuesday at Terry Graham's crime scene. But a messenger was also known as an angel, Shelia's family nickname.

She slipped the headset off her ears and let it hang around her neck. She dialed her sister again. "Come on pick up, pick up," she said in a low voice.

When all Shelia's numbers went directly to voicemail, she called Scott Nillson. "Shelia's got to be the target," she said when he answered.

As soon as she disengaged the call, she punched the code for dispatch and sent someone to find Chrissie, then punched in Bimal's number.

"Crime lab, Bimal."

"It's Kel Nyte. DK text me a while ago. I need you to get a fix on his location. And check my sister, Shelia Savell's, numbers."

Chapter 54

Scott Nillson and another uniformed SPD patrolman walked to either side of Dirk Nyte's Grand Marshal's Chrysler Sebring convertible. Ahead of them a pair of motorcycle units led the procession as if they were a planned part of the parade. Scott's idea had been to flank the vehicle, and keep their eyes on the crowd for anything suspicious. With the cheering throng lining the sidewalks on both sides, the task was impossible at best, so over Dirk's objection, they forced him to wear a Kevlar vest under his shirt. In the evening heat, perspiration beaded his forehead.

"You doing all right?" Scott asked as he came along side of the vehicle. He slid his phone into his holster.

"Never better," Dirk replied and looked to the other side of the street to wave at some children who stood, swaying foot-long battery powered torches. "Never better."

"I need to run ahead. You sure you're okay?" he asked.

Dirk stopped waving and stared back at him. "What's happening?"

"Don't know, but I've got to go."

Meanwhile, Shelia punched a text back. "What choice?"

The silence that followed was only seconds but it felt like hours. She jumped when a ping came through the monitor mounted speakers. A small dialog box glared out from the dark display and asked permission to take control. She had no choice but to surrender. She aimed the mouse pointer at the "Yes" option and clicked.

A scene from the parade route resolved. A high-stepping marching band approached her building from a block away. The music she could hear from the street below matched the rhythm of the steps of the band. Then the view panned the crowd on the Fourth Avenue sidewalk and stopped in front of her building.

As she watched, the picture zoomed in on Danny eating cotton candy off a white paper cone. His lips were pink and looked sweet. She never wanted to kiss his mouth more. Across his cherub face, a happy, innocent smile beamed as he dove in for another bite. Tearing off a piece, he used two fingers to poke the treat onto this tongue. He looked toward the au pair, said something, and then he turned his head past her. He glanced over his shoulder toward the entrance of her building. *He's looking for me.*

"You see him?" The woman's voice goaded from the computer speakers.

"Yes," she answered, with her heart in her throat, the one syllable squeezed out with such effort it sounded like a final confession at the end of a hangman's noose.

"You see that twinkling trinket necklace? It was a gift from me not twenty minutes ago. He was very happy with it."

"Damn it," she said finding her voice. "Leave my son alone."

"That's up to you."

"What do you want?"

"Patience, Angel."

Angel, a nickname her dad had called her since she was a little girl, was known within the family circle, but few outside were privy to his pet name. On occasion it would slip out when they were in public. *Is DK someone I've met, or is this another case of him having an inside resource?*

"You see, I gave him that bauble so I could pick him out from the crowd. Look close at his chest. The lights almost cover it up, but do you see it?"

She leaned close to the monitor and grabbed it with her hands as if she wanted to pull Danny to her breast. Making a frantic search, she found what DK referred to. A small red laser dot hovered just above Danny's heart. She drew on a breath that wouldn't come.

"My God, yes!" she gasped. "Don't do this, please."

"Like I said, you have a choice. He doesn't have to die today."

She released her right hand from the monitor and forced herself to control the frantic shaking as she reached into her pants pocket for her personal phone.

"I must say, you do look lovely today, albeit a little frazzled. It's too bad." The lilt of the mechanically altered voice sounded like he was in jovial mood.

"You can see me?

"Through your webcam and I wouldn't advise turning it off, either." The sudden change in his tone had a ring of finality. "You don't want to piss me off any more than I am already. You know I have a clear shot at Danny. Any inconvenience and I won't hesitate to take it."

She tore her eyes away from her son's image on the monitor and stood.

"Where you going, Angel? You can't hide from me."

Shelia stepped away from the webcam and silenced the tones on her phone. Facing the window, while she keyed in a message to Kel, she scanned the building under demolition across the street. With his line of sight to Danny, he could be taking cover somewhere in that hollowed out structure. From her elevation on the 15th floor and with the sun dipping toward the western horizon, the side of the building facing her was obscured by shadow.

Having overcome her initial heart-wrenching, breath-gasping reaction, keeping her tone even, relieved

358

that DK couldn't see her hands, she asked, "You said, 'It's too bad?' What do you mean?"

"Too bad things have to end this way."

"What way is that?"

"With a life or death decision especially on a day that had promised to be so much fun for you and your family."

She knew she didn't need to ask but did anyway. "What are my options?"

"Your life or your son's. It's your choice."

Terror returned cinching a choke hold around her chest. She didn't want her words to come out like pleading, but she was powerless to stop them.

"But why? What's this about? Why are you after Dad?"

Without looking toward her hand, she pushed the send button on her cell.

"Asked and answered," he said.

"You're so angry with him, and I'm sure for good reason. Why not just tell him?"

"After tonight, he'll know and never forget.

"Stupid girl, stupid, stupid, stupid girl," he continued. "And they tell me how smart you are—the rising star. Haven't you learned anything? Don't you realize I've taken control of your life? Everything you do is redirected to me. Every action you take from now on I'll dictate."

"What are you talking about?"

"Your text to your princess. Kel's not coming to your rescue."

"My God! How'd you do that?"

"Let's just say I have connections. But is that really the question you want to ask? Sit back down, now!"

The tangled thoughts in her head needed time to unravel. If she and Danny were to survive, she had to separate her emotions from the facts. True, he controlled every form of communication at her disposal, the computer and all three phones. She needed a low tech solution, something he couldn't track, like two tin cans and a sting, a carrier pigeon, or a signal fire, but none of those options were available. The only thing she could depend on was her mind—her litigation skills—but she had never sparred with a lunatic.

"Okay, you've made your point," she said, turning back to the webcam. The words came out as matter-of-fact as if she was ordering a pizza without anchovies, but her mind raced, searching for a way to change the direction of an inevitable train wreck.

"I concede. You have control and my attention," she said, taking a step toward the desk. "So if I choose to let my son live, what do I have to do?"

Delivering the last line felt more like having a root canal without drugs than a concession. She couldn't say "If I choose to die?" because she hadn't yet conceded it was an option. She had to believe there was a way to save them both. She sat down behind the desk.

"Good girl. That's more like it. You listening now?" he asked.

"Yes. *Oh my God, I can't believe this*."

"Just so you know how deadly serious I am, watch this."

She was relieved to see the laser dot vanish from Danny's chest. The video panned down the street, and a convertible car came into view a few blocks up the street.

"Recognize him?"

"My God, Dad. Don't do this, please. You've made your point. I'll do whatever you want. Don't shoot him."

"Him? No, not him. I want him to feel the pain his action caused. That's why you or Danny must die tonight."

"What pain did he cause you? I don't understand."

"And you never will, Angel."

"Only my family calls me Angel," she said, "You certainly aren't part of *my* family."

"This is all *about* family. Years before you were born, Dirk called me his brother and then abandoned me. So we're all part of one big dysfunctional family, aren't we? Stop trying to distract me. Watch the screen."

As the scope moved away from her dad, she felt a momentary release of the terror tightening inside her until the crosshairs came to rest on a woman sitting in the bleachers in Westlake Park.

"No!" Shelia screamed. "Enough innocent people died this week. You don't have to spill her blood."

361

He didn't respond.

"Damn it, don't do this!"

As she spoke, the sights jerked up and came to rest on a light fixture on the side of a building three blocks away. The light shattered, and the view on the screen dropped to the shards of glass spraying down on the crowd below.

"My God," Shelia said, her voice faltering from terror.

"You see, even after all these years, I'm still an excellent sniper. So, yes, I can pick Danny out in that mob, but I'd rather not. Think about it, Shelia, you have the power of life and death in your hands. You can choose life for yourself and let Danny die. I'm not sure you'll ever escape the regret, but over time, you'll heal enough to live your full life, even if you have to do it with a shrink on speed dial.

"But I can't see you doing that. You wouldn't be much of a mother, would you? If you choose to save your son, though, you'll never know what caused your end, just like the others this week. Trouble is you'll die, and it's doubtful that Danny will ever understand it, either. Even if he remembers you, what is he, four? The last time I saw my son he was three—oh the innocence. Still, he won't understand and may just grow up thinking he caused you to commit suicide."

Chapter 55

Kel cupped her hand over her eyes to shield them against the declining sun as the Seattle skyline came into view. The top edge still blazed but was quickly being swallowed by a bank of clouds pouring over the Olympic Mountains. From the rear window seat of the six-passenger Bell 407, she dialed the phone. Bimal's voice entered her ear.

"Anything?" she shouted.

"One phone's on. There have been a couple of calls in the last few minutes to one of your sister's phones, but no activity around the time you said he text you. He could be using the phone as wireless hotspot."

"What does that mean?"

"Like a modem."

"A modem…?" The picture of Marcel, battered from the Sunday night brawl, interrupted her question. He had sat in the hospital bed at Harborview Hospital on Monday typing with his mime fingers on an invisible keyboard and then pretended to send a text to a telephone.

"Damn it, he's switched to computer," she said. "I need his location now."

"He's pinging a tower in downtown Seattle. He's disengaged the GPS so I can only get you within a quarter mile."

After Bimal gave her the street boundaries, she disconnected the call. Putting the aircraft's headset back to her ear, Kel turned to the men sitting on the opposite window. Deputy Tarza and Sergeant Villa were busy shoving 12 gauge shells into the magazine tube of their SLP semi-automatic shotguns.

"It's got to be the Mangorn," she shouted into the microphone.

"That's on the parade route," the pilot bawled, looking over his shoulder. "It's in the no fly zone."

"For civilians maybe. Get me there now."

"Suicide?" Shelia screamed at the computer speaker.

"Of course, what better way?"

"No one who knows me would believe I'd kill myself."

"Happens every day, Angel. The news reports that someone off'd themselves and no one saw it coming."

"I'm not your angel."

"Of course, how could I be so callous? That aside, I'm getting weary of all this chatter, so make your choice, you or Danny."

"Every mother's instinct I have is to save him. What if you're bluffing?"

"Let's see, how many people died this week in my lesson plan? Does that sound like a bluff? What's it going to be? No more stalling."

"Isn't there another option?"

"No, like your computer, it's binary—zeros and ones. You live or he lives, and you have thirty seconds left to decide."

"First, what assurance do I have that if I kill myself you won't shoot my son next?"

"You have to trust me."

"Do you think that's likely?"

"Negotiations have been concluded. Tick tock, missy. If you don't decide, I do, and your son sleeps with the real angels tonight."

"If I agree to sacrifice myself for my son, how will you know I've done it? What am I supposed to do? Do you have a gun hidden in my desk? Is there a razor blade so I can slash my wrists? Are there pills I can swallow?"

"No, those are too easy."

"Then what?"

"You're going down to the 12th floor and jump into the crowd below from the terrace."

"Jump!" she screamed. "I could never do that."

"Then say goodbye to Danny now."

She looked back at the monitor and saw the camera centered over her son's innocent little heart. The twinkling necklace almost disguised the red dot, but she could see it as if it were a lighthouse beacon on a clear night.

"No," she shouted.

"So, you've made your decision?"

"Yes."

"Good, now take your phone with you so we can keep in touch, and no unnecessary stops at a coworker's office or the ladies room. If I don't see you on the 12th floor balcony in two minutes, Danny's blood will be on the sidewalk. Move now!"

"I don't know if I can get there in time. That's three floors."

"One minute 55 seconds."

"The phone doesn't work well in elevators or the stairwell. What happens if I lose you?"

"One minute 47 seconds."

Flying over the high-rises, Kel realized Danny could possibly be a target, too. She called Scott.

"Do you have Shelia yet?"

"No," he said, panting for breath. "We're just coming up to her building now."

"Look, Shelia's son could also be in danger. Get him to safety."

"In this mob? Are you kidding? How could anyone find him?"

"He'll be near the Mangorn. His name is Danny, and the nanny's name is Drina. Hurry."

Chapter 56

As Kel disconnected the call, they hovered over the helipad atop the Mangorn Building. The phone rang again. She tapped the button on the Bluetooth.

"He just turned another phone on," Bimal said. "And the GPS is on."

"Where is it?"

"Patience, I need a few seconds."

"I'm all out. I need to know now. Where is he?"

"He is in the middle of the block on Fourth Avenue between University and Union."

"The Mangorn, that's where I am."

Leaning forward, she shouted to the pilot, "Put this thing down."

"Wait, Kel," Bimal said. "He might be across the street."

"Across the street? Damn it, of course." She disconnected the call.

"No, not here," she said into the microphone.

The pilot nodded and gave a gentle tug on the control. The Bell rose a few feet and banked left over the parade route on Fourth Avenue more than four hundred feet below.

Kel looked out the window and down twenty-three floors. In the lights of the Mangorn she saw the outline of the condemned terra-cotta building Shelia had tried to save. With the sun having dropped behind Mount Olympus and no lights coming from the inside of the shell, the final glow of twilight defining the ridge surrounding the roof gave the only indication of the speck they would have to land on.

"Put it down there," she said, pointing to the rooftop.

"Cannot do, not big enough for touchdown."

"Can you get me in close?"

"How 'bout close enough you won't stub a toe?"

Shelia ran down the stairs two at a time and arrived on the 12th floor. The door was secure, and her pass key wouldn't open it. She looked at her phone's display. Only one bar showed, but she heard DK say, "You have ten seconds, Angel."

"I'm on the 12th floor now, but I'm in the stairwell and can't get out. Even if I could, I don't know if I can get out to the balcony. I have to go back up. I need more time. Please."

"Damn it," he said.

"What's happening?" Shelia asked. Something had changed, she knew it, but whether it swayed in her favor she could not discern.

"Nothing to concern your pretty little angel wings with. You have two more minutes to get to the balcony before Danny meets Jesus face to face."

"That's not enough time. I have to climb to an unsecured floor and then hope the elevator will take me to 12."

"Why aren't you moving?"

A few moments before, Scott had entered the lobby of the Mangorn Building, and found a man in a blue blazer, white shirt, and skinny dark tie behind the security desk. "I have to get to Shelia Savell's office now. This is a high priority police matter."

"Yes, sir, right away," said the young man. As he moved out from behind the counter, a blush made a sudden appearance against his otherwise pale cheeks.

Scott turned to follow him to the elevator but stopped when he heard another voice.

"What's happening?" said a young Latin American woman. She held the hand of a little blond boy.

Coming through the revolving door right behind them, a uniformed police woman stepped into the lobby.

"Are you Danny?" Scott asked, walking toward the two civilians.

Danny looked to the au pair as if asking permission to speak.

"What's going on? Am I in trouble? We were just waiting for Mrs. Savell, Danny's mother."

"You're in no trouble, but I need you to wait inside." Seeing the lobby window was tinted, impossible to see in from the outside, he pointed to it. "Maybe you can watch the parade from over there. Why don't you stay with this officer?"

"Si," she said, "but I don't understand."

"The officer will explain," he said, looking to the police woman.

"Sure, let's go over here," the officer said. "Danny, would you like to sit on my shoulders? You can probably see real good then."

As he turned back to the security guard who was holding the elevator, the lobby door spun again. Scott turned and was relieved to see three patrolmen, one a motor officer who had also been accompanying Dirk, enter.

Affirming their presence with a nod, Scott said to the guard, "Shelia Savell's office."

The sound waves of a helicopter's blades echoed off the surrounding buildings with such intensity DK could feel them in his chest. Looking up he saw the aircraft swoop over the top of the building across the street. With Fourth Avenue bright with the lights of the Torchlight Parade, the white underbelly and the bold word "Sheriff" across the tail boom were easy to target.

Having just realized Danny and the au pair had disappeared from the sidewalk, he raised the barrel of a Mauser Airsoft sniper rifle.

Kel looked down toward the building across the street. She couldn't see any movement. DK had to be there for his final act of terror, but even though the building was a dwarf among its towering neighbors, every floor would have to be searched, room by room.

As she scanned each level, holding the aircraft's headset to her right ear for communication with the pilot, a white flash appeared in her peripheral vision, followed by the thunk of metal piercing metal.

"We're taking fire," she screamed into the microphone.

"No shit," said the pilot, pulling the stick hard right away from the building. "We got to land somewhere else."

"Like hell, you put me down there."

The g-force of the sudden lurch pressed Kel against the passenger window. She continued to scan the condemned building, searching for any indication of where the gunfire had erupted. As she probed the shadowed hulk, a second muzzle flash burst, and, just inches from her face, the window imploded, sending a shower of glass shards into the compartment and the ping of a single bullet ricocheting through the cabin. Twisting to her right, she dropped her head away from the airborne shrapnel.

"You hit?" Sergeant Villa yelled.

"No," Kel said and then looked up to Villa.

He was unfastening his seat belt and reaching across to Deputy Tarza sitting opposite him. Tarza's left hand was wrapped around his arm just below the right shoulder. Blood ran between his fingers, turning the sleeve of his dark brown uniform shirt even darker.

"Must'a caught that rebound," he said. "Bastard got a lucky shot. Guess I'm not going to be much help down there after all, Sarge." He nodded toward the street.

"Harborview," Villa shouted to the pilot.

"Like hell," Deputy Tarza said. "Drop these two first, and then I'll take a ride to the hospital."

Chapter 57

Scott, the three patrolmen, and the security guard, arrived at the 15th floor. With their guns drawn, Scott led the three officers through the elevator doorway, leaving the guard in the car until they cleared the elevator lobby.

Hearing a sound to his right, Scott turned to find another elevator door at the far end just closing.

"Wait, SPD," he shouted and ran to try to stop it. He was one step too late when the double doors slid shut.

"Damn it. That could have been Shelia." Turning to the guard who walked out the elevator, he asked, "Any way of knowing what floor that lift is heading for?"

"Not from here. Could from the lobby, but no one's there."

"Okay, then, where's Mrs. Savell's office?"

"According to our floor map," the guard said, holding up a magenta-colored three-ring binder, "she'd be on the west side. This way."

Scott stationed two of the patrolmen in the elevator lobby, one securing each end's point of entry, and with the motor officer, followed the guard. After the rosy-cheeked guard slid a pass card through an electronic reader, a click released the glass door, and he pushed it open.

"Which way?" Scott asked as he followed the security man through the opening.

"About half way down." He pointed to the left.

"Wait here," Scott ordered.

Shelia's elevator stopped on the 12th floor. *Thank God*, she thought, and then realized thankful was the least thing she felt. She was delivering herself to the murderous whims of a mad man, but she couldn't focus on the terror facing her, only Danny's salvation.

As the elevator doors slid open, she looked at the display on her phone. Three bars showed.

She lifted the device, holding it in front of her mouth. "I'm heading for the balcony now," she shouted. "Please don't hurt Danny."

"You only have a few seconds left before I pull the trigger."

"Please, God no, wait. I'm at the door. Damn it, it's locked."

"Ten, nine…"

"Stop, please. Don't shoot, please."

"Seven."

She slid her access card through the reader. The light turned red.

Scott and the motorcycle patrolman ran down the hallway between the secretary cubicles on the left and the windowed lawyers' offices on the right. Outside each door, a name plate identified the occupant. After passing four doors, they came to the one marked "Shelia Savell." Without hesitation, Scott burst inside the lighted room and made a quick assessment. Shelia wasn't there, but from the work scattered across the desk, it looked as if she had plans to return. No signs of struggle indicated she was in any trouble, so, if she actually was, she had been coerced by some other means to leave the room.

While Scott secured the room, the second officer entered behind him and walked to the window, looking down to the parade below.

Satisfied there were no clues to Shelia's state, Scott turned to leave. "We're clear here."

The motor officer turned to join him and stopped when he faced the desk. "Look at this," he said, pointing to the computer monitor.

Scott turned back and stepped around behind the desk to look where the officer pointed. The letters were a simple, black Arial font set against a white background, but the words had been penned by a demented mind.

"Damn it to Hell," he uttered and couldn't tear his eyes away while he read the words.

"Fifth the angel of the court

Recompense with no retort

Falls from grace, she cannot fly

Chooses death without goodbye"

Chapter 58

The pilot swung a full clockwise circle and brought the aircraft over the towers on the west side of Fourth Avenue. They made slow, forward progress until he pulled the Bell over the building next to the terra cotta structure.

"Get ready," shouted the pilot's voice in her ear.

"I don't see it."

"It'll be below you in seconds. You guys get one chance. If we're lucky, we'll surprise the bastard, but in case he's on the roof, we're going in dark. Open your doors, step out on the skids, and be ready to jump on my go."

"All in a day's work," Deputy Tarza said with a wink to Kel.

She glanced at him and tossed him a smile. "Take care of yourself."

Tarza, still holding his injured right arm, turned his right hand into a thumbs-up sign. With a wink, he said, "Thumbs airborne."

The cabin lights went out.

She felt for the door handle, and as she slid the door open, she recalled stories her daddy had told about jumping out of choppers into firefights in Vietnam. She never pictured herself in a similar setting, but now that she was about to make a leap that could cost her life, she felt no fear.

She removed her seatbelt, sat on the floor, and hung her legs outside until she found the skid with her feet. Standing, she turned around and took the handrail on the outside of the aircraft.

"Ready," she shouted into the microphone.

When the aircraft lunged forward, Kel slammed her eyes shut and caught her breath. The several-story vertical drop reminded her of a free-fall amusement park ride, a thrill she never relished. Steadying herself, she tore her right hand away from the handrail and pulled her Glock from its holster.

The chopper came to a sudden stop and the pilot's voice screamed in her ear, "Go, go, go!"

Tossing the headset into the cabin, she let go of the handrail and jumped into the darkness.

"One," said the woman's voice through her speakerphone.

Shelia slid her pass card through the reader again. This time, the light went green. Shoving the door out of the way, she burst onto the deck.

"I'm here! Don't shoot Danny."

There was no response.

Hearing the throb of an engine and a loud whirring above her, her eyes followed the sound across the street. The only thing visible was the green and white position lights and the dark shadow of a helicopter against the lights of the high-rise a block to the west. It rose into the night sky.

"I'm here!" The hysteria trembled her voice to where she could hardly speak.

"Climb out on the edge," said a new voice through her speakerphone. No longer masked by the voice changer, it was a voice she heard had before.

"Who is this?"

"Not your worry. I still have Danny in my sights, and I'll take him down if I don't see you step over that rail right now."

Shelia looked back across the street. She knew DK had to be there, but the dark shell facing her gave no indication of where.

"Okay, I'm stepping over the edge. Oh my God, is there no other way to save my son?"

Shelia raised her left leg over the rail and sat on it. *One more to go,* she thought, but it was as if her foot had been nailed to the deck.

"My God, I can't do this. Just shoot me. You'll still have your revenge."

"That's not the deal. Now we know how much you love yourself. Just like good ol' dad. Too concerned about self-preservation to make the final sacrifice. Seems you've chosen with your cowardice."

"No wait. Look, I'm swinging my other foot over."

Holding onto the handrail behind her, she felt the edge of the deck with the heels of her feet. *God help me.*

"Good girl. Now, don't look down. The next step is the easy one. Just close your eyes, lean forward, and let go."

"Where's the closest place someone could jump?" Scott said as he ran back to the building security guard standing inside the glass door to the elevator bay.

"Jump?"

"Yeah, commit suicide."

"Uh, don't get asked that question every day."

"Damn it, this is life or death, man."

"Uh, uh, uh…12th floor, there's a balcony there."

"Lead the way."

Before searching the floor, Scott had pulled the Stop button on the elevator. Now the five men raced to the open door.

"Twelve," Scott shouted.

The motorcycle officer slammed the Stop button with the heel of his hand and then hit the 12 button. Nothing happened.

"Let me," said the guard, and pulling his access card on the elastic tether binding it to his belt, he swiped it across the reader and pressed the button again."

The elevator moved.

As soon as Kel felt the roof under her feet, she squatted down, prepared to meet DK.

She heard a voice as the sound of the helicopter faded into the distance. "This way."

Kel pulled her flashlight and pointed the beam. It fell on Villa. He had run across the roof to the opposite side and now knelt next to a door providing access to the building. Under his left arm he embraced two shotguns, and in his right hand he held a box of shells. He looked away as her beacon hit his face, so she lowered the light and ran after him.

"This is your scene," he said. "How do you want to play it?"

"Slow and careful. We'll take the stairs, clear each floor, and then meet back at the stairs before descending to the next level. When I saw the muzzle flashes a few minutes ago, they looked to be mid-building but I couldn't tell how many floors down."

"He could have repositioned."

Kel nodded and eased the access door open. Casting her flashlight beam through the opening, she made a quick search down the stairway.

"Clear, let's move."

"Want this?" Villa asked and held out Deputy Tarza's shotgun.

Stepping into the doorway, she said, "Thanks, but this'll do me just fine." She held her Glock in front of her and descended the concrete stairs. Villa's breath, labored with tension, right behind her.

The door had been removed from its hinges on the next level, leaving a wide opening to the floor. She motioned for Villa to check right, and then they stepped from the stairwell into a large, open room. Except for floor to ceiling columns, there were no walls to obstruct their view. Quickly sweeping their beams around the room, they found it to be clear.

As they made their way back to the stairwell, the crack of a rifle exploded somewhere below them and echoed through the building.

Meanwhile, Scott and his men arrived at the 12th floor.

"Where's the balcony?" Scott asked the guard as the door opened to the elevator lobby.

"On the west side, follow me."

"No! You wait here."

The building guard, a year out of high school and a short distance track runner, disregarded Scott's order. He shot through the elevator doorway and sprinted across the open lobby.

"Wait, damn it," Scott shouted after him. "This is a police matter."

He didn't stop. Scott gave chase with the other officers at his heels. The gap between them opened further.

Sliding his access card through the reader, the guard charged through the doorway onto the balcony. Shelia stood on the outside of the railing. With a soft, assuring voice, he said, "Ma'am, don't do it."

The voice surprised Shelia, and she turned with a jerk, jarring her left foot. It slid off the edge, throwing her off balance, and she grabbed for the rail, wrapping her arms around it. As she did, the phone slipped from her hand. Her lifeline to Danny fell out of reach.

A shot blasted behind her, and the young guard crumpled to the deck in front of her.

"Oh my God!" she screamed.

Scott reached the door before it closed and stepped over the guard. "Shelia, don't jump."

"I have to save Danny." Tears of terror choked the words back, making them nearly inaudible.

The other three officers crowded through the doorway. While two of them took a kneeling position, pointing their service weapons across the street, the motor officer knelt by the guard.

"Danny's safe. We have him. I spoke to him and the nanny on my way up." Scott looked at the officer next to the guard.

He lifted his fingers away from the man's carotid artery and shook his head.

"Are you sure?" Shelia said.

"Yes. Let me help you."

As Scott reached out to take her arm, another pop echoed between the buildings, and a slug hit him in the chest, knocking him backwards into the doorway.

Facing the balcony, hanging on to the railing, the two men down were more than Shelia's knees could take. They buckled.

Hearing the second shot ring out as they approached the turn in the stairwell between floors, Kel said, "That one's close"

A volley of distant rounds echoed through the vacant building and ricocheted off the concrete. "Reinforcements," she added.

"That's good news," Villa said. "Maybe they can keep him busy until we find him."

As he spoke, the vibration of her cell phone startled her at first. She grabbed it off her belt.

"Bimal?" she said with an agitated whisper. "This better be good."

"Not so sure it is. In the last couple of minutes he powered up a third phone. You're right on top of it."

"Damn it," she said and disengaged the call.

"What's that?" Villa asked.

"Whatever it is, it can't be good. Watch for something suspicious."

"Can you give me a hint?"

"This guy knows bombs. He may have rigged the place. My guess is stairwells."

"Shit, that's comforting," he said, glancing down the stairway in front of him.

"Sorry I got you into this, Villa. Not too late to turn back."

"Never ran from a good fight. Don't plan to now."

"Then let's finish it."

Training her flashlight beam down the next dozen steps, she cleared the stairwell and took each riser at a slow, deliberate pace. When they reached the next level, like the floor above, the door was missing. They stepped through the opening.

Chapter 59

The two officers who had taken a kneeling position on the deck fired toward the muzzle flash across the street a floor above them. The first one called dispatch, "Shots fired, one dead, officer down."

The motor officer turned away from the dead guard and toward Shelia's scream. Her feet slipped off the edge and then her body dropped. The fingers of one hand remained visible, grasping the bottom of the railing.

He reached between the wrought iron bars and grabbed her by the forearm.

"Can you reach my other hand?" he asked, extending his other arm through the bars.

She looked up, her free hand flailing toward his. Clutching it, he stood, pulling her up.

"Could use some help here," he said.

One of the other officers holstered his pistol and moved to the edge where Shelia was suspended in midair. Putting his arms around her waist, he pulled her over the rail. The motor officer, whose hands were under the rail, let go of Shelia's arms to grab her legs. When she was halfway over, another shot came from the window across the street. The officer with his arms around Shelia's stomach pulled her the rest of the way over the rail, but not before blood and tissue sprayed into his face.

Kel heard the third shot, and, realizing it was still below her, ran to the stairwell. Villa met her at the doorway, and they descended the stairs, taking them two at a time.

Reaching the landing of the next floor, Kel's flashlight caught an object wedged between the wall and a water pipe.

"Sergeant," she said, anxiety and panic reducing her breath to a whisper. She pointed to the object on the wall.

"Is that what I think it is?" he asked.

Only a few moments before, Shelia had begged DK to shoot her so she wouldn't die in the fall. Now, as the officers drug her over the railing, terror that the next bullet would rip through her body gripped her anew. She and the motor officer tumbled to the deck together, landing on the still body of the security guard. The officer's left arm was slick with blood.

"He's been shot," Shelia said as another bullet disintegrated the window behind her.

"You get inside," the officer who had taken her by the waist said. "We'll take care of him." Then dropping to the floor several feet from the third officer, he took aim at the window across the street and squeezed off three rounds in rapid succession.

Shelia found her phone on the deck and scooped it up as she slid toward the door on her stomach. Slithering past Scott's body, she fought the urge to flee for safety, grabbed his arms and pulled him through it.

"Can you get yourself inside?" the second officer said, turning toward the motor officer.

"I think so," he said and groaned. He rolled off the guard's body and made his way through the shattered window opening.

"It's meant for us," Kel said and took two rapid steps toward the bomb. She peeled the C4 from the wall.

"What the hell?" Villa whispered. "That could go off at any second."

"With all that gunfire out there, I'd say he's too busy right now. Besides, it has a cell phone detonator. If I pull this wire, this thing's harmless—I think."

Chapter 60

Shelia dragged Scott to a small lounge and put a concrete pillar between him and the bullets still ripping though the building. As she slumped to the floor next to him, she threw her face into her hands and gave in to the terror that had gripped her in the last few minutes. Bracing against the uncontrolled tremors surging through her body, she lost the battle against tears.

Next to her, she sensed movement.

"Damn asshole," Scott groaned. He opened his eyes and lifted his hand to rub his chest. "Feels like a Mac truck slammed into me."

Shelia dropped her hands from her face and smiled. Placing her hand on his shoulder, she said, "Glad you're still alive, Scott. Are you sure Danny's okay?"

"Talked to him myself."

"My God, thank you. If you hadn't come...I...I'd be dead right now."

Supporting his torso with his elbows, he slid up to a sitting position and leaned against the post. "Kel sent me, Shelia. It's her you should thank."

"You think?" Villa said.

"Don't you remember basic bomb training from the academy?" Her best defense against uncertainty had always been a sense of humor. "What's the worst that can happen?"

"That we get blown to Hell."

"That wouldn't be so good," she said, holding the explosive up. As she grasped the green wire, her heart pound hard against her breast bone.

"Why the green one?"

Kel could hear the tightness in his throat.

"I like green, you prefer red?" She took the red lead, looked toward Villa and, with a quick jerk, pulled the tip from the plastique. "Whew, looks like we're not going anywhere just yet."

While the two officers continued firing toward the windows in the condemned terra cotta, the motor officer low crawled on his stomach using his right arm to pull himself toward Shelia and Scott. He drew up next to them.

"Thought you were dead," he said to Scott.

"Early rumors—that, and Kevlar," Scott said with a chuckle. "Oh God, that hurts! I think he broke a rib."

"While I was grabbing her," the motor officer said, nodding toward Shelia, "I saw a couple of flashlights on a floor or two above the perp."

"That's got to be Kel over there. Look, you're hurt bad. You stay here. Shelia, call 9-1-1 and get medics rolling. I'm going to help with cover fire."

Kel and Villa stepped back to the concrete wall next to the door and took cover. She looked around the jamb. Her flashlight beam revealed that, unlike the other floors, this one had interior walls. Rich walnut paneling, not yet removed by the recyclers, formed a hallway.

Using the flashlight beam to scope a path down the passage, she found the floor clear of rubble. Thirty feet down, a gap in the paneling opened to the left. She turned the light out and moved into the hallway.

Since the guns had gone silent on both sides of the street, she tried to push aside the fear that something dreadful had happened to her sister. But it nagged at the back of her mind like a developing migraine. She leaned against the wall next to the opening and was about to charge into the room when shouts and shrieks of the confused spectators on the parade route drifted into the building. Cutting through the chaos, a loudspeaker from a police cruiser announced, "Everyone clear the area immediately."

With her pistol pointed to the ceiling, she wondered if they had taken her daddy to safety yet, or if he was even in the proximity of the gunfire. In the ambient light from the city pouring through the open doorway, Villa appeared squatting against the wall across from her. He pointed the shotgun toward the opening.

"Goddamn it!" a man's voice shrieked from inside the room. Following immediately, the discharge of several rounds from an automatic pistol echoed though the empty space.

"It's over, Klineman," Kel shouted, waving Villa's shotgun off.

"Not yet. I'll drop you, Princess, just like I did Angel. Beautiful sight, her arms flailing helplessly as she plunged to the street."

She wouldn't allow herself to believe it. She had sent Scott to protect Shelia, and she trusted him. "I don't buy it, Darrell."

"Darrell Klineman's dead. Has been for decades. And now it's time to finish the hunt."

Just a few hours before when she saw the picture of Darrell Klineman, she put the eyes with the man but she still needed confirmation. And now she had it. She recognized the voice as soon as he spoke, but using the word "hunt" gave absolute validation. Three times in the last five days DK had spoken that word directly to her— once while he pinned her to the floor of Susanne Lowen's condo with a Taser and once on the phone while he stood over Roger Kinnear's murdered body. The last time she heard it, the word came from Jared Collins at Susanne's memorial.

Before she could speak, a hail of bullets from across the street tore holes and splintered the antique paneling above her. Waving Villa to head back to the stairwell, she hesitated for two seconds and then followed, stooping low.

Chapter 61

"Hey Princess. I told you we'd meet again."

Jared's voice came from the hallway where seconds before she had couched. The stairwell thrust Kel into complete darkness. The sound of bullets tearing through the walls seemed amplified as they echoed off the stairwell's concrete walls, and then they went silent. Next to her, Sergeant Villa panted heavy. Until the last hour, she didn't know him, but Villa standing on the first riser, armed with two shotguns, she gave her comfort.

"Be ready to move," she whispered, "this could go to Hell in a hand basket real quick."

She turned her head toward the opening and shouted, "Give it up, Collins, there's no reason you have to die today."

"So you know who I am." Jared stopped in the hallway three feet beyond where Kel knelt seconds before.

Keeping her voice even, she said, "Daddy remembers you as Lone Wolf, a good soldier he told me. He thought you were killed in the retreat, but when your body wasn't returned only then he realized he had left you behind."

"Yet here I am in the flesh."

"He still has nightmares about that day."

"I lived those nightmares in real time and when I *did* get home, they didn't stop. Because of him, I lost my family, including the only woman I ever loved."

Kel sensed the hatred in his voice. The syllables clicking off his tongue were as percussive as the distant snare drums she heard even now tapping a marching cadence from blocks away.

"But that's the catastrophe of war. Governments throw away innocent lives in their greedy quests. Dirk can't be blamed for what happened to you or any of his men, for that matter. It was out of his control. People die, are physically or emotionally maimed for life, and sometimes go missing in war, but—"

"I knew you of all people would understand."

"I do. I sympathize with you. Our government says my Lance is dead, but they never brought him home for me to bury. Yet I don't feel the urge to bring his superiors to some self-designed justice. We can't act out the lesson plans we might want just because life dealt us a bad hand."

"Dirk let my son be taken away from me twice."

"Willie?" she asked, her tone bordering on reverent.

"So you figured that one, too?"

"You made it easy. You gave me your DNA. Jared, Willie was my friend. I miss him, too."

"At least you got to know him. He hardly knew me as dad, let alone a war hero or best-selling author."

"You said Dirk took him twice. What did you mean? Why did you want to point me to Willie?"

"Because after he was killed, Dirk turned his back on him just like he did me."

"Jared, he hasn't forgotten Willie. There's an ongoing investigation."

"Which without me would never have been solved. His death is an SPD cover-up."

"What? Are you saying the department knows who killed him?"

"I'm saying the department assassinated him."

"That's preposterous," she said, unable to mask her surprise. "Who exactly? And how do you know this?"

"You know it, too. I checked the history on my computer at *The Globe* after you left my office on Tuesday. There could only be one reason you were checking into Tribune Investments. If you're the detective I believe you are, you've made *his* connection."

"Do you mean Jake deLaurenti?"

"So you say."

"Is that why I can't raise him? Where is he, Jared? Have you killed him, too?"

"Those, Princess, are questions you may never find the answer to. But I'll say this, polluted waters run deep."

"Is this another of your riddles?"

"That's enough talk."

Realizing she wasn't going to get an answer and that negotiating with a sociopath with a death wish was beyond her bachelors in psychology degree, she shouted, "Put down your weapons. You're under arrest."

"Not likely," Jared said.. He slapped a fresh magazine into the automatic pistol.

The stairwell became claustrophobic as bullets ricocheted off the concrete walls. The sound so deafening, Kel threw their hands over their ears as she stumbled behind Villa in the gloom up the stairs half a flight to the turn. As she came around the corner, grasping for the unseen railing, something hit her hard in the side, and her foot slid out from under her. She cracked her shin against the concrete riser and fell to her knees.

"Damn it," she said under her breath, grabbing her side.

Villa, above her on the step, groaned.

"You hurt?" she asked.

"Caught one in the leg."

Her left side began to burn. "Can you continue up?"

"Think so."

"You go," she said, reaching to the pain and feeling the warm ooze of blood from a bullet hole. "I'll hold him off."

"You sure?" Villa turned on his flashlight. Seeing the blood on her shirt, he said, "You're hit, too. I'm with you."

"It's just a nick. So don't argue. This is my war. He chose me."

Villa hesitated, shook his head, and made his way up the stairs, using one hand to put pressure on his wound.

She felt for the handrail and pulled herself to her feet. The burn turned to an ache and radiated into her abdomen. A half flight of stairs below, she heard the metallic snap as Jared slipped a new magazine into the pistol.

"Still with me, Kel?" he asked. He pulled a phone from his pocket.

"Not going down that easy." She reached to the wall on the downward side of the stairwell. The scuff of Jared's foot against the floor gave her an indication that he was walking toward her. She leaned against the wall, weakness creeping over her.

"It might be easier than you think, Princess."

"I know you won't believe this, but I have you surrounded. It's time to end this."

"I certainly don't see anyone, but you are right. Lesson's over."

From somewhere below her, the detonation of an explosive device ripped through the stairwell. The concussion knocked her back to the floor. Before she could stand to run further up the steps or slam her eyelids closed, a torrent of broken concrete debris rebounded off the walls and risers, raining down around her. She threw her hands over her head, and her Glock skittered away.

Once the thunderous reverberation stopped, Kel opened her eyes. She was enveloped in a dense cloud of dust and smoke. Filling her lungs with the first gasp, she coughed to expel the contaminated air. She pulled a cloth handkerchief from her pocket and held it over mouth. The deafening sound had muted her ears, but within seconds they began to ring back to life. She shook her head to expedite the clearing.

"You all right?" shouted Villa from a flight above.

"Okay," Kel said, gritting her teeth against the throbbing pain in her side. "Stay put."

She reached to the floor to search for her pistol.

The explosion knocked Jared to the ground. Hearing voices inside the stairwell, he stood. Withdrawing the pistol from his belt, he pointed it toward the cloud billowing out the doorway.

"You told me I was surrounded, Princess. Still don't buy it, but one thing you probably don't know about me is that this isn't the first time the government has sent a team to kill me. They called it black ops in '82. I was unarmed when they arrived that day, but I buried them all anyway. You haven't got a chance. That first blast? It was just a warning. Next bomb's for real, Kel. Final lesson for dear ol' dad."

While Jared ranted, she located her Glock. She made her way back to the wall and pulled herself to her feet. With the cloth over her mouth, she eased down the stairway, feeling her way with her feet so as not to slip or displace any of the rubble littering the treads. Each step increased the agony, but she continued down toward the opening.

"I would strongly recommend you don't do that again," she said when she reached the doorway. "The next one could be lethal."

"My point exactly," Jared said.

He raised the automatic pistol and was about to fire when above him a series of shotgun blasts began tearing jagged holes through the ceiling, Just short of hitting him, Jared backed quickly toward the room he had been using as his blind to coax Shelia to her death. As he moved, he raised the automatic pistol toward the new unseen threat and fired several bursts in response. As he reached the opening, several rounds exploded from the stairwell doorway. He ducked inside and hit the floor.

"Still time to disarm, Collins. Your lessen plan's finished."

"As you wish," Jared said and stood. He tossed both guns into the hallway. "You know what the irony is?"

"No, why don't you tell me," Kel said, kneeling with her Glock pointed down the empty hall.

"If I had died in the jungle that day," he said, stepping into view, "the world would be no different because of it."

"Except that several people you killed this week would still be with us."

"Quit trying to shrink me. You can't fix this. Too many years of what they'll call displaced anger."

He took slow steps toward her. As he walked, his body fell into the shadow, and Kel could see him no longer. Only his voice indicated his approach.

Why," he continued, "do we try so desperately to hold on to life, anyway? In the end, it's all a shit-filled abyss. I survived war wounds to end up in a cage. Every day for fourteen years I was torn between hoping a bullet would put me face down in some godforsaken rice paddy and plotting my survival. Then on the day that should have been my release, I became a political inconvenience. And when I did make it home, my life had moved on without me. I was no longer needed or wanted by anyone, yet I lived on."

"You've made your point, Jared. You've succeeded. Dirk understands your grief."

"Now you're whining. Just like Angel and your dad, trying to save yourself. Give it up."

Hearing his voice drawing closer to the stairwell, she moved out of the doorway and tucked in behind the concrete wall. For a moment she had forgotten her wound, but now a wave of nausea swept over her. She leaned back against the cool cement barrier.

"No, Jared." She took a couple of deep breaths to continue. "I'm trying to *save* you. I have the advantage. You're in an exposed position."

"You're not going to shoot an unarmed man. Neither is your buddy on the next floor. That wouldn't be kosher, would it?"

"Just lie down on the floor where you are, and it'll all be over."

"I don't think so," he said. "You're the one sitting in the trap."

"I wish you'd reconsider."

"Can't do that, Princess." His voice had the finality of last words from the trapdoor at the gallows.

Despite her jagged breath and the pain intensifying with each second, Kel felt his presence slip through the doorway. "I told you next time we met I may not be so nice."

"Don't do this, Jared."

In the light from the phone display in his hand, Kel could see an unnatural smile form on his bearded face. Her instinct was to throw her hands up to protect her ears but she stared back at the hardened image before her. In his face she saw that he planned to kill them both, but she had moved and rearmed the bomb in the hallway moments before.

Now she wished she hadn't. She reached to pull him behind the wall next to her, but she was too late. The call engaged and detonated the C4. As the pellets ripped into his body and he catapulted into the opposite stairwell wall, in the flash of the explosion, she saw that with his last flicker of cognizance, he realized he had failed to complete his final lesson.

After he crumpled to the floor, and the debris cloud choked the air for the second time, Kel felt a darkness supplant her consciousness. She pressed hard against her wound trying to stop her life from ebbing away. She threw her support to the wall. *I have to hold on,* she thought, but it was as if the voice came from another's mind. Then, out of the pain, the blackness, and the regret, her body surrendered. Weakness took her knees. She fought the force, but she sensed her body had begun a slow descent down the concrete. Then, just before all thought receded into the vapor, a face appeared. It was ethereal, nothing but smoke. *Chrissie, I love you mo...*

Chapter 62

The sun caressed Shelia's face. She didn't feel it. The American flag-draped oak casket in front of her held her attention. Flanked by Danny and her husband, Jackson, she sat on a plastic folding chair in the front of several rows of mourners under a green awning. She pulled her eyes away from the speaker and let them drift past Danny to Chrissie. A chair sat empty beside her, and with two crimson roses in one hand, Chrissie dabbed at the tears on her cheek with a tissue in the other. Shelia turned her thoughts back to the speaker.

"I'll conclude by saying," Mayor Sudan said, "that Dirk Nyte was my friend, sometimes my conscience, sometimes my confidant, sometimes a thorn in my flesh, but always my friend and foremost an honorable man. Not many in the public eye can make that claim—not that *he* would—but he was one of the few.

"Anyone who knew him knew a man without pretense or vice. He was a master at showing his cards and then winning anyway. Not because he was a strong competitor but because he was right. And not that he was a perfect man. No one passes from womb to tomb without wearing a few scars, and no one slips the veil of this existence without leaving a few in the passing. But it's not these wounds that live on after a man. It's his choices. Did he choose to ignore the pain he caused, blame someone else for it, or accept his own failure? This will be his legacy."

He continued while he pulled a sheet of paper from his inside coat pocket. "Just a few weeks ago before Dirk entered the hospital for the last time, he stood where no one should ever stand, over the casket of a child—his child. On that day, he said these words."

Unfolding the paper, he slid his glasses down his nose a half inch and began to read.

"'After all that Collins did to people I knew, cared about and loved profoundly, I can't hate *him*. His acts, yes, but not the man. Hatred is the coward's way out of the hard work, a device we manipulate to explain and blame, to medicate terrible, unthinkable loss. But its bitter taste robs us of something vital. To replace our heartache with animosity is to trivialize those we lost. We *must* celebrate their lives, we *must* mourn our sudden separation, but we must also search deep into our hearts to understand Collins's pain. To do less is to allow it to happen again.

"'No one knows what circumstance would drive us to similar acts. He was a soldier, a man under orders to commit unspeakable brutality on the same innocent people who were conscripted to perform the same unspeakable atrocities on him. His life in that context alone would have been changed forever. But then, already out of his control, through graver circumstance, the unimaginable happened. His heart still beat and yearned to be home, but while life for others went on as if he no longer existed, he was forgotten by those who should have fought for him, should have sought for him, and should have loved him.

"'He had choices,'" the Mayor paused and looked to the gathering over the top edge of his glasses, "'or did he? What would you choose if your life was stolen from you? Can we sit here today and say with absolute assurance that we could never express ourselves through acts of violence? I suggest that until you understand the depths of his anguish, the cage to which he was confined from that day in 1968 until last Friday night, you don't know, and neither do I.

"'So, no, despite what has happened in your lives and mine, I cannot give an inch to hatred. I must rather seek to forgive, for when I forgive it holds me captive no longer. Only then can I truly mourn my loss, and you can, too.'"

The mayor looked up from the page and concluded, "Pity we can't all ascend to such an ideal as Dirk posits for us."

Nathan Ballesteros, the new chief of police, walked the freshly folded flag to where Shelia and her family sat.

"With the department's deepest sympathies and gratitude, Counselor," he said and took her hand. "That we all had such integrity."

Releasing her hand, he turned and stepped to where, with the other pallbearers, Kel stood like a sentry near the casket. She turned to Scott, squeezed his shoulder, and then took a few steps back to separate from the others.

"Detective," Ballesteros said and extended his hand, "the words your father spoke at your brother Roger's memorial leaves me convicted. If mankind was filled with the kind of grace as he demonstrated every day, we cops would be out of business."

"Now that's something to pray for."

He lifted his twin black eyebrows, and his eyes widened. "I'm glad to see you've recovered enough from your wounds to be here this afternoon."

"Nothing but a matching casket could have kept me away, sir," she said and glanced toward the crowd as they formed a single line to file by Dirk for the last time, "but the doctor released me just yesterday. I *am* going to take a few days, but I'll be back next week."

"Has Captain Silva assigned you a partner?"

"No, but he wants to add me to Willie's taskforce. Fresh perspective and all."

"Right where you wanted," he said, and his face sketched a look of disquiet that faded quickly.

"If Collins was correct, Jake was a dirty cop. But he said something to me just before he died, 'polluted waters run deep.' I've had a lot of time to muse over his final riddle. I believe it has a double meaning. First, I'm sure we'll never find Jake's remains. With Seattle being surrounded by deep bodies of water, there could be limitless places to make his body disappear forever."

"And second?"

"He was telling me Jake didn't act alone. He wouldn't give me anything else 'cause at the time he thought he was about to kill me, but I think there's more to it. Silva agrees. Truth is, I'd go after it on my own time even if Silva didn't agree."

"Of course you would, you're a Nyte. Wouldn't expect anything less."

Chrissie came to Kel's side and slipped her arm into her mother's. Ballesteros smiled at her and nodded.

"My condolences, again."

His uniformed driver waited off to the side, and as he walked away, Kel looked toward the crowd. The procession was near the end and most had begun to make their way back to vehicles parked along the paved roads crisscrossing the cemetery. She wasn't surprised to see that Lieutenant Martinez was not among the attendees. While still in the hospital recovering from surgery, she read in *The Globe* he had been placed on administrative leave for his part in the DK murders. Her daddy may have been a gracious man, but Dirk's limits were the abuse of power. Martinez had been the leak revealing Roger and Dirk's relationship.

"I love you, Chrissie."

"I love you more, Mom," Chrissie said, holding out one of the roses in her hand.

Kel remembered the last time they had played their game the night Jared had summoned her with his manifesto. They had not been able to finish their ritual since.

"I love you most," Kel said, wrapped her arm tight around her daughter's waist and took the flower.

"I'm going to miss Pops so much."

"We all will. You ready?"

Arm in arm they walked over to Shelia and her family who stood facing the casket. Each one in turn laid their rose on the lid and said goodbye in their own way—some with a tear, some with a word, some with a hand resting on the polished wood.

After everyone finished, Kel placed her rose on the floral casket spray and said, "Go now, Daddy. Mom's waiting for you."

Acknowledgements

Amy Harke-Moore saw something of merit and awarded <u>Dead of Nyte</u> first place in the "Novel Beginnings 1st Chapter Contest." Then as my editor, she taught me, among many other things, many lessons on point of view and head hopping. From this, many people and scenes ended up on the cutting room floor, so to speak, but the finished product is worth the bloodletting (most of it mine).

My first readers—David S. Moore, Thom Rowe, Gene Zurcher, Silvia Shelton, Linda Garcia, and Deb—their honest critique brought light in dark places, saved Kel from breaking the law and made her a better mother.

Thank you seems too trivial to give to my wife, Anita. A first, second and third reader, her insight helps pull the story out of me. She believes in me when I don't and encourages me when I want to give up. Even now she's saying write the next in the Nyte series.

Made in the USA
Charleston, SC
09 September 2013